DISCARD
S0-BBC-982

SEAN RUSSELL

THE INITIATE BROTHER
GATHERER OF CLOUDS

Moontide and Magic Rise:
WORLD WITHOUT END
SEA WITHOUT A SHORE

The River into Darkness:
BENEATH THE VAULTED HILLS

BENEATH THE VAULTED HILLS

BOOK ONE OF

The River Into Darkness

SEAN RUSSELL

DAW BOOKS, INC.
DONALD A. WOLLHEIM, FOUNDER
375 Hudson Street, New York, NY 10014
ELIZABETH R. WOLLHEIM
SHEILA E. GILBERT
PUBLISHERS

Jacket art by Robert Giusti.

Book designed by Stanley S. Drate/Folio Graphics Co., Inc.

DAW Book Collectors No. 1063.

DAW Books are distributed by Penguin Putnam Inc.

This book is printed on acid-free paper ∞.

First Printing, August 1997
1 2 3 4 5 6 7 8 9

DAW TRADEMARK REGISTERED
U.S. PAT. OFF. AND FOREIGN COUNTRIES
—MARCA REGISTRADA
HECHO EN U.S.A.

PRINTED IN THE U.S.A.

I'm sure that every writer, at some point, has received encouragement and advice from kindly teachers, and in this I'm no different. This book is dedicated to them (for teachers receive so little credit for their work), especially the late Helen Fawcett, Chris Evans, Catharine Jones, and Larry Kendal, wherever he is.

The journey out through darkened lands
A way beneath the vaulted hill
The tidal years sound elder bells,
Though falcons cry and thrushes trill.

Men of such stature, of such undeniable greatness, cast shadows beyond our limited world.

HALDEN: ESSAYS

BENEATH THE VAULTED HILLS

Prologue

HE sat before a window that stood slightly ajar and read by starlight. There had been a time when he'd preferred the warm light of day, but in the decades since the passing of his centenary, he'd become more inclined toward the cool illumination of the stars or even the moon. He studied the stars, of course, and one could hardly do that by daylight, but even so, he found the pale light so much more restful. Or perhaps he had just seen enough of the world.

Recently there had been a particular wandering star that he'd been observing nightly, using his improved telescope—an invention of Skye's, ironically. This star had a strange halo about it and a fiery tail. Things even the ancients did not know.

But more than anything he *felt* its passing. Felt it pull on all the heavenly bodies and, in turn, the effect this had elsewhere. Here, in the house of Eldrich, for instance.

The mage marked his place with a feather and closed the ancient book with care, placing it on a small table. He rose and walked out onto the terrace, looking up at the heavens. Eldrich had been reading Lucklow's treatise on augury—its practice and its perils. Especially its perils. The chapter on interpretation particularly fascinated him. Interpretation was the key, and it was the least certain aspect of the art.

The wandering star, for instance. It meant something—he was utterly sure of that—but try as he might, he could not understand what. And there was no one else whom he might ask.

"Do I feel lonely, being the last?" he asked the stars. He waited a moment and then decided that they could not reply. Only he knew . . . and would not say.

From beyond the garden wall he heard a wolf raise up its voice, the howl reverberating in his own breast. His familiar, off in the hills and wood, hunting as it must.

A spring night . . . still, awaiting the voices of the frogs and insects. Only the choral stars singing their ancient melodies.

He looked up and found the wandering star. *"Perhaps we have roamed long enough,"* he whispered.

Augury tempted him. He could feel it. Perhaps this time he would have a vision that was absolutely clear, and his course of action would be obvious. Obvious beyond all doubt.

"A fool's hope," he said aloud. Certainly he was too old for those.

The world was in motion. There was no doubt of that. Everyone poised to play their part, to make their sacrifice, if that was what was required. After all these many years he could not have a mistake. Not the smallest error.

Eldrich tilted back his head and gazed at the stars, wondering again if he had calculated correctly. If he could make an end of it soon.

Chapter One

It is, perhaps, less than true to say it all began in a brothel, but I found Samual Hayes hiding in such an establishment and this marked the turning point if not an actual beginning. How Samual Hayes had become misfortune's whipping boy, I will never understand.

The journal of Erasmus Flattery

HAYES thought it particularly appropriate that the streets of the poor lacked public lighting of any kind. One passed out of the light of the better areas into near darkness, only dull candlelight filtering through dirty panes and casting faint shimmering rectangles on the cobbles. At night one often saw dark feet and legs passing through these rectangles of light, or if the passerby walked closer to the window, one would see a silhouetted head and shoulders floating oddly above the street. Hayes had sat in his window often enough to mark this strange anatomical parade passing by—incomplete men and women flitting into existence before each dull little window, then ceasing to be, then coming to meager life again.

Paradise Street—he wondered if the man who named it had foreseen its future—lay near the boundary between the light and darkness, an area of perpetual twilight, perhaps. Almost a border town where few seemed to make their homes permanently. Most were on their way into darkness—a handful were moving toward the light. It was a place where a young man might end up if his family had sacrificed their fortune to foolishness and keeping up appearances, as was the case with Samual Hayes.

For him Paradise Street was also a place to hide from one's creditors, as astonishing as that seemed to him—a young man who, for most of his life, had never given money a second thought.

He passed through a candlelit square of light and looked down at his hands. There he was, not gone yet. Still more or less substantial. Perhaps there was hope.

"His High and Mightiness is still among us, I see," came an old man's voice out of the shadows. Hayes stiffened, but walked on, feeling his resolve harden as well.

He would have thought his fall from grace into this world would have made him one of them, perhaps even engendered some sympathy, but for some few it made him an object of enormous disdain. *How could anyone born to privilege have fallen so far as to land in Paradise Street?* That is what they thought. Only a fool or a weakling could take such a fall. And there were moments when Hayes feared they were right. It made him all the more grateful for the kind treatment he received from some of his other neighbors.

As he came up to his rooming house, he realized that there were perhaps a dozen people gathered in the shadows across the street, but they were uncommonly quiet.

"Mr. Hayes!" said a woman who was one of the local busybodies. "There's men taking your rooms apart. Look, sir." She pointed up at his windows.

Shadows were moving in his room, though Hayes knew he'd left no lamp burning.

"Flames!" he heard himself say. He realized that everyone stood looking up, but no one made a move to interfere.

Someone laid a hand on his arm as he went to run for his door. It was an old soldier who lived down the street. "Them's navy men, Mr. Hayes," he said with distaste. "Mark my words. Navy men, whether they wear their fine uniforms or no. You'd be best to give them a wide berth, sir. That's my advice, for what it's worth."

"Navy men?" Hayes' rally to save his possessions was stopped short. "Agents of the Admiralty?" There was clearly some mistake.

"And they aren't the only ones, Mr. Hayes," the woman said. "When they arrived, they surprised others already in your rooms. Those'ns jumped out the window. My Tom saw 'em, didn't you, Tom?" she said to a boy who clutched her hand.

The boy nodded and took his fingers from his mouth. "They floated down, landin' soft as pigeons, if you please. Soft as birdies."

The woman looked back to Hayes, as though awaiting an explanation.

"But who were they?" Hayes said, asking a question instead. "Robbers? I—I have so little to steal."

"If they were robbers, Mr. Hayes, they were uncommonly well-dressed ones. 'Gentlemen,' Tom said, and the old blacksmith saw them, too. 'Gentlemen,' he said as well. I don't know what you've been up to, Mr. Hayes, but there are men around asking after you—navy men. You'd best be on your way before someone turns you in for the few coins they'll get. There are enough around that would do it, too, I'm sorry to say."

"I'll talk to them. There's some explanation, I'm sure. . . ."

The old soldier touched his arm again. "I'm sure you didn't do whatever it was they think you done, sir, but you'd best go. When authorities come bustin' down your door, they don't want to hear no explanations. The gaol is no place for the likes of you, Mr. Hayes. Find the most well-placed friend you have, sir, and go to him. That's your best hope—that and a good barrister. Be off now, before some'un turns you in, as Mrs. Osbourn said. Good luck to you, Mr. Hayes."

A group of burly men appeared around the nearby corner and in the light from a window Hayes saw someone pointing toward him, and he was sure the men he was leading weren't residents of Paradise Street.

Hayes slipped back into the shadow, making his way along the fronts of the buildings, hugging the wall. He pulled up the collar of his frock coat quickly to hide the white of his shirt and neckcloth. Fifty feet farther he broke into a lope, as quiet as he could, passing ghostlike through the rectangles of stained light.

He dodged down an alley, slowing now for lack of light, feeling his way, his heart pounding and his breath short, though he'd hardly run at all. *Fear,* he realized. *I am running in fear from the authorities.* This was how men disappeared into the darkness of the poor quarter.

There were shouts behind him and the sound of men running, then suddenly slowing. A lantern swung into the alley at his back, but it was too far away for the light to touch him.

In a hundred feet he came out into another street and turned left. His instinct was to head for the lighted streets—the safe streets—but the men chasing him were not cutthroats who kept to the dark, and in the streetlights he would be seen more easily.

But still he found himself gravitating that way, mothlike. It was the habit of a lifetime; a desire to escape, to not disappear entirely.

He continued to hear the men shouting. Hayes pushed himself on, fighting to catch his breath, not even sure if they were still following him—afraid to look back.

He was heading toward Brinsley Park, and Spring Street—the beginning of the lighted boulevards. *This is madness,* he told himself. The darkness was his ally now. The place he thought constantly of escaping, and now it sheltered him. He should cling to it, wrap it around himself, for it was all that protected him.

But if he stayed here, in the twilight quarter, someone would give him away—for he would never be anything but an outsider, here. Not safe in the darkness or the light. Better the light, then. Too many disappeared in the darkness.

Hayes took the risk of pausing before he went out onto the lit street that bordered Brinsley Park. For a moment he stood listening to the sounds down the darkened alley he was about to leave. His pursuers were likely not far behind.

Almost more than hear, Hayes sensed noise down the street, not on top of him but too close. Composing himself, he stepped out onto the lamplit street, monitoring his pace so that he would not stand out, yet making the best time he could.

Couples walked at their leisure, especially on the street's far side, which is where he wanted to be, as far from his tormentors as he could be. Weaving between carriages and tradesmen's carts, Hayes strode quickly to the opposite side, realizing that this was a mistake—because of the size of the park there were no streets leading off from that side of the avenue for a distance equal to several blocks. More than anything, he needed to make as many turns as he could to confound his hunters, and now that wasn't possible. They might think he'd scrambled over the iron fence into the park, keeping to darkness like any criminal would, but the fence was so high. . . .

He pressed on, fighting the urge to look back—a man who appeared to have pursuers would be noticed, no question of that.

Men and women passed, arm in arm, chatting and laughing. A coach clattered by, a young man leaning out its window, toasting the passersby theatrically; his drunken companions laughed and as one of them tried to fill his glass, a crimson stream of wine splashed over the cobbles.

"Hayes?" someone called.

Hayes looked about wildly. Bloody blood and flames, someone was announcing his name to everyone on the avenue!

"Samual Hayes?" the voice came again; from the carriage, he realized. "Driver! Heave to, man."

Slowing, the carriage veered toward the curb, frightening pedestrians, clearly not in perfect control. Hayes was not sure who had called to him, but he took one look back and made a dash for the still-moving carriage. As he approached, the driver set it off again, laughing inanely, for it was another young gentleman with the reins in hand. Hayes forced himself to sprint, and as the door swung open, he reached out and grabbed the carriage, feeling hands take hold of him and drag him in where he sprawled on the floor.

Half a dozen men his own age looked down at him, grinning. "Why, Samual Hayes," one of them said, "have a drink," and proceeded to pour wine all over Hayes' face.

"Hume!" Hayes managed, almost choking. He pushed himself up, fending off the bottle.

The young gentlemen were laughing madly.

"Aye, have another drink, Hayes." Hume began tilting another bottle toward Hayes, but he managed to push this one away, too.

"Flames, Hume, but you came just in time. I was being chased by footpads."

"On Spring Street?" someone said, clearly certain he was joking.

"You'd have been better off with the footpads, I'll wager," someone laughed. "We're celebrating Hume's impending demise. Marriage, that is."

Hayes struggled up into a crouch and stared out the rear window. He could see them now, a group of men at the run, but too far back to be distinguished. Too far back to catch them, that was certain.

"Blood and flames," Hume said, twisting around to look out. "You were serious."

"Let's go back and give them what-for," someone called out. "I've a rapier in here somewhere."

"No!" Hayes said quickly. "Drive on."

"Hah! Out of the frying pan into the fire, Hayesy. You're with us now and our intent is far more wicked than any footpads. Driver," the young man called *"The brothel!"*

"The brothel!"

"The brothel!" the others took up the cry, and the carriage careened off down the street, only the fragile common sense of horses keeping the gentlemen from disaster.

The anemic light of coach lamps smeared across rain-oiled cobbles and lit the moving flanks of horses without having a noticeable affect on the overwhelming darkness. Avonel of an evening in early spring.

Erasmus Flattery stepped down from the hired coach and, with barely a nod, shook some coins out of his pocket for the driver. This was the address, he was sure. A doorman held an umbrella for him, interrupting a drizzle so fine it seemed more like a cool, falling dew, or the actual substance of darkness dribbling down from the heavens.

"Sir. . . ?" the doorman said expectantly, and Erasmus realized he was standing there as though unsure he would enter—like a young man who'd lost his nerve. In truth he had always avoided such places, though not on moral grounds. He was not a prude. But brothels were the haunts of foolish young men, and the old attempting to deny the truth of time. Either way it was a house of delusions, and, as such, repugnant to Erasmus. But then, Erasmus had come out of perverse curiosity.

Only the Marchioness of Wicklow could ever have brought off such an event, for who could refuse an invitation from Avonel's principal hostess? Only a prude or a man who had much to hide, clearly. Any woman who did not attend would unquestionably be admitting that her husband frequented such establishments and that therefore she could not bear to even enter the place herself. No, the Marchioness had weighed things out with a kind of ruthless precision and cruel irony that Erasmus thought had to be admired. Of course, as a bachelor, he was in no danger here. His wife would not be watching, wondering if any of the matron's comely employees seemed to treat him with just a bit too much familiarity.

So here gathered the cream of Avonel society, pretending to be engaged in something exciting, risque, and watching each other like predators. Erasmus thought that the Marchioness had gone a long way to expose the truth of Avonel society this evening. He, for one, was almost certain he could smell the sweat.

Erasmus was escorted quickly up the short walk and into a well-lit lobby. Smiling young women relieved him of cloak and hat, gloves and cane.

"Lady Wicklow's party," he said, and one young woman turned to the matron who approached and, still smiling, repeated his disclaimer.

The matron was a cheerful looking woman whose age could not be disguised behind even the layers of makeup she had applied. Erasmus thought that if you took away the makeup, she would look far more like the competent wife of a particularly boring, country squire than the proprietress of such an establishment. She should have been serving tea and exaggerating the accomplishments of her children.

"Mrs. Trocket at your service. And you are. . . ?" she asked as she curtsied, surprising Erasmus with a bright look of both intelligence and humor.

"Erasmus Flattery, ma'am."

Her face changed as she heard the name, and though she held a list of guests, it was immediately forgotten. "Ah, Mr. Flattery. It is a great pleasure, I'm sure."

She motioned for him to escort her, clearly pleased to have a member of such an important family visit her establishment. The name, Erasmus thought, did occasionally prove useful—when it wasn't a curse.

"Well, you'll find we've created a place of refined entertainments for the discerning gentlemen—and lady—for we do not cater to gentlemen alone. Not at all."

All of the "ladies" Erasmus could see were clearly in the employ of the able Mrs. Trocket, and they smiled at him less than coyly as he passed. One blew him a kiss. They wore gowns that one would not see in most Avonel homes, that was certain, and several seemed to have forgotten their gowns and wore only the most exotic Entonne lingerie. He tried not to stare, but they really were the most fetching creatures. And they laughed with the gentlemen present, flirting in the most open manner. Erasmus thought suddenly that the place was a bit too warm.

The air was redolent with the smell of perfumes which did not quite mask a musky odor that pervaded the rooms. Erasmus did not have to wonder what that scent was, his body reacted to it of its own accord, and likely would have had he never encountered it before. Love had its own scent.

They passed into another room, not so different from the first, though perhaps not so well lit. Here musicians played, and the men had shed their coats or loosened neckcloths. The women seemed to have joined in the spirit, and were less encumbered by clothing as well. Some couples—or even threesomes—were dancing drunkenly, pressed close while others were locked in more passionate embraces, too drunk or too aroused to care that they were in public. On either end of a divan a naval officer sprawled, like tumbledown bookends, insensible with drink. So much for their evening with the ladies, Erasmus thought, though it would not likely stop them from boasting, all the same.

A woman put her hand on Erasmus' arm as he passed, and she did it with such familiarity, meeting his eyes so calmly, that for a moment he thought he knew her, and he was sure he looked at her with the greatest surprise. Mrs. Trocket led him through the next door.

They entered a hallway with large rooms to either side, and through the open doors he could see that several "refined entertainments" were underway. He glimpsed near-naked dancers through one set of doors, and heard singing from another. A farce, played out in elaborate and outrageous costumes, was in progress in yet another room.

"We try to have something for everyone," Mrs. Trocket said, noting his interest. "And things change often—nothing stale at Mrs. Trocket's. Amusement with wit and charm, that is our goal. A bit too . . ." she used an Entonne word that did not have an exact Farr equivalent, though its meaning lay somewhere between "racy" and "fashionable," ". . . for many of the worthies of Avonel. But for a young man such as yourself . . ." She smiled knowingly.

Erasmus was thirty—not so young by the standards of Farrland—and was, despite his name, no longer easy prey to flattery.

Up a broad flight of stairs and finally into the most eccentric library Erasmus had ever seen. It belonged in an ancient abbey or college for studies in the arcane. The room was polished oak from the floor to the very top of the shelves—some two stories up—and was all nooks and alcoves and stairways and carrels. Balconies were suspended precariously overhead, backed by cliffs of books. Sliding ladders, at odd angles to everything else, ran up to bronze railings.

People stood on these ladders, surveying the crowd or holding forth to groups who gathered about their feet.

Erasmus realized that Mrs. Trocket had left him alone. Perhaps she had even bid him farewell.

The room was crowded with people, and there was such a hum of conversation that he thought of his beehives in far off Locfal. It was, to Erasmus' eye, a typical gathering of the educated classes of Avonel, though to one well-versed in such things, it might have been a more fashionable group than was common. Erasmus did not much care for such distinctions.

He noticed that everyone seemed a bit more animated than usual, as though they were trying to hide their discomfort, or perhaps they were merely thrilled to find themselves in such a place, for certainly none of the ladies had been in a brothel before. Many of the men looked distinctly uncomfortable, and Erasmus was sure it wasn't because this was their first visit—but they had unquestionably never been here in the company of their wives. They were likely terrified that some young woman was going to recognize them, though Erasmus knew that the able Mrs. Trocket would have advised her young ladies beforehand. Still, it was good sport to watch the husbands shying like nervous foals.

Scattered among the people attending the party were both servants and working girls and they talked and laughed with the guests and plied them with spirits and delicacies. The atmosphere here, in the center of the Marchioness' circle, was less bawdy and brazen than Erasmus had seen in the other chambers. Passions were well under control where one's reputation could actually suffer some damage. After all, the usual code—that one did not speak of who or what one saw in a brothel—would not be in effect this night. People would likely talk of nothing else for days.

Erasmus began searching the room for familiar faces, and though there were many that he knew by sight, he couldn't find anyone he thought might offer interesting conversation, and he saw several he knew for a fact had never said an intriguing thing in their lives. He thought the rather intense looking man across the room seemed vaguely familiar, and then realized that it was his own face in a looking glass, and this made him laugh.

Well, he certainly won't have anything to say that I haven't heard before, Erasmus thought.

He backed up against the wall of books, and thinking he would keep people at bay if he were engaged in some activity, he took a volume from the shelf and opened it. In two lines he realized that it was erotic fiction, and returned it to the shelf. What pleasure could such an activity provide if one could indulge it openly? All the books he could see were of the same variety, so he turned back to the gathering.

"Isn't it divinely wicked?" a young woman said to him, and he realized he was looking at a daughter of the Shackleton family, though his memory would not cooperate by supplying a name. She waved a glass of wine expansively, the look of drunken delight not varying measurably. "Only the marchioness would dare such an evening." She looked at him suddenly, her manner inquisitive if a little unfocused. "Don't I know you?"

"Erasmus Flattery," he said, and watched her expression change from drunken delight.

"Really?" she managed, remaining fairly collected. "You've been to our home, I think."

Erasmus nodded.

"I so wanted to ask if the rumors were true, but I was too shy, and my mother warned me to mind my manners. But tonight I've had enough wine. . . . Is it true you served Eldrich?"

He shook his head. "Vicious rumor. I once visited a school chum at Lord Eldrich's home—he was a great-nephew or some such thing. But it was all very ordinary, and the legendary Eldrich never appeared. Not even to my school chum, if he's to be believed."

"Too bad," she said, her look of delight fading a little more. "Too many good stories end up that way. The truth is a bit of a bore, isn't it?"

Erasmus shrugged.

"Well, that's what I've found anyway," she said resignedly, placed a hand on his chest rather clumsily, then backed away into the crowd, waving theatrically, as though she had lost all capacity for the unself-conscious gesture.

Dora, Erasmus thought as he watched her disappear into the crowd. Dora Shackleton, although "Simpleton" might be more appropriate.

Nearby a gathering of people swayed and bobbed, all trying to view the object of interest that lay at the very center of this movement. Drawn by what force Erasmus did not know—perhaps merely because the audience was almost entirely young ladies—he found himself looking over the heads of the watchers. Heads of lustrous swaying hair that fell to bare shoulders and beyond.

"But you see she is completely relaxed," a man was saying. "In fact, she will wake from this refreshed, as though she had slept the night through and experienced only the sweetest of dreams."

The man bent over a young woman seated in a chair. He sported both an ostentatious mustache and a monocle and looked too much like a player on the stage—the foreign count whom no one trusted, despite his charm. He laid a hand on the young woman's shoulder, but she did not stir, and kept her eyes closed. Indeed, she seemed to be asleep sitting up.

"But what will she do?" a woman asked, a little embarrassed by her question.

"Or not do," another added, and they all giggled at her boldness.

"Clara will do nothing in her present state that she would find objectionable while awake. She is mesmerized, but her morals are perfectly awake, let me assure you."

"Can you cure illnesses, then?" someone asked. "Some make such a claim."

"Some illnesses, yes. I have had encouraging results treating nervous dyspepsia, insomnia, dropsy, and brain fevers, to name but a few. Consumption, I regret to say, it will not affect, though it will take away some discomfort from the consumptive patient. Irrational fears I have treated with great success. Recurrent nightmares I have solved utterly."

"Can people really remember back to their very childhood, Doctor? To their birth, even?"

"I have seen long-lost memories surface, often, but I cannot claim perfect success. I treated the great Lord Skye, who as you know can remember nothing that took place before his childhood accident, but we were unable to recover his past. It is lost, I believe. Lost when he suffered his terrible injury."

"But his intellect was not affected . . . ?"

"Only his speech, slightly. But otherwise we do not know. Perhaps if he had not suffered his tragedy, he would have shown even greater genius. But what is a memory? Can it be weighed or measured? If one is forgotten, does the brain weight less? How is it that we hold so many in our minds? And where are they kept?" He looked around at the gathering as though expecting answers, but when none were forthcoming, he continued. "There are those who claim the mind and the brain are not one and the same, but clearly when the brain is injured, so also is the mind. Thus Skye lost his memories—as though they were destroyed when his brain was damaged. But in an undamaged brain I believe the memories are never truly lost, but only misplaced. Memories of every event and smell and taste and emotion, all there, like perfect novels in infinite numbers. The novels of our lives. It is one of the mysteries that empiricism has yet to explain." He turned to the sleeping woman. "But let us see what Clara can remember. Perhaps she has some memories long forgotten. Clara? I want you to turn your mind to your childhood. . . . Your very earliest memory."

Erasmus drifted away. He had seen such displays before. Fascinating the first time or two, but largely quackery, he thought. This man had made more modest claims than most, who were milking the ignorant for their hard-earned coin with promises to cure all manner of illness and deformity, and much more. Which only made this man slightly less of a charlatan.

But what is memory?

Perhaps not an entirely foolish question, Erasmus thought, but he was more interested in knowing why one could not forget. Or how one could forget. For that he would hand over his own money, and gladly.

A young woman offered him a glass of champagne. She was wearing nothing but lingerie of black lace, sheer black stockings, and an astonishing tumble of dark curls.

"You look, sir, as though you might require some help erasing that troubled expression from your brow," she said in a lovely warm voice. Erasmus was usually easy prey for a beautiful voice.

"I cultivate looking troubled," he answered. "It keeps people at a distance."

"Ah," she said, stepping aside to let people pass and pressing herself softly against him. "Are you trying to keep me at a distance, then?"

"It's very likely, I fear." Erasmus glanced around the room. "I'm looking for friends, actually."

"Do they have names?" she asked, speaking near to his ear in a tone so intimate that Erasmus could hardly help but respond.

Erasmus hesitated. "I believe so, though they've never told them to me."

This caused her to pause for a moment, then she laughed.

"Ras! Short for rascal, I see," came a voice from behind. Erasmus felt a hand on his shoulder and turned to find Barton, an old classmate from his Merton days. "Come out for an evening of wickedness, I see?" The man was beaming at him a bit foolishly, as though overcome with delight at finding Erasmus Flattery in a brothel, of all places.

"I was invited by the marchioness," Erasmus said, not quite sure why he was trying to explain his presence.

"Oh, to be sure! As were we all." Barton laughed. "But have you seen the contortionists? Well, I tell you, it will fire your imagination. Possibilities undreamed of!" He laughed again, and snatched a glass from a passing tray. Barton's face was red, even his now completely bald pate was flushed. "You look a bit out of sorts, Ras," he said sympathetically, and then suddenly looked a little self-conscious himself, as though afraid he'd been caught in the act of frivolity. "I hear you're setting your stamp on the Society. Making quite a name for yourself," he offered, perhaps searching for some topic that would put Erasmus at ease.

It was not a good choice—Erasmus did not like to be patronized. He nodded distractedly, and the woman who still held his arm pressed against him again, calling for his attention.

Barton smiled and drained his glass. "Well, mustn't keep you from your friend," he said, nodded to the woman on Erasmus' arm and turned to go.

"But, Barton . . ." but Barton was gone.

The woman, pressing her arm into Erasmus, leaned close to his ear and made a rather outrageous suggestion. Erasmus disentangled himself. "Ah, '*If it were not a phantom moon, and your affections, Lady, were but true.*' "

She looked at him, confused.

"Denis," Erasmus said. "*The Prince Alexander.*" And seeing that this information did not help, he added: "It's a play, my dear."

She released him, her look of confusion not fading, and Erasmus set out into the fray. Tight little alleys opened up in the knots of people, and he pushed his way down these, awash in the scents and sounds, the colors and shapes.

He jostled someone accidentally and a rather poorly dressed young man shot him a look.

"Erasmus?" the young man said. "Farrelle's ghost, Erasmus!"

"Samual?"

The young man put a finger to his lips. "Don't say it so loudly." He looked truly frightened, shrinking down a little so as not to be noticed.

"Hiding from a fiancée, are you?" Erasmus smiled.

"No, nothing like that. Far worse, in fact." Samual Hayes looked about him quickly. "I'm hiding from the law, Erasmus."

Erasmus almost laughed, thinking it a joke—Samual Hayes in trouble with the law!—but then he realized that the young man was completely serious. "Martyr's blood, man, what have you been up to?"

"Nothing," Hayes said quickly, "I swear. Yet I am being pursued all the same."

"Mr. Flattery?"

Erasmus turned to find a naval officer approaching, smiling. The navy men were always extremely amiable to him, not for anything Erasmus had done, but because a recent ancestor had been an admiral and something of a war hero. Odd how the accomplishments of one's family seemed to somehow rub off on a man.

"Captain Adelard James. We met once at the duke's country home. At a dinner, this two years past. . . ."

"Of course. A pleasure to see you again, Captain. You were off to Farrow, wasn't it?"

The man looked pleased that Erasmus would remember. "That's it exactly. Yes, we talked much about the island. Have you been back since we last spoke?"

Erasmus shook his head. "No, I'm afraid not." He turned to introduce Hayes, but the young man had disappeared. They talked for a moment about nothing much in particular, and then parted. Erasmus stood wondering what in the world Hayes had been on about.

Barton reappeared suddenly. "Finished with that little bit already?" he asked, speaking too loudly. "Well, never mind, there's always more here, Ras. Do you know, I've just been told that the Countess of Chilton is in attendance? Can you believe it? I'm dying for a glimpse." He raised a bushy eyebrow comically. "Come along, old man, and we'll see if the rumors are true. See if a dart of pure desire strikes right to our very hearts."

They had taken an astonishing length of time to make their way to this room, searching as they went. Hoping for a glimpse of the woman said to be the most beautiful in the known world. Barton touched Erasmus' arm suddenly, and he turned to look in the direction his friend was staring. There was someone there, no doubt, in the middle of the press of both men and women—like a queen bee surrounded by her attendants. And the similarity seemed very apt to Erasmus. It was as though they all hovered about, rubbing antennae, caught up in a collective orgy of adoration.

He could not see the woman who was the focus of this adulation, but he could see the reactions of those around. They were transported, foolish with delight at finding themselves in the company of this woman. And it was not just the men. The women seemed hardly less affected. Erasmus felt it himself, and he still had not caught a glimpse of the countess.

"Can you see her, Barton?" Erasmus asked, for Barton was a good half a foot taller and looked over virtually everyone's head.

"Almost," he answered, not shifting his gaze away from the spectacle.

Suddenly someone in the throng moved to one side and Erasmus thought he caught a glimpse of a beautiful smile.

"Now, now, gentlemen. Not polite to stare. Actually, the countess has gone, and what you see there are merely the people who were so unbelievably fortunate as to actually have spoken with her."

"Sennet," Barton said, turning to a dapper young man who looked on in vast amusement. "Do you know Erasmus Flattery?"

"No, but certainly I know your brother, the duke. Your servant, sir. And I should add that I know you by reputation. I'm not an empiricist myself, but, even so, one cannot help but hear the name of Erasmus Flattery. Not these days."

Erasmus never knew how to respond graciously to praise, and as usual changed the subject. "Were you serious?" Erasmus asked. "Are these merely the people who spoke with the countess?"

Sennet bobbed his head, his long, rather sharp nose performing a precise arc in the air. Erasmus thought the marquis—for this was undoubtedly the Marquis of Sennet—was the most oddly formed man. His chin seemed to have been drawn out too far, his forehead sloped back. Freckles of vastly differing sizes were scattered over his face, and yet all of this seemed to be offset by the most kindly eyes, large and filled with humor, with deep lines at their corners from much laughter, Erasmus suspected.

"Yes," Sennet said, his amusement apparently growing. "Isn't it wonderfully absurd? It's really a madness. A collective madness." His look became just a bit more serious, as though something in this disturbed him.

"I've never actually seen the countess myself," Erasmus said, wondering if there was as much regret in his voice as he heard. "Is she as beautiful as everyone claims?"

Sennet tilted his head to one side. "One would have to say yes, I think. It is very odd. I actually believe there are other women in Avonel just as beautiful—perhaps even in this room—but they do not have the effect of the Countess of Chilton. It is a force of personality. . . . I don't think I know a word to describe the effect, for she is more than enchanting." He shook his head and laughed. "Well, you see, I am as besotted as everyone else. Though I shall not duel with others who do not declare her the most beautiful woman who has ever lived, which apparently happened this week past."

Erasmus thought this a good thing. He seemed to remember hearing that Sennet was a formidable swordsman, and had once won a duel with the master of Avonel's principal fencing academy. A feat that had given him something of a reputation these past three years.

"No, I make it something of a rule," Sennet said. "Never risk your life over a woman who cannot remember your name. Sensible, don't you think?"

Erasmus' answer died on his lips, for he saw Samual Hayes half-hidden behind a column, trying to catch his attention.

Erasmus excused himself and made his way over to the young man.

Young Samual was the only son of neighbors of the Flattery family. The Hayes family were kindly if not terribly competent people, who had lost their estate not too long ago from bad investments and profligate spending. Not an uncommon story, unfortunately.

"I have to get out of here," Hayes said as Erasmus came near. "It's the navy men; they're after me." He paused, avoiding Erasmus' eyes. "But I have no place to go."

Erasmus reached out and took Hayes' arm. Better to find out what went on here. He owed it to the young man's parents. "Come along, then. You can hide at my home—at least until you've told me what's happened. Don't look so frightened, Hayes; unless you've murdered the prince royal, it's unlikely agents of the navy will try to rest you from me without a proper warrant, and I rather doubt the officers present this evening have one in their pockets. They have other things on their minds."

Erasmus steered Hayes toward the door, wondering if he would miss anything that evening, but then decided that he had only come out of boredom. An unhealthy reason in the first place. The rescue of a family friend seemed infinitely preferable.

Chapter Two

It was not a secret in Avonel that the Earl of Skye had a preference for a certain type of woman—petite, white-blonde, green-eyed, and young. An Entonne accent was desirable but not absolutely necessary. For a man of surpassing intellect, his tastes were hardly extraordinary.

The woman who answered the door, however, was not only a complete stranger, but she had none of the characteristics that Skye expected. In truth, he thought her a rather unusual looking woman. Not more than twenty-three, he guessed, but he had seldom seen a woman so . . . faded. Her hair, her skin, they appeared to be drained of color. The hair was red, but of such a lifeless variety. If anyone were to return from death, Skye thought they would look like this—as though part of their life had been drained away. Yet her eyes had the gleam of youth and even standing there, holding the door, he sensed a vivacity about her.

She curtsied with grace. "Lord Skye, it is an honor. Please, come in," she said pleasantly. Whoever she was, she was no one's maid servant.

He hesitated on the doorstep. "This is the right address?"

"You've come to visit Miss Finesworth?"

He nodded and she beckoned him in.

"You have me at something of a disadvantage, Miss. . . . I do not know your name."

"I am a friend," she said, and smiled as though she had been put up to this and found his reaction rather amusing. "Come up, sir," she said, not offering to take his coat or cane, nor was there any servant to do so.

It was turning into something of an odd assignation, Skye thought. Where was Miss Finesworth? She had assured him the house would be empty.

At the stair head the young woman opened a door and preceded him into the room.

"What in bloody blazes!" Skye stopped abruptly. There were three naval officers slumped so limply on chairs that Skye feared they were dead.

"They are drugged," the young woman said matter-of-factly.

Skye felt an urge to bolt, but he stood, staring, almost dumbfounded, at the scene.

"But why?" His voice came out in a whisper. "Why are they here?"

"To arrest you, I'm afraid," she said. "You see, the young woman you were to meet, Miss Finesworth, was to pretend to be an Entonne spy who had offered her allegiance to Farrland. She would claim that you had come here to give her plans for the cannon, so that Entonne could produce naval guns of their own." She waved a hand at the unconscious officers. "These gentlemen were then to take you away. To gaol, Lord Skye."

"That's . . . that's preposterous. It's . . ."

She crossed to a table and slid a large roll of papers across the smooth surface. "You will recognize these, I think?" she asked, releasing the ribbons that bound them. She spread them quickly open and looked over at Skye.

Not sure why, he went to look.

He let out a long breath. "My drawings of the naval gun. The Admiralty had them."

"Yes, and sheets of specifications. Instructions for casting. Everything one would need to produce cannon."

Skye stepped back stunned to silence. "Who are you?"

"A friend, Lord Skye. Someone who would not see you harmed." She touched his arm gently. "You needn't fear me. Without my intervention you would be on your way to gaol this moment. You have made an enemy, Lord Skye. A formidable and somewhat ruthless enemy. Moncrief, I assume, but perhaps you know already."

"Moncrief!? But he is my friend! I dine with him. I . . ." he blustered into silence.

She stared at him with what appeared to be compassion. "I would be surprised to learn that Moncrief has any friends, Lord Skye. You threaten him in some way. You are a favorite of the King and have His Majesty's ear. Perhaps too much for Moncrief's liking."

Skye leaned on the table. "It is unbelievable. Moncrief would not dare attack me."

"Moncrief dared to attack Enttone, Lord Skye. What is a mere citizen to him? Even one as influential as yourself. After all, he has brought men down before. Powerful men."

"Why have you done this?" Skye asked, stepping away from the table, eyeing this peculiar looking woman.

"You have many admirers, Lord Skye. We would not see you fall victim to . . . anyone. Trust me when I say this. We are your friends. It is best that you leave now. Tell no one you were here. Is your driver to be trusted?"

Skye nodded.

"Then you should be gone."

Skye nodded again, turning away without further urging. He was not sure what went on here, but escaping this place seemed imperative.

At the bottom of the stairs, he turned to the young woman. "If this all proves to be true, Miss, I will be in your debt."

She nodded. "So it would appear, Lord Skye. But for now . . ." She opened the door for him, and with a quick bow he went out, opening the door to the carriage himself, and sending his surprised driver on.

He slumped back in his seat, a hand over his face. Had he just escaped ruin? It didn't seem possible. Flames, but he should not wait in Avonel to find out.

Chapter Three

Memory is fiction, a narrative we write and rewrite to explain an ever-changing present, a story in which we are the hero, the victim, the wronged or the incomparable lover. And if memory is fiction, what then is history?

Halden: Essays

THE ride to Erasmus' home passed almost entirely in silence, as though Hayes were afraid the driver might overhear them. Erasmus thought that something dire must have happened to frighten the young man so. He looked positively haunted, and this was not helped by the fact that he was rather poorly dressed and smelled of wine—though he appeared perfectly sober.

It came out that Hayes had visited the brothel only because he'd been rescued by friends who were on their way there. They were celebrating the coming marriage of one of their circle. An odd practice, Erasmus thought. Apparently the groom-to-be had been stripped naked and tied to a woman, who was also without clothing, and they would not be released until they had performed the act before the groom's so-called friends. All rather difficult in that they had been tied in such a way as to make consummation almost impossible. Somewhat more entertaining than anything Erasmus had seen, but then his exploration of the brothel had been cut rather short.

They arrived at Erasmus' town home and were let in by his man servant, Stokes, who looked askance at this young vagabond Erasmus had brought home.

After Stokes had found Hayes some clothing and let him clean up, they met in Erasmus' study on the second floor. "I will tell you, Hayes, you look like you've survived the war."

"Do excuse me, Erasmus, I—I appreciate you taking me in like this."

"Yes, well, come and sit by the fire and warm yourself." Erasmus motioned to his servant. "Brandy would seem to be in order. And coffee. Will that answer?" he asked Hayes, who nodded.

Erasmus took the second chair. "I think you should tell me what's happened, Hayes. There will be time for pleasantries later."

The young man nodded, rubbing his hands up and down his thighs as though to bring some feeling into them. He stared into the fire, martialing his thoughts.

The young Samual that Erasmus remembered was barely detectable in the man seated before him. The good-natured, apple-cheeked child was gone, and in his place was someone leaner and harder. The bones of his face showed through, as though hardship had caused his skeleton to expand and strengthen. This young man looked like he could stand up to some adversity, which no doubt he already had.

"I don't need to acquaint you with my recent family history, Erasmus. Suffice it to say that, since leaving Merton, I've been living in . . . one of the city's more picturesque quarters." Hayes shook his head as though he could not quite credit his memory. "I came home this night to find my rooms had been invaded by . . . well, my neighbors claimed they were navy men. And I was pursued by others and only managed to escape by pure luck." He looked up at Erasmus. "I really had no place to go. No friend good enough to burden with my troubles."

"Don't worry, Samual, you're both safe and welcome. There are one or two advantages to having a brother who's a duke. You haven't any notion of why these men were in your rooms, I take it?"

Hayes shook his head. "None."

"And you're sure they were men from the Admiralty? You saw uniforms?"

"No, but the people in that quarter of the city have an uncanny ability to spot the representatives of the Crown no matter what their dress. If they say they were navy men, I would wager all I have they were right. Not that it would be much of a wager, I'm afraid."

Stokes appeared just then with coffee and brandies. Erasmus

wanted to reassure Hayes that his life would not always be thus, but by the time Stokes left, the moment had passed.

"Well, perhaps it is a case of mistaken identity." Erasmus stared at Hayes, who gazed fixedly down into his brandy. The silence was protracted and more than a little awkward.

"It makes little sense to come to me, Samual, and then not trust me," Erasmus said softly.

Hayes shook his head and shifted his gaze to the fire. "I have been racking my brain all evening trying to think of any reason, any reason at all, that the Admiralty would be interested in me. Interested enough to sack my rooms."

"And. . . ?"

Hayes looked up at him. "I can think of only one thing, and even it makes almost no sense."

"Out with it, Samual."

"I had been doing some research for a gentleman. Someone who wanted utter discretion. It was paid work, you see," he said, a little embarrassed.

"No shame in that. Not to my mind, anyway." Erasmus waited, his patience wearing thin, though he fought to hide it.

"Well, the gentleman has some involvement with the Admiralty. That is the only explanation I can think of. But, for the life of me, I can't imagine how the work I did could lead to naval officers searching my rooms." Hayes rose from his chair and paced two steps across the hearth, clearly troubled. He stood looking down at his hands oddly, turning them over and over before the flames.

"It is such a strange thing. . . ." He hunched down before the fire.

"Perhaps you should tell me about this work you've done, Hayes. I might notice something someone with less distance would miss."

Hayes nodded, still looking into the fire. "It is a story I want to tell you, Erasmus. You, in particular." He glanced up. "But I would have to ask for complete secrecy in this matter."

Agents of the navy were involved, Erasmus reminded himself. "If your story bears upon the security of the nation in some way, Hayes, I cannot guarantee that I'll be able to keep your confidence."

Hayes stood up quickly. "But it doesn't, Erasmus. I swear it."

Erasmus considered. It was not that he didn't want to offer

Hayes some help, it was just that he didn't want to become more involved than was necessary. "You said that you particularly wanted to tell me this tale. . . ."

Hayes nodded hopefully. "Yes, for you see, the story involves a mage, or at least I think it does. That is what I hope you can tell me."

Erasmus shifted in his chair, wary now. "I will tell you honestly, Hayes, that I have little special knowledge of mages, despite what people will persist in believing."

A tight smile of polite disbelief flickered across Hayes' face. "Of course . . . I simply thought. . . ." He stopped and looked away again.

"If, as you say, the matter is innocent, I will honor your confidence. That is all I can promise."

Hayes nodded. "It all began about two years ago with a professor at Merton. You see, he called me and a classmate to his study one day and asked if we'd be interested in undertaking some research for a prominent gentleman—he would not tell us who it was, for the gentleman desired absolute discretion. We had to agree before we were told his name. Our professor did assure us that the gentleman in question was above reproach and it was all on the up and up. I agreed readily, for I would be paid, and my classmate, Kehler, agreed as well.

"We were sent off to meet our prospective employer, completely in the dark as to what we would be doing, and I dare say we would have thought it something of a lark if we hadn't known the man by reputation." He glanced up at Erasmus, clearly still impressed by this mysterious gentleman. "I can't say more than that he is a person of some standing.

"We speculated a great deal about what our task might be, but I can tell you, Erasmus, we were not even near the mark. Do you know anything about a little village called Compton Heath?"

Erasmus shrugged. "Just the name."

"And I should have said that's really all there was to know—except for this one peculiar incident that the gentleman was interested in." Hayes reached down and took a sip of his brandy. "I don't know how he ever learned the story, but his fascination with it was obvious. As he told it, he could not sit still but paced across the room speaking as though he were explaining a great discovery.

"According to our employer, a stranger appeared one day in

Compton Heath: a man dressed oddly, who spoke no tongue that any recognized. He seemed more than a little disoriented and distraught, as well as a bit fearful of the people, though from all accounts they treated him kindly. A doctor was called who determined that the man suffered nervous dyspepsia and required rest and quiet.

"A priest, skilled in languages, was located and came to hear the man's strange speech. The priest confessed that he could neither name the man's language nor even from what region it might originate. Some theorized that the stranger had been shipwrecked and was the only survivor, and that he had come from a land in some unexplored part of the world where there was a rich civilization. The imagination being what it is, these people also believed the stranger was a man of importance in his own land—a prince or a wealthy adventurer. The problem with this theory, of course, was that the town of Compton Heath lay some twenty miles inland, and it seemed unlikely that this man would have traveled so far without first encountering other towns or homes and their people.

"But then the stranger was not quite right in his mind, so it was not entirely out of the question that he had wandered so far. The local officials took the man under their wing, not quite sure what should be done. He became something of a local curiosity, and men of learning traveled from neighboring towns to see him for themselves and to hear his strange tongue.

"But this situation did not last long. One evening a grand coach arrived, from where no one knew, and when it left the stranger was no longer domiciled in Compton Heath. The officials claimed the man had disappeared of his own free will, though few believed them. In fact, the town worthies were clearly frightened and did not like to speak of the matter at all. Afterward the rumor went about that a mage had sent for the stranger, though this can be neither proven nor disproven."

Erasmus was silent for a moment, and Hayes turned his attention to him, trying to read his reaction to the news of a mage's involvement. This was clearly the question he hoped Erasmus would answer, for everyone knew that Erasmus Flattery had once lived in the house of the mage.

"What year did this happen?" Erasmus asked.

"1453."

"Over sixty years ago."

Hayes nodded. "As we traveled to the village, we speculated endlessly about the gentleman's interest. It seemed extremely odd to us. The gentleman in question is of a serious bent of mind, I will tell you, yet this story seemed the kind of thing that would be taken up by people who believed in fairies and spirits. We could not quite understand, for certainly we could give no credence to such a tale ourselves."

"So that is what you discovered?" Erasmus said. "There was no truth in it?"

Hayes looked a little troubled. "We set out only to disprove it, of course, but that was to be more difficult than we expected.

"We arrived in Compton Heath more than half a century after the fact, but we could imagine no other way to begin. The incident had not happened so long ago that there would not still be a few who had been alive at the time: people who had seen the stranger and heard the man's odd tongue." Hayes' brow knit together, and his look grew more serious. "But nothing was to be as we imagined. We were not in the town long before becoming convinced that, indeed, something strange *had* occurred there on or about the dates that we had been given. Certainly the townsfolk earnestly believed it, at any rate. And though many were willing to speak to us about it, those who had been directly involved in the incident—those few still alive—would not even see us, despite all our best efforts and charm. It was utterly frustrating. Everything we learned came second- or third-hand, and though it all corroborated our employer's story, none of it came from anyone directly involved. We had been instructed to be absolutely thorough in our inquiry, but it was impossible. The people who had been directly involved, some of whom were said to have met the stranger, would not speak with us. They would not even open their doors so that we might plead our case."

Hayes sat down in his chair and leaned forward, hands on his knees. "I will tell you, Erasmus, after a week in the village we were more intrigued than ever, for the silence of the people involved seemed terribly peculiar. A bit macabre, even. We finally agreed that our last hope remained with the doctor who'd taken an interest in the stranger—the one who had diagnosed nervous dyspepsia—for he was the only man who we had not approached who might still be alive.

"We were especially interested in him because several people in Compton Heath told us that the doctor had kept notes of his observations of the stranger, and not just his medical observations. A few months after the stranger's disappearance the doctor had moved on, and there were only rumors of his whereabouts, but even so I thought we must pursue it. We feared we would find him as silent as the people of Compton Heath—if he were alive at all—but felt there was little other hope of fulfilling our obligation to our employer."

"While in Compton Heath we did find some intriguing bits of information," Hayes said, sitting back, "though, of course, much that we were told was contradictory, so it was difficult to discern what might be true. Apparently the stranger could write, not as we do, of course, but he wrote nonetheless. An old woman showed me what was alleged to be a sample of this script, and for a small fee she allowed me to copy it. I'm not sure she isn't laughing with her friends about this yet, but all the same, I paid her the money and took my copy away, as not a few others had before me, I suspect."

"Do you have that writing?"

Hayes shook his head. "I'm afraid it is being held hostage in Merton with many of my other possessions, pending the payment of some back rent."

"Ah. And that is the story?"

"Not quite," Hayes said, glancing at Erasmus, a bit of triumph in his look. "You see we eventually found the physician who had first examined the Stranger.

"It was not an easy task," Hayes said, "for the man was prone to moving and not leaving a forwarding address, though this did not seem to be for the usual reasons. The good doctor appears to have been as dedicated to the payment of his debts as he was to shifting his domicile. He moved almost yearly for most of his life, before finally settling in the village of Nearbrook, on the Tollingham Canal.

"It is my guess, now, that the good doctor felt he had finally managed to outrun whatever he believed to be pursuing him—or perhaps he had just grown too old to keep running. We found Ripke, for that was his name, living in the house of his daughter and son-in-law, who was a physician as well. I regret to say that the beginnings of dementia were evident in the doctor's speech and manner, although he had not yet succumbed completely. There were times when he spoke with clarity, and his memories were not so intermingled with his delusions.

"It was the oddest meeting, Erasmus. His daughter began by

assuring us that the old man would not speak to us of this matter. Indeed, that he would not speak of it even with her. We asked if we might talk with Doctor Ripke all the same in hopes that we might change his mind, and this was eventually allowed.

"And talk we did. We sat in a small garden above the canal, the old man tucked beneath an ancient, threadbare blanket, for he would use no other. He seemed something like a child who believes that once under the blankets he is safe from all the monsters hiding in the dark. The conversation ranged freely, as you might imagine, though it was not all unpleasant. At times his old self, or so I imagined, would come forth and he displayed real charm, and even some concern for others. Then, very unexpectedly he would lapse into tirades, for he believed himself a victim of terrible persecution.

"The man took a liking to me, I think, and at a sign from my partner, Kehler, I took over our inquiry, Kehler being content to sit and listen. It was some time before I could steer him round to the topic of interest to us, but finally after some cajoling, he fell into a long silence, and then said, 'Damn him, I shall not take it to the grave!' I think he had been keeping the secret so long, and living in fear, that he could no longer bear it. 'Let him take me now and be done with it,' he kept repeating, as though some terrible fiend would learn of our conversation and come for him. Occasionally he would even fall to accusing us of being agents of this thing he feared but never named.

"It was a long difficult process taking three days, and I don't think I would ever have been allowed to press my questions as I did, for obviously the interview was a detriment to the old man's already precarious state, but his daughter was clearly even more interested than I. She sat just out of the man's sight and listened carefully to every word, hardly able to believe that her father was telling the story at last." Hayes stopped to drink, his throat dry. "I learned a number of things from Ripke that our visit to Compton Heath had not uncovered. The stranger was certainly civilized, not a wild man as some claimed. He was modest regarding his body and submitted to the doctor's examination only after it was demonstrated to him that he would not be harmed. His hands bore no calluses or signs of labor. He was clearly curious, even amused at times by things he saw. The workings of a clock caused him great merriment, apparently, and he obviously understood the ways of mechanical things. Given writing implements he not only wrote in a script no one had ever seen but produced a number of sketches of objects, the purpose of which could not be readily grasped."

"Farrelle's flames!" Erasmus blurted out. "Do these drawings and script exist?"

Hayes shook his head sadly. "No, but I will come to that part of the story. The stranger began to learn Farr; quite rapidly I believe, and it soon became clear that he knew more about many things than his supposed teachers. He drew a fairly detailed anatomical drawing of the human body, and clearly had strongly held beliefs about how it functioned—Ripke was of the opinion that the man might well have been a physician in his own land. If what Ripke said was true, the stranger suggested things about the functions of the heart and lungs that are only just now being considered. For instance, Ripke is convinced that the stranger did not believe that air in the lungs cooled the heat of the blood but rather *infused* it somehow, and this enriched fluid was carried to the extremities of the body to nurture it, like fertilizer does a garden. Or so I understood him to say."

"This is what some medical men are proposing now," Erasmus said, a bit surprised.

Hayes nodded. "So it is." Though he did not seem nearly as astonished as Erasmus. "Just as Ripke and the others began to realize what a miracle they might have on their hands, a large carriage arrived in Compton Heath late in the night." Hayes took a long drink of his brandy, and seemed suddenly very sad. "Ripke was not present when the coach appeared, but as Compton Heath was a small village, he soon had word of it. He hurried to the house where the stranger was lodged and found a scene of terrible confusion. Horsemen held back the few onlookers from an ornate carriage that had pulled up in the lane, and when the doctor tried to enter the house to determine what went on, he was stopped by the horsemen, who would provide no explanation. He stood helplessly by as he saw the bewildered stranger bundled into the carriage, and as the door opened, in the darkened interior, he saw a man, or at least his silhouette, calmly waiting.

"At this point in the telling, Doctor Ripke went into a spasm of cursing and cowering that finally sent us away for the rest of that day and part of the next. When we were allowed to return, only I was able to speak with the doctor. He would see no others. I found a haggard looking Ripke waiting, for he had been awake raving all night. But he was more lucid than at any other time during our visit, as though the fit of madness had run its course and left him too exhausted to continue with such mania. I took a seat with him before the fire—for though it was a warm day, he huddled next to the hearth as though it were the worst day of winter—and he suddenly reached out and took hold of my hand. You cannot imagine the look he gave me then, as though he pleaded with me for his own life. 'Pursue this no further,' he said, his voice all but gone from his night of raving.

"When I asked why, he would not answer but curled up in his chair, drawing his ancient blanket up over his head, and from underneath I heard him muttering, and then crying pitifully. I could learn nothing more from him, and finally his daughter took pity on the man's state and sent me away."

"But what of the writing and the sketches?"

"They disappeared at the same time as the stranger."

"And no one could reproduce them?"

Hayes shook his head. "Ripke tried, but each time he put pen to paper, he would be overcome by a strange fear. A fear so great that it drove what he had seen out of his memory. And his notes, taken at the time, could not be found. His daughter thought that he hoarded them in a wooden box which he kept locked and hidden away, but when he died, a few months after our interview, her husband opened the box and found nothing but pages of gibberish. Lines that connected in no way that conveyed meaning. The artistic equivalent of a madman's ravings."

Erasmus felt a sudden chill himself, for he could almost see the poor doctor huddled up by his fire, slipping back into madness. "And who was it took the man away?"

"I was hoping you would tell me, Erasmus. This doctor was filled with a terror that he could never escape. I might dismiss this as just the dementia of one old man, but several others who were present that night suffered similarly—two much worse, in fact. They self-murdered not long after. Was this the doings of a mage? That is my question? Could one place such a terror on a man? Would they do such a terrible thing, for surely this Ripke had done nothing that could offend a mage? Unless there was some part of the story he was not telling. A stranger appeared in his village, and the doctor endeavored to learn something of the man, and did nothing to cause him harm. That is all." Hayes stared hard at Erasmus, clearly unsettled by what had happened to this poor doctor. "Could this have been the workings of a mage?"

"I fear it is entirely possible," Erasmus said quietly. "I . . . yes, they could instill such a fear in a man, and it would not likely go away with time—not in the years that men live, at least. That this man Ripke lasted as long as he did with some apparent sanity is the miracle."

"You speak with some confidence, Erasmus," Hayes said.

Erasmus glanced at him, his annoyance not hidden, but Hayes did not look at all abashed.

"Yes, well, I had an experience while I was in the house of Eldrich that left me with some special knowledge." He pressed the tips of his fingers together, staring into his past, Hayes was sure; and it was not a happy past either.

"Perhaps it is an evening for stories," Erasmus said softly, as though he spoke to himself. "I will tell you of this one incident that might give you some evidence of the mage's indifference to our ideas of what is just." Erasmus paused, as though reconsidering, but then pressed on. "The millennium was but four years off when I was taken to the house of Eldrich," he began. "To this day I have only the vaguest idea of why this was done. Some feat I had performed as a child, I would suppose, though for the life of me I can't remember what.

"My father, the duke, must have made the arrangements, though he never bothered to explain his reasoning to me—a pattern that continued through the rest of his days.

"There were three other boys in the house at the time. One was two years older, had been there longer and kept to himself; another was younger and had attached himself to a women servant. That left Percy and me.

"Percy was three months older, several inches taller, and though quick of wit, he left it to me to lead in our friendship. His family were mildly successful shopkeepers, I understood, but even at that age I cared little for social distinctions. He was a good and true friend, and we stood by each other in a situation that, though never truly threatening, was less than hospitable and more than a little strange.

"Percy had less idea of why he was there than I did, and the fact that his family had no influence at all makes me wonder if my own family's prominence had anything at all to do with my being there.

We knew that Eldrich was said to be a mage, and we were both terrified and fascinated by this. That is to say, by day we were fascinated, but once darkness fell, terror reigned. Most nights, after the lights were doused, we slipped into the same bed and clung to each other, almost paralyzed with fear, until we finally fell asleep. We were never sure what we were afraid of, though we speculated endlessly.

"For months we didn't see Eldrich himself, so we imagined that he was a hideous near-monster, or perhaps turned into one after nightfall. The one truly frightening thing we did see was Eldrich's familiar, a great wolf that roamed the halls, often by night. This beast never actually threatened us in any way, though we did much to stay distant from it, but we did on occasion hear sniffing outside our door—and there were many more times when I suspect we imagined it. This put a fear into us that cannot be truly conveyed, for there is no one so accomplished at terror as a ten-year-old.

"We were given a pleasant enough room to share and put in the charge of a tutor who was to see to our studies. He was a good-hearted old man who reeked of tobacco smoke and the fecund soil from the gardens in which he loved to dig. In the spring he also smelled of horse droppings.

"Mr. Walky, as he was called, was a man of prodigious learning—or perhaps I should say he had been a man of prodigious learning in his day. By the time Percy and I came to him, his mind had begun to . . . 'decay' I think would be the right word. It was solid enough in places, and growing if not quite flourishing in others, but, overall it had begun to lose its foliage, and the trunk was sadly rotten at its center.

"Walky often called us by the names of former students, and lost track of our lessons, his mind wandering off. Very occasionally he would tell us the most wondrous tales of the past, and sometimes even tales of the doings in the house of Eldrich. To children, these seemed more like stories than history—like ghost stories, some of them—and it was difficult for us to discern those that were real from those that were fanciful.

"Had I been only a little older, I would have been wise enough to set these down in ink, but I was not yet perfectly proficient in my letters, and—to be honest—the thought never occurred to me. They seemed so much like tales from old books that I didn't for a moment imagine that they would not be recorded elsewhere. But I realize now that they weren't—at least not anywhere that could be found.

"Percy and I had a great deal of time to ourselves—too much, really—and, I confess, we got up to some mischief occasionally. For this Mr. Walky would give us extra work and refused to tell us stories, though earning his temporary disapproval was far more injurious, for we had no other friend or ally in that strange world.

"In all the months I lived in Eldrich's house I never actually spoke with the master himself and, in fact, only saw him perhaps three times. The first I was sitting in a window seat staring out at the garden. It was a cool autumn day, windless and with an odd, thin cloud layer through which the disk of the sun was visible, though just. In the distance occasional holes in a more dense cloud layer would open and shafts of light that we then called 'mage rays' would illuminate some far-off patch of the countryside, the colors of fall appearing there like some promised treasure.

"I was supposed to be reading a book, but as I had not the habits of mind that I later developed, I was staring out the window, daydreaming. At some point I realized there was a man standing in the garden, looking down into one of the fading flowerbeds. He was a tall gentleman dressed in black but for a white shirt. On his head he wore no wig and his dark hair, curly and loose, framed his pale face which, at that distance, was hard to distinguish.

"I had about two seconds of mild curiosity before I had a sudden realization: this was the legendary Eldrich! I knew it as though I had seen him a thousand times. *This was the mage.* My heart began to pound like mad, and I leaned forward to press my forehead to the glass so that I might have a better look. At that very moment the man looked up, perhaps attracted by the movement in the window. And I swear to you that I thought my heart had actually stopped.

"The look this man fixed on me. . . ! I was sure he could read my thoughts, learn every bit of wickedness I had ever thought or done. I nearly fell out of the window seat I was so terrified. He had noticed me! And all those months I believed he was unaware of my existence, but now I knew this was not so. I could tell by the look. He knew me. Eldrich knew me!

"I flew back to my room as though pursued by the foulest murderer, and burst through the door in such a near hysteria that I alarmed Percy even more than I had been frightened myself.

"For a long moment I could not speak, but only gesticulated

wildly, opening and closing my mouth to no avail; finally I managed, 'Eldrich.' And Percy, who thought I meant the mage was on his way to our room, went completely white with horror. He began to tremble uncontrollably and actually became so light-headed that he collapsed onto the bed, and his eyes threatened to roll back in their sockets.

" 'What does he want with us?' he whispered when he had recovered a little.

" 'He wants nothing of you,' I told him. 'At least not that I know of. But he saw me! Saw me shirking my studies. Flames, what if he turns me into a goat? Or fixes me with a stutter?'

"It sounds ridiculous, now, but at the time I had never been so terrified. We both stared at the door as though it would burst open at any moment and the mage would be carried in on a blast of wind, and we would find out at last for what terrible purpose we had been sent to this place.

"We stayed like that until a servant came to call us to supper—he must have wondered why, when he opened the door, we were clinging to each other, cowering as though we were about to be spitted, our eyes the size of saucers. Of course, Eldrich never appeared and we recovered from our fright after a few days, but we never laughed about it, nor teased each other. No, anything to do with the mage was not a laughing matter. And I will tell you honestly that I am not convinced that this fright was simply the natural result of two young boys living in strange circumstances. Can you imagine what kind of man would take amusement from so terrifying children?" Erasmus stopped, unsure if he would go on, but the memories kept flooding back.

"While I was there, the older boy tried to run away, but reappeared the next day looking decidedly sullen, and could never be convinced to speak of the matter. This proved what we suspected: we were prisoners, and though it might have been more like boys at boarding school than prisoners in gaol, a stranger boarding school I had never heard tell of.

"One of the things Walky taught us, once the weather grew fair, was the art of swimming. He scoffed at our protests that it would ruin our constitutions, and called us old wives. His own good health, he claimed, was due to regular physical labor and swimming. He even said that the mage himself swam, though we did not believe that Lord Eldrich would stoop to such a frivolous activity.

"We not only learned the art of swimming, we grew to like it and while the weather remained warm, complained if a day went by without us being allowed into the water. Walky used this as a carrot for us. 'Finish your maths, my young lions, and we shall go for a nice swim. Be about it now.'

"He often called us his 'young lions,' especially when he was pleased with us or when he was in a particularly agreeable mood. I did not know it at the time, but old half-mad Walky, as we thought of him, was a good friend to us, and concerned with our welfare.

"Sometime later in my stay at Eldrich's house, Walky's grip on reality seemed to slip a little more. Occasionally he would forget what lesson he had begun and make odd requests of us. Once he asked me to name the three herbs used to purify water, which I had to tell him was not in my course of studies. Another day when he was particularly distracted—to the point of mumbling to himself—he demanded I recite the incantation for locating springs, and when he saw the look of incomprehension on my face, he began a strange rhythmic chant in a language neither Percy nor I had ever heard. After a moment of this strange behavior, Walky faltered in mid-word, looking at us in astonishment. Quite abruptly he fled the room.

"We did not know what to say, and for a long moment sat there in stunned silence. But there was no doubt about what we had heard. It had been magic! We both felt the power of it. Walky had been performing an enchantment!

" 'Do you know what I think?' I said to Percy. 'Walky must have been a teacher of mages.'

" 'He'd have to be a hundred years old—maybe more,' Percy protested, always practical.

" 'Nevertheless, that is what he is doing in Eldrich's house.' I was utterly sure of what I said.

" 'Then he must be a mage himself,' Percy said.

" 'Maybe not. He might prepare the young ones before they go to study with the mage proper.'

"There was a long silence while we considered the ramifications of this insight, neither of us wanting to actually put into words what it meant. We did not look at each other, and the silence stretched on. I remember hearing the insects buzzing outside the open window.

" 'Are we to be mages, then?' Percy said, his voice very small and filled with awe.

" 'No,' I said quickly. 'It can't be that.' But I was not so sure." Erasmus fell silent, lost in his memories of those days, long past.

Hayes leaned forward. "And was that it?! Was that why you were there?"

Erasmus looked up, startled. "What? No, of course not. I don't know to this day. . . ." He felt his head shake in denial, though of what he was not sure.

Chapter Four

THE final hour of darkness held the city close, not willing to release it until touched by the burning sun. The birds that lived in the eaves and openings of houses stirred and cooed their waking songs, like men and women sleepily readying themselves for their day's toil.

Anna's carriage entered the courtyard through an arched opening and she heard the gates close behind her. By the main door, a lamp chased the darkness from that small corner of the courtyard, illuminating the wisteria vine climbing the posts of the entry porch.

It's done, she thought. *For better or worse, it's done.*

The door to the carriage opened, and she was handed down to the cobbles, where she stood a moment, not quite ready to go in.

Banks appeared beneath the wisteria.

"Anna?"

"Coming," she said, still not wanting to. A walk in the garden to clear her head and calm her was what she would prefer. She had never felt such elation and such anxiety at the same time. The two emotions seemed to be struggling within her, producing a nervousness that was entirely uncharacteristic.

Banks took a step toward her, and rather than have him come and lead her inside, she relented and went toward the door, sweeping past the concerned-looking young man so that he could not take her arm in his too-possessive manner.

The house was warm, the air redolent with smoke and the smells of coffee.

"Everyone is here?" she asked Banks.

He nodded. "Yes, there have been no mishaps. Your part went well, I take it?"

"Not as I expected, but well enough. We are in the library?"

"The dining room, in fact."

She set out for the dining room where she found the others seated around the table, talking with animation despite the hour.

"Anna," Halsey said, standing, as did the others. Halsey was the oldest of the group, the leader by both seniority and acclamation.

"We've just been speculating about Skye," Kells said. "So tell us what happened."

She took the chair that Banks pulled out for her and collapsed in it, suddenly tired. The high back pressed into her skull, and she shut her eyes a moment.

"All went much as we expected. Not as well as we might have liked, but not as badly as it could have–not nearly as badly." The sound of a coffee cup arriving on the table before her brought her upright. "He . . . he was shocked, as you might imagine, but I think, on balance, the earl believed me. The unconscious sailors helped make my point. As the earl left, he owned that he was in our debt. . . ." She lifted her cup and let what she'd said sink in.

"Well," Kells said, "that is hardly bad news, though it was the least we could expect from a gentleman. We did save him from gaol, after all. From utter ruin, in truth." Kells nodded. He was always quick to judge. Quick to act. In some ways she felt closest to him for that. As usual, Halsey said nothing, weighing her words, considering every possible interpretation that might suggest disaster.

"But what will Skye do now? Did he say?" Delisle was five years older than Anna, and asked most of the questions—even the obvious ones, which was good, she'd come to realize. Many things would never have been discussed openly without him.

"I don't know, and I didn't ask. It was a delicate moment. As we agreed, the most important thing was that Skye realize and believe we had saved him—for no reason other than our admiration of him. I think he did believe that. What of your own tasks?"

Delisle glanced quickly at Banks. "I wish we could say things went so well. We were almost apprehended in Samual Hayes' rooms. A pack of navy men came up as we were there, and we had no exit but the window. I fear they are still wondering how we jumped from such a height and apparently sustained no injury. It was the worst luck, but once we were up the stairs, there was nowhere else to go."

"It never occurred to us that the Admiralty would send men to search Hayes' rooms at the same time as they sprung their trap for Skye," Banks said. "I still can't imagine why they did it."

Halsey was shaking his head just a little, sitting back in his chair, a look of some disbelief on his face. He was not happy with what he heard.

"You had no difficulties?" Anna asked the old man, her tone quiet and deferential. He had never been entirely in favor of this endeavor and now seemed to be having his worst fears confirmed.

"Difficulties? No," he said softly. "I have always managed what must be done, even when it is murder." He shook his head again, clearly disturbed. "So, Skye did not offer to open any gates for you?" he asked, fixing Anna with a gaze. She wondered how a person made their look so hard.

"He offered nothing, not that I expected he would. Not yet. But I still do not doubt that my vision was true. He *will* open a gate for us. I'm sure of it."

"Yes, but who will wait inside? You still do not know, I collect?" Halsey's gaze didn't soften, nor did it release her.

Anna shook her head. Visions were not so easily explained, and augury was imperfectly understood, even by the ancients. Anna could recall her vision in detail if she closed her eyes, yet she still could not say who stood beyond the gate. A man who held a book and a white blossom, but as he turned toward her so that she might see his face, a light blinded her. Nothing more. Skye would open the gate to knowledge and power, that was the vision's meaning. Who held the book, she was sure was irrelevant.

"Let us not have the argument again," Kells said. "It will not come out differently. Eldrich still plans to bring an end to the arts in our time. The years of caution are past. We cannot wait Eldrich out—not now. When the mage is gone, the arts will disappear with him."

Yes, Anna thought. She had seen it. Eldrich disappearing down the corridors of a forest, leaving behind a world devoid of its former power, devoid of all magic. She shuddered at the memory. The forest had seemed so lifeless, though to most it would appear still green and growing. She could not imagine wanting to live in such a world.

"But, Anna," Banks said gently. "You've not seen what we recovered from Hayes' rooms." He slid a letter across the table. "There was much more—a journal, a sheaf of notes—but we were caught unawares and left it all behind in our panic."

Anna picked up the letter.

"It is from this other young man Skye employed," Delisle said. "Fenwick Kehler. We have wondered where he got to. It appears he has been researching in the Farrellite archive in Wooton!"

My Dear Hayes:

I had begun to despair of ever accomplishing my task here, no matter how hard I searched, but recently things have changed. You would not believe what I have found, sir! All that we ever dreamed and more! The archive is a mine of knowledge lost and forgotten, one must only find the vein one seeks. I will tell you much more when next we meet. I hope to be granted a few days' leave come late spring and will travel to Avonel in all haste.

I hope this letter finds you well.

Yours as always,
F. W. Kehler

"It says very little," Anna said, surprised that Banks would think this so significant.

"So one would think, but we saw Hayes' journal. Pages and pages about the Stranger of Compton Heath. And much speculation about Baumgere! Assuming that Kehler is still in the employ of Skye, the letter says a great deal. One should realize that Kehler must write with extreme caution. After all, he is clearly delving into matters of which the priests would not approve—and they are likely not above monitoring the correspondence of their guest scholars.

No, if read in the proper light, this letter says a great deal. Skye might open the gate, and the man standing inside could well be this young scholar, Kehler. Who can guess what he has found in Wooton? We know the priests have been hoarding knowledge for centuries, and not all of it of a religious nature."

Anna shrugged. "Do we know what has happpened to Hayes? Do the Admiralty have him?"

No one answered for a second.

"We don't know," Kells said. "It is possible. Now that Skye has escaped their trap, it will not look good if they have taken this young man into custody. He is, after all, innocent of any crime. I don't know what they'll do with him. And who knows what the worthy gentlemen of the Admiralty will think if he tells them what he has been researching for Skye."

"We needn't worry about the Admiralty," Halsey said suddenly, his aged, gravelly voice sounding tired and somewhat sad. "For now we must watch for any sign of Eldrich's hand in all of this. We wait and keep our distance."

"Certainly caution has served us well all the long years," Anna heard herself say, "but those days are at an end. If we are too cautious now, we'll sacrifice everything. The arts will be lost to us forever. And Eldrich will have triumphed."

"You will learn a terrible lesson, Anna, if you persist in underestimating him," Halsey said, some frustration in his voice. "*He is a mage.* Even if Eldrich is the least skilled of mages, he is still more powerful than you can imagine. You do not begin to understand what he can do. It is entirely possible that Skye does his bidding, or that the men who attempted to ruin Skye did so on behalf of the mage, whether they were aware of it or not. And we have leaped to Skye's rescue. We have revealed ourselves. Revealed ourselves after centuries of hiding. We have been reckless enough. Now we must wait.

"It is one thing to say that the time for caution has passed and another to go running foolishly into the arms of Eldrich. I will not allow it. Imprudence now will be our ruin. Let us see what Skye will do. I don't want to find that he has opened this much vaunted gate only to discover that the man who awaits us is no man at all—but a mage."

"Perhaps Anna should attempt to see again. After all, we have contacted Skye. We have passed a way-point—a significant one."

Delisle glanced a bit guiltily at Anna. "Things might be clearer, now."

Anna sat immobile. The thought of attempting augury again brought up something near to panic. She had gone down that path too often, at great cost, and more often than not there was nothing to show for it. Halsey had begun to protect her from it recently, protect her from the others who saw augury as the solution to all doubt, despite the fact that it never was. She waited for the old man to come to her rescue so that she would not have to start making excuses . . . start showing her fear.

It draws the life out of me, she thought. *Can't you see that?*

Halsey did not look at her, but suddenly nodded his head, the smallest motion. "Can you bear it?" he asked looking up at her, the sadness he had nurtured all evening suddenly manifest, like the scream of a newborn.

"Of course," she heard herself say. There was no other answer. She was no less dedicated than the others who would do anything to keep Eldrich from accomplishing his purpose.

But why is he doing it? she asked herself again. She did not know. The mages were selfish and willful. They needed no more reason than that.

They are taking the magic with them . . . somewhere.

She saw the image of Eldrich, disappearing down a corridor of the forest. Saw the world left behind. A world where augury would no longer be possible. A world where her talent had even less chance of blossoming than it did now. No chance, in fact.

She pushed back from the table, not waiting for the others. Better to lead than follow. She was the one born to talent. She was the one who would lead one day, if all went as they hoped.

She went out into the garden, into the starlight, listening to the night as she walked. Forcing her heart to be still, her mind to become calm.

I cannot be afraid, she chanted over and over again. There was a difference between not showing fear and not being afraid, and simply not showing fear would not pass here. It could even bring her to . . . well, she did not like to think about that.

They went to a small pool among the trees. Anna stopped here and breathed in the night, drew the darkness into her lungs, the starlight, the shadows. Still, they were so still. She listened for the songs of the stars—the choral stars.

The stars appeared before her as she closed her eyes, wavering, and then holding steady. She began a whispered chant, bending quickly to make a mark in the earth, to draw a figure of pale light.

When it held steady, she rose and stepped into the figure, not needing to open her eyes, for the lines burned in her mind, burned so that she could feel them.

It is not pain, she told herself, though she longed to shut out the glowing lines, longed to scream.

It is not pain. She repeated the lie, knowing it was the only way to survive.

A burning heat searing her nerves like fire, like the coldest ice. Pain so terrible in its intensity that it did not seem human. Mankind could not feel such agony. Like birthing a child and then experiencing your own horrible death as the child howled.

Anna screamed, opening her eyes suddenly. Staring down into the dark sky of the pool, where the stars hung like points of white hot fire.

I'm looking into my own mind, she thought, and then stiffly tossed a pebble into the water. The stars wavered, swaying back and forth and she felt herself falling. But still she stared, waiting. Waiting. Opening herself to the emptiness, to the agony, but only for an instant. It was all she could bear. All anyone could bear. And then she shut her eyes, feeling the earth beneath her knees, hands taking hold of her.

She had seen nothing. *Nothing.*

Chapter Five

THIS particular visitor always arrived unannounced and, somehow, unexpected. Considering the amount of time that Sir John dedicated to contemplating this gentleman, and the dread he felt whenever Bryce actually appeared, it was impressive that the man invariably seemed to arrive when Sir John's guard was down. The maid thought it very peculiar, and Sir John was sure that his own reaction made her even more suspicious. There was, however, nothing he could do about it. These visits were not a matter he controlled or even had influence upon—and not many things transpired in Avonel that Sir John could not influence.

It was understood that Sir John never kept this visitor waiting, no matter the hour or circumstances. He looked at the clock again in disbelief. Not even half-five–still dark, and only morning by the most liberal interpretation of the term. He bent over and stirred the coals of the fire, carefully arranging dry kindling. Mornings were cool, though that would soon change, but a fire was still a pleasure if not an absolute necessity. There was a crack from the cedar, and a thin thread of smoke streamed up. Flame erupted with a sigh.

Sir John was still dressed in his nightclothes, and felt strangely vulnerable, not that he usually felt any less vulnerable when Mr. Bryce came to call, no matter what the circumstances.

"Congratulations on your baronetcy, Sir John." Bryce stood at the door to the drawing room. No apology for arriving at such an hour, not that Sir John expected any.

"May I?" Bryce gestured toward a chair.

"Please. Brandy? Wine? I have a fine claret from the southern slopes of Farrow." Sir John insisted on pretending it was late at night rather than obscenely early in the morning. It made it all easier to deal with, somehow.

"Claret, please."

Sir John poured them each a glass and took a seat by the fire. Bryce was, without a doubt, the most self-assured man Sir John had ever met—not arrogant or full of himself, but apparently without self-doubt. And the effect of this confidence on others was profound. Sir John was quite sure the King himself would defer to the man.

The odd thing about it was that Sir John, who prided himself on his ability to understand his fellow man, could not quite explain how Bryce managed to convey this degree of confidence, nor what lay at its center.

The truth was that Bryce was invariably extremely polite, even sensitive; things that Sir John did not associate with this kind of self-assurance. Power was what he thought of when he met a man with confidence, and Bryce was not typical of men who possessed power.

Sir John thought Bryce almost inhumanly precise. His dress was impeccable, his speech exact and explicit, as though it conveyed his thought perfectly and without effort. Sir John had never spoken to a man who did not occasionally grope for a word, or use some term that was less than exact—except for Bryce. The man was meticulous in every way—disturbingly so. Sir John could not escape the feeling that he was dealing with someone who had passed beyond normal human functioning.

Sir John could not imagine Bryce ever making a mistake, needing sleep. He was certain the man did not sweat. Bryce existed on some other plane and descended only occasionally to the muddled world of men, who must seem only slightly more organized and thoughful than beasts to him.

Bryce sat regarding him for a moment, sipping his wine. "I suspect the seeds you've sown have begun to bear fruit, Sir John."

As a political animal Sir John had spent many years learning to keep his feelings and reactions to himself, but he was under no illusion that he could hide such things from Bryce, so no doubt what Bryce saw was the flash of fear that Sir John had just experienced.

"What has happened?" Sir John asked. Who had fallen? Moncrief or Skye?

"That is what I hope you will be able to tell me. I suggest you pay a visit to your friends in the Admiralty. Bring every little detail you gather to me. I will weigh them, Sir John. Do not presume to know what is significant yourself. Only I can decide that. Do you understand?"

Sir John nodded. This little lecture was unnecessary, for he was well aware that he had not the slightest insight into the man's intentions. At Bryce's instructions, Sir John had nurtured this feud between Moncrief and the Earl of Skye—though feud was hardly the right word; Moncrief never let his vendettas become public. It was one of the reasons the man was so feared. He would go about knifing you in the back and all the while you would have not the slightest sign of what was about to befall you. But by any name, Sir John had encouraged Moncrief's jealousy and loathing of Skye. Not a task he had taken on with great joy. Sir John might not understand all the discoveries Skye had made, but he had no doubt that the man was a genius, a genius and largely benign. Benign in a society where Moncrief was the most voracious of predators, but where predators were not in the least uncommon.

"I will visit you again this night. That will give you ample time. . . ."

This was most definitely not a question, and a day would certainly not be anything like the time Sir John needed. "I . . . yes, that will be adequate."

"Good." Bryce looked at Sir John and attempted something like a smile. Like all other human emotions, pleasure and joy seemed beneath him, and any attempt at imitating them was doomed to sad failure—though Sir John certainly never found any amusement in such attempts.

"You do not look pleased, Sir John. Were my assurances that we intend no harm to Skye not enough?"

"More than adequate, but I suppose I still worry. Setting Moncrief against someone . . . I don't know if there is any animal so vicious as the King's Man."

"Yes, it is a wonder . . . the way he walks through civilized society, as though he were actually part of it. . . ." Bryce shrugged. He was not given to philosophizing about mankind. "You admire Skye."

"Yes," Sir John said quickly. "Yes, I do. But not for the reasons he is admired by everyone in the nation."

Bryce did not say anything, but waited patiently.

"I admire him for his convictions. It is no secret that Skye has had great misgivings about the use of his invention. The cannon is the deadliest weapon in the history of warfare, after all. Some say we have hardly begun to understand its uses. And look what has happened already. The battle off Cloud's End was pressed too far, many think. It is said that the admiral of the Entonne fleet tried to surrender, but even so his ships were destroyed. They have taken poor Admiral Stewart to task for this, but it was policy. I have no doubt of it. The goal was to destroy the Entonne fleet to the last ship." Sir John shook his head. "Barbaric, really. And so many seamen lost. It did not matter what flag they sailed under, they should have been allowed to surrender. It was nothing short of murder.

"Lord Skye is not pleased with the way the Farr government has used this advantage he has given them, and I dare say he would be less willing to give them such a weapon again."

Bryce actually raised an eyebrow at these words. "A man of conscience," he said, and Sir John nodded. Bryce seemed to consider this for a moment and then his focus returned, his gaze fixing on Sir John.

"Well, you needn't worry about this moral dilemma much longer. You see the Entonne now have the ability to produce cannon and gunpowder on their own. In fact, they have been engaged in this activity for some months."

Sir John sat forward in his chair. "How in the world. . . ? Was it Skye?"

Bryce shrugged. "I don't know how they discovered this. It was apparently not so difficult to manage, really, not once the cannon had been invented. Even the Admiralty must have realized their advantage would be brief. No doubt that played a part in their decision to destroy the Entonne fleet—press their advantage while they still had it."

The Entonne had the cannon?!

"You look rather surprised, Sir John. It was inevitable. And will the world be different when Entonne has the cannon? No, it will be the same as it was for the last three hundred years: neither country having an advantage. Better to have balance."

"But my government should be informed."

Bryce's manner seemed to indicate that he thought this a matter of little consequence.

"If you think it's important. I suppose it might profit you to be the first with the news. So you see? Do I not act with your best interests at heart? Was that not always our arrangement? Have you not been granted a baronetcy as a result of my efforts?"

"Are you suggesting that I'm not worthy of this honor?" Sir John said, the words out of his mouth before he realized what he said.

Bryce only smiled. "You are thrice worthy, my dear Sir John, but worth has little to do with the granting of titles, as you well know. You have long been worthy, but never influential—at least not influential enough."

"But whose purpose does this baronetcy suit, I often ask myself."

"My employer's, Sir John, make no mistake of that. My employer's. But will it not benefit you as well? Do you not have the joy of it? Does it not gratify you to be addressed as 'Sir John'? Speak honestly."

"You know it does," he said quietly, feeling a little overwhelmed.

"And I know your fear, Sir John. You worry that you will be asked to compromise your principles. Or that my employer will demand something of you that will bring about your ruin or the ruin of your good name. Is this not so?" He did not wait for an answer, as though he didn't require confirmation of another's thoughts. "But rest assured; my employer does not wish you ill. You're a good and loyal servant, Sir John. Why would he endanger one such as yourself? When one has a champion race horse, only a fool would demand it run to the hounds. My employer, Sir John, is the least foolish of men, let me assure you."

Sir John felt himself nod. One could not disbelieve Bryce. As with so many things, he was likely above lying. If he did not want

Sir John to know something, he merely did not tell him. He had no qualms about that. There was always an insidious logic to any claim Bryce made. Sir John often wondered if he were not merely under the man's influence, bespelled by his superior logic and overwhelming self-confidence. Was he losing sight of his own principles, or merely learning to see the world more clearly, tutored by this stranger who came to him at all hours?

Bryce waited patiently, almost watching Sir John's thought processes.

"I will find out what I can," Sir John said.

"My employer also needs to know where Skye is now."

Sir John nodded, not at all sure he could find him.

Bryce showed no acknowledgment, but reached into his coat and removed an envelope. "There is a venture you will find interesting, Sir John. A short canal to join the Singe and the Trent Rivers, undertaken by reliable men. All the details are here." He handed the envelope to Sir John, who took it quickly. Mr. Bryce actually smiled at him. "In a few months your debts will be discharged, Sir John. I think you can indulge in a man servant now. Next year you shall have a carriage, the year after a larger home. You have been following your budget assiduously, I trust?"

"To the letter . . . or number in this case." And I have not been out to gamble, not once. Bryce had been right; the desire had faded. Even though he had failed to master it for more decades than he cared to count, it had disappeared. And even more remarkable, his debt, which he had previously thought insurmountable, was nearly paid.

Bryce did not even bother to smile politely at this weak jest. "It is a profitable arrangement, is it not?"

Sir John nodded.

Bryce rose. "I shall let you get on with your valuable work, Sir John. No, please, I will let myself out."

But who is his employer? Sir John asked himself.

Sir John went to the window, though he hung back a little so that he would not be seen. Bryce emerged onto the street below, into the light of the still glowing streetlamps and the pale luminescence of approaching dawn. There was no carriage waiting, not even a hired hack. Mr. Bryce crossed the street with a determined air, like a man on his way to an appointment, and just as he stepped up onto the curb, he stopped, and looked directly up at Sir John, and nodded.

Involuntarily Sir John stepped back from the window. *Surely he could not have actually seen me up here,* he thought. Surprisingly unnerved, he sat down heavily in a chair.

How could he have known I watched?

Chapter Six

SHE hated confessions. She did not care to listen to other people bare their souls, and she cared even less to hear her own voice speaking in that pathetic, too-intimate tone. Yet here she was, standing before the fire, the portrait of her late husband staring down upon her sternly—though he had never, in real life, turned such a look upon her—and she was revealing things that embarrassed her deeply. Confessing things she would much rather keep to herself, and she did not know why. And to Marianne Edden, of all people!

"I thought he showed signs of interest," Lady Chilton said, annoyed by the meek little voice that escaped her lips.

Silence. A blessed moment of silence. Perhaps she had finished. May Farrelle help her retain some dignity.

"I am impressed. You seem to have found the one man in all of Farrland who is immune to your charms," Marianne said dryly, rather unaffected by the countess's plight. "But you rate genius rather too high, I think. I myself know several men of undeniable brilliance, and I must tell you that I think them the greatest bores in the nation. I would as soon hear a mother talk of her children than listen to these 'men of brilliance.' There is no one so self-absorbed as a man convinced of his own lofty intellect—a condition that far too many suffer from, I must say. But if he is the only man among the hordes who are smitten with you, well. . . ."

"All right, Marianne, I will stop feeling sorry for myself. You have made your point." The countess shook her head. There was no room for melodrama around Marianne Edden. She was a novelist and had the novelist's eye for such things.

And then the countess found herself speaking again. "The most humiliating part," she said, unable to stop, "was that I attended the marchioness' evening only in hopes that I might see him. I went to a *brothel* because I had dropped a hint that I would be there, and he did not even bother to show his face! A brothel! And what did I hear people discussing but his latest passion, and she's hardly more than a child. . . ." She put a hand on the mantle and leaned against it. There, it was out. Perhaps now she could stop.

"Is that not like a man?! A beautiful and accomplished woman pursues him, and he chases after a doll. Now there is *genius* for you! A genius at making a perfect ass of himself!"

The countess did not answer. Oh, it was good to hear Marianne offering her support, but it had little effect on how she was feeling. *Shake yourself out of this*, she thought. *You of all people should not complain because you are not being madly pursued by a gentleman.* The thought caused a different feeling of distress. There was a madness that whirled around her, and had for many years, and she could not control it except by staying out of society, which she could not do entirely. She could not hide herself away.

The countess was a widow, it was true, but she was still young. Certainly she could not be condemned to living out her life alone, or worse, with a partner who was only vaguely satisfying. Men pursued her with a kind of ferocity that other woman almost never experienced; surely one of these countless men would be the match she sought. The wall against loneliness.

"When will you show me these paintings he is so interested in?" Marianne asked.

The countess felt a tiny shudder at the mention of the paintings. "I will have them removed from their cases for the gentleman who is to authenticate them. What was his name?"

"Kent. Averil Kent."

"Yes. So you might see them this afternoon, if you like."

"This day I shall be otherwise engaged, but I should like to see them at some point. What is Skye's fascination with them, do you think? Have you ever found out? He hardly seems the kind of man to be interested in things mystic."

The countess ran her hand along the mantlepiece and looked up at the portrait of her late husband—even with his disapproving look, she found more comfort in this painting than in the pieces by Pelier.

"So one would think. I don't really know what it is about Pelier that so fascinates him. He is not an open man, Skye." She shook her head, thinking that she meant that he was not emotionally open, for about most subjects he would happily speak at length—but about his interest in the Peliers he was very close. She suspected that, about this one thing, he was embarrassed.

"There is something more to his interest than mere art. Perhaps now that I have them in my possession, I will discover what it is that so intrigues him."

"Perhaps, though I fear you will not tell me," Marianne said. "You are rather unfair, I must say. I share all my gossip with you, and it is not just gossip but gossip of the very first rank, and you . . . well, you are positively *discreet.*" She said the word with impressive disdain. "Hardly ladylike. You are only supposed to be discreet in the company of others—not with your dearest friends, of which I presume I am one."

"You most definitely are, Marianne, but I have so little to tell you. It is terribly unfair, I agree, but do I not introduce you to everyone you could ever want to meet? Do you not gather reams of material for your novels from the people you meet through me? There is some return, I think."

Marianne nodded a little reluctantly. "I suppose I cannot deny that entirely." She looked up at the clock on the mantlepiece. "I fear I must be going. My public awaits me."

The two women said their good-byes, and the countess was left alone. She settled herself in the chair so recently vacated by Marianne and stared at a still life across the room. It was hardly a remarkable work, merely competent, but it soothed her all the same. The Peliers, on the other hand, she found unsettling, to say the least. There was something about them. . . . Like looking at another's dreams—or nightmares perhaps. Not that they were horrific, just disturbing and oddly unreal. They seemed more the result of delirium—the fever dream—than of a normal imagination.

Why was Skye so fascinated by them? It was almost unseemly that an empiricist would be so captivated by a man like Pelier, who was said to paint "visions," some of which later, it was claimed, came true.

"Foolishness," she said aloud. Yet Skye was hardly foolish. Oh, he was a little vain, and took too much pleasure from his great reputation, but he was not foolish—not yet at any rate.

The countess was surprised not to have heard from the earl. She had sent him a note as soon as the paintings had arrived the previous afternoon and had expected a reply almost immediately. He might not be in thrall to the Countess of Chilton, as so many others were, but she expected the Peliers would bring him at a run.

Very odd.

Why does he not care for me she wondered? *Why, when so many others are driven to foolishness*? The mere thought disturbed her. Two men had dueled over her recently. She turned red with embarrassment and distress. Dueled over her, and she had never met either of them! Strangers. . . . And one had been wounded fairly seriously. What if he'd been killed? Did they never think of her? How would she live with that?

I will be driven to hiding myself away, she thought. *But not yet. I need to be sure that there is not the least chance of interesting Skye. Not the least chance.*

Kent sat in the parlor, waiting as patiently as a man could to meet the most beautiful woman in Farrland, and very likely beyond. He sat in a chair across the room from a looking glass, staring at the poor, anxious wretch who looked back at him so guardedly.

Take hold of yourself, man, he chided himself. *It's not as bad as you think.*

His head knew this to be true; after all, Kent was something of a favorite of the ladies of Avonel. Oh, he knew he was not an outstandingly handsome man, but he had his good qualities. He gazed at the man in the looking glass and willed him to appear more at his ease.

That's better, he thought. *Yes, sit up as though you were vital and confident—no matter what the truth might be at the moment.*

No, he was not so difficult to look at. His brow was high and smooth, his eyebrows well formed. If he were looking at his ideal portrait, he would certainly repaint the nose if he had the chance, for it was a bit larger than he would like. And his chin could be bit more in proportion—not quite so strong. His eyes, of course, were very fine—a grayish blue that changed with the light. He'd worn a blue frock coat that brought out the color of his eyes. He had always known how to dress—had even become something of trend setter this last while. Yes, the man sitting across from him would do. Many a woman would be happy with less. Oh, taller. He would like to be a bit taller, but he wasn't short by any means, and his form was perfectly acceptable. No, many a lovely woman had settled for men no easier to look at. Even the countess' first husband was said to have been a rather ordinary man, in the physical sense.

Footsteps sounded in the hallway outside and he rose in anticipation, his mouth a bit dry, but the sound passed on and faded, leaving Kent feeling a disturbing sense of loss. He was so unsettled that he went to the mantlepiece to examine a miniature portrait, as though he would hide the fact that he had risen nervously in expectation, only to have no one arrive. *But no one is watching*, he told himself. Still, he felt he had looked foolish.

He hardly registered the subject of the portrait; a man like many another. His mind was on the woman. Kent had seen the countess on more than one occasion—his recent success had brought him entrance to such circles—but he had never actually been introduced. Which meant that in many ways he was still on the outside. Yet, here he was, invited to the countess' Avonel home, even if it was in a professional capacity.

He dearly hoped that the countess would buy one of his paintings. It would set the rest of the aristocracy scrambling to follow suit, and would send the prices up. This thought produced a bit of anxiety. But not as much as the idea that the countess would take a disliking to him. That was his great fear. Not only would it likely ruin his career, but such a humiliation was not to be recovered from. He would be forced to leave the country.

I do not expect her to fall into my arms at first sight, he told himself. *I'm not such a fool as that. But if she could find my conversation pleasant, and be at least a little charmed by my wit. . . . If I could enter her circle—even its outer rings—so that she would invite me to her home on occasion and acknowledge me at the theater, then I would feel at least that I am not a complete buffoon.*

Kent knew a little about the countess, as did almost everyone in Farrland. She was said to be very bright, easily bored, literate, artistic, aloof in her manner. The men who managed invitations to her famous salons were all of the first rank, known for their personal charm and sophistication. Mere physical beauty did not qualify one for invitations to the home of the countess—a woman renowned for physical beauty. Nor did a title seem to much impress her, for several of her favorites were not of particularly notable families.

I am almost there, Kent told himself. Recently his paintings of nature had gained him entrance to the Empiricist Society—an achievement of which he was justifiably proud. And his landscapes would soon have him made a Fellow of the Royal Society for the Arts. Averil Kent, F.E.S., F.R.S.A.

By accomplishments alone he was almost ready to step into the countess' world. But accomplishments were not enough. The countess must meet him and judge him worthy.

"My late husband, the Earl of Chilton," a woman said in a voice so warm and full of color that it melted into Kent's very heart. He turned to find the countess standing just inside the door. "Or perhaps you were more interested in the artist? Montpelier, I believe."

Kent bowed a bit awkwardly, unsettled by her sudden appearance. "It is a lovely little piece, Lady Chilton," he managed. "Lord Chilton was a striking man."

"Do you think so?" she said, a very slightly mocking smile appearing on her lovely mouth.

Kent nodded. What was it about her? Why did she drive men to utter foolishness? He fought the urge to stare.

"I never really thought of him as striking, not even as handsome. But he was kind beyond measure, and deft in politics, and fair, and considerate. And he seized life like no other. Though his life was cut short, I am sure Lord Chilton lived more than many whose spans tripled his own." She looked over at the small painting in its silver frame with a look of great affection and some sadness.

The countess held out her hand suddenly. "And you are Mr. Kent, I take it."

"Averil Kent, Lady Chilton. Your servant." Kent touched his lips to the offered hand, and realized as he did so that he blushed, though the countess gave no indication that she noticed.

She gestured to a chair and Kent gladly sat while tea was called for.

It struck Kent that the countess did not possess the ideal feminine figure, for in truth she was too tall and slim. Almost willowy, he thought. Too girlish and not womanly enough, and this surprised him, for no one would hear the slightest suggestion that she was less than perfect. Her dark hair, nearly black, was perhaps perfect, for it was thick and fell in lustrous curls about her heart-shaped face.

With his painter's eye Kent quickly noted her features. Large blue eyes set too wide apart and slightly elongated, which was unusual and gave her face an exotic appearance. He realized that there was a mole hidden in her right eyebrow, though no one would likely notice. Her lips were full and complemented the shape of her eyes. Kent thought the structure of her face very fine. Unquestionably she was a beautiful woman but not really so striking as to cause the furor that she did.

And if that were true, why was he responding as he did? He hadn't felt so nervous since he had first begun to court. It was her voice, he realized. It was so rich with color—he could almost see it. A palette of the most vibrant hues. When she spoke, her voice penetrated into his very center and something there began to vibrate as though in harmonic empathy. When she spoke, he wanted to close his eyes and just feel the effect, as though he was being caressed.

"My friend, the Marchioness of Wicklow, has a very fine landscape you did of the Whye Valley, Mr. Kent. I admire it greatly. Have you done others?"

"Of the valley?" he said, almost unable to hear the words for the warmth of her tone.

"No, landscapes."

"Ah. Yes," he said trying to pull himself together. "The countryside has been my principal subject these past few years, though the natural world has also drawn my attention."

She smiled. Kent got the distinct impression that he was talking to a woman who was unhappy. Something about her features—slightly frozen—as though she were tired of keeping up the facade. "And this is what gained you entrance to the Empiricist Society?"

Kent nodded. "I'm surprised Lady Chilton would know."

"You are thought to be an artist with a considerable future, Mr. Kent. And I am an admirer of the arts and a friend to the artist."

Kent felt a slight shiver as she said this, as though she had inferred that she admired him. Tea arrived, interrupting the conversation and giving Kent a chance to try to collect himself. He hoped his blush had disappeared, though his face felt warm yet.

"I'm given to understand, Mr. Kent, that you are an expert on Pelier."

"I must say, in all modesty, Lady Chilton, that this is precisely true."

She laughed, which he found gratifying. "But I think you are being too humble, sir." She gestured with her teacup to the doors behind Kent.

"Would you be so kind as to give me your opinion of these pieces?" She rose, taking up her cup and saucer, and led Kent through the adjoining chamber and then into the room beyond. He thought she walked a little stiffly, as though undertaking some task she found distasteful.

The paintings were not hanging but resting on a side table and leaning against the wall. Though Kent had a long-standing interest in Pelier and his work, he realized that focusing his mind on anything other than the countess at that moment would take an act of extreme will. For her part the countess stood back from the paintings, an odd look on her face.

"As you will see, they are signed Pelier, but there seems to be some doubt as to the veracity of the claim."

Kent set down his cup and moved closer to look. The first was a typically ambiguous piece: three figures gathered about a marble crypt. If it had meaning, it was impenetrable, as was the case with many of Pelier's works. They were reinterpreted regularly to fit events. The second was even odder. A man, dressed unconventionally, his back to the viewer, crossed a bridge over a stream, but the bridge changed its form from one end to the other, as though two different designs flowed together in the center. On one bank of the river it was morning, the light pouring down upon the flowering trees of a spring day. The other bank was neither spring nor morning, but depicted a fall afternoon. In the background Kent could see the ruin of an ancient cathedral, and then he realized that there was an old-fashioned carriage drawn up in the shade of the trees. It seemed to be waiting.

"How very odd," Kent said. "Do you see the way the river flows in two directions? As though the bridge were downstream from either side." Kent shook his head and smiled: the wonderful ambiguity always made him do both of these things.

"Do you have a lens?" he asked.

The countess rang for a servant who quickly fetched a lens. Kent bent closer to the canvas, examining the signature, the technique, the brush strokes, the palette.

The inscription on the tomb was not in any script that Kent knew, he realized, making it likely a Moravian painting. Pelier had almost unquestionably been a member of this secret society. It might be a message for fellow Moravians. But there was something about this painting. . . .

"I believe, Lady Chilton, that this one, at least, is a very skilled forgery. I am sorry to say it. Was it sold to you as a Pelier?"

"It was a gift, Mr. Kent, and the kind soul who gave it me did not claim with certainty that it was genuine. What is it that makes you so certain that it is not a Pelier?"

Kent gestured with a hand. "Do you see the white in the marble of the tomb, and here in the gentleman's shirt? It was not made from lead, I'm sure. Pelier used only white made from lead. And the brush strokes, though a very close imitation, are not quite as I would expect. Pelier had a very light touch that is particularly difficult to imitate. The signature is astonishing. I should have believed it to be real if not for these other things." Finally Kent pointed to the area of sky. "But this is the true error in the painting. I have often thought that Pelier's handling of cloud and light in the sky was unparalleled. This is only competent. No doubt about it, Lady Chilton. A wonderful forgery, but a forgery all the same."

The countess shrugged and smiled. "Oh, well, it was a gift given in kindness and that is what matters. It is rather ironic that I have it at all. I pretended to admire these paintings at someone's home—out of politeness, you see—and the next day they arrived at my door." She stepped back and looked at the painting. "And they are forgeries, to boot."

"Oh, no, Lady Chilton. This first is a forgery. But the man crossing the bridge. This is a Pelier. I'm quite sure of it. Look at this tremendous sky! If he had painted nothing but skies, I would have counted him a master all the same. No, this one is quite genuine, and more than that, I have never heard tell of it. It happens, now and then—a real Pelier is found. It will set the art world abuzz—not to mention those who spend their time interpreting and reinterpreting Pelier's work."

"How exciting for all concerned," she said, looking at the painting and wrinkling up her nose.

"The countess is not an admirer, I collect?"

"Oh, I suppose there is nothing wrong with Pelier, but . . ." She made a face. "Do you believe Pelier was a seer, Mr. Kent? Or was it all a terrible ruse?"

Kent considered a moment. Somehow he felt his answer to this question was "the test." His fate hung on his reply.

"Well, I will say without hesitation that Pelier was no charlatan, which is to say that he believed that his paintings were inspired and prophetic, though he did not claim to know what they meant. Whether he was a seer . . . ? It depends on whose interpretation you read. I think there is little doubt that he predicted the great earthquake of 1378. If you look at the two paintings that deal with this incident— Have you seen them, Lady Chilton?"

She shook her head.

"One shows the ruin of the city of Brasa, so much like the actual ruin after the disaster that it cannot be mistaken. Thirteen doves fly overhead against the perfect clouds and sky. The number 78 can be seen on a fallen house, and there is a cherry tree in blossom, which would make the scene February—exactly when the tragedy occurred. A young girl runs naked down the street, obviously a victim of burns, as so many were. And a team of gray horses still in harness can be seen running wildly across the distant hillside, their carriage lost." Kent met the countess' eyes, wondering if she thought him a fool. "I think it is clearly a case of prophesy. I cannot explain it any other way."

"I see. And did Pelier really paint in a trance with his eyes closed?"

"I very much doubt that his eyes were closed, but he would not allow anyone in the room as he worked, so we will never know. Pelier did say that he did not know what the painting would be when he set brush to canvas and that he was 'inspired' as he liked to explain it. He made very few claims for himself, Lady Chilton, it was only those who gathered around him toward the end. They were responsible for his myth—these men and those who came after."

"It is a fascinating story," she said looking at the paintings again. "I am a little sorry that only one is genuine," she said, but Kent was sure she did not mean it. She still stood back unnaturally far, and everything in her manner spoke of great discomfort. These paintings unsettled her in some way.

Kent looked back at the paintings. "But the other could easily be a copy—perhaps even a very faithful one. Many were made, and there is no precise catalogue of Pelier's works. Once a canvas was complete, he did not much care for what happened to it. He was simply driven to make the painting. I tend to agree with those who believe there were some forty paintings that were never recorded. Sold for near to nothing or given away. Lost now these many years. A genuine Pelier, like this, turns up every decade or so, and there are any number that might merely be imitations made for gain, or actual copies done by his various devotees."

"You do not subscribe to the school that tries to find meaning in every element of his paintings, do you?"

Kent shook his head. "No, I tend to think that is a bit off the mark, nor do I believe that an event must be found for every painting. Some, however, I think were genuine acts of prophesy, and although this runs against my beliefs, I can't think of any other explanation." Kent shrugged, a bit embarrassed. He had told the truth when it might have been better to have lied. But it was done now.

"Well, Mr. Kent, I certainly agree that there is more to life than we perceive daily, that is certain. After all, there is still a mage alive in this very land, and one cannot deny all the acts of the mages, augury among them. That a man painted pictures that alluded to events in the future is not impossible, I think."

"I agree entirely, Lady Chilton," Kent said, his enthusiasm, and perhaps relief, obvious. "That is what I have long said. . . ."

"Lady Chilton?"

Kent and the countess turned to find a maid standing in the door. "Pardon me, ma'am. There is a letter. . . ."

There was an odd second of hesitation. Kent thought he saw a hint of annoyance flit across the countess' face, and then her manner changed. "Oh," she said, then turned to Kent. "Would you excuse me for a moment, Mr. Kent?"

"Certainly."

The countess swept out, leaving Kent to watch her go, more graceful than a dancer, he thought. He could hear quiet voices outside, for the door had been left slightly ajar. Kent found himself gravitating toward the door, straining to hear, not really sure why. Perhaps the countess would say something about him, give him some hint as to how he had been judged.

But the whispering fell silent, making him wonder if he'd been heard. *That would finish your chances,* Kent thought. *Sit down, man!* But he stayed where he was, straining to hear.

A rustling of paper. "Castlebough," the countess said. "Have things ready. I will leave today if it is possible. The morning at the latest."

Kent stepped away from the door and pretended to examine another painting.

"Not another forgery, I hope," the countess said, but Kent could see her manner had changed. The letter had erased the discomfort caused by the Peliers, though she did not seem utterly sure and joyful, as though she had heard from a lover. In fact she still seemed rather sad.

"No, not that I can tell," Kent tried to smile but found the countess' manner distressed him, as though he could hardly bear to see her unhappy—a complete stranger.

"More tea?" the countess asked, clearly prepared to continue their visit in all politeness.

"I think Lady Chilton has other matters more pressing. Please, don't let me detain you."

She stopped, looking at him, her manner very solemn. "You are very kind, Mr. Kent. Yes, I am called away. Perhaps we might try this again? I was so looking forward to getting to know you a little better."

Kent was touched by the apparent sincerity in her voice. "Nothing would please me more. I will be away from Avonel briefly—a painting expedition—but when I return. . . ."

"Then we shall indeed meet again." She seemed to have a thought. "Do you do portraits?"

"I'm afraid I don't, Lady Chilton."

"Unfortunate. But perhaps I could visit you in your studio? I would very much like to possess an Averil Kent and want to be certain not to get an imitation."

"It would be an honor, Lady Chilton," Kent said, bowing his head.

"Hardly," she said, "but for some strange reason my influence in Avonel society is entirely out of proportion to my actual accomplishments. I might increase the demand for your work, Mr. Kent. Unless you are a man of independent means and disdain the making of money from your art?"

Kent met her eyes briefly, shaking his head almost imperceptibly.

"Good. I despise dabblers. Real artists who must make their living by their own hand—these are the men and women who have made Farr art what it is. Not the Lord Dinseys and Sir Gerrard Bainbridges." She paused and fixed him with a pensive look. "If we are to be friends, Mr. Kent," she said, her rich voice dropping to a tone so intimate that Kent almost forgot himself. "I must tell you that I cannot bear to be treated like . . . Well, as though I am something other than human. Do you understand?" Her manner was most sincere, her last words almost a plea.

Kent nodded, feeling suddenly a deep sense of loneliness from this, the most desired woman in all of Farrland.

"Until we meet again, Mr. Kent," she said, offering her hand.

Kent touched his lips to her perfect skin, and found himself out on the street, walking in the wrong direction. The tiny glimpse he had of the woman behind the persona of the Countess of Chilton had left him utterly confused. Was she lonely? Could a woman in her position have a life that was less than perfect? Did she have doubts? Or dream of life being other than it was? What was it that called her away on a moment's notice?

He stopped on the street, looking around as though lost in a foreign city. After a second—as though recovering from a mental lapse—he realized where he was.

"What are you thinking?" he said quietly. "You would be seen as a fool, certainly." But he went off down the street wondering how many days it would take to reach Castlebough, and whether they might meet along the way, so that he would not have to wait so long to hear that voice again.

Chapter Seven

To call it an uneasy alliance would be something of an understatement, but the compact between Moncrief and Admiral Sir Joseph Brookes had survived a decade and continued to totter along as precariously as could any alliance between two men whose ambitions were not entirely mutually exclusive.

Brookes was the older of the two by some fourteen or fifteen years, placing him in his middle sixties, though he appeared to be much older than that. Not that he was fragile or frail in any way, for he was a vital man, hale and strong yet, but he was gray and wrinkled from his years at sea as were few men who lived even to their eighth decade on the land.

Like most navy men, Brookes was highly conscious of his appearance and groomed and dressed himself with a kind of self-awareness that was usually the prerogative of a dandy—yet he was not in the least vain. It was merely a habit required by the service—a point of pride that had almost nothing to do with narcissism.

Despite its fragility, the alliance was founded on rather solid foundations. Sir Joseph Brookes had become Sea Lord largely, though not exclusively, through the efforts of Moncrief. Not that he lacked qualifications—that was certainly not the case. Brookes was an efficient and even somewhat imaginative leader. But one did not rise in the service of the King without well-placed patrons.

In return for Moncrief's continuing support, Sir Joseph put at the disposal of the Kings's Man the intelligence-gathering organ of the Admiralty. Of course the palace had agents of its own, but they were forced to operate under the scrutiny of the government—a situation that Moncrief found . . . inconvenient.

The Admiralty, however, was almost an independent principality—and the Sea Lord was the prince of this not so tiny nation within a nation. One of the reasons Sir Joseph had lasted as long as he had in the position was his political acumen. Like the sovereign of any small nation, he had developed an unparalleled deftness for balancing the needs of his own principality against those of his more powerful neighbor—in this case the King and government of Farrland. He was a master at disguising his own plans as actions for the benefit of Farrland—and sometimes they even were.

"We've found the woman," was the first thing Brookes said as Moncrief entered.

The King's Man had taken one of the leather chairs in the Sea Lord's office. He leaned on his cane and stared at Brookes, making his displeasure known, and though he felt some relief at this news, he did not allow it to show. "So we know who it was put her up to this betrayal?"

"The hell of it is, we don't." Brookes was not a man to be easily intimidated. When one has faced both battles and storms at sea, even a King's Man does not look so frightening—but all the same, he did not look comfortable. "She was discovered this morning floating in the harbor—drowned."

Even Moncrief could not keep his face entirely impassive at the news. "Surely Skye would never have done such a thing," Moncrief said. "Was she in the employ of the Entonne all along, then? The plans for the cannon are missing, I take it?"

Brookes nodded. "Yes, unfortunately, they are. Whether she was an Entonne agent . . ." He shrugged, maddeningly.

The plans for the cannon were missing! It had to have been the Entonne. Farrelle's flames! Had he and Brookes given away Farrland's military advantage in their attempt to bring down Skye? Moncrief felt a little ill, suddenly, and sat back in his chair leaning heavily on one arm.

"I suppose I should hear what happened," he said at last, his mouth dry.

Brookes took a long breath. "It is a little difficult to be certain.

Our people were in place in the house, just as we had arranged. The doorbell rang, and Mary went down to answer it, and that is all the officers can tell. They awoke some six hours later. Both Mary and the plans had disappeared. And that might have been the end of the story if we had not found Mary this morning, as I have said."

"That is it? That's all we know?"

Brookes shook his head. "Almost. All we know for certain, at least, but there are a few other small details. Two of the men present swear they had neither food nor drink while they were in the house, nor for several hours before, yet they all seem to have fallen unconscious at precisely the same time."

Moncrief snorted. "Well, clearly, they're lying. I'll wager they were all drinking and are afraid to say it. Who admits dereliction of duty, after all?"

"So one would assume," the Sea Lord said, "but I spoke with the men myself, and I tend to believe they were telling the truth—or at least most of it."

Moncrief was surprised to hear that Brookes would actually speak with men involved in such an action. Best to keep oneself a step removed. That was always Moncrief's policy.

"But they were obviously drugged. . . ."

"So one would think. But how do we explain the men who took no refreshment?"

"If they are not lying, then they must be mistaken," Moncrief said. "Liars or fools—take your choice."

Brookes did not look convinced of this.

"If you will indulge me for a moment, Lord Moncrief, I will bring in two witnesses to an event you might find edifying."

Moncrief was a little shocked at the suggestion. He did not want to get too closely involved—as Brookes clearly had. "If you think it absolutely necessary," he said, making sure his reluctance was clear.

Sir Joseph nodded, seemingly unaware or unconcerned. He tugged on a tasseled bellpull, and his secretary's pockmarked, but rather dignified face appeared in the open door. "Sir?"

"Send them in, will you."

The secretary made a motion that resembled a bow and disappeared. A moment later the door opened, and two individuals came reluctantly in with heads bowed and taking small, timid steps. One was a seaman, who held his straw hat in hand, and the other was a woman—a harlot, Moncrief was sure.

"This is Abel Ransom, purser on His Majesty's Ship *Prince Kori.* And Miss Eliza Blount—*seamstress,*" Brookes said. "Would you be so kind, Mr. Ransom, as to tell us what you saw last night."

The seaman nodded, his eyes only flitting up occasionally. Moncrief wondered if a man of so little rank had ever entered this office before—unless it was to scrub the floor.

"If it please you, sir, I was on the dock by Halls and Hale, sailmakers, late this night past when a carriage drew up along the quay." He glanced up apprehensively, as though he did not expect to be believed. For a moment he struggled, fear apparently having driven all memories from his head.

"Well, go on, Ransom," Brookes said, none too patiently.

"Yes, sir. Two gentlemen and a lady disembarked from the carriage, sir. I couldn't see them clear for the light was poorly, but one gentleman was older, sir. Older and a bit cranked, sir."

"Bent," Brookes translated for Moncrief.

"Yes, sir, bent and not so spry. He was speaking to the lady, though we could not hear what was said. We was in the shadow of the door . . . talking, you know.

"The woman left the gentlemen, walking a bit stiffly toward the quay's edge, but she didn't stop, sir. I swear. She just walked right in. Didn't jump, sir, but walked in as though she didn't see the water. The two gentlemen went to the edge, sir, and watched for a few moments, doing nothing to help her, as though she were in no difficulty. And then they loaded themselves back in their carriage and set off." He looked up, his apprehension changing to defensiveness "We went to see what had happened, sir. But the tide was at full ebb, and she was not to be found. Drownt, I'll wager."

Brookes looked over at Moncrief, raising his eyebrows.

"And you did nothing to help?" Moncrief asked.

The man glanced at the woman. "Well, sir, we didn't realize she was in trouble, you see. The two gentlemen stood by so calmly, we didn't know what to make of it. 'Perhaps she can swim,' thought I. These folk do the oddest things for sport, sir, if you don't mind me saying. They'll row a boat for pleasure, sir. And some are said to swim, though I've never seen it myself. It was all so peculiar that I just didn't think clear."

"And you, Miss?" Sir Joseph said. "Do you agree with Mr. Ransom's tale?"

She nodded quickly, clearly hoping to not have to speak at all.

Moncrief realized that under the makeup hid a girl of perhaps sixteen or seventeen. Older than some, perhaps but still too young. Having daughters himself, Moncrief was both appalled and filled with pity.

"Speak up when you're spoken to, girl," Brookes said.

"Yes, sir," the girl managed, her voice coming out as a whisper. "Just as Abel tells it, sir. If it please you, sir."

"Very little pleases me," Brookes said, though he was not really talking to the girl. "Have you any questions, Lord Moncrief?"

"I suppose I need not ask who the woman in question was?" Moncrief said quietly to Brookes, who nodded. "Can they identify the men?"

"Can you?" Sir Joseph asked the pair.

"I'm sorry, sir. It was very dark."

"I'm sure," Brookes said. "Have you anything more to ask?" he said to Moncrief.

The King's Man shook his head.

"I will have them kept close by in case they can offer anything more," Brookes said as the man and woman were led out. "But do you see what I mean? Is it not an odd story?"

It was Moncrief's turn to shrug. "The woman was threatened. It was either into the harbor or some terrible violence would be done her: a choice we might have made ourselves."

"Yes, I suppose, but both Ransom and the girl are sure there was no threat. Only quiet conversation. When the woman went into the harbor, they were completely taken off guard. No wonder they thought it innocent—some lark of the gentry, though no one was laughing, I will wager."

"So how do you explain it?"

"I can't explain it, but it was damnedly peculiar, don't you think?"

"To say the least." Moncrief was not at all sure what to make of it.

"But do you see, there is a pattern of a kind?" Sir Joseph said. "Two of the men waiting for Skye swear they touched neither food nor drink, yet they fell as insensible as their mates who had. Then this odd occurrence at the harbor. Now let me add something more. The officers sent to look into the rooms of one of these young men that Skye employed encountered others who arrived before them with the same intentions." He paused for a second. "These gentlemen vacated the rooms by the only means available—they leaped from the window. This seemed peculiar enough, as the window was quite high, but they apparently landed without harm and disappeared into the darkness. The officers who were present assure me that they would have been badly hurt if they had performed this same leap—and naval officers see men fall from the rigging often enough to know."

Brookes raised his bushy gray eyebrows—like great storm waves, Moncrief thought. Raised them as though what he had just said made some sense.

"And your point, Sir Joseph?"

"Men fell asleep as though drugged when they had ingested neither food nor drink. A woman walked calmly into the harbor and drowned. She did not cry out or plead for her life, but simply went into the water as though nothing would come of it. And finally, men jumped from a great height to escape our men, and landed so easily that they were able to *run* off. Landed so softly that the men who chased them out barely heard a sound. These things are all more than peculiar, they are . . . well, I fear they are not natural. . . ."

If anyone but Sir Joseph Brookes had made this statement, Moncrief would have laughed aloud, but the Sea Lord had an uncanny intuition and had been proven right too often for Moncrief to scoff, no matter how outrageous the proposal.

"Do you think it's Eldrich? Is that what you're suggesting? Flames, Joseph, the mage has not left his estate in . . . decades. The rumors are that he is not long for this world."

"Yes, the rumors always abound where the mage is concerned. He makes very certain that no truth ever escapes from his own lands—unless it serves him. No, we cannot be sure the mage is anywhere near death, I think. Nor can I say with assurance that Eldrich was either involved or not involved, I only know that something happened in the city last night that was not quite as it should have been, and it all centered around Skye. Perhaps the King is not his only protector."

The two men sat brooding for a few moments, as though the idea was so far beyond their usual experience that they could not even begin to imagine what it might mean, or what they should do. And then Moncrief interrupted the silence. "What has become of Skye?"

"We don't know."

Moncrief shook his head. "I have done everything I can to insure that he doesn't reach the King, or even send His Majesty a message, but this can't be kept up forever. A few days at most. . . . We must assume that Skye knows who was behind his attempted ruin?"

"Not necessarily. Surely Mary suspected but had no proof, and the officers involved I trust utterly. No, we are safe from prosecution at least—how else we might suffer I cannot say. If the King were to believe Skye over us . . ." Sir Joseph rubbed one of his eyes gently and Moncrief realized that the man had not slept this last night. "But I have a feeling, Lord Moncrief, that Skye and the King are the least of our worries. Something else is afoot. Something very odd. If we assume that the men who jumped from the window on Paradise Street and the men who sent the woman to drown in the harbor were not the same gentlemen—for they would have had to have been in two places almost at once—then there would appear to be more than one man who has at least some knowledge of the arts. That leaves us with two possibilities. They are servants of the mage," he paused, as though surprised by his own words, "or they are some group of whom we know nothing at all."

"The former seems much more likely to me."

"I would have to agree, but let me tell you something else. The officers who went to search Samual Hayes' rooms came back with a journal and a number of interesting letters. Most from his friend Kehler who has been studying at the Farrellite archive in Wooton. You will not believe what they've been up to. It seems Skye employed them to delve into this matter of the so-called Stranger of Compton Heath. Have you heard of this?"

"Something, yes. Some kind of a lunatic who appeared in the town, and the locals made claim that he was from an unknown land. Wasn't that it?"

"More or less. But the odd thing is Hayes and Kehler came away convinced that the man was not mad at all. They also seem to believe that it was a mage who took the man away."

Moncrief was at a loss for words, and unsettled by how out of his depth he suddenly felt. Moncrief who controlled the government and much of the kingdom, besides. "Joseph, I haven't even the beginning of a notion as to what goes on. Have you?"

"I can't claim that I do, Lord Moncrief, but no matter how absurd it might seem, it begins to look as if Skye has some interest and perhaps even some involvement in the arts. Whether it is Eldrich or some other, I cannot say. But it seems to me that we should know if the arts have come to life again around the Entide Sea."

Moncrief also wanted to know what went on here, but if a mage were involved. . . . "I question the wisdom of interfering with Eldrich. He will not look kindly on us meddling in his affairs. I don't care how old or infirm Eldrich has become—he is still a mage."

Brookes nodded. "Yes, but I would never advocate interference. Observation is all I am suggesting. If there is some other who practices the arts, we should know his purpose—or at least be reassured that he means us no harm. If it turns out to be Eldrich, then we will break off our operation. If we are reasonably sure it is not Eldrich, then I would think it advisable to inform the mage."

"It is still a risk, but I agree, however reluctantly." Moncrief stopped as he began to rise. "But, Brookes, we should be sure your best people are involved and that they understand how important it is for them to keep their distance. We must limit the risks as much as possible."

"Certainly, Lord Moncrief. Leave that to me."

Moncrief rose, but had a sudden realization—clearly the surprising turn the conversation had taken had reduced his capacity to reason. "How will you begin, Brookes? You lost track of Skye."

Brookes had risen to his feet as well. "Yes, but only temporarily, I think. If Skye reappears in Avonel, we will know, for we still have one of the earl's servants in our pay. But I don't think it will be so difficult to find Skye. He had these young men looking into the story of Baumgere, and I am all but sure that interest will give him away. I will wager that Lord Skye has retreated to the village of Castlebough—a town conveniently near the Entonne border should he need to quit Farrland altogether. I'm sure he has only temporarily dropped from sight, for the earl is far too well known to be able to hide for long. We will soon know his whereabouts, and then we'll see what goes on in our kingdom. Something very odd, I think. Something very odd indeed."

Chapter Eight

THE sound was rhythmic and syllabic but too low to be distinguished. Chanting, Erasmus was sure. He could almost make out the words, though they did not seem to be Farr. Anxiety began to grow in him. The day was clear and warm, but here, among the green hallways of the wood, it was cool, the sunlight filtered to muted greens. Smoke; he could smell the smoke. It seemed to burn his nostrils, but then there was a hiss, and it turned sweet and aromatic. Leaves had been tossed onto the fire. Luckwort leaves, but they did not calm him as they should. Knowing what came next, he wanted to shout, but try as he might, he could produce no sound.

He pushed aside a branch, hurrying now, feeling the horror of what was about to happen drive him. But something was wrong; he seemed to be gliding so slowly, like a bird hanging on the wind, making little progress.

And then the scream. He stopped, standing on the pathway between the trees and the angled trunks of falling light. More than anything he wanted to look away, close his eyes to it, but he could not. Not quite. And then the child appeared, engulfed in flame, mouth open in a silent scream of unimaginable agony. Every nerve shrieking in anguish. The child stumbled toward him, arms out as though begging for help, to be held. And then it stumbled, looking at him still, the recrimination clear.

Why? Why did you do this to me?

The burning child toppled forward, and the last thing Erasmus saw was its face. *His* face. He was burning. Not some other. He was aflame.

Erasmus woke from the dream, covered in sweat. He stumbled up from the divan where he had fallen asleep and made his way to the doors looking down into his garden. He sucked in the cool air, almost sobbing. Alive. He was alive and unharmed. It had not been he who burned. Thank Farrelle. Not him.

The dream was never easy to drive from his mind, and Erasmus was grateful that it came infrequently. He paced back and forth across his study, unable to sit, running his hand back through his hair over and over.

"Blood and flames. Bloody blood and flames."

He often wondered what caused the dream to return, but, as always, he could not say. Perhaps nothing caused it. It just would not let him be. His penance.

"We did not know," he said aloud. "How could we?"

He tried to think of something else: his conversation with Hayes, but Stokes arrived with Erasmus' wash water. The servant wore an odd, pensive look that was not quite in character.

"You look either troubled or ill this morning, Stokes. Now which would it be?"

"Never ill, sir," he said quickly. "Nor particularly troubled . . . but your young man has been up since I don't know when, pacing, sir. Back and forth across the library. Across the main hall. He seemed to be considering leaving, sir, or so I thought."

"He's here now, I hope?"

"Oh, yes, sir. He's had a pot of coffee all to himself and is vibrating like a harp string. He seems anxious to speak with you, sir. Keeps asking when you might be up."

"I'll be down directly. Don't let him leave before I've spoken with him."

Erasmus continued with his toilet, not letting Hayes' impatience ruin his morning ritual. Stokes came back a few moments later to shave him, and lay out his clothes, and with the warmed steel scraping across his face, Erasmus again considered the conversation of the night before.

The tale of the Stranger would have seemed nothing more than folklore if it hadn't been for Hayes' encounter with this physician, Ripke. That had a ring of authenticity to it that Erasmus was not about to deny. And Erasmus' intuition told him that the man who'd come in the carriage to collect the Stranger was no man—not in the sense that he understood the word. It was a mage, and Erasmus thought he might even be able to supply the mage's name. If a mage was interested in this Stranger, then Erasmus was interested, too. So Hayes had better be prepared to reveal a little more—the name of the gentleman who had employed him would be a good start.

As he went down the stairs, Erasmus wondered what the Admiralty's part was in this affair. Unless they really did believe the Stranger was from an undiscovered land, for certainly most of the vast globe remained a mystery. Perhaps they'd learned something on a recent voyage. . . .

Hayes was sitting at a small table in the breakfast room, looking out into the garden. As Erasmus entered, he jumped up, obviously relieved to see him. There was a certain anxiety in the young man's manner that did not disappear, however.

"Ah, Erasmus. I can't thank you enough for your help and generosity, but I've decided that I must get messages to both Kehler and our employer as soon as possible."

"Not before you've eaten, I hope." Erasmus took a seat at the table and dropped a napkin into his lap, reaching for the coffee pot. "Sit down, Hayes. I've been thinking as well."

Hayes took his seat slowly, as though he were ready to run out the door without any further discussion.

"The agents of the Admiralty might well be looking for you yet, so I'm not sure I like the idea of you racing around the city on your own. If they've come after you because of your link with this gentleman who employed you, they're likely after him as well."

Hayes shook his head. "I've thought about that and decided it's very unlikely. You see, my patron is beyond . . . well, not beyond the law, but certainly even agents of the Admiralty would not dare apprehend him without . . ." He hesitated. "Let me just say that the man is not unknown to the King."

Erasmus stopped with his cup in the air. "*Are you telling me that it is Skye?*" Erasmus could hardly credit this idea, but who else could

Hayes mean? A man of great reputation and standing who had some involvement with the Admiralty. An intimate of the King, a man whose interests wouldn't lead one to believe he would be interested in stories of mysterious strangers. An empiricist, obviously. *Skye.* It could be no other.

Hayes hesitated, chagrin obvious on his rather tired countenance. "I'm not telling you . . . at least not intentionally," he added quietly.

Erasmus sat back in his chair and stared at his friend. If he had been told the man in question was his own brother, he would have been less shocked.

"What possible interest could Skye have in such a tale?" he asked finally.

Hayes shrugged, reaching down and picking up his spoon as though suddenly interested in silverware. "Erasmus, I hope you understand that the earl does not want his name connected with our inquiry—he was most adamant."

Erasmus nodded dumbly. "But why is he interested?"

Hayes turned the spoon over and dropped it so that it rattled off the floor. Erasmus bent down quickly and retrieved it, reaching out and taking hold of Hayes' wrist so that the young man would look at him.

"Why?" he said quietly.

Hayes shook his head. "I don't know. It . . . I don't know. We speculated endlessly about this, but you must know that one does not ask the Earl of Skye impertinent questions."

Erasmus nodded. The earl had a reputation for impatience with anyone who presumed too much of their friendship. "Well, I agree that a message should be taken to him directly. And this young man, Kehler . . . what's become of him?"

"He has continued in the employ of Lord Skye, though not here in Avonel. I'm not at liberty to say more."

"Do you intend to see him in person—Kehler, that is?"

"No, I'll have to write him."

"Well, eat, and we'll pay a call on the Earl. I think, given the circumstances, we can risk doing so without warning him."

"You'll come with me? But, Erasmus, he'll know I've told you."

"Yes, well, that is a problem because I'm not sure you should appear at his door, not with the Admiralty looking for you." Erasmus thought a moment. "We'll approach it like this. You write a letter to the earl, and we'll take a carriage to his home where I'll deliver it. You can stay in the carriage unless the earl is there and wishes to speak with you. I'll claim to be merely a loyal friend helping without explanation. Skye and I are both members of the Society and I'm known not to be one of the gossips. Will that answer?"

Hayes looked enormously relieved to have an ally and went immediately to write the note, not having touched his food.

The ride to Skye's town home was not so long, as it turned out he did not live far from Erasmus. Hayes stayed in the hired carriage, as planned, while Erasmus rang the bell.

As he stood on the step, he turned around to survey the street. If Skye's home was being kept under surveillance, it was being done with some discretion. An old woman stared down from a window across the way, but she didn't have the look of an Admiralty agent to Erasmus' mind—a busybody was more likely.

The door opened and a man servant nodded respectfully as Erasmus handed him a calling card. "Erasmus Flattery. It is imperative that I speak with Lord Skye. I have a letter that I must deliver."

"I'm terribly sorry, Mr. Flattery, but Lord Skye is not at home. I'll certainly see that the letter is delivered safely, however." He reached out a hand which Erasmus ignored.

"I've been charged to place it in the hand of Lord Skye and no one else."

"I am sorry, sir, but that isn't possible at the moment. . . ."

The servant looked up at the sound of the carriage door opening. "Mr. Hayes!"

Hayes ran quickly up the steps. "Yes, is the earl not at home? I desperately need to speak with him."

The servant shook his head, apparently pleased to see Samual. "No, sir. Lord Skye set out early this morning and didn't say where. It was most peculiar. You don't know where he'd have gone, do you, Mr. Hayes?"

"I'm afraid I don't. You haven't had men from the Admiralty about asking after your master, have you?"

"Not a one, sir, though your colleague, Mr. Kehler, was by this morning. He left a letter as well."

Hayes shook his head in worry, looking at Erasmus as though

unsure what to do. "Kehler didn't say where he was staying, I don't suppose?"

"I'm afraid not, sir. Will you leave your letter with me, Mr. Hayes?"

Hayes was about to say yes when Erasmus stepped in, pocketing the letter quickly. "No, but thank you. If Lord Skye does return, would you ask him to contact me?"

The servant eyed Erasmus oddly, as though he were a little offended that Erasmus did not seem to trust him. "As you wish, sir."

Erasmus steered Hayes down the stairs and into the carriage.

"Whatever led you to do that?" Hayes asked. "We don't know when Skye might return or if he is even actually away. It would be better if he had my note at the soonest possible opportunity."

Erasmus nodded. "Perhaps, but did you not think that servant was more curious than was polite?"

Hayes was brought up short by this. "But he knows me, and was likely concerned about his employer."

"Perhaps so, but it is the practice of the agents of the Admiralty to pay servants for information about their employers. I would rather err on the side of caution." Erasmus tapped on the ceiling to have the driver move on. "It seems your colleague is in Avonel. What's his name? Kehler?"

Hayes nodded, thinking. "Yes, but where, that is the question. Under normal circumstances he would be my guest. As things stand, however, he could be rooming anywhere."

The little window between the driver and the carriage slid open. "I'm not sure where I'm to go, sir," the man said.

"Nor am I. Hold your course for a moment while we decide." He turned back to Hayes. "I assume Kehler has some friends in the city? Besides yourself, that is?"

"Emin, primarily, but he's abroad till midsummer." Hayes considered a moment. "We could try the Belch."

"Of course," Erasmus said. "The old Gulch and Swallow."

They pressed on to the inn where Hayes thought they might find Kehler, a place well known to Erasmus, though he had not been there in years.

The Gulch and Swallow Inn was called "House Hopeful" by many of its patrons for the simple reason that budding empiricists gathered there, both for organized discussion, and for discourse that could only be described as unruly. The truth was that, beyond their various interests, the patrons spent an inordinate amount of time gossiping about the doings of the *Society for Empirical Studies* and its fellows, for House Hopeful (also referred to as the "Belch and Swallow") was filled with young men who longed to become fellows of that august Society.

They spent uncounted hours discussing how one would best go about bringing one's efforts to the notice of the Society, as well as dissecting the tactics of every successful candidate.

Of course House Hopeful also provided a stage for the conquering hero, for who could resist returning to the "old neighborhood." And no matter how gracious the newly appointed fellow was in victory, or how much he assured the others that their turn would come, there was always a little triumph there, and a bit of jealousy as well.

Erasmus thought that these young men could speed their fellowship considerably by simply using the time spent in the Gulch and Swallow to further their original studies, not that he hadn't squandered his own fair share of hours in this very establishment. Youth, it seemed, had an undeniable need of company. It was rather like misery in that regard.

Neither of them spoke as they rode. The measured clip-clop of hooves on paving stones was hypnotic, lulling Erasmus into a contemplative state. The dream came back to him, but he pushed it out of his mind—much easier to do in broad daylight. They were not long in coming to their destination.

Erasmus followed Hayes through the door and stood for a moment, letting his eyes adjust to the darkness of the room. There was a faltering of the conversation as many of the young men present noted that one of the gods had descended to walk among them. Though perhaps Erasmus' reputation was not yet so large as to strike awe into the hearts of young empiricists. He might have been considered a mere demigod.

Hayes surveyed the young men present, acknowledging the occasional nod, and then he waved to someone, and crossed the room to him, Erasmus in his wake.

"Pleasures of the day to you, Dandish. Have you seen Fenwick Kehler?"

Dandish almost vaulted out of his chair, glancing nervously at Erasmus. "Yesterday. He was in here for an hour or more, asking after you, too, as I remember. He was talking to Ribbon most of the time." Realizing that Hayes didn't intend to introduce him, the young man turned to Erasmus. "Sanfield Dandish at your service, Mr. Flattery. I'm a great admirer of your work in horticulture and botany, sir."

Erasmus offered the young man his hand and a tight smile, never comfortable with even genuine praise. "Kind of you," he said.

"You might try old Sam," Dandish suggested. "He likely spoke with Kehler."

Hayes ordered ale and left Erasmus at a table while he spoke with the tapman. He was back in a trice. "Sam's not sure where Kehler's found lodging, but likely in this quarter. There are a number of rooming houses that cater to visiting students and scholars. I'm sure I'll find him." Hayes picked up his ale and sipped it, staring at Erasmus. "Look, Erasmus, it doesn't seem that agents of the Admiralty are out in force searching for me. They haven't been in here, apparently, and this is a spot they'd likely not miss. I see no need for you to spend your day searching out Kehler. Leave me to it, and I'll bring you any news I might gather; that is, if you don't mind having me as a guest another night. I still feel a little trepidation at the idea of returning to my rooms."

"You are thrice welcome, Hayes, but see if you can bring Kehler back with you. I'm curious to hear his story as well. I could have Stokes put another room to rights and put you both up, if you'd like."

Hayes brightened at the offer. "You're too kind, Erasmus. I'll see if I can find Kehler, and we'll see what he's discovered in the archives of Wooton. I'm a little surprised that he's in Avonel so early in the year. It makes me a bit suspicious. If I'm not at your home by eight, it will mean the Admiralty have me. I trust you'll know what to do, for I certainly don't."

"Leave it to me, Hayes, but stay alert and be careful who you give your name to."

Erasmus spent the afternoon puzzling over the story that Hayes had told him. It had brought unfamiliar emotions to the surface. He had even spoken of his time in the house of Eldrich, which he almost never did. No, it was all very odd. The worst of it was that

Erasmus was certain he could feel the hand of the mage in the story of Compton Heath. The unseen hand.

"He does not sleep," Erasmus whispered to the window. *"Not yet."*

Erasmus was quite sure the rumors that Eldrich neared his end were not true—at least not in the way that others interpreted them. Eldrich, Erasmus was quite certain, would not pass through until he felt his time had come. But the idea that the mage was lying on his deathbed, aged and feeble, was simply not possible. Eldrich would likely remain hale and vital up until his last hours in this world. People simply did not understand mages—not these days, anyway.

Erasmus went out onto a small balcony which looked down into his garden. Unlike most people of stature in Avonel, his home did not provide him a view of the sea. He found that the vast, open horizon begged too many questions and he felt that enough questions plagued him as it was. No, Erasmus much preferred his small garden. It gave rest to his soul in a way that the expanse of ocean never could. A garden whispered no questions.

The onset of twilight released the spell over the shadows dwelling beneath the shrubs and trees so that they began to swell, flowing slowly out into the open. A distinct demarcation between light and shadow began to climb the foliage of an ancient oak, and the corner of the house cast a shadow in dark relief on the lawn. Soon all of reality would blend in darkness, and everything would lose definition. Erasmus would dream and lose definition himself.

The world when Eldrich is gone, Erasmus thought. *A commonplace world.*

A hard tap made him start, and his manservant, Stokes, appeared. He opened his mouth and then stopped, a bit surprised. "Would you not like a lamp, sir?"

"Please," Erasmus said, trying to calm his heart, feeling much as he had when a boy, expecting Eldrich to sweep in on a blast of wind.

Stokes lit a lamp, and then lit another on Erasmus' desk. The light seemed to have a calming effect—like oil on stormy seas.

"Most unusual, sir. There is a Farrellite priest at our door asking to speak with you."

"Does he want money? Can you not tell him we are not of his faith?"

"It seems he has not come asking money, sir, but wishes to

speak with you, though he'd not say why." Stokes looked a bit out of sorts. Though not a believer himself, Erasmus was, like most people in Farrland, respectful of the priests, if only as a concession to good manners.

"I am half-inclined to send him away," Erasmus said, thinking aloud. "Could he not take the time to send me a note telling me the purpose of his visit? These priests . . . !" He looked back out into his garden, which was slowly being consumed by darkness. "Oh, bring him up. I suppose I shall find out what he wants."

Stokes bobbed his head and went out, leaving the door slightly ajar so that his employer might hear the guest approaching.

A moment later Stokes opened the door and let in a small man dressed in the robes of the Farrellite faith. "Deacon Rose, Mr. Flattery."

Erasmus extended both his hands as was expected, though he disliked doing it. He tried to remember where a deacon fit in the Farrellite hierarchy. Above a parish priest, he thought, though the old root of the word was servant—servant of the martyr in this case. Certainly not servant of the parishioners.

"Mr. Flattery," the man said softly, his manner very humble, which annoyed Erasmus even more—falsely humble, he was sure. The deacon grasped both of his hands and said a quick blessing in Old Farr. "Thank you for seeing me without prior notice, Mr. Flattery. I apologize. It is not a habit of mine to burst in upon people unannounced, I assure you."

"Don't apologize, Deacon. Will you take wine or brandy? Coffee or tea?" Erasmus gestured toward two chairs.

"Brandy would be very welcome, I must admit. I have been traveling for the last three days and only came to Avondel this morning."

"Well, then, you need a brandy, Deacon." Erasmus was about to ask if the man had eaten, but stopped himself. He had never been too friendly with the priests of Farrelle, for he believed them to be a cynical, self-serving group that did much to slow progress in Farrland.

The priest collected up his robes and sat, smiling at Erasmus in a way that was kindly but not too familiar. Deacon Rose was a small man, his shape well disguised by robes. His hair, both gray and black, was cut short in the common style of the priests and he wore the round, crimson skull cap that denoted his rank. Rose might not have been a particularly handsome man, but he had a face that exuded a great deal of charm and humor, and his eyes suggested real kindness, although there was a trace of great determination there as well.

Erasmus was about to begin the small talk that was expected on such occasions—comments on the weather, etc.—but decided that the unexpected visit was hardly polite and so went right to the heart of it.

"What is it that I might do for you, Deacon Rose?"

The priest gave an odd smile that was half a grimace, as though he was hurt by the lack of politeness, but such was the burden of bearing the one truth. "And well you may ask, Mr. Flattery. But let me assure you, to begin, that you need do nothing for me. I have come regarding a mutual friend for whom I have great regard and concern. It is for his sake entirely that I am here.

"You see, after my arrival in Avonel earlier today, I went seeking this young man, and though I was not fortunate enough to find him, I was told in one establishment where the young gather that someone fitting his description and answering to his name had visited earlier, and, to my great surprise, I was not the first man who had come seeking him this day. Only an hour before the notable Erasmus Flattery had been asking after the same young man."

Stokes arrived with brandies and lit another lamp before leaving. Erasmus should not have been surprised that this visit had something to do with Hayes and his friend Kehler, but somehow he had been caught off guard.

"Erasmus Flattery was a name I knew well because of my own interests, and this brought me here. You see, Fenwick Kehler is a student at my college and, I have to say, such a student as we see only once a decade, if that. Mr. Kehler has the makings of an exceptional historian, perhaps even a great one. That is why I'm so concerned."

Cynical though Erasmus believed the priests to be, this one seemed genuinely worried about his student.

"The problem, Mr. Flattery, if I might come right to the point, is that young Kehler has been searching into the archives. I fear he has poked into matters the church considers to be private. Things that, strictly speaking, he was not to have had access to." For a second the man looked embarrassed. He began rubbing his hands together slowly, and then turned the single ring that he wore. "Yes,

I know, many people think we are hiding things in Wooton, but that is not precisely true, or at least is not what they likely think." He looked up at Erasmus suddenly, and there was a keen intelligence in that look. "Perhaps Mr. Kehler has spoken to you of this . . . ?"

Erasmus said nothing, but gazed coolly at the priest.

"Of course, that is your affair and not really my business," the priest hurried to add. "But let me only say that Mr. Kehler has looked into documents that would give him merely part of a story."

Erasmus almost interrupted to plead ignorance to the subject, but the priest began to speak again, turning his gaze out the window and continuing to toy with his ring. "The whole affair of Honare Baumgere is a grave embarrassment and something of a mystery to us. And all of this speculation . . ." He looked back at Erasmus. "It's such utter foolishness.

"But that is not my real concern. You see, Mr. Kehler's making free with our archives has caused quite a stir. He was granted great trust, and did . . . well, did what he did, unfortunately, and now he is in grave danger of expulsion. Not the end of the world, you are no doubt thinking, but the worst of it is that our young Kehler is from a family of extremely modest means. He is entirely dependent upon the good graces of the Farrellite Church for his tuition and other expenses. Oh, he does some work in the library in return, but not enough to recompense, and now, you see, he has put his situation in grave danger. He has not the means to return to Merton, or even some lesser university. I fear that we are about to see the end of an exceptionally promising career, Mr. Flattery." He shook his head. "I am not quite sure what to do, for you see he will not face up to the consequences of his actions. As soon as it was learned that he had broken his word to us, Mr. Kehler slipped out of the monastery and away. Now a man of his age and learning should have the mettle to own up to his wrongdoing and, at the very least, apologize. Yet he ran off like a child, to the disappointment of many who had done much to further his studies and who had esteemed and trusted him."

He reached out and touched Erasmus' wrist. "That is why I have come to you. If he does not return and take responsibility for his actions, he will certainly be expelled, which would be a terrible loss to the world of scholarship, not to mention the effect it will have on his life. I'm sure he has great regard for you, Mr. Flattery. You are a fellow of the Society, as all young men wish to be these days. Can you not speak with him? I assure you there is no great mystery to be uncovered in the archives of Wooten. He is throwing his career away for nothing." He spread his hands. "Nothing." The deacon looked up at him, anxiety overcoming his facade of peace and charm.

Erasmus was affected by the man's concern, though it was against his better judgment. "Let me explain, Deacon, it would be something of an exaggeration to say that Mr. Kehler and I were acquaintances. I suspect I would have less influence on him than you hope."

Deacon Rose looked a bit surprised. "I did not realize. I thought perhaps it was a relationship of long standing. In a way it would make sense that Mr. Kehler would cultivate your friendship. Did he ask you about mages, Mr. Flattery?"

Erasmus was a little taken aback by this. "I really feel any conversations I've had with Mr. Kehler were private matters, Deacon. I'm sure you understand."

"Quite so. But even if you have not been long acquainted, you could do the young man a good turn. Could you not have a word with him, Mr. Flattery? I suspect he would respect your advice. Think of poor Kehler. What will become of him? He has no trade, no family connections. We are talking about a great career being cut short over mere stubbornness. And that is a tragedy. *Youth,* Mr. Flattery. Only a young man could be so impetuous. Only a young man could fail to see the consequences of his decision. The future, no doubt, seems infinitely bright to him, but we both know that much can happen in the course of a few short years. I fear he will live to regret this decision. Regret it most terribly."

Erasmus wondered what Kehler was up to in the Farrellite archives. He was still in the employ of Skye, and Skye was proving to have some very peculiar interests.

Scholars had long believed that a great deal of Farr history was hidden in the archives of Wooton. Perhaps a great deal of information about the mages. "I'm not sure where Kehler has gotten to, but if he can be found, I'll speak with him. I can promise no more than that. I have no faith that he will heed my council."

The priest reached out and took both Erasmus' hands. "Thank you, Mr. Flattery. May Farrelle bless you for your good heart. And Kehler will thank you as well, one day." He muttered another blessing in Old Farr.

The priest sat back in his chair, taking up his brandy, and looking at Erasmus as though he were a particularly prized student. "As I said earlier, Mr. Flattery, we have a common interest: viticulture. Years ago, now, I held a position in the south countries, and at the abbey there we cultivated the vine—oh, and made wine as well—but my love was the vine and the grape. To work in the fields beneath the sun of high summer, to see the clusters swell upon the vine . . . I miss it terribly. I have a few vines growing at Wooton, but it is too far north—though I am finding some better results these last few years. Certainly you haven't done all your work up in Locfal?"

"Some of it, but I have a small holding on the island of Farrow."

The priest reacted as though Erasmus had mentioned the name of the man's lost love—the loss that had sent him into the priesthood. "Oh, how fortunate you are, Mr. Flattery. I have traveled to Farrow only once, and for far too short a time, but there can be few places better suited to viticulture, I think. Have you seen the famous Ruin?"

Erasmus nodded.

"Is it not marvelous? Astonishing really. Life is filled with mysteries, Mr. Flattery, and I am glad of it. I'm much saddened by these young empiricists who wish to explain everything. Contemplating the mysteries is a worthy meditation, in my view. It teaches humility and fills us with proper awe for this world we have been blessed with. Don't you agree?"

Erasmus shrugged. "I thought it was the business of the church to explain mysteries."

The priest did not look at all ruffled, his amiable manner not changing in the least. In fact, he seemed almost pleased that Erasmus might dispute with him. "The Farrellite Church is not monolithic, Mr. Flattery. There are schools of thought—many of them—and though we agree on the central issues, there are many more on which there are differing views. This is very healthy, I think.

"Perhaps I'm something of a mystic. I believe there are mysteries that were not meant to be comprehended by men. Not in this life at least. But these mysteries are there to fill us with awe. To intruct us in ways we cannot explain. They are like the best art in that regard. Their contemplation opens doors within our own thoughts. We see things we would not otherwise have seen. And they fill us with joy at their beauty. Those who study the words of Farrelle in an attempt to comprehend the mind of the martyr are entirely misguided in my view. These writings were never meant to be understood, but were created to stimulate the minds of his followers. They were not meant to be the basis of doctrine but of inspiration." The man paused, a bit embarrassed perhaps, but clearly this was a subject near to his heart. "May I tell you my view of mysticism?"

Erasmus nodded his consent, interested, in spite of himself, by what the man was saying.

"Imagine that you were trained as a dancer, and for many years that was your calling. But then you realized that it was necessary to your art to learn greater mental focus, and so you took up the meditative discipline of the Belthamite Hermits and pursued this for some time. When you had completed your study, you discovered that there was much to be expressed by the hands and the motion of the arms and so traveled to Doorn to work with a master there. And then, perhaps some time later, you returned to Avonel and one day, for no particular reason, picked up a fencing foil only to discover that all of your years of training had made you a great fencer, yet none of the specific disciplines you studied seemed to be in any way connected to fencing. This is mysticism. You read the teachings of Farrelle. Meditate on the ways of a running stream. Labor in a public garden to feed the poor. And if you do all of these things mindfully, one day you have an epiphany that has somehow grown from all of these things, yet does not seem to be made up of them in any recognizable way. All of these things lead to a greater understanding. Yet understanding is an inadequate word, for it is not an 'understanding' that you can explain. It is more like a blossom opening inside you. It is beautiful and awe inspiring and teaches you greater compassion and might allow you to accomplish much in the world. But can you give it a name? No. That is the way of the mystic, Mr. Flattery, and one does not have to be a believer in mysticism to experience it." A sudden grin creased his much-lined face.

"Now you see what I have done? Began talking about viticulture, a subject dear to both of our hearts, and end up lecturing you about mysticism. I do apologize. I am carried away by my own enthusiasms. It is a great weakness and has turned me into something of a bore, I'm afraid. Do forgive me." The priest rose suddenly.

"But I have taken up enough of your valuable time, Mr. Flattery. I thank you again for agreeing to speak with Mr. Kehler. It is noble of you, and I'm sure that Kehler will one day thank you for it."

Deacon Rose was still thanking Erasmus as he passed out the door to the street. Erasmus stood for a moment before the door, lost in wonder, and then realized that he looked like a man performing his devotions before an altar, and this sent something of a shiver through him.

He turned and went back up the stairs. This priest was not so charming as he thought—or at least not so cunning. Fenwick Kehler had discovered something in Merton that had the church very worried. Erasmus had no doubt of that. Something to do with Strangers, perhaps. Strangers and mages.

Chapter Nine

AVONEL had dozens of private clubs of varying degrees of exclusivity. The most exclusive, and therefore the most private, were the clubs that bore no markings to distinguish them in any way from the surrounding buildings. Some of these did not even have public names, and were referred to by their members simply as "the club."

Every club had a purpose, though it was not always the purpose inscribed in the association's charter. For instance, the club that Sir John had come to this night was ostensibly a gaming club, but its actual purpose was to put certain of its members in such debt that they would, for the foreseeable future, owe their allegiance to the "club." Sir John had once been so far in debt to this particular organization that he expected to do its bidding for the rest of his career—furthering the interests of its members at great cost to his own credibility as a minister of the government. That was before he met Bryce.

Now he expended effort to further the interests of Bryce's mysterious employer, though this had not brought him into conflict with his conscience nearly so regularly. Still, more than anything else, Sir John longed to be free. To owe allegiance to no man but his King, and to his country. That was why he had gone into government service in the first place: idealism. He shook his head. Hard to believe he had once been idealistic when you saw how things had turned out.

Sir John wondered if his news of the Entonne development of the cannon had leaked out yet. It could not be kept secret forever, that was certain. He was only afraid that the first the navy would hear of it would be when an Entonne man of war opened fire on a Farr ship. He could not allow that, but before it happened, he planned to make some political coin from his knowledge. It was, after all, a commodity like gold or grain; a value could be placed on it and it could be traded, and that was precisely what Sir John intended to do.

"Sir John! How good to see you. We've not had the pleasure of your company in a good long while."

It was one of the senior members of the club. A man Sir John had once done many favors for.

"No, not for some time," Sir John said.

"Feeling lucky tonight?"

"Indeed I am." Sir John felt so incredibly fortunate that he did not intend to gamble a single coin.

The man touched his arm, smiling widely. "Well, you know your credit is always good here."

Sir John looked down, nodding. The man's smile caused such a surge of anger and resentment. He knew what it really meant: We knew you'd be back. *I am back*, Sir John thought, *but I am changed. Now I can resist. I don't quite know how or why, but I can resist.*

He moved on through the rooms, nodding to a man here or there. Feeling a little let down by this encounter. *They thought me so weak, so in thrall to my demons.* The realization undermined his confidence a little.

He remembered well his conversations with Bryce, as he had come to know the man. Bryce had once said, daring insult: "I will tell you what it is, for it is no mystery to me. You believe you are a man blessed: intelligent, of good family, first of your class, healthy and vigorous, and handsome to the ladies. You believe so completely in your good fortune that you cannot accept your luck would desert you at the tables. How could it? And so you go back, to prove your good fortune is no accident, as though you cannot accept this failure. Your luck will win out—it must. And so you have lost a fortune, thrice over."

Bryce, almost a stranger then, had been so utterly right. Sir John had known it the moment Bryce had uttered the words. A man so blessed should not lose at something so trivial as cards or dice. Really. It was absurd. But he did, repeatedly.

And then he had come to his agreement with Bryce—his deal with the devil. Bryce would clear his debt to the club, though not his other debts—those that had been accrued because gaming took all his money—Sir John would have to deal with those himself. And so it had happened. Bryce had accompanied him to the club one night, they had sat down at a table with the men who owned Sir John's debt, and they had played at cards. And Sir John had won! He had won as he always believed he should.

And then, when his debt was cleared, Bryce had stood up, and announced it was time to go. Sir John had never felt such frustration. Go!? But the look Bryce fixed on him told him that there was no arguing. When Bryce left the table, Sir John's luck would go with him.

He asked Bryce how he had done it—this was before he realized that one did not ask questions of Bryce—but the man would say nothing. Sir John was left with the impression that Bryce must be the sharpest of players, handling cards so deftly that no man could see what he was doing. Sir John did not care that he had won by cheating, for he always suspected he had been cheated anyway.

But the most incredible thing was, after that night he had no urge to gamble. None whatsoever. He did not even come down to the club to socialize. The desire was gone. He no longer felt that he had to test himself—test his good fortune. In fact it seemed a foolish pastime now. He could barely understand how he had been trapped in such folly.

He went into the largest room, searching among the faces, hoping to find the right gentlemen in attendance this evening. Few of the men at the tables looked up—intent on their cards. A wine tasting was underway in the next room, with a number of men from both the dragoons and the navy seriously engaged. One, the scion of the Palle family, raised a glass to him as he passed. Sir John smiled.

Ten minutes later he found one of the men he looked for; the Marquis of Sennet. The marquis leaned back against a wall with his thumbs tucked into his waistband and, with a rather bored air, watched several men playing a game called skittles on a pocketless billiard table.

"Lord Sennet," Sir John said, leaning a shoulder against the wall.

"Lord? We are being formal tonight, aren't we? Have you come back to lord it over certain gentlemen?" he asked, and Sir John laughed. "Tell me, Sir John, how did you do it? It has been the subject of endless speculation around these rooms for twelve months past."

"Well, I sacrificed a ram and painted pentagrams on my chest in its blood. I went to the ruin of the old abbey on the city's edge and sold my soul to a dark spirit. . . ."

"The usual, then?"

"Well, I sacrificed no virgins, not even symbolically."

"I see." Sennet looked back to the game as everyone groaned.

"I have a bit of news that might interest you," Sir John said, lowering his voice. "In fact, I'm sure it will."

"Do you?"

"We should speak more privately."

"In the library?"

Sir John nodded, setting off for the stairs. In this club one could usually rely on the library being vacant. It was not the literary set that came to gamble.

Sir John cast a glance back at the gaming room, and all the men intent on their fortunes. It seemed a rather pathetic scene to him. He shook his head, not without some sense of moral superiority, he realized, and continued on.

The library was indeed deserted. He found a copy of the day's news and made himself comfortable by the cold hearth. A few moments later Sennet appeared, his curiosity well in check.

He slouched into one of the chairs and stared at Sir John as though he did not believe for a moment that he could tell him anything of interest.

"I have some news about the Entonne—not even a rumor yet."

"News of the Entonne is always intriguing."

"And I'm very interested in knowing what goes on with Skye. There have been some rumors. . . ."

"I might be able to help you there." The one thing about Sennet was that he could be trusted to return an equal measure of information. It was one of the things Sir John liked about the man.

"My friends in Entonne tell me that their countrymen are casting cannon, and producing gunpowder as we speak. In two months, perhaps fewer, they will have armed ships."

Sennet sat up in his chair, his look changing completely. Sir John almost smiled. It was hard to catch Sennet unawares.

"You've told the King's Man?"

"Not yet."

"Martyr's blood," Sennet said, his agile mind running over all the implications of this news. "We all knew it would happen, but not so quickly." He looked up at Sir John, clearly impressed. "You shan't make Moncrief happy with such news—not one bit."

Sir John said nothing. No one in Farrland would be happy at this news—except, perhaps Skye.

Sennet broke into a grin. "Well, you caught me looking at the wrong hand, Sir John. Well done. But then you've long been a better conjurer than most." He tipped an imaginary hat to Sir John. "You must have the finest of friends in Entonne. Very well placed." Sennet looked at him with a little admiration, his mind clearly trying to divine the names of these sources. "But your question—" His look became more serious. "I don't know if you realize what a hornets' nest you've broken open. Flames, but Moncrief is playing a dangerous game.

"I am not sure what you've heard, but I have a friend in the Admiralty. . . ." Sennet let the sentence die. "This night past Skye had gone to meet a woman. Though it was unknown to him, she was once an Entonne agent now likely in the employ of the Admiralty." He tilted his head at Sir John, who did not catch the inference.

What in the world was Sennet suggesting? And then it struck him. Moncrief's jealousy had run out of control! "They were trying to entrap him," he said, not needing confirmation. That would be Moncrief's approach. Ruin Skye by destroying his reputation. It would not be so hard. Have a woman who was reputed to be an Entonne agent claim that Skye was bringing her the design of the ship's gun, then have agents of the Admiralty apprehend them in the act. Treason. Even the King would not be able to save Skye from that.

But Sir John, and now Sennet, knew that the Entonne already possessed the cannon! They needed nothing from Skye. If this got out, Moncrief's plot against Skye would explode in his face.

"What happened exactly, do you know?" Sir John asked.

"Not in detail, but I'm sure you can guess. It went awry somehow. Moncrief actually visited the Sea Lord—went to the Admiralty building! They're more than distressed. No one knows where Skye is at the moment, and I'm sure that Moncrief and the Sea Lord are living in terror that he will appear in the palace, lunching with the King. If it gets back to His Majesty that Moncrief and Brookes plotted against Skye . . . well, there will be no saving them."

"Did Skye realize what was afoot and escape?"

"I don't know. Perhaps. But there is more. This morning a woman who fit the description of this former Entonne agent was found floating facedown in the harbor."

Sir John shook his head, realizing suddenly that he had underestimated Moncrief's jealousy. The man was less balanced, and now more desperate, than he had suspected.

Sennet smoothed his frock coat with exaggerated care.

"I sense there is something else, Lord Sennet."

"I don't know what to make of it. I'm even a little embarrassed to tell you."

Bryce's warning came back to him. Bring everything you learn back to me, and I will judge it.

"Please, Lord Sennet, put aside your reticence. I will pass judgment on the information only, not on its source."

Sennet nodded. "Something very odd has happened. My friend in the Admiralty, even he is not certain what it is. But it seems there is some hint of . . . well, the arcane." He looked up at Sir John, a bit defensive, but interested in his reaction, too. "Does that make any sense to you?"

Sir John shrugged, suddenly feeling as though he had been set adrift. *The arts?* Is that what he was suggesting? "Perhaps. Can you say more?"

"Not really. My friend was not very clear. You might delve into the death of this woman—the one found in the harbor." He shook his head. "I was told that Brookes and Moncrief both looked as though they had seen ghosts. And they interviewed some sailor and a trollop. My friend believed they knew something about the woman's death. Bloody peculiar."

"So it seems." Sir John shifted in his chair, anxious to leave. Anxious to relay what he'd learned to Bryce—to see the man's reaction.

"You had best be careful who you tell about the Entonne and their naval gun, Sir John," Sennet said, sensing that his friend was about to leave. "Moncrief will not want that information to get out too soon, I shouldn't think."

"No, I'm sure he wouldn't, though there can't be many who know about his plot against Skye and therefore could put two and two together." He stared at Sennet, who shook his head.

"I'm sure that's true. Still . . . if Skye knows what was planned, then he will likely not keep it secret, though accusing Moncrief without evidence would be a mistake. Especially as it is well known the two men dislike each other. It might seem merely an attempt to slander the King's Man, and that would be foolish. I can't imagine Skye acting rashly."

"No." Sir John had thought his own news of great value, but Sennet had repaid him with coin to spare, if for no other reason than he was now on his guard against Moncrief. He would likely have gone to Moncrief with his news of the Entonne and the cannon. And where would that have led?

Sennet had discharged his debt, that was certain, but Sir John was willing to trade on his credit a little.

"You don't know where Skye has disappeared to?"

Sennet shook his head. "It is a mystery. Is it idle curiosity or do you need to know?"

"I need to speak with him. I have information that he must have."

Sennet considered this request, gazing at Sir John as though weighing his ability to pay. "It has come to my attention recently that the Countess of Chilton has a certain regard for Lord Skye. She would not likely give him away intentionally, but . . ."

"The countess? Really? I should have taken up empirical studies."

Sennet smiled politely.

Sir John was willing to make one more withdrawal against his credit. "I have a last request. Have you ever had dealings with a man named Bryce or heard tell of him?"

"Bryce? What is his given name?"

"I—I don't know," Sir John admitted, a bit embarrassed. "He is a mystery to me. Tall man, dark, very sure of himself. Extremely fastidious. Precise in his speech. I cannot really tell you more."

"But aren't you describing the stranger who sat at the gaming table with you the night of your phenomenal luck?"

Sir John nodded.

"But everyone believes he was a friend of yours. A . . ." He did not want to say "sharp." "You really didn't know him?"

Sir John shook his head. A small lie, only. He barely knew Bryce.

"Well, that is interesting. I don't know if I can learn anything with so little to get me started. You can't tell me anything more? Is he a gentleman of leisure, or does he follow some profession? What schools? I suppose you know nothing of his family?"

"I can tell you nothing more. No, that is not precisely true. He has a head for figures, especially where money is concerned, and is a shrewd investor."

"Ah, there you go. If he is an investor, then he can be found."

"Well, that might or might not be true. I am not absolutely sure he invests himself. . . . Though one would think he must."

Sennet took out the smallest pocket watch Sir John had ever seen. "I will do my best, Sir John."

"I will be in your debt," Sir John said, meaning it more than figuratively.

"Hardly." Sennet turned to him, very serious suddenly. "Do be careful with what you know about the Entonne. I would not like to see Moncrief hush it up because it could potentially hurt him. Some innocent Farr sailors might die to learn what is already known. I suggest you find some other way to send that information to the King, and not through the Admiralty, that is certain."

"Moncrief is my superior. I can't bypass him and go directly to the King myself." He fixed a look of appeal on Sennet. "You could take this information to the King for me, and Moncrief would know nothing of its source. If anyone could manage that, you could."

Sennet nodded. "Very likely, but aren't you afraid that you'll lose credit for your discovery?"

So, there would be a greater cost for this interchange than he'd anticipated. "It's immaterial who receives the credit. Better Moncrief not know it came from me, and you're absolutely right—the King must know immediately. Can you manage it?"

Sennet nodded. "Leave it to me, and if there comes a time when it is propitious to do so, I will share the credit with you. Is that acceptable?"

"More than acceptable," Sir John said, feeling his peerage slip away.

"Then I will be about our business, Sir John. Good luck with locating Skye. If I learn anything more, I will send you word immediately."

Yes, no doubt you will. You're about to receive all manner of honors for the information that I have given you. Sir John realized that he felt a little more amused than resentful. He had discovered what Bryce wanted to know, and that was what mattered, for good or ill.

Sir John wandered down through the club in something of a daze, barely acknowledging the men who spoke to him. The thought that it was he who had started this entire affair—setting Moncrief up to be ridiculed by Skye—was finally making its significance felt. He had known that Moncrief would never let such an insult go unanswered. Had Bryce been out to bring down Moncrief all along? Was that his purpose? Astonishing. Who Bryce's mysterious employer was suddenly took on more meaning. Moncrief had enemies, that was without doubt, but which one of them employed Mr. Bryce?

But there was something else in his conversation with Sennet that stood out—for its strangeness if for nothing else. *"There was some hint of the arcane."* Was this why Bryce had cautioned him to relay everything he heard to him? Sir John shook his head. What was he caught up in?

Sir John stepped out the front door of the club and was about to ask the doorman to find him a hack when the door of a large carriage opened and a man leaned out.

"Sir John?"

It was Bryce, waiting at the curb.

Sir John stepped up into the carriage and settled into a seat, more than a little surprised.

"What in the world brought you to be here at this hour?" Sir John asked.

"You might call it a hunch," Bryce said, smiling only slightly. "Have you found Skye? Do we know what happened?"

"I have the name of someone who might know Lord Skye's whereabouts, or so I hope. Whether she will help us or not remains to be seen. As to what happened, it seems that Moncrief, in a fit of jealousy, tried to entrap Skye." He told Bryce what he had learned from Sennet, holding back only the last piece of information.

Bryce merely nodded. "And that's it? That's what you learned?"

"No, there is one more thing. . . ." Sir John watched this mysterious man very carefully, though he didn't expect to be able to read Bryce's reaction—he never could. "My friend tells me that there was some hint of the arcane in this matter. Perhaps something to do with how the woman died."

To Sir John's amazement, Bryce smiled. Not a smile of mockery or disbelief, but one of great satisfaction. As though he'd been told that the woman he desired most in the world was mad for him.

"Well," he said, and no more.

"Does it have some significance?" Sir John asked, unable to stop himself.

"That is for my employer to decide," Bryce said, though he still looked pleased, and not annoyed as he always did when Sir John asked questions.

This made Sir John suddenly bolder. "So you will bring down Moncrief. Is that what you've planned all along?"

Bryce looked surprised. "*Moncrief?*" he said as though hearing the name for the first time. "Sir John, Moncrief is no concern of ours. None whatsoever." And with those words he folded his arms and turned to look out the window.

Chapter Ten

IT was some time after dinner that Hayes returned to Erasmus' home. He looked as though he'd run across the entire town on his own two legs, he was so red in the face and out of breath.

Stokes led him into the study, his manner toward this young waif considerably softened.

"Ah, Hayes. Without your friend Kehler, I see." Erasmus paused. "Is something wrong?" It appeared that Hayes was more than just red in the face, he was unsettled. "Nothing ill has befallen your friend, I hope?"

"No. Not that I'm aware of. But I just had the strangest encounter. As I came up to your door—I was just lifting the knocker—someone called out Kehler's name. I turned around to find this little man hurrying across the street. He came to the bottom of the stair and realized I wasn't Kehler at all. Then he mumbled an apology and scurried off. The strange thing was that he was a Farrellite priest and Kehler has been studying at their college in Wooton."

"Deacon Rose."

"You know him?"

"Only since this afternoon. He came here looking for Kehler. He had been by the Belch and learned that I was in there asking after him. He came here hoping I would help him find your friend. It seems Kehler has been delving into things he was not meant to find, and this has the church in rather an uproar. This man Rose claimed that Kehler had betrayed their trust, and now was in danger of expulsion which would ruin his career, for he was dependent upon the church for his tuition."

Hayes snorted. "I've never heard such rubbish. Kehler's people aren't wealthy, but they're certainly able to pay his school fees. No, I don't think the Farrellites are searching for Kehler for charitable reasons." Hayes reached into his jacket and pulled out a letter. "Kehler left this with a friend." He started to offer it to Erasmus, appeared to change his mind, and then pushed it into Erasmus' hand.

Erasmus slipped the letter from the envelope—a single page written in an appalling hand.

My dear Hayes:

I've instructed Colghan not to trust this letter to anyone but you. I do hope it finds you. I tried to see you while I was in Avonel, but you'd fled your rooms and there were all kinds of rumors as to what had happened.

I've been on the run as well; from my good teachers. It seems they have not properly appreciated my search for the truth. Well, be that as it may, I have found some things that would amaze you. I dare not say more in a letter, but hope to be able to tell all in person. I've chosen the road of honor, I'm sure you will understand.

I am leaving you this one line of text which is a complete mystery to me. Can you find someone at Merton who might be able to read it?

There followed a single line of characters which caused Erasmus to sit down abruptly.

"Erasmus?" Hayes sounded worried. "Are you well? You've turned white as a ghost. Shall I call Stokes?"

Erasmus looked up at Hayes who stared at him with great concern. "He found this text in the archives?"

"So I would assume. Can you read it?"

Erasmus shook his head. "No. No one can read it. No man at least. It is the writing of the mages. . . . I saw it—in the house of Eldrich." Erasmus raised the letter again, still unsettled and oddly saddened. "Where is Kehler now, do you think?" he asked, his voice very soft, as though he had just learned of a friend's death.

Hayes did not answer, and Erasmus looked up.

"I think it would be better if you told me, Hayes. I'm beginning to suspect that your friend Kehler has involved himself in matters he does not clearly understand. And we mustn't forget that the Admiralty searched your rooms—perhaps they have some interest in this matter, as well."

Hayes took a seat, clearly struggling with promises he'd made to Skye and Kehler. "Kehler wrote that he'd taken the road of honor," he said, his voice very subdued. "It is a reference to a priest. A man who died years ago. Honare Baumgere. Do you know to whom I refer?"

Erasmus shook his head. "No, but the priest mentioned his name—almost in passing—as though he wanted to see my reaction to it."

Hayes raised his eyebrows. "Baumgere was someone Skye was interested in. I mentioned that in Compton Heath they sent for a priest learned in languages? That priest was Honare Baumgere." Hayes took a long breath, and let it out slowly, his gaze fixed on some point well beyond the room. "Later—many years later—Baumgere excavated a . . . structure near the town of Castlebough in the Caledon Hills."

"I've heard something of that. Wasn't it a crypt?"

"That's how it's known, though there is no reason to believe it was really a crypt other than the fact that it vaguely resembles one. But it is a puzzling piece of architecture. Some say it is as unique as the Ruin on Farrow, for we don't know who built it or when, or even its purpose."

"And Skye has some interest in this? It connects to the Stranger in some way?"

Hayes nodded stiffly.

"Samual," Erasmus waved the letter at him, "this is the script of the mages and though it might one day become a matter of academic interest, I can assure you that while Eldrich lives, it is still a jealously guarded secret. If the priests are keeping texts in this language in Wooton and Kehler has found them, then it is no wonder they are searching for him. Eldrich will be in a blind rage if he discovers the church has been hoarding texts dealing with the arts.

"You see, when the Farrellites lost their war against the mages, they swore they would never practice the arts again, for they had used the mages' own arts against them. All of the texts they had gathered were to have been surrendered to the mages. If they have held some back, or even discovered a text since that they've hidden, Eldrich will not be merciful. I can assure you of that. The worst of it is, your friend Kehler might end up suffering as much as the priests. Remember, mages are not known for being just or fair. I think it best that you tell me what you know and then we set out to locate Kehler. I only hope we can find him before he does something foolish. What say you, Hayes, will you trust me with the rest of your story?"

Hayes thought for a moment, his boyish face very serious, which mysteriously made him look even younger. Then he nodded quickly, pulling his waistcoat down. For a moment he was very still. "Baumgere was a scholar of some note," he began, "who, for many years, was an archivist at Wooton. Sometime in his middle years he was struck by the urge for a more pastoral life and was granted the living of the church in Castlebough. Do you know Castlebough? It is not far from the famous Bluehawk Lake. I think it the most beautiful country. Right in the heart of the Caledon Hills. The village is not as well known now as it was—oh, fifty years ago—when it was the fashion to take the waters there, but people still travel to Castlebough for their health.

"Baumgere had always been a scholar—had likely never given a sermon in all his days—but he was apparently a respected man within the church, and if that was what he wanted, then his superiors were happy to oblige. After a scant three years in Castlebough, Baumgere left the church, odd enough in itself, but then he discovered the buried 'crypt' near the castle.

"He began to wander the hills, as though still searching for something. People would see him occasionally, in the company of his servant—a massive man who was both deaf and dumb. They were said to have excavated other locations in the area, but if they found anything, no one saw.

"Baumgere purchased a manor house outside the town, proving he had a bit of money, though he had always claimed that he did not come from a moneyed background, not that he made many claims for himself, for he was a secretive man.

"There are any number of rumors from this point in the story. The ones Kehler seems to believe—and he knows much more about this than I—have to do with writing on the crypt. It was said the edifice bore a significant script, though Baumgere had this writing eradicated as soon as it was discovered, which must have taken some labor. Apparently you can see where the work was done. No one knows why.

"There is another odd fact. . . . Baumgere apparently owned a painting of the crypt, by Pelier, no less—which means it was done over two hundred years before Baumgere discovered the crypt. Everything that Kehler could find indicated that the crypt was unknown in that time—still buried, in fact.

"The painting is typical of Pelier's oracular style, complete with symbols and portents. Unlike most of Pelier's paintings, his interpreters did not have an explanation for this one. If it foretold some event in the future, no one seemed able to suggest what that might be.

"The painting apparently showed the tomb with the writing still intact, and three individuals paying their respects or perhaps examining the tomb, it is difficult to say. There was supposed to be a gentleman, a somewhat grotesque man thought to be a servant, and a veiled lady dressed entirely in black. Oh, and there might or might not have been a dark figure hidden in the shadow of the door. In the background one can see the old keep that sits above Castlebough, and Kehler believes that Baumgere used this to locate the crypt.

"Apparently Skye had been looking for some time for the Peliers that Baumgere owned. He had spoken of them to Kehler almost at their first meeting, and this had influenced Kehler's decision to attend Wooton. Many thought that Baumgere's effects were taken by the church, including the Peliers and whatever writings the man might have left behind."

Hayes rose from his chair and went to the window, closing it to within an inch, for the night was growing a little chill. He leaned forward cautiously and looked down into the street.

"Is he there?" Erasmus asked, almost whispering.

Hayes shook his head. "I can't tell." He picked up his story, not relaxing his vigil. "I find it odd that the Farrellite Church appeared to take no interest in their former priest, but then I suppose he did nothing to interest the church—not until later on." Hayes sat on the window ledge now, where the lamplight threw odd shadows on his face; creasing it with lines of worry. "It is said that when Baumgere was on his death bed, the priest who was his replacement came to administer last rites. But upon hearing Baumgere's confession, he refused to perform the absolution, storming from the house in a passion and leaving the man to die the true death—an astonishing event in the history of the Farrellite Church, even if he was no longer a priest. So Baumgere passed through like any man who had not found the faith. And then, oddly, not long after, the priest who refused him the absolution was found hanged from a tree in the forest. Self-murder! A mortal sin according to the teachings of the Farrellite Church. And that is more or less the end of the tale.

"Baumgere left no money to any individual nor to his church, and no one knew his story unless he confessed it on his deathbed, which is what everyone believes. Whether the priest who heard his confession ever passed the story along is not known." Hayes stood up and smiled at Erasmus. "So you see, it is fertile ground for speculation."

"I should say so. Do we assume this script that Kehler sent you has some connection to Baumgere?"

"It's quite likely, but he didn't say, as you saw."

Hayes turned to look down into the street again. Erasmus could just make out his reflection in the dark glass. "One can never be sure what Kehler is up to. His interests are . . . peculiar."

"Such as?"

"Lost knowledge. Secret histories. Things he believes the church has long known but kept hidden from the lay public. One can never be sure with Kehler. He very much keeps his own counsel—rather like you, Erasmus. The story of the Compton Heath Stranger sent him off on a completely new direction. Before that, his interests had been very academic and rather respectable. Skye opened up a world of mystery for him. An area that academia ignored. You cannot imagine his excitement. He hoped to find something about the Stranger of Compton Heath in the archives. He thought Baumgere might have written something that would be found there."

Erasmus considered for a moment. There were pieces missing from this story—entire chapters, he was sure. "Is there some connection between the Stranger of Compton Heath and the structure that Baumgere found?"

Hayes made an odd motion—almost a shrug. Almost a lie, Erasmus thought. "Anything is possible."

"I imagine Kehler must have a theory about Baumgere and what he searched for?"

"Yes, I think he does." The same reticence. Lying did not come easily to young Hayes—at least not lying to friends. Perhaps he felt he'd said too much already.

"But you cannot say, I collect?"

A long moment of hesitation, as he looked down into the street, or stared at his own reflection. "Perhaps if we find Kehler, he will tell you more. That is all I know. Oh, there is one more thing. . . . Apparently Baumgere's own gravestone has a line of characters inscribed on it that can't be read. Perhaps Baumgere's final word, or merely a black jest by the headstone carver; no one knows." Erasmus nodded, staring hard at Hayes, who gazed down into the darkened street. The hollow *clip-clop* of a passing horse drifted up to them; a log in the fire shifted.

"You are thinking that you should travel to Castlebough to aid your friend—and to warn him," Erasmus said softly. "And I do not think your concern is misplaced. If the church has texts in the language of the mages. . . ." Hayes glanced at him, his look of helplessness lifting a little. "It seems imperative that Kehler know what he has stirred up. I can arrange my affairs to leave by noon. What of you, Samual? Will you come with me?"

For a moment Hayes only stared at Erasmus, and then he stood up, almost shaking himself, shaking off the lethargy and helplessness that was the legacy of Paradise Street. Then a thought came to him, and the light that had ignited inside him dimmed. "But Erasmus, I must tell you I haven't. . . ."

Erasmus held up his hand. "Don't even speak of it. We are talking about Kehler's well-being here. He is potentially in danger from both the church and Eldrich. No, let us not quibble about money. My father, bless him, left me enough that I might live in complete idleness. Rescuing Kehler is far better use than I would otherwise put it to."

When Hayes finally took himself off to bed, he left the letter from Kehler behind. Erasmus took it up, and for a long time stared at the line of foreign script. Just the sight of this writing brought up old memories and the accompanying turmoil. Yet he could not put the letter down. For a moment he thought of throwing it in the fire, but the idea of it bursting into flame was unsettling.

"He has escaped from memory," Erasmus read aloud. *Escaped from memory.*

Chapter Eleven

THE Caledon Hills crowded up against the western border where they grew to near mountain status, before falling away to a high plateau just inside Entonne.

Sparse population and rugged geography meant that only a few roads managed to find their way through the twisting valleys and gorges. The geology of the area was dominated by a thick stratum of whitestone that current thinking said was formed at the bottom of a shallow sea, millennia ago, though it now resided high above sea level.

The pale stone had been worn and broken by the long ages and left irregular hills standing, sometimes quite rounded but often steep sided and angular. Rivers wound through valleys and plunged between high cliffs into gorges where the water roiled and foamed and then fell in precipitous drops into deep turquoise pools.

An ancient forest spread its branches over most of the Caledon Hills and here one could find species of oak, beech, and walnut that were not common to any other area of Farrland. A particularly fragrant pine, called the Camden Pine, grew on the north sides of hills at higher altitudes, and the rose family had spread a few of its species—from bitter apples and hawthorns to flowering rosebushes—across the hillsides and valleys.

Long known for the abundance of game, the hunting lodges of

the aristocracy were scattered among the hills, and here and there a fertile valley provided a patch of farmland. Deep, clear lakes became the destination of travelers drawn to the lonely beauty, and in particularly picturesque locations towns catering to such travelers sprang up.

Hayes looked out over the valley below and then toward the northern hills. They had stopped the carriage at this point, not just to rest the horses after the climb but because it was a well known viewing point, and the fact that they were not the first to find it did not reduce the pleasure.

In the distance Hayes was sure he could see the remains of a large structure, though, when built of the same stone as the surrounding hills, it was sometimes difficult to tell—limestone had a tendency to break into blocks that looked surprisingly man-made.

Erasmus was slowly sweeping a field glass across the scene.

"Is that an old lodge there, on the hill to the right?" Hayes asked.

Erasmus focused his glass and then shook his head. "A tower. Perhaps even a small castle."

It was the other thing the Caledon Hills were famous for; the ruins of castles and other defensive structures. In the long years of warfare that had plagued the nations around the Entide Sea, the hills had seen more than their share of battles, and castles had been built and torn down and built again for over a thousand years. No doubt there were several under construction at that very moment, though closer to the present border in the great passes between the high hills. It was difficult to move a large army any other way—in fact, it had so far proved impossible.

Erasmus took a few steps to the right and leaned against a low stone wall so that he could look west along an arm of the valley. A small lake lay there, reflecting the colors of the late afternoon, the image of a cloud floating white and ghostlike in its center.

"There," Erasmus said. "That will be Castlebough, I think. Do you see?" He handed Hayes his glass.

It took Hayes' eye a second to adjust, but then he saw, at the lake's end on top of an angular hill, a town huddled around the ruins of an old citadel. "True to its name, there is a castle, or at least the remains of one."

"A keep of the Knights of Glamoar," Erasmus said, surprising Hayes by knowing anything of the history of such an obscure little village. "The place where this man Baumgere discovered a mysterious crypt. And the place where our good Kehler is likely pursuing his obsessions, as you call them. Let us hope that we are here before the agents of the Admiralty, and that the agent of the church has not guessed where Kehler might be."

Hayes swept the glass up the valley. A hawk hanging above the lake suddenly let go of its perch on the sky and plunged toward the water. He lost sight of it before it struck, as though it had vanished into the clear air.

"Look! Erasmus! A wolf, by the lake." He handed Erasmus the glass. "Halfway along the left shore. Do you see?"

Erasmus swept the glass along the lake's edge, then back. "No . . ." he said, his voice oddly tentative. "No. It seems to have gone." He lowered the glass, his look utterly changed. As though he had seen something that had unsettled him. "We should be on our way." Erasmus motioned Hayes to precede him toward the carriage, but when Hayes looked over his shoulder, he saw that Erasmus was looking back, his manner very grim.

He must be reminded of the wolf he said prowled the home of Eldrich, Hayes thought, and felt a wave of pity for the child Erasmus. He could not imagine such a strange experience—so unlike his own rather carefree boyhood.

They traveled on, Erasmus even less communicative. He sat very still, staring out the window by the hour, his chin supported on his hand, looking like a man bereaved. He didn't know why, but somehow Hayes thought that Erasmus mourned for his lost childhood and for the terrible legacy of memory which haunted him still.

Sir John stood on the edge of the road, which dropped several hundred feet into the gorge. He glanced down and then quickly up again. The sight of the roiling waters—white and impossibly porcelain green—caused all his muscles to tense. He stood there on the cliff edge like a stick man—unbending, awkward, utterly discomfited.

In contrast, Bryce hovered on the cliff edge as though he had not noticed that a step to his right would send him into the sky, briefly, before drowning him in the river below. He might have been a bird for the amount of concern he displayed. A mere instant of loss of balance and either of them would see their life end.

Bryce pointed suddenly. "There—do you see them?"

Sir John squinted, leaning slightly and then pulling himself back abruptly. A field glass was what was needed here. But then perhaps he did see something move. Perhaps a yellow carriage. They had been told at the last inn that the countess was not far ahead of them, and at the pace they had been traveling, it was no wonder. Sir John half expected them to arrive before her.

"I'm sure you're right, though I'm surprised that the countess travels with such a small retinue. Two carriages only." For a second Sir John thought he'd lost his balance, and stepped quickly back from the edge, his heart pounding.

Bryce looked at him closely and then smiled—half from amusement, half from pity. "I think we should let them travel on for a bit. I'd rather not be seen." He turned his head suddenly, his look intent. "Do you hear that?"

Sir John listened, but could hear only the river, the sound of the breeze bending the trees, and the poor trees uttering their complaints. A raven called.

The horses had pricked up their ears, suddenly excited.

"Is someone coming?"

"Yes. Let us wait and see who it is. If your Admiralty men are still chasing after Skye, I want to know." Bryce bent down suddenly and retrieved a pinecone, throwing it over the precipice. Like a school boy he stood and watched it fall, veering to one side suddenly as it neared the water, caught by a current of wind gusting through the gorge. Then there was the smallest splash. Bryce stood for a moment as though watching the cone's progress, and then he turned to look down the road just as a two-horse team appeared around the corner, pulling a trap.

The only occupant of the carriage sat a bit taller in his seat as he approached, obviously peering at the two men on the road. And then, as he came closer, he raised his arm and waved.

"Sir John?" he called as he pulled his team up.

"Why, Kent, what a surprise. Where are you off to?"

"Castlebough," Kent said. "And yourself?"

Sir John hesitated, not sure if Bryce would want their destination known, but then Bryce spoke up. "The same. You must be the illustrious Averil Kent. . . . Percival Bryce, your servant, sir."

"And I am yours, Mr. Bryce," Kent said. Sir John did not know Kent well, but even so, he thought the young man looked a bit uncomfortable, almost as though he had been caught doing something he'd rather others knew nothing about. There was an awkward silence for a moment, and then Kent tipped his hat.

"Perhaps we'll meet in Castlebough, then," Kent said. "Pleasures of the day to you, gentlemen."

Sir John and Bryce followed Kent's progress for a moment.

"Odd to meet Kent here," Sir John said as Kent disappeared around a bend. "He must be on one of his painting jaunts."

Bryce laughed. "He is pursuing the countess, Sir John. Could you not see it?"

Sir John looked at his companion in surprise. "How can you be certain?"

"Oh, it was written in his manner. In the tilt of his head. His slight embarrassment at meeting someone he knew. Did you not see the way he peered ahead so hopefully when he saw our carriage, and then the disappointment when he saw who it was—or who it was not, I should say. Do not doubt it. The poor man is here in pursuit of the Countess of Chilton, like any sad hound chasing a bitch in heat. I pity him; he is in for a bad time of it, I think. Let us hope he is not fool enough to end up in a duel over such a woman."

"Such a woman, indeed!" Sir John said. "Do you disparage her, then?"

Bryce turned to him rather sharply. "I meant only that she is a woman who draws men to her even when she does not mean to, Sir John. Do I disparage her? No. On the contrary. I pity her. More even than poor Kent." Bryce looked off down the valley. "I pity her utterly."

Chapter Twelve

A man may either move westward through life, following the light, or eastward toward the gathering darkness. It is a kind of orientation of temperament that is set in our earliest years; an emotional compass. One either pursues one's dreams or one's memories, and it is an exceptional man who, once his compass has been set, can alter it even a point or two.

Halden: Essays

WHEN Hayes came down to break his fast in the morning, he discovered that Erasmus had been gone over two hours. Hayes cursed himself for a lazy fool and considered going out after his companion, but then decided that this would invariably lead to Erasmus returning while Hayes was out, and so on, so he decided on food and staying in one place.

Around the site of Castlebough were several hot springs, the waters of which were said to be healthful, and these almost more than anything accounted for the town's survival. Certainly the terraced gardens and small pastures he had seen on the slope below the town did not provide commerce, and the few travelers who stopped there on their way elsewhere would not support anything but the smallest inn.

But Castlebough boasted nine good-sized inns, and these catered almost exclusively to people coming to take the waters. To Hayes' satisfaction Erasmus had chosen one of the better establishments, the *Springs,* and here he had found them each a room on the same floor. As Hayes had no worries about finances on this journey (Erasmus insisted on paying) he felt something like a gentleman of means again. He had never realized what a great sense of freedom one felt at being able to spend money without concern—not until he had been forced to count every penny.

Imagine, he thought, going into an inn and having to ask the cost of a meal before ordering! It had never even occurred to him to do such a thing before, and though he had become used to it in time, at first he had found the experience rather humiliating.

Well, I have been humbled enough to last a lifetime now, he thought. *I shall never worry about growing arrogant or vain, that is certain.*

Now, if they could only find Kehler. Hayes wondered, not for the first time, what his friend was up to, for Kehler was secretive even with him, and Hayes was very likely his closest friend in the world.

May we find him before he gets himself in too much trouble, Hayes thought, though he realized that, more than anything, he wanted to know what Kehler had discovered. His curiosity was burning.

The dining room was not half-filled with people, all of whom appeared to be taking their leisure—not residents of Castlebough, that was certain. There were a few elderly people who might actually suffer infirmities, but most he saw were hardly old—in their thirties or forties—nor did they look to be suffering from any illness. If anything, they seemed to be on a holiday. He could hear some of them discussing plans for the day: a boat trip down the river which would actually take them through a cave; a sail on Blue Hawk Lake; an excursion to various ruins. Hayes felt a bit jealous of their leisure, supported as it obviously was by resources he did not have.

"Ah, Hayes. . . . You've finally managed to face the day," Erasmus said as he found his companion. "Have you been here long?"

"No, not at all. Just long enough to overhear the plans of our fellow guests, and to begin to feel a bit sorry for myself. You have come along just in time to save me from that particular emotional quagmire."

Erasmus pulled up a chair and ordered coffee. "Well, I have been out to look at our town and to check the other inns. None seem to have a Mr. Kehler in their care, nor anyone who fits his description, so I hope we have not come so far to find he has already been and gone."

"But he was two days ahead of us! I can't imagine that he has already left." Hayes was a bit distressed by the idea that he might have brought Erasmus Flattery so far, on an errand of mercy, and found it was only a fool's errand, after all.

"Well, I'm told there are any number of residences in Castlebough that are owned by people from the lowlands. Some of these are let out by the week, and others are lent to family friends. You don't know if Kehler has friends who might keep a home here?"

Hayes shook his head.

Coffee arrived, and Erasmus took it up without cream or sugar. "Then I suggest we go have a look at this mysterious crypt, then perhaps at the house that Baumgere owned. I have been asking the staff for directions—not so uncommon it seems. Baumgere and his mysterious excavations have drawn any number of people before us, apparently. Kehler might find his mystery well picked over. I wonder what he hopes to discover?"

Hayes shrugged.

Erasmus fixed an odd look on his companion, and the younger man turned his attention to his food, realizing that Erasmus believed he was holding back information. It was always difficult to know where one stood with Erasmus, for the man seemed to have made up his own mind about which of society's strictures he would obey and which he would blatantly ignore.

"As soon as you're ready," Erasmus said, having bolted his coffee. He rose from his chair. "I'll be in my room."

Forty minutes later the two gentlemen were walking up one of the steep streets of Castlebough. It was a typical town of its type, built of local stone, the main street jagging back and forth up the hillside with numerous alleys and stairways joining the levels. A spring somewhere high up had been tapped for the village water supply and this ran down among the houses on a circuitous route, appearing here and there and could often be heard whispering beneath the paving stones. Hayes thought it a picturesque little town, trim and neat, and no doubt kept in this state for the visitors.

As they emerged above the last houses of the town proper, they found the old stair they had been directed to and headed up. The graveyard they wanted was on the hilltop behind the old castle, and though one could reach it by road, the stairway led to a shorter, if slightly more adventurous path.

Conversation soon ceased as they saved their wind for the climb. The stair ended at a path that wound up into the wood, then suddenly set off up a steep gully. Here stones had been set as steps occasionally and in one place a rusted chain acted as a hand rail; they pulled themselves up on this with some effort. Eventually they found stairs again, then a ledge, a final staircase, and then they emerged on the top.

Both Erasmus and Hayes threw themselves down on a stone bench to catch their breath. Before them spread a wondrous view, out over the town and down to the lake. To the north they could see the hills lifting up like seas toward an indistinct horizon that seemed impossibly distant and mysterious. If Hayes stared hard, he was certain that he could see another mountain beyond those he had thought were the farthest, and then others beyond that.

In the west the high hills lifted up to a jagged meeting with the cold sky, and here there was still snow to be seen, bright and pure in the morning sun.

"If Kehler proves not to be here, I will feel we've been amply rewarded just by this view," Erasmus said, making Hayes feel a bit better, for he was worried that Kehler was gone, or worse—the priests had found him first.

They sat for a moment more, not speaking, but absorbed by the scene. Then Erasmus got to his feet, and Hayes followed. Reluctantly they turned away.

The castle had been greatly reduced by the villagers taking away cartload after cartload of stone to enlarge the town below, but even so there were still the remains of some high walls and towers. Hayes could see the blue sky through some of the openings, and tufts of dry grass and small yellow flowers sprouted from cracks and ledges.

A vine of morning glories had taken hold on the west wall, and these were open now, nodding in the light breeze. Behind some wild berry bushes they found an old graveyard. The most magnificent hornbeam Hayes had ever seen presided over the site, its trunk nearly three feet thick and its branches twisted and gnarled as such trees tended to be.

There were perhaps a dozen headstones half-obscured by brush and tall, golden grasses. Hayes bent over the stones and began to examine them closely. After a moment he called out, "Look! Baumgere's grave, but only his name remains. The inscription has been obliterated." He bent close, running his fingers over the few discernable lines. "Was this vandalism, do you think? Or could it have been erased for some other reason?"

Erasmus shook his head, but offered no opinion. There were a few bits of what might once have been a design or parts of an inscription left, and Erasmus looked long at these before taking out a pen and ink and copying them into a little note book.

"And will you make sense of the remains, Mr. Flattery, where so many others have resorted to mere fantasy?"

Both Hayes and Erasmus turned to find the source of this strange, high-pitched voice, and there, a dozen feet away, stood an outlandishly dressed man who could not have been four feet tall. They were both so surprised by the sight that they stared dumbly.

"Randall Spencer Emanual Clarendon, at your service," the dwarf said, making a sweeping bow. "And you are the illustrious Erasmus Flattery, I take it?"

"At your service, sir, and my particular friend, Mr. Samual Hayes."

"Your servant, sir," Hayes said, offering a hand to the man who reached up his own small hand to meet it.

Randall Spencer Emanual Clarendon was impeccably dressed in expensive and elaborate clothing of bright colors, and carried at his side a short rapier in a beautifully tooled scabbard. His high boots bore enormous silver buckles and his shirt studs glittered with pale stones that Hayes believed were diamonds. He wore no wig and tied his fringe of gray hair in a tail with a bright blue ribbon. His pate was bald and colored by the sun, his eyes the blue of mountain lakes, and beneath a magnificent white mustache, his full mouth smiled as though he enjoyed the reaction of the men before him, for certainly they stared like country boys with their first view of a noble.

"You know who I am," Erasmus said.

"Yes, forgive me. It is a small village, and the news quickly spread that Erasmus Flattery was domiciled among us. Your studies of the noble grape are well known to those of us who are dedicatees. There is, you see, quite a large vintners' society here. Some of the most successful oenologists and viticulturists spend part of their year in Castlebough, and you might imagine what the talk is among them." He smiled winningly, showing a gold-capped tooth. "I hope you will have time to come to our meeting, Mr. Flattery, and your companion as well. Are you a horticulturalist also, Mr. Hayes?"

"I'm afraid not, though I admire a decent bottle of wine." Hayes felt there was a hint of pity in the look this statement elicited.

"Well, you might find it of interest all the same. We have converted more than a few gentlemen to our cause in the past. But,

Mr. Flattery, there is more of a connection between yourself and the village of Castlebough. The famed Admiral Vinzen Flattery kept a house here for a number of years, and came often with his wife to take the waters."

"I had no idea," Erasmus said. "The admiral was not known to me, unfortunately, though still alive, I think, when I was born. I shall have to see this house."

"And I would be happy to show it to you. But I've come looking for you because I'd heard you had been asking questions about our mysterious Baumgere. I thought I should find you before those who would try to sell you copies of the inscription, or maps that lead to supposed treasure or what not. Not that you would be taken in by them, I'm sure, but they will waste a gentleman's time. I once took an interest in Baumgere and his story and would be pleased to put my small knowledge at your disposal and act as your local guide, if you will permit me."

Hayes and Erasmus looked at each other, their decision clear. "We would be delighted," Erasmus said.

Suddenly something erupted out of the grass, causing Hayes to spin around. A massive wolfhound darted past him and came panting up to Clarendon, who was obviously its master.

"This is Dusk, my particular friend," he said. "Put out your hands and let him sniff you. I hope neither of you wish me harm, for he will attack if you do. He can sense things men cannot and will not be persuaded that a man who does not like me should be allowed to go happily about his business. Fortunately I am not widely disliked, or I fear poor Dusk might have met his end by sword before now. Ah, there, you see, he has found you worthy, and that is a judgment worth more than many a man's, I will tell you." He stroked the dog behind the ears, barely having to reach down to do so, for Dusk came almost to Clarendon's shoulder.

"As Castlebough is so small, Mr. Clarendon, perhaps you have heard of a friend of ours. We were hoping to meet him here. A young man named Fenwick Kehler?"

"Kehler? No. . . . I know no one of that name, but I will ask. And please, call me Randall." The dwarf gestured toward some nearby trees. "Baumgere's discovery lies back here. You are trying to discern the remains of the mysterious inscriptions . . . ?"

"Did they really exist?" Erasmus asked.

"Oh, indeed they did, though not for many years now. The inscription erased during the time of Baumgere, as you have no doubt learned, though whether this was done by Baumgere is not known. The story, you see, has been . . . *embroidered* over the years, and the unfortunate truth is that the factual evidence—what is indisputably known—is very slim." He took a deep breath, and looked at the headstones, an air of sadness settling over him. "That Baumgere chose Castlebough for his home has fueled the fire of speculation, for there are few regions around the Entide Sea as fertile for such theorizing as the Caledon Hills, with its uncommon history and many real mysteries. And perhaps the story of Father Baumgere *did* have its beginnings long ago, in some event that took place here in these hills. That is what many say." He motioned again to the trees. "If you have the time, I will show you the mysterious 'crypt,' as it is called, and we can sit for a while and I will tell you what I can remember."

Randall led them into the bower of silver-barked beeches, then down stone steps between lilac trees. The path circled around and then emerged in what almost seemed a small quarry.

There before them, carved into the whitestone, stood the facade of a small structure. Four pillars stood proud from the stone, the heavy eaves of the roof facade appearing to rest on them. A doorway had been cut into the stone, and a bronze door hung from heavy pins. This door stood ajar and slightly askew, as though it had been forced open and damaged in the effort. Hayes was quite astonished by what he saw, for though it was not large, the tomb projected a sense of grandeur.

"There was an inscription over the door, as well as on the lintel," Randall said. "All gone now, as you can see." He turned to the others. "You look surprised, Mr. Flattery?"

Erasmus did not take his eyes from the structure. "It is not quite what I expected. It is . . . well, humble in its scale, yet grand in its design, as though merely a model for the real thing."

Randall turned back to the tomb, gazing at it for a moment. "That is precisely true. And what did the designer mean to convey by this contradiction? That the person buried here was more than others realized? That his or her true greatness was not recognized?" He stood a moment longer and then sat down on the stairs, his eyes still fixed on the facade.

"I have sat here like this often, and therefore the building, if it can be called that, is extremely familiar to me, yet it seems more a mystery each time. Perhaps this is what happens when the truth of an object eludes you—it seems somehow to be resisting your efforts." He shook his head and smiled. "But it is just a facade cut into the rock, empty inside, as you will see if you venture in. A chamber not twelve feet square carved into the bones of the cliff. No secret doors or hidden chambers. Perfectly solid rock. The body or ashes long ago moved elsewhere, or perhaps it was never meant to be a crypt at all. Who can say, for it is only known as such for its vague resemblance to such structures. It might have served some other purpose entirely." Randall looked at each of the others, and then down at the stone he tested with his hand.

"As you no doubt remember from your days at school," he began, "the Caledon Hills have not always been part of the Kingdom of Farrland. Once they were claimed by what is today Entonne, and at other times they were autonomous or semi-autonomous. Seven hundred years ago this was the Duchy of Atreche, and only nominally under the control of Farrland. Early followers of Farrelle hid here from their persecutors, and more than one mage has chosen to make his home among these enchanted hills. Great feats of chivalry were performed here—in this very spot as well as a thousand others. And the hills have witnessed tragedies, too. It is a harsh land, really. Agriculture is difficult; whitestone offers no metals to be mined. Only the forester and the huntsman can live to profit here. But despite that, the hills have a beauty that I think incomparable, and many before me have thought the same, so they were drawn here to find a life, and often had to fight to preserve the lives they made.

"The Order of Farrellite Knights, called the Knights of Glamoar, raised their great citadels here, eradicating the Tautistian Heresy which had taken root among people who had fled Entonne and Doorn. And then the knights themselves were branded heretics, and fell finally to the army raised by the Bishop of Nearl during the great turmoil.

"Many think the Knights of Glamoar left a treasure hidden among the hills, for certainly they had wealth enough, and this treasure some believe was the source of Baumgere's wealth. And perhaps it was, but it is hard to imagine that Baumgere found the directions to this treasure among the Farrellite archives. Although it is said that a great deal of Farr history has been devoured by the church." Dusk had wandered off, sniffing the ground and the air, and suddenly he came bounding back again, checking on his master and eyeing the strangers.

"But what do we know of this man for certain?" Clarendon continued, sounding like a lecturer. "Baumgere did appear to come into at least a little wealth after he left the service of the church, and there is no obvious source for this. That is all true. I will show you his home on the edge of the village and you will see what I mean. It is not only large and ostentatious, but it is an architectural oddity as well. The home of a true eccentric.

"Undoubtedly Baumgere had done something that made the local priest, who by the way was his friend and admirer, refuse him absolution. Now there are only certain varieties of sin that will see a man denied absolution, and they are well known: heresy, though what constitutes heresy changes over time; sacrilege, of course—robbing a grave, for instance is sacrilege. Murder, oddly, will not see you denied absolution, as long as you seek forgiveness from the church and repent of your sin.

"But if you are a priest of the church, there are a number of other things that can damn you and leave you wandering in the netherworld. Treachery during the religious wars would have seen a man denied absolution. Betrayal of a mystery of the church will have the same result. And so will acquiring knowledge beyond one's station—a parish priest cannot have certain knowledge possessed by a bishop, you see.

"I have long said that much of the speculation about the source of Baumgere's wealth could be repudiated by merely considering the possibilities laid out for us by the refusal of absolution. If we eliminate betrayal of the church in time of war, we are left with heresy, sacrilege, betrayal of a mystery of the church, acquiring knowledge beyond one's station."

"You seem quite sure that this denial of absolution related to Baumgere's acquisition of wealth or to his discoveries, Randall," Erasmus said.

"Ah, that is true." Clarendon smiled, as though pleased to find that Erasmus had not gained his reputation without reason. "But I set out only to tell you what was known to be utterly true, not to subject you to either my own opinions or the speculation of others. Forgive me, for you are obviously correct: these things are not necessarily connected as cause and effect. As difficult as it is, I will try to stay with what is known, although resisting the desire to speculate in this particular instance is almost impossible." The small man ran his hand over the stone again, as though he searched for something there. "Father Joseph, the priest who refused Baumgere his absolution, self-murdered within a week of Baumgere's death. Utter disillusionment? Loss of faith? Or perhaps melancholia that was in no way related to Baumgere and his secret—for certainly Baumgere *had* a secret. Of that even I am certain. But one must believe strongly in coincidence to accept that these two things were not related, just as one must believe strongly to deny a connection between Baumgere's mysterious discovery and the denial of absolution; or Baumgere's years in the Farrellite archives, his unexpected departure from the service of the church and his sudden wealth." Clarendon laughed.

"You see, I cannot confine myself to the particulars! Do forgive me, gentlemen. I am doing my best." He appeared to focus his will. "Baumgere was an interesting person. He never rose far within the hierarchy of the church though he was said to have been an excellent scholar—something admired by the Farrellites. But perhaps he was not a political animal, which one must be to rise in the church of the martyr—it is like government or the court in that regard.

"Baumgere had few friends and kept his affairs to himself. I therefore suspect this was apocryphal, but a prominent citizen once claimed that Baumgere had answered his inquiry about the source of his wealth by saying, 'Why is no one concerned with my true riches? My real wealth is in my knowledge,' he said, 'the years I spent immersed in the study of our history. These are the basis of real riches, and no one seems to be at all interested.'

"As I say, I don't believe this story to be true but mention it only because it has become an integral part of the myth. Baumgere might not have been so rich as people thought."

"And the headstone, and the ruined inscription on the tomb: where do they fit in?" Hayes asked.

"Ah. An excellent question, Mr. Hayes, for where things 'fit in' as you say is certainly the crux of the matter. There was an inscription on the headstone that did disappear, though whether this was an act of vandals or done for some other reason cannot actually be proven. The inscription on the crypt, however, was unquestionably eradicated—and almost certainly by Baumgere.

"I have only one thing to add to this particular instance—and I have shared it with very few. But, Mr. Flattery, I will make this knowledge available to you, for it is possible you might have something to add to the matter." The small man stared at Erasmus as he spoke, then he stood. "Come. Let me show you."

Clarendon crossed to the tomb again. He put one knee on the ground and bent to point out something in the design carved there. "You see, this is a floral motif circling the column."

Hayes bent closer to look at what was a very common design—a vine and flowers in high relief.

"This is said to be wisteria, and though it is clearly stylized, I have often wondered if the clumps of flowers are flowers at all but bunches of grapes. You are a botanist and horticulturist, Mr. Flattery, what would you say?"

"That is the grape vine, Randall. You are absolutely correct."

Clarendon brightened. "Ah," he said with some satisfaction. "Now," he said rising and pointing to the lintel above the columns. "Look there. It is the only break in the pattern. What do you make of that, Mr. Flattery?"

Hayes could see three flowers carved there, their stems intersecting.

Erasmus leaned back and looked up. "The two outer flowers are almost certainly roses, but the other flower I cannot name. I have not seen it before."

"Exactly. One flower is unknown and the others are roses. Vale roses I am told by a man who has a great knowledge of roses."

Erasmus stepped back abruptly, suddenly quite guarded.

Clarendon looked up at Erasmus. "I see you know what this symbol means, Mr. Flattery."

Erasmus shook his head, though it was not a strong denial.

"Teller," Clarendon said, and nothing more, but he stared at Erasmus who met his gaze.

Hayes looked from one man to the other, wondering what in the world they meant. Teller? "Who was Teller?" Hayes heard himself ask.

Clarendon did not take his eyes from Erasmus. "He was a man who once apprenticed to a mage: Lapin being the most likely candidate. But he did not complete his apprenticeship, for his mentor died." Clarendon's gaze seemed to become even more intent as he said this. "There is a possibility that Teller assisted the Farrellites in their war against the mages. We do not know what happened to him after that, though he may have lived for some good number of years. Some believe that Teller started a secret society dedicated to learning the arts of the mages—those he did not already possess. During the Winter War the mages destroyed what was left of Teller's society—or so historians believe. The token of Teller, and later his society, consisted of three vale roses arranged as you see the blossoms here."

"But there are only two roses here," Erasmus said quickly.

"That is true, Mr. Flattery, but I am content that it is Teller's token all the same."

"But this crypt is certainly not five hundred years old," Erasmus protested.

"It is difficult to say. Authorities believe it might be much older, but it has been buried and not subject to the usual weathering, so it cannot be dated with certainty. It might have been built long after Teller's death, and his ashes moved here."

"But if Teller's society somehow survived beyond the Winter War, why would they do anything to call attention to themselves? It would have been foolish of them to build a tomb," Erasmus protested. "The mages had tried to eradicate them once. Why do anything that might bring down the wrath of the mages? It makes no sense."

Clarendon shrugged. "This tomb sat undisturbed and unknown until the time of Baumgere. It is only in the last century that Castlebough has become of interest to the outside world. Perhaps it was not such a great risk. Or perhaps the world had changed enough that they did not think it would matter. But it is interesting, don't you think?" He placed his back against one of the pillars. "But you began an apprenticeship with Eldrich, Mr. Flattery, and did not complete it. . . . Perhaps you might shed some light on what happened so long ago to Teller?"

Erasmus shook his head. "I began no apprenticeship, I assure you. . . ." Erasmus' denial was interrupted by a wild barking and snarling.

"Dusk!" Clarendon called, and immediately began to run in the direction of the noise.

The barking came from inside the castle ruin. Hayes and Erasmus followed Clarendon, though he was slower due to age and size, but neither of them wanted to find the apparently enraged wolfhound before his master.

After a moment of searching through the ruin, they rounded a corner to find Dusk staring up at a wall, snarling and taking the occasional leap, trying to scale the steep stone, and snapping his powerful jaws at some invisible foe.

"What have you treed, Dusk?" Clarendon called, trying to catch his breath. "Come out of it now."

Hayes followed Clarendon, who took hold of his dog, and looking up found a man balanced in a niche in the wall looking quite terrified.

"Kehler!" Hayes exclaimed, completely surprised.

"Please, Hayes, call him off. I cannot hold myself here a second longer."

And indeed Hayes thought that this was true. Poor Kehler was red with exertion and his arms were beginning to tremble.

"You may come down, sir," Clarendon said, pulling back the still growling dog. "I have him."

Kehler hesitated, perhaps comparing the relative sizes of man and straining dog, but then his body decided for him and he slipped, falling awkwardly onto the soft grass below.

Hayes helped him to rise, unable to hold back his laughter, and Kehler came up brushing at his clothing.

"I hope you are not injured, sir?" Clarendon inquired, not letting go of Dusk.

"No, only frightened half out of my wits. Martyr's blood, but that is a fearsome beast," Kehler said, eyeing the dog.

"But he will not hurt you now, Mr. Kehler. Have no fear. He means only to protect me, and was unsure of your intentions." He turned his attention to the still growling wolfhound. "Now, Dusk, that will be enough. This is a friend."

The dog and Kehler were properly introduced, though neither looked as though they would trust the other immediately.

Kehler collapsed onto a grassy bank, looking up at the two men and the astonishing little man they accompanied.

"I cannot tell you how surprised I am to find you here," Kehler said.

"Nor can we tell you how happy we are to find you," Hayes answered. "Where are you staying? We tried all the inns."

This seemed to unsettle Kehler a little. "I'm not staying in the village. Have you been asking for me by name?"

"And how else would we inquire about you?" Hayes asked. "By

reputation? Your accomplishments aren't yet so grand, I'm sorry to tell you."

"And these gentlemen are not the only ones searching for you, Mr. Kehler," Clarendon said, his manner very serious. "A Deacon Rose has been asking about town for you."

"Demon Rose!" Kehler said. "Farrelle's flames! Do not give me away, please," he pleaded, his face contorting in fear.

Chapter Thirteen

Memory is nothing more than a receptacle of our past; the future a fabric of dreams. And the much vaunted present, that which we are all to seize with a passion, is but the smallest measure of an instant, the single tick of a clock, a medium for translating the future into the past, dreams into memory.

Marianne Edden:
A Reflection on the Death of Michael Valpy

THE evenings were cooler in the highlands, and the countess stood at the closed door looking out over the balcony into the valley. Dusk seemed to alter the distances so that the farthest hills appeared not so much to be disappearing as slipping away. A moment more and they would be out of sight.

A light flickered to life behind the countess, casting her reflection back off the glass. She almost stared, as though a stranger had appeared before her. An unhappy stranger.

"And do you see him there?" came the voice of her companion.

The countess shook her head.

"I never thought I would see the day when the most desired woman in the kingdom would chase after a man like a lovesick girl. And even more astonishing, he would seem to be running. Are you certain that he likes women?"

What had she been told? That all of his woman had looked the same—petite and very blonde. The countess was neither of these. She touched her forehead to the cool glass. Did he think of her as only a friend—the way she thought of several men who were mad for her? Did those poor souls feel as tortured as she?

"Elaural?"

"Excuse me, Marianne. Yes, he likes women. What is in doubt are his feelings for this particular woman."

"He must be playing at indifference. The oldest ploy. Introduce him to me, and I will soon have an answer for you."

The countess did not doubt that. Marianne Edden, she believed, was the most perceptive woman in Farrland. This insight into others had gained her great fame. No, that was not precisely true, and Marianne could not bear inaccuracy. It was her ability to put these perceptions into words that had gained her fame, for Marianne was the finest social novelist of her day.

"Well, come away from the window and try to take your mind off the damn fool. I will even play at cards with you, if you like, as much as I detest the activity. Anything to not see you pining away like a lady in a bad novel. It is undignified."

The countess turned to her friend. "I thought you felt dignity was a foolish concern."

"Dignity? No. I am entirely in favor of dignity—it is this exaggerated pomposity of the aristocracy that I cannot bear. Pomposity is not dignity—it is not even *dignified.* It is an ass' attempt to hide his own mediocrity. A dignified shopkeeper—there is someone worthy of respect. Someone who does not believe he has a special place in society, yet bears himself with self-possession and grace—and not without humor. A shopkeeper who believes that he fulfills his role in the world to the best of his ability. Who is honest and fair because he believes in honesty and fairness—not just when he thinks others are looking. A man who suffers the setbacks and humiliations of life without constant complaint. Dignity."

Marianne bent over and thrust a dry stick into the fire until its end began to smoke and glow. She used this to light a pipe, and then rose up in a great cloud of smoke, puffing like a beast of burden.

This was the portrait of Marianne Edden that needed to be painted, the countess thought: all but obscured by a cloud of bittersweet-smelling smoke, as though she had risen from the flames like a demon . . . or a martyr, and cast her all-seeing eye on the weaknesses and foibles of the mortals scattered about her. The countess smiled for the first time that evening.

"I'm sure I do not suffer setbacks and humiliations with quite the fortitude of your noble shopkeeper, but I shall try not to complain, as a woman in my position has no right to do, I'm sure."

Marianne settled her large frame into a chair, a look of distraction on her face. The countess always imagined that Marianne Edden was a woman who had mistakenly been raised as a farm boy—the mistake only discovered when she was twenty, and the attempts to correct what had been done only partially successful. To call Marianne masculine was not accurate. Oh, she was certainly not "ladylike," as the term was used. One could not imagine Marianne suffering the vapors. Or suffering fools, something Farr women seemed to have been bred to do.

Marianne had once paid some medical students to allow her to be present at the dissection of a corpse—saying that she needed to know more about the substance of man to write the truth about him—and not only had she failed to suffer as the more sensitive sex should, but she went around to people's parlors appalling their guests with graphic descriptions of what she'd seen!

"She is not your average . . . citizen," the countess had once heard her described, which had made her laugh. Even for understated Farr society, that was an understatement.

"What is it, precisely, that you see in this man?" Marianne asked, as though it were not a personal question at all. As though it were something that caused her great confusion and perhaps the countess could set her straight.

The countess could not help but smile at this innocence. "Well, he is a genius. . . ."

"*I'm* a genius, and I don't have the most beautiful man in the kingdom pursuing me. In fact, in my case intelligence appears to have the opposite effect. But go on. Clearly this faculty has more attraction for you than most."

"But he is guarded, as though there were things he must hide. He almost never makes an effort to impress with his wit and conversation, as others do. As though it is merely a game that he cannot be bothered with. As though he would not put his gifts to such use. When he speaks, he is very sincere, choosing his words with great care. And when he pronounces, for he is not known for making long speeches, everything he says is worth listening to with the utmost care. Although it is infrequent, I have seen Lord Skye refute the arguments of every man present with only a few well chosen words, and no one could gainsay him. As though his own thoughts were unassailable."

"A man not in love with the sound of his own voice seems very unnatural," Marianne mused, as though the thought disturbed her.

The countess was suddenly overwhelmed with her inability to

say what she felt. She had not the powers of her companion and that was certain.

"Should we not have some tea?" she asked suddenly.

"Ale would be more to my liking," Marianne said, looking at the countess with some distaste, obviously appalled by the idea of tea. It was dark, after all.

"Then I shall call for ale," the countess said. She rang for a servant, asking for both ale and tea, not quite ready to join Marianne in her passion for working man's tastes.

A bubbling mustache appeared on the satisfied face of the novelist as, a moment later, she lowered her glass. "You should try this, Elaural," she said, using the countess' given name, her love for things working class not allowing titles—at least not in certain circumstances. The countess smiled sweetly, she hoped.

Marianne leaned forward to poke at the fire, her short hair swaying in the lamplight.

She would have such pretty hair were she to let it grow, the countess found herself thinking. *But she will not be admired for her appearance, but only for her mind—why it would be wrong to be admired for both, I cannot fathom.*

But in some way the countess admired the stand Marianne Edden had taken. It was courageous if a little eccentric. The countess believed it natural for men and women to admire each other. To flirt and court. Did not the very animals do the same? Natural. But then it was easy for her to be sanguine about such a thing—she had not been born with crooked teeth or a hideous nose. Men admired her—too much for her liking. But to be ignored. . . . She couldn't imagine how painful that might be. *Will be,* she reminded herself. Age would see to that. She would have the experience soon enough, and the thought disturbed her as it always did.

"Will you consent to my seeing these portraits now?" Marianne asked suddenly.

The countess felt a small shiver run through her. "If you like, though they are not portraits." The Peliers were still in their cases, where she had purposely left them. The truth was that, as much as she wanted to be rid of these paintings, she feared that once they were gone she would never see Skye again.

Reluctantly, the countess went to the wooden case in which the paintings had been transported. "Could you lend a hand? The frames are not light."

The two women lifted the first painting from the case and unwrapped it carefully, and then the second. They leaned them against the wall on a side table and shifted the light so they could be clearly seen. For a long moment they stood there, gazing at the paintings by lamplight which, the countess thought, made them, if anything, more eerie.

"What is it about these paintings that disturbs you, Elaural?" Marianne asked softly.

The countess shook her head. "I don't know," she whispered, not even attempting to deny the truth.

"But are you drawn to them, as well?"

The countess nodded, as much as she would have liked to have disagreed.

Marianne turned her attention back to the paintings. "And this man of yours has an obsession with these?" the novelist said flatly.

"I would not say that, but he believes they are significant in the larger mystery."

"This is the story you told me as we traveled? What was the man's name?"

"Baumgere."

"But one painting is a forgery, you say?"

The countess nodded. "Though it might be an accurate forgery—an exact copy. That, at least, is what Mr. Kent believes."

Marianne leaned closer to look at the signature.

"There is something peculiar about these paintings. I feel it myself. And this man." She gestured to the figure crossing the bridge. He looks like a man going to the gallows. Look at his face. He knows his fate has been decided and continues only because there is no alternative. Something or someone awaits him, and he cannot turn back. Now here is a character to be pitied. This is the Stranger Skye spoke of?"

"That is what he believes. The spire in the background belonged to a church that burned years ago in the village of Compton Heath."

"But what became of the man?"

The countess shook her head. "He was taken off in a carriage, though by whom, no one knows. The story has it that it was a mage—but then that makes for a better story, doesn't it?"

"Yes, it does," Marianne said. "I wish you were not involved in this matter, Elaural. Skye . . . Skye has his own obsessions. You would be best to involve yourself no further. You don't even know what he is seeking—or do you?"

The countess shook her head. She didn't. Something more than he was telling her, that was certain. It was not just curiosity. It *was* an obsession.

Where had the stranger come from, and what was it that this priest sought? Was that what drew Skye? Did he know what Baumgere was searching for?

"What does the writing on the crypt say? Does Skye know?"

"No. Apparently it cannot be read, or so Skye says."

"And I understand one may not gainsay the great Skye?"

"You may, but at your peril."

"I will warn you only this one time, Elaural. I am famous for my intuition, and I do not have a good feeling about this matter. There, I've said my piece." The slightest pause. "It would be different if this man was mad for you. . . ."

"I thought you'd said your piece?"

"I have." She turned away and went into the other room.

A moment later the countess followed, shutting the door tightly between them and the Peliers.

Marianne looked up, her face still somewhat grim, as though the paintings had left her feeling ill. "This crypt is nearby?" she said, forcing her voice to sound normal.

The countess nodded.

"Then we should at least see it while we're here. I hope this genius of yours will contact us soon. It does seem a bit inconsiderate."

"He is not my genius, and I am sure there are reasons for what he is doing. I would like to see the structure myself—I do not know if it can be properly called a crypt. Apparently it is one of the sights around Castlebough."

"Well, we cannot miss the sights. We should have something for our trouble after traveling so far. Perhaps a ghost will rise from the crypt and answer all our questions."

The countess shook her head, trying to force the feelings caused by the paintings to subside. "I don't think you're taking this as seriously as you should, Marianne. I think tomorrow it will be time for you to go back to your work. I am going to keep my word on this. You will be locked into a room with pen and paper every morning at ten sharp, and not let out until you have slipped three pages under the door for me to judge."

"I was being facetious, Elaural. I will show you the word in my dictionary: *facetious.*" But it was banter by rote—neither of them laughed.

Chapter Fourteen

A memory is a dream turned to disappointment.

Halden

"I WAS something of a prodigy of the local Farrellite School, but my father, who was more shrewd than his lot in life would indicate, took me out of the clutches of the priests." Clarendon lifted a glass of wine. "He realized there was a possibility of making money from my talents, and money was the one thing that had always eluded the poor man." He paused to taste his wine. "Do you find the finish bitter?" he asked Erasmus.

They had come down from the ruin late in the afternoon to Clarendon's house. Kehler had insisted on coming later, after darkness fell, and had arrived looking more than a little apprehensive. He still would say nothing, and the others gave up asking, hoping he would come to it in his own time.

Erasmus thought there was quite a contrast between the lad-next-door looks of Hayes and his sharp-featured friend. Kehler's motions were all quick, and he held his head lowered at the neck in such a way as to leave the impression that he was ready, at an instant, to duck out of sight. The two were about the same age, but Kehler already showed gray at the temples and crow's feet pressed into the corners of his eyes. But there was also something between these two young men, some commonality despite their divergent appearances. They were both a bit haunted, perhaps for vastly different reasons, but it was unmistakable.

Erasmus tasted the wine again, his focus entirely inward. "Bitter? Very slightly so, perhaps. I almost think I enjoy it. There is an odd aftertaste, like slightly burned apple."

Clarendon tasted his own wine again, inclined his head to one side, and closed his eyes. "Yes. Yes, I see what you mean. You must meet the others, Mr. Flattery, they will make you most welcome." He looked up at a painting on the wall—a circus troupe under the light of torches and great lanterns, and then seemed to remember that he had been telling a story. "Originally I would perform arithmetical calculations in my head—problems posed by people who came to see the show, for we had joined a traveling show: General Albert W. Payne's Traveling Company. Unfortunately the 'General' took most of the money, and my father squandered what was left on fine clothing, women, and drink. He was not a very original man, I'm afraid," he said, as though apologizing.

"Many feats were performed. I memorized enormous blocks of text in one reading and parroted them back without mistake, or merely glanced at a thirty digit number and then wrote it down. I once sat the final examinations in mathematics at Merton making not one error and halving the previous record for time. I was at that time three months shy of my tenth birthday. I gained quite a reputation, and made even more money for the owner of our traveling company. Not long after this my father died—choked on his own gorge while insensible with drink. There was a struggle between several of my relatives, people I hardly knew, and the General, to decide who would be my legal guardian. In the end, one of the women in the show, whom I had always called 'aunt,' produced a signed certificate of marriage proving that she and my father had been joined in sacred matrimony—when he was drunk beyond knowing, I'm sure.

"It was something of a scandal, really, but finally my 'aunt' managed to outbid my dear family and the General, who only offered the judge money. Aunt Liz, who was a stunning young woman, managed to offer the judge something he did not already have, and perhaps had never possessed—the apparent adoration of a beautiful young woman, however briefly it lasted.

"My life changed on that day. Aunt Liz and I left the company immediately. She had been a dancer and tumbler in the show, which was lewd in the extreme, and perhaps she had even worked in the tents when the show was over, I don't know, but she was as shrewd a businesswoman as ever palmed a coin, I can tell you that. She took what money she had managed to save, which would indicate she really was working on the side, and hired tutors. A retired professor from Merton to teach me higher maths. An elocution instructor. My crooked working class accent was hammered straight, and I was also allowed to read as much as I wanted—and I wanted to read all the time. Very soon Aunt Liz had Farrland's most respected scholars vying with each other to instruct me, for I have a flawless memory and an ability to perform calculations that would take other men hours or even days, though they might take me only a few moments."

Hayes watched the small man's face, utterly entranced by the story, but sensing a sadness in Clarendon as he exposed these memories.

"Soon all the performances I did were in the private homes of Farrland's wealthiest citizens, or in grand halls. Once, I was invited to be a guest of the Society, where they posed the most difficult questions of all, though I acquitted myself well. I began to feel like less of a spectacle, less of a freak, though the old feelings were not entirely gone. I was called The Petite Professor, or the Dwarf Savant. Professor Memory. All manner of appellations. And among all the educated people I even made a few real friends. And I also made money. Lizzy saw to that. She was my guardian goddess, and I loved her hopelessly." He swiveled as though to look out the darkened window, raising a hand to his face, but turning the movement into a mere gesture, placing the hand beneath his chin.

"When I was seventeen, my darling Lizzy fell victim to a cad. A Colonel Winslow Petry. They were too quickly married. . . ." His voice trailed off. And then he resettled himself in his chair, straightening his small back. "And so I was forced to begin again. For the second time in my short life I had lost everything. Lizzy and the money, too. But fortunately I had a head for figures, and in one sense that's all money is—numbers, marks on a page. I knew what to do to make it, even if it gave me little joy, and the lesson of my father taught me to preserve what I acquired.

"Lizzy and her colonel went off, spending the money we had made. To this day I can't think of it without the deepest sadness. She was the one person I had trusted utterly. . . . After that I traveled continuously for six years. Through Doorn and Entonne. To every corner of the lands around the Entide Sea. Everywhere I went, I moved in society. I learned to play the pianum, though I am not so skilled at that as I am at other things I have turned my hand to. I became a devotee of the arts and met many artists and writers. And it was through this that I was saved." He looked up at his guests, his face brightening a little.

"I was so fortunate, after all my years of travel, to meet the Haywood family—do you know them?"

"The porcelain people?" Hayes asked.

"The very ones. I was invited to their home to give one of my demonstrations, and I almost did not leave. Such open-hearted people, such complete joy in my life, I had never encountered. I was captivated by them in a way that you cannot imagine. You see, they invited me into the fold, as it were, as they did a select few they took a genuine liking to. They rescued me . . . from cynicism, bitterness, resentment, all the ugly, unworthy things that had become lodged in my heart. And I cast all of these things out, like demons, and made myself anew. Through the Haywoods I learned that my gifts were to be treasured, and that I was no more a freak than a man who sits before a pianum and holds the audience in his hand, playing upon their emotions with his own given skill. I was gifted, perhaps supremely so. As for my small stature . . . well, in their home it did not matter."

"You see, I had never thought of myself as an intellectual, but only as someone who could perform tricks, tricks of the mind to be sure, but tricks all the same. In my own view I was no different from the performing animals in General Payne's traveling show, or from the other freaks whose physical deformities were a source of fascination and horror to the general population. But the Haywoods made me realize that this was not true, that in fact I was the equal of a professor at Merton—even more so, for I disremember nothing and can perform calculations in my head that others can never equal.

"Through them I actually taught for a year; higher mathematics at the University in Belgard. It will sound odd to you, but the Haywoods humanized me, for I was always an outsider in my own mind—a near-human. A dwarf; different in both mind and body." He smiled almost beneficently. "And so you see before you a man, small in stature, yes, but large in mental abilities. A true man of parts, as they say. And through the good graces and efforts of the Haywoods, I was even able to develop my other sensibilities." He raised his glass as though toasting his benefactors. "And that, more or less, is my story. I have made enough money that I no longer perform as I did, but devote myself to my interests and my many friends, for as you know people born with my particular physical characteristics often do not live a normal span of years, and I want to be sure to waste as little time as possible." He drank from his glass.

"And so here we all are, having lived our separate lives, followed our separate journeys, yet somehow we have all arrived here at this exact moment. If, like me, you have grown suspicious of coincidence, you might think that there is some reason for this. Why have we all come to this place tonight?"

Hayes was not sure the question was rhetorical. He even found himself wondering the same thing. What were they all doing there?

"But you have an interest in the mages, Randall," Erasmus said, "and you know something of Teller, and this is truly arcane knowledge. Has this long been an interest?"

Randall looked down at the table, and Hayes thought the man was trying to decide what he would tell Erasmus, for though it was obvious that the dwarf was an admirer, Erasmus was still a near stranger.

"I came by this interest accidentally. You see, I discovered Castlebough through a physician who attended me. He suggested I come here for the cure, which I did, and for me, at least, it worked. During that visit I fell in love with the village and the surrounding countryside. It is a healthful environment, I think. Clean air, salubrious water, exercise, and few of the aggravations of the city.

"I come here in the spring and usually stay for the entire summer. In the winter I travel. This winter last I visited Farrow." He stood suddenly in his place, but it was only to lean forward to fill Kehler's glass. "I am naturally curious and thought to learn something of the history of my new home. And what a history it has! The citadel above saw some of the most terrible battles of the Wars of Heresy." He shook his head, the sadness coming back. "And, of course, there was the mystery of Baumgere, which has intrigued the village for years. Unlike the inhabitants of Castlebough, however, I had an enormous advantage during my research. In my travels I have had occasion to meet men of great knowledge, and I have looked into private libraries to which few have been granted access.

"It is astonishing the way knowledge is scattered around our world," he said suddenly. "Some written in books of which only one copy remains extant. Much passed down by word of mouth, and very temporarily stored in the minds of the most unlikely people in the most out of the way places. And then there are the great libraries and the innumerable attics of the known world. . . . The things people confide in their correspondence! So, yes, it began with an interest in this local legend—the crypt of Baumgere and the denial of absolution—and led me to this man named Teller, and then to the mages." Clarendon looked up at the others, his manner almost defensive.

Hayes could see that Kehler was staring raptly at his host, listening to every word, and to all that was suggested but never stated. It was a wonder that Kehler managed to contain himself.

"The society that Teller founded was almost certainly destroyed during the Winter War—about 1415—almost five centuries after Teller. Five centuries! What did they learn in that time?" He looked at each of his guests, as though sure they were keeping the answer to the question from him. "I do not know," he said, dropping his gaze. "I do not know. But enough that the mages felt they must hunt them down and destroy them. Destroy them after they had managed to keep themselves secret for five hundred years."

"The mages had no need of hunting them down," Erasmus said, surprising everyone.

Clarendon looked up, his eyes suddenly alive with interest.

Erasmus met no one's eye, but stared at the empty chair across from him, as though he addressed someone seated there. "The Tellerites—and I use this term for lack of any other; what the society called themselves is unknown, and the mages would not speak their name—the Tellerites were caught—trapped, I think—all together. Trapped and destroyed."

"How?" Kehler asked quietly.

"I don't know, though it seems likely they had gathered to perform an important ritual. I haven't been able to learn more. I can't even say where this happened nor, with any certainty, when, though Randall's date of 1415 is probably very close."

"But what do you make of the crypt and the gravestone by the citadel?" Clarendon asked.

Erasmus shook his head. "I don't know. If some remnant of the society had survived the purge . . . well, I think it unlikely they would do anything to draw attention to themselves. Is that the tomb of

Teller? I very much doubt it. What purpose it served is a mystery. As to the gravestones . . . well, you said yourself that it is only rumor that connects them to Baumgere."

Kehler leaned forward in his chair, barely suppressing his excitement. "But where? Where were the Tellerites destroyed? Could it have been here, in Castlebough? Could that explain the grave?"

"No," Erasmus said. "I don't know where it occurred, but I am more certain about where it did not, and I can say almost without doubt that it did not happen here. There is a very old song that originated among the Cary minstrels, and is as ambiguous as all their works." Erasmus sat forward in his chair, and softly he began to sing in a thin, though expressive voice.

"A shepherd, a maiden, an orphan of ten
A night 'neath a kint in fragrant spring
Seven men came walking by torchlight and star
And low by moonlight were heard to sing,

A delro, a delro
Ai kombi aré.
We have come to the gate,
The gate of Faery.

Five passed through the moonlight more ghostly than men
Singing by starlight in tongues unknown
Passed by the orphan, the maiden, the man
Down into the labyrinth, to the mouth of stone.

A delro, a delro
Ai kombi aré.
We have come to the gate,
The gate of Faery.

The darkness ascended, devouring the sky
And wind cried in fury and toppled the tower
The heavens were scarred with letters of fire
Shattering stone with words of power.

A delro, a delro
Ai kombi aré

The sun would not rise at its appointed hour
And the stars wandered, lost, across the sea of the sky

Five men slowly walking in sullen power
Past orphan, and maiden, and the one devoured.

A delro, a delro
Ai kombi aré,
We have come to the gate,
The gate to Faery.

A delro, a delro
Ai kombi aré."

Erasmus sat back in his chair, staring unseeing at the others. No one spoke for a moment, and then a breeze moved the curtains, causing Hayes to start. He laughed nervously, the sound dying like a pinched-off flame. A moth came in from the night and fluttered wildly over the heat of a lamp, unable to resist the light.

"But what could it mean?" Hayes asked.

"The destruction of Teller," Randall said firmly.

Erasmus nodded.

"And the language . . . ? It is the mage tongue?"

Erasmus shrugged. "Perhaps. I don't know. The song is partly fancy, certainly. *'We have come to the gate, the gate of Faery.'* But there is something there, as there usually is in the minstrels' songs. A buried truth. Seven men passed in the moonlight. Five came behind, 'more ghostly than men.' Five mages. A great spell was cast, or a series of them. Five men returned 'in sullen power,' past the witnesses, one of whom was devoured—went mad, I think. Mad with fear. That is the story."

"But you know something more, Mr. Flattery, for you would hardly make such an assumption from so little evidence." Randall fixed his gaze on Erasmus again, though this time Erasmus did not even look up to meet his eye.

"You will not say." Randall smiled kindly. It was not a question. A long silence. "Not now, perhaps," the dwarf said, "but when you know me better. . . ." Randall stood and filled Erasmus' glass with wine, then did the same for the others. He raised his glass, and his guests stood as well. "To mysteries, gentlemen, for they keep me alive. To unexpected meetings, for they, too, are mysterious. And to coincidence, which I believe in not at all."

Chapter Fifteen

HAYES sat in a chair in his room and watched Kehler pace back and forth across the small square of carpet. Occasionally he would go to the window and twitch the curtain aside just enough to peer down into the dimly lit courtyard. For a moment he would stare, perhaps searching for malevolent forms in the shadows, and then he would return to his pacing.

"Deacon Rose is a lot more dangerous than you realize. Certainly more dangerous than Erasmus believes." He stopped and made a visible effort to calm himself, taking long, slow breaths. "No, Deacon Rose is to be avoided at all costs." He looked over at Hayes in a way that was uncharacteristically measuring. "But where is our much vaunted employer?"

"I agree with Erasmus; I think Skye would come here," Hayes said, trying to ignore the gaze that was cast upon him. "Though I can't imagine the famous Lord Skye could be long in Castlebough without everyone knowing."

Kehler resumed his pacing, went two steps, and then stopped, looking at Hayes in some surprise. "What in Farrelle's name were agents of the Admiralty doing in your rooms?" he said, going back to an earlier part of the conversation. "They can't be interested in this matter we've been chasing . . . can they?"

Hayes lifted his hands in a gesture of helplessness. "I wouldn't think so. No, it must have something to do with the naval gun. Perhaps they're afraid Entonne agents were trying to steal the plans from Skye. Would they not begin to look at all of his acquaintances, then? And here I am, in terrible financial distress, recently applying for a position in the foreign department. Do I not look like the perfect person for the Entonne to enlist? That is my guess, at least. I do hope Skye will exonerate me, I don't much like living as a fugitive. Things have gotten so bad that I'm acutely aware of the nearness of the border. I've even made a plan for slipping across into Entonne if it becomes necessary." A short, sad laugh escaped him, and he shook his head.

"I'm quite sure it won't come to that, Hayes. You have Erasmus on your side, which means the Duke of Blackwater will stand behind you. And certainly Skye will vouch for you—for us. I'm one of the earl's associates, too, don't forget. At worst we'll be exiles together."

This almost brought a smile to Hayes, but not quite. "Yes, well, that is some comfort, but at the moment I am rather adrift. I'm sure my landlord in Avonel will have sold off my few belongings by now, and here I am, entirely dependent on the good graces of Erasmus Flattery." The sadness pulled at his face, pinching it so that his eyes almost glistened. "I have seldom had less hope for my future than I do now."

"I don't think you need to worry overly about your future, Hayes," Kehler said, a sudden smugness very poorly disguised.

Hearing this, Hayes looked up at his friend with some hope. "Why do I have a feeling you're about make me a devil's offer?"

"Nothing of the sort, my dear Hayes. Well, not too much of the sort." The words might have been jocular, but Kehler's manner had become very serious. "To be candid, Hayes, I am not completely satisfied with my relations with our employer. Perhaps it is the perennial grievance of assistants, but I feel I have done the lion's share of the work and see Skye taking all the profit." He stopped to think. "The truth is I don't understand what it is that Skye hopes to learn or do with what I've found, but I suspect he will not put it to any use but his own." He looked directly at Hayes. "I've made some discoveries in Wooton that will leave you a little breathless, I think."

"And I'm anxious to hear about them, but, Kehler, you undertook this matter for Lord Skye. Does that mean nothing to you?"

"Indeed, it does. I delivered a letter to the earl's home outlining several of my discoveries and have heard nothing from him. Hardly a fair return for my efforts. But I promised Lord Skye that I would deliver my information, and keep the earl's confidence—by which I meant that I would not reveal his part in the matter. But what *I* do with my findings is another thing entirely. Now, what would you say if I told you that we could satisfy both our curiosity, make what I hope will be a major discovery, and net you a substantial sum of money into the bargain?"

"I would say, bully for Kehler, of course, but you must know—considerations of Skye aside—Erasmus seems to think that you're involving yourself in matters that could well be dangerous. If the Farrellites have been hiding knowledge from the mages, Erasmus believes they will go to almost any length to keep it from Eldrich. Thus the priest is pursuing you, or so I assume. Perhaps you should tell me precisely what you have discovered."

"All in good time, Hayes. All in good time. Our first order of business is to slip away from all concerned—agents of the Admiralty, priests, friends, and well-wishers, all. I've collected the gear we'll need." Kehler gestured toward the door.

"But where are we going?"

"To complete what Baumgere began, but grew too old to finish. To make our names in the world. Come along while there is time, for I can assure you of this, Hayes—it is an opportunity which shall not call twice."

Chapter Sixteen

THERE was something about Skye that Marianne Edden could not quite grasp. Possessing an intuitive faculty that she thought justifiably celebrated, it was difficult to accept that someone could so completely elude her. Skye shifted slightly in his chair, and she watched his every move, hoping somehow that this meditation on him would help. She had even placed her chair so that she could watch him unobtrusively.

Her eye wandered for a second to the countess—compared to Skye Elaural was as easy to read as a child. She could hide nothing, not from her friend at least. But Skye. . . .

Marianne had never met him before, and she was not unaware that there were people who would consider this evening of historic importance. The meeting of two of the great minds of their time—one scientific, the other literary. It was lucky that none of these people were present; they would have been exceedingly disappointed.

Skye sat staring at the Pelier paintings, only occasionally breaking away to attempt polite conversation. His mind was clearly not on his hostesses—and most pointedly not on the admiring countess.

Alone in a room with the most brilliant novelist and the most celebrated beauty of his time, and he hardly seems aware of us, she thought, not entirely immodestly—it was not, after all, Marianne who went about proclaiming her brilliance, at least not usually.

"Have you learned anything of the script?" the countess asked, her voice very small. She was obviously aware that Skye barely noticed her.

He turned to her with a confused look, and then her question registered. "Oh. . . ." He went back to the painting, his gaze not even lingering on the face that other men could hardly tear their eyes from. "Nothing useful. It has been suggested that it bears some similarity to the writing found on the Ruin of Farrow, which is an intriguing idea. There is also some evidence that it might be a very old Farr language, one not spoken for some centuries, though perhaps known to the mages far more recently. Unfortunately the two men who might be able to tell me the truth of this are not inclined to be helpful."

"Who might they be, pray?" the countess asked, obviously making an attempt to capture his attention, something she managed effortlessly with other men.

The way Skye shifted in his chair . . . there was something not quite right here, Marianne was sure of it.

"Well, Eldrich, obviously, and the other is Erasmus Flattery. Do you know the man? He is a brother to the Duke of Blackwater, I think."

"No," the countess answered, clearly feeling a sense of failure. "No, I'm afraid not. But is this Erasmus Flattery not an empiricist? A colleague of yours in the Society?"

Skye nodded, a slight grimace appearing. "Yes, though he seldom attends, and is not well known to any fellow at the Society. Something of an eccentric, this Flattery." He paused uncomfortably, then went on. "He lived in the house of Eldrich when he was a boy. Did you know that?"

"Well, I knew it was a rumor, but I have never given it much credit. Have you, Marianne?"

"I confess that I have not formed an opinion on the matter of Erasmus Flattery's boyhood."

The countess cast her a look of mild annoyance, but Marianne could not resist. The situation seemed so patently false and strained to her. Why did Elaural continue to humiliate herself with this man?

"Well, it is quite true," Skye said quickly. "Flattery spent some three years in the house of Eldrich, if you can imagine. But he will not speak of it, avoiding all questions with some energy. Too much energy, many people think." A long awkward pause followed, and Marianne braced herself mentally for what would follow. Did the countess not see what was happening here? Did her usual instincts abandon her in this man's presence? Farrelle help her, Marianne thought, it must be love.

Skye cleared his throat quietly. "The great irony is," he began, trying to force a casual tone, "Erasmus Flattery might actually be in Castlebough—at least there is a rumor to that effect." He stared hard at the paintings, careful not to look at either of the women. "It is an odd coincidence that Flattery is here at this time." He glanced quickly at the countess, then back to the painting. "Imagine having spent time in the house of a mage and never saying a word of it. The man is keeping a small part of our most fascinating history to himself. It seems so odd that I have heard some suggest that Flattery is bespelled and cannot speak of it." Skye snorted. "Apparently he also spent some time studying the Ruin on Farrow and says little of that either, though he has claimed that he discovered nothing new. I wonder if that is true." He leaned forward to gaze at the inscription on the tomb. "Can he tell me what tongue this is? Can he, perhaps, read it?"

"What makes you think the mages knew this language?" Marianne asked, hoping to deflect what was coming.

The earl hesitated. "I have seen a note—written by one of the mages—Lucklow, to be precise. Not a very remarkable note really, considering its source, but beneath his signature letter **L**, there is a line of characters astonishingly similar to the characters we see here. I admit it is unlikely that Erasmus could answer my question, but who else might have such knowledge? No one that I'm aware of."

"But what would that mean?" the countess said, sounding genuine for the first time that evening. The news had excited her interest. "How would Pelier have known such a script, if, as you suggest, it is the script of the mages? And why would one find the same script on Farrow? The discovery of the island is comparatively recent—in the last four hundred years."

Skye raised a finger, his face brightened at the countess' interest. "Exactly. How would Pelier have been familiar with this writing? Either he was truly gifted with the sight and merely reproduced his vision, having no more idea what it meant than we do ourselves, or he somehow had knowledge that only the mages possessed.

"It is well known that Pelier was a member of various arcane societies, though there has been so much speculation about this that the truth is certainly beyond retrieving now. Perhaps he belonged to some group that had knowledge of this script. There are rumors of such cabals: men who had some knowledge of the ways of the mages. I am convinced that at least one of these groups actually existed, though it was destroyed years ago."

"But why do you care?" Marianne asked, and she watched Skye's face change, his manner suddenly suspicious, vaguely hostile.

"It is the great mystery," he said easily. "The fascination of every man in Farrland, and every woman, too, I dare say. The mages and their arts. Men who lived twice or thrice our span of years, and could perform feats that were far beyond our own meager powers. That is reason enough for such a fascination."

"But what of this Stranger and the priest, Baumgere? What have they to do with your great mystery?"

Skye shrugged. "That is what I hope to learn, Miss Edden. Where did this Stranger come from?"

"You don't think it a hoax, then?" Marianne said, pushing Skye more than was polite.

The great empiricist shrugged. "I cannot prove that either way, but if it was a hoax it was managed with astonishing cunning, for some very astute men were taken in."

"But was he from another land—a civilized nation yet undiscovered?" Marianne could almost sense Skye closing down, becoming more and more reluctant to answer her questions.

"He was from some other place," Skye said, clearly becoming uncomfortable.

"But what does that mean, 'some other place'?"

Skye shrugged, guarded now.

"Really, Marianne," the countess interrupted, sounding a bit anxious. "You are being difficult this evening. We all have our interests. I venture that you are seldom required to justify your own."

Marianne bowed her head. "Do forgive me, Lord Skye," she said smiling at the countess' rebuke. "I have been told that I have no tact at all, and apparently it is true."

"No need, Miss Edden," Skye said solicitously, relaxing visibly now that her inquisition was over. "No need." He said nothing more, and they turned their attention back to the paintings again, no one sure what to say to save the moment.

"Do you really think there is some possibility that Erasmus Flattery can read this script?" the countess asked quietly.

Skye shrugged. "It's not impossible."

The countess took a deep breath. "Well, if you send him to me, I will find the truth for you," she said.

Skye turned to her, his eyes bright with . . . what? Smugness, Marianne realized. It was what he had hoped for all along.

"Do you really think you could?" he asked.

"Have no doubt of it," the countess said, clearly happy to have his full attention finally. "Some men find me difficult to refuse."

Skye almost leaped to his feet. "Then I will find him within the hour. Write a note, and I will see it delivered to him this night." He turned to Marianne in his joy, and realized she was not so enthusiastic as he. But this did not cause him to reconsider.

Erasmus heard the note being slipped under his door, and after a moment rose from his bed to see what it was. Sleep after all, was not so easily found that night. There was enough starlight and moonlight in his room that he found the envelope easily—a rectangle of gray against the dark wooden door.

For a moment he stood by the window trying to make out the hand by the poor light—was it from Clarendon? Hayes? Perhaps even Deacon Rose? Finding a candle, he lit it from the coals of his fire and slit the note with a pocket knife.

My Dear Mr. Flattery:

I have just been informed that you are also visiting Castlebough (the joys of small towns) and wonder if I might entice you to visit. I have long wanted to make your acquaintance, and will confess that I have a very small favor to ask. I look forward to our meeting.

It was signed by the Countess of Chilton.

"Indeed," Erasmus said to the room. "What in the round world does the countess want with me?" Erasmus slumped into a chair.

There was no question of him having suddenly become an object of interest to the smart set in Avonel. That was not possible. No, it was this "small favor" that had occasioned the sudden interest. And if that were the case, it had either to do with botany or the ways of the mages, and somehow Erasmus did not think it had anything to do with botany, though he was not sure why. Even so, one did not pass up an opportunity to meet the Countess of Chilton. It was the kind of thing that would intrigue people a decade hence. *"You actually met the countess?" "Yes, but none of the rumors are true. We were nothing more than acquaintances."*

Lost in thought, he sat by the window until his head suddenly rolled to one side, and he forced himself to take to his bed.

No report had been exaggerated.

That was Erasmus' first thought upon meeting the countess. She was, if anything, more lovely than he had imagined—and his imagination was usually unrivaled in this regard. He found he was hardly able to take his gaze away from those exquisite eyes, that perfect face. *Certainly,* he thought, *no man can look at those beautiful lips without wondering what it would be like to kiss them.*

The morning sun cast elongated rectangles on the floor and turned the border of the countess' tresses into a flaming nimbus about her heart-shaped face.

I should have worn my blade, Erasmus thought, *I am prepared to fight a duel for her already. It is no wonder that men are driven to foolishness around her.*

"It is very kind of you to come, Mr. Flattery. And on such short notice. I am honored."

"It was the summons I'm sure every man in Farrland dreams of, Lady Chilton. I would have come on a moment's notice."

"Well, you are not letting down the family name, I see." She smiled charmingly to let him know that she teased and motioned to a divan set in the light of the windows.

Erasmus took his seat stiffly, and Lady Chilton sat at ease near him.

"You are known to be a man of some genius, Mr. Flattery," she said, perhaps not to be outdone, "so I will not patronize you. I was speaking truthfully when I said I had long wished to make your acquaintance, but as I wrote, there is a small favor I will ask, if you will allow it."

"Lady Chilton, certainly any favor you ask will be too small. Please, do not hesitate." Erasmus was glad that she did not indulge in an hour of aimless chitchat before coming to the point. Glad and a little disappointed. One did not want a visit to the countess to end any sooner than it must.

She turned her attention to two paintings that Erasmus had not even registered, though he had walked right past them.

He felt a certain disorientation looking at the paintings, though he could not say why. There seemed to be subtle breaking of the rules of perspective, and a hyperrealism, as though the painting were really part of a fever dream. And then he realized that the crypt in one painting was the same as he had seen above Castlebough. *These were the Peliers Skye had found!* He turned back to the countess, his manner guarded.

"It is the inscription on the tomb that I am interested in," the countess said.

"Lord Skye has put you up to this, I see," he said, his voice colder than he meant it to be.

The countess averted her gaze a little. "I rather put myself up to it," she said softly.

Erasmus stared at her, feeling sorry that he might have caused her discomfort. One could hardly look at this woman and want to cause her anything but pleasure.

"But you are correct in your assumption," she said. "How did you know?"

"I . . . I had heard a rumor that Skye found the paintings once owned by Baumgere." He inclined his head toward the paintings.

"I see. And can you read this text? Skye believes it might have been a language used by the mages. He also wonders if it bears some passing resemblance to the writing on the Ruin of Farrow. I understand, Mr. Flattery, that you are an authority on the Ruin, among a great many other things." She turned her gaze back to him, her look a mixture of defiance and guilt.

The countess could see by his face and the stiffness of his posture that Erasmus Flattery was not pleased with this development, and she was not so happy herself to be using him so. There was something in his manner that also told her that Erasmus was hiding more than most realized. She wondered if Skye was right—Erasmus *could* read the writing.

"It is a mystery to me," he said firmly.

The countess looked down at her fingers worrying the cushion's edge. "Have I offended you, Mr. Flattery? It seemed an innocent enough request to me." She looked up again, meeting his eyes fully, watching the effect this had. Yes, this man, at least, was not indifferent to her charms.

"Offended me? No," he said, though obviously she had unsettled him.

"Does this have to do with your service to Eldrich? I understand that you mislike speaking of it."

"Not at all." He hesitated, looking down for an instant, but he could not keep his eyes from hers. "Do not apologize, Lady Chilton. It is I who am sorry that I have no answer to your question."

"Oh." She blew air through her lips in dismissal of his apology. She favored him with her most charming smile. "There are some who say that you were bespelled by Eldrich and cannot speak of those years. . . ."

He laughed.

She had managed to save the moment.

"I am not bespelled, Lady Chilton. My brief time in the house of Eldrich was so utterly without incident that I refuse to bore people with the tale. I was a boy. I was sent to the house of the mage where I lived for three years almost to the day. During that time I was under the guardianship of a tutor who was so ancient that at the end of three years he still occasionally got my name wrong. I studied the things every schoolboy studies. I stole sweet-tarts from the kitchen. I confess I missed my mother and family. And then I was sent home, and at no time was I offered an explanation—either then or since. Oh, and I forgot to say; I never met the mage himself. I did, however, see him, or so I believe, on more than one occasion, though never close to. A tall man with black hair and a stiff gait. And from this rather odd experience, people think I learned the secrets of the mages." He shrugged and smiled a bit helplessly.

"I see what you mean. Tea, Mr. Flattery?" She motioned for the servant to come in, realizing that Erasmus was more than relieved. He was hiding the real story, she was certain. She wondered what it would take to pry it out of him?

She sent the servant off and poured the tea herself.

Erasmus Flattery, she decided, was not a bad looking man. Oh, he was not fashionable, though certainly well enough dressed, but his entire manner was not what was currently acceptable in Avonel society. No, Erasmus Flattery committed the unforgivable sin of allowing his passion to show. He was a man of great intensity, and did nothing to hide it, unlike the fashionable gentlemen of Avonel who feigned boredom in almost any situation. Farrelle help them, they were so indifferent (except to her, it seemed). She found Erasmus' manner rather refreshing.

Erasmus exhibited none of the openness and naivete that characterized many empiricists and scholars. Instead he seemed guarded, like a man who had seen a great deal and not all of it pleasant. She had seen men who had been in battles who wore this same look.

"I understand there is a move afoot, Mr. Flattery, to allow ladies to attend some of the lectures at the Society," she said, turning to small talk, though small talk of his own world.

"There is, though I will tell you that I have little hope of its success. The old men are still very much in control there."

"Are these the gentlemen known affectionately as the 'fossils'?"

Erasmus laughed. "Very affectionately, I assure you!" He tasted his tea. "There is a plan to offer lectures to the public for some very small fee. Not on the Society premises or under its auspices, but most, if not all, of the lectures heard at the Society meetings might be offered. It would be a good thing, I think. The best we can manage until the old men step down."

"Well then, may the fossils soon pass on into the collections of the cosmic museum."

"Hear, hear."

"Tell me about this ruin on Farrow, Mr. Flattery. It is rather romantic, don't you think? This great mystery sitting there all these centuries, its purpose unknown, its builders long passed from history. What on earth could it have been for?"

Erasmus shrugged. "I don't actually know, though I fear it might be something less than romantic. My best guess is it was a kind of calendar. Almost an instrument used to calibrate the movement of stars and planets, to gauge the exact moments of certain celestial events. The longest day of summer, the shortest of winter. It likely had ceremonial purposes as well, though what those were is anyone's guess."

"But it is sitting there nearly intact, and has been for who knows how long, and yet all the other ruins on the island are buried beneath the earth, the walls fallen to foundations. How is that?"

Erasmus sipped his tea. "The other ruins bear no resemblance to the Ruin of Farrow. They are of different stone, and not built in the same style. I think they predate the Farrow Ruin by some time. Perhaps centuries."

"Astonishing," she said. "I must make a trip there. I don't know why I haven't." Her own voice sounded so false to her that the countess could not believe that Erasmus was not offended by her manner.

Look what I do here, she thought. *This poor man has secrets he wants to keep, perhaps for good reason, and I have set out to charm them from him.* A wave of self-revulsion swept over her. She thought of Skye jumping up from his chair like a boy when she assured him she could get the information he wanted from Erasmus Flattery.

How little he cares for me that he would use me so, she thought, and felt a sadness near to tears. And now I will use this good man equally poorly. She looked over at Erasmus and felt that they were both victims in this.

"I must ask—though please don't let me pry—are you not haunted by what happened to you in your youth? If such a thing had happened to me, I'm sure I would think of nothing else. Your good father never offered an explanation?"

"The duke was not in the habit of explaining himself to anyone." Erasmus looked up, reacting to the sympathy on her face. "And yes, I do wonder." He looked down into his cup for a moment. "I'm sure there was a reason. I mean there must have been. It seems very likely that I performed some feat in my youth that brought me to the attention of Eldrich. It has long been known that mages required some kind of native talent that allowed them to be trained in the arts—just as a singer must have a voice. Perhaps I showed some signs of this, but either was found wanting, or more likely, the mage held faith with the others of his kind, and trained no apprentice."

"But if he did not intend to train you, why on earth were you taken into his home?"

Erasmus looked out the window. "Perhaps Eldrich was not absolutely sure that he would not take an apprentice. No one knows for certain why the mages have stopped the practice of training the next generation. It is a mystery that will likely never be solved. But Eldrich may have reconsidered. Or perhaps true talent, in the measure needed to become a mage, has become very rare."

"Overwhelmed by reason, perhaps?" the countess said.

Erasmus smiled. "Perhaps." He met her eyes for a second then looked away, obviously unsettled by his own hopes, his feelings.

The countess felt badly for him. She was, after all, attempting to raise those hopes—not too much, just enough to get what she wanted.

What a truly awful woman I have become, she thought.

"Tell me, Mr. Flattery, how have you enjoyed becoming the 'illustrious Erasmus Flattery'? Has it given you great pleasure, I hope?"

Suddenly, Erasmus sat very straight and met her eyes, his manner no longer congenial, or so eager to please. "The script, Lady Chilton," he said more coolly than men commonly spoke to her, "is not the same as that found on the Ruin of Farrow, though a few characters have enough similarities that I would venture they are not so distantly related. I can't tell you how Pelier could have written it, nor can I read it. Is that what you wanted to hear?"

The countess felt herself shrink inside. "You do me disservice, sir," she protested softly.

"Do I, indeed? Then please accept my humble apology." He set his cup on the table and looked as though he were about to rise.

She reached out and placed a hand on his arm. "No. It is I who should apologize. I. . . ." She searched for the right thing to say, but everything suddenly seemed false. "I should not have misused you so, Mr. Flattery. I hope you will forgive me. You see . . . I have found these last few years that . . . I am not always satisfied with my conduct . . ." She looked down at her hands which made small movements that seemed rather helpless at the moment.

"The attention you receive, Lady Chilton," Erasmus said softly, "it cannot be easy."

"It is not," she said quickly. "Though it is no excuse for my behavior, and I have no right to complain. Some women have no suitors at all. Imagine the pain of that? No, I must not complain. But . . . I am really not so charming." She smiled painfully.

Look at the effect of this on him, she thought. *Farrelle help me, I have tried to be honest for once, and I think I have melted his heart.*

"What is Skye's interest in this?" he asked with some difficulty. "These are the Peliers Baumgere possessed?"

After what she had just done, she felt that she had no choice but to answer. "I believe they are, though I have been informed that one—the painting of the tomb—is not a Pelier. Skye believes it to be a close copy—including the inscription that you see on the tomb—of an original, but I am not sure why he thinks that."

Erasmus turned his attention back to the painting. She wondered what he was thinking at that moment, for his look was very dark and serious.

"Is it not remarkable, Mr. Flattery, that Pelier would paint such a thing—and then this man Baumgere would dig up the very crypt depicted?"

"Most remarkable, Lady Chilton." Erasmus shook his head as though baffled, and then turned back to his hostess. "I'm sure I have taken enough of Lady Chilton's time. It has been a great pleasure."

She was certain her mouth dropped open. Men never volunteered to leave her presence. More often than not she had trouble ridding herself of them.

"It—it was very kind of you to come, Mr. Flattery, and I hope you will do so again."

They both rose at the same time.

The countess could hardly remember such feelings of confusion. Look what she had been reduced to! Skye had her performing seductions for his own ends, and even if they were emotional seductions only, even so. . . . She felt such a sense of emptiness at her center when she thought of what Skye had her do.

You did offer, she reminded herself. But he did not protest, as a gentleman should.

And here was this poor man, Flattery, who had never done her harm, nor any other that she knew of, and she had used him so badly. And insulted him in the bargain. Treated him as though he were a fool.

She could almost feel his pain at this experience. Invited to tea with the Countess of Chilton for no reason but this information that he did not want to share. Terrible.

Anger toward Skye boiled up in her. Helpless anger, for she knew she could never let it show before him. He did not care for her that much. He might simply walk away, and she would never see him again. Was this anger focused on him, or upon herself for her weakness?

She accompanied Erasmus to the door, so lost in these thoughts that she could not even attempt polite conversation. The silence walked with them, like another; a ghost in their company that they could feel but not see.

At the door they stopped, both wary. She thought they circled each other, unsure if they would fight or embrace.

Erasmus bowed stiffly. "Lady Chilton."

"Mr. Flattery," she said the last syllable disappearing from her lips unexpectedly. An awkward second, then Erasmus reached for the door, but she snatched his hand away and did not release it.

"If you ask me not to repeat what you have told me, I will swear to keep it to myself." She realized she stood close to him now, holding his hand in both of hers, almost clasping it to her.

"It . . . it does not matter," Erasmus said.

She searched his eyes unself-consciously. "Then I will keep this secret, at least. I know you can read what was written on the painting. No. Do not deny it. I know. And I know there is more to your story of Eldrich. But that, too, I will not tell."

Erasmus held her hand tightly now, almost causing her pain. And he stared at her, his look unreadable. She thought he would either explode in fury or take her in his arms, she could not tell which.

He managed to open the door a crack with his free hand. Then she stood on tiptoe and bussed his cheek before he went out the door, saying only her name as he took his leave.

She watched him make his way to the gate, not looking back, and then he turned onto the street and was lost from sight. Still the countess did not close the door, but stayed drinking in great draughts of the cool highland air.

"What has come over me?" she said aloud but could find no answer in the confusion of feelings that seemed to be whirling inside her. Why had she suddenly felt such guilt at the way she used this man? It was not the first time she had applied her charm for some specific end—nor was it the hundredth.

Because now I know how it feels, she thought.

"Poor man," she whispered to the street, though she was not entirely sure which man she meant.

Chapter Seventeen

ERASMUS sat at a table on the terrace on the warmest morning that had been seen yet that year. His mind was on his meeting with the countess, which troubled him more than he had expected. Had she not warned him that her interest was his knowledge? Why then did he feel such a sense of dejection and emptiness?

Erasmus had also begun to wonder what had happened to Hayes. On his way out that morning he'd left the young man a note saying that he had been briefly called away and would find Hayes here at noon. They were to meet Kehler within the hour.

Erasmus was hoping they would get some explanation for Kehler's flight to this place—more than he had heard from Hayes, at any rate.

What had Kehler learned in the archives of Wooton? Could he have made the same discovery as Baumgere? If so, were the priests pursuing Kehler to offer him money for his silence, as, apparently, some thought they had Baumgere?

Erasmus took his timepiece from his pocket and cursed silently. Almost one! Was this Hayes' idea of a reasonable hour to rise? Erasmus could not be more patient. Draining his coffee he jogged up the steps to Hayes' room and pounded ungently on the door.

Nothing. No sound of movement within. No voice calling out. Again he hammered on the door so that it shook on its hinges.

Nothing. He went back down the steps two at a time, looking for the manager.

In five minutes they returned with a key for the room, finding it empty, the bed made as though it had never been slept in, and most of Hayes' belongings gone.

"I do not care for this," Erasmus muttered.

"The young are impetuous, not to mention intemperate, Mr. Flattery," the manager said soothingly. "I'm sure nothing dire has befallen your charge."

"You are, are you?" Erasmus said, annoyed by the man's tone. "Ah. . . ." A folded note was pinned to the wardrobe door.

"There will be your explanation," the manager said, as though proven right.

Erasmus jerked the note free and opened it.

My dear Erasmus:

I have gone with Kehler to look into the cavern called the Mirror Lake Cave. He believes that it was here that Baumgere searched and failed. Perhaps it is mere optimism, but Kehler believes there is still a great discovery to be made there. I have been sworn to secrecy, but only a fool would go into such a place without alerting others. Do not come after us immediately, but if we are not returned five days hence, you might confidently mount a search. It is our intention to look beyond the Fairy Galleries. I will mark our way with the letter H. Apologies for this, but Kehler would take no others.

Your servant,
Samual Hayes

"All is right with the world, I take it?" the manager asked.

Erasmus glared at the fool of a man and then swept out the door without a word.

Clarendon unrolled the survey across the table, placing weights on each corner.

"There you are, Mr. Flattery," Clarendon said, "just as I told you."

Erasmus had never seen anything like it. He was looking at a "map" of a cave system, and it was truly labyrinthine. Passages crossed over and under each other, or even paralleled each other only feet apart. He tried to compare the plan view and side view and was soon confused. The complexity was staggering.

"There must be miles of passages here," Erasmus said, dismayed.

"More than thirty, apparently, and likely even more that have not been explored or yet discovered. There might be a more current survey than this. I will find out." Clarendon put his finger on a chamber. "Here are the Fairy Galleries, so called. I have not been in this section myself, though I know men who have. We can certainly speak with them, but perhaps we should wait the five days the letter suggests before we gather the men for a search."

"I don't want to gather men for a search. I want no one to know of this at all—at least not until we are absolutely certain they are lost. No, I will take this map, or the more recent one if it exists, and go immediately to the cave entrance. If they have not emerged in a day or two, I will go in after them."

"Yourself, alone?"

Erasmus nodded.

"Well, I cannot allow that. It is more treacherous than this map might indicate. You must take me, at least, Mr. Flattery. You would be imprudent not to."

Erasmus began to protest, but Clarendon raised his hand, his mustache bobbing oddly; a sign of determination, Erasmus thought. "I am far more vital than you guess, and in a cave, where passages can often grow very tight, the smaller man can perform the greater deeds. And you forget—I have been in the caves before." He paused to consider. "We should not go unprepared, that would be dangerous, Mr. Flattery. But preparations take time. Let us plan to leave the day after tomorrow." He looked down at the survey, then raised his head and met Erasmus' eye, a sly smile appearing. "Tonight there is little we can do and I have promised to deliver Erasmus Flattery to a gathering of devotees of the grape. Tomorrow I will put my staff to work on the preparations, and the next day we shall set out well rested. I will tell you honestly, Mr. Flattery, that we stand little chance of catching up with these young men even if we were only hours behind them. They are younger than we and have the fires of both youth and curiosity. We will not catch them up until they have slowed their pace, and that will be in the Fairy Galleries—two days' hard push into the cave. They are young but hardly foolhardy, I think, so I do not worry that they will come to grief; at least it would be very unlikely. Be of good heart, sir, we will find them safe, I'm sure."

Erasmus and Clarendon walked to the meeting, for Castlebough was small and the evening pleasant. This night the gathering was to take place at the home of a man who, like most of the Society's fellows, did not reside year round in the town.

As a result of all the comings and goings, the society had a constantly changing membership, and one never knew who might be present, though Clarendon assured him that several men Erasmus knew at least by reputation would be there. Erasmus had agreed to speak briefly about his own work, and to answer questions.

The two men made their way through the streets and down stairways by the light of stars, the glow of the occasional streetlamp, and what illumination leaked from unshuttered windows. They were like two shadows moving, one elongated by a low source of light, the other made short by light from above.

The house they went to was very pleasant, built in the general style of the town with much dark wood inside, all carefully polished. The gentlemen were welcoming and gracious to Erasmus, and if he did not feel he'd found his place in the world here with these men, he at least felt highly appreciated. Odd that so many people he had never met held him in such high esteem.

Clarendon introduced him to the man who had surveyed the great cave, who had brought along the current survey at Clarendon's request. Although the man had reached an age where he no longer went into the cave himself, he consoled himself by meticulously recording the advances of others.

"I once thought I should complete the picture, Mr. Flattery," the man said. "Explore every last tunnel and chamber, but it was bigger than me, I fear. Nature's energies far exceeded my own. Sometimes I look at the still-growing plan and think we must be near the end, but then remember that I thought the same thing twenty years ago when only half what we now know had been discovered.

"Layel, the famous geologist, walked over miles of hillside around the cave, examining the drainage patterns and finding any number of sink holes, most of them choked closed, and he told me he would not be surprised if we eventually found ourselves linking to another system of caves as large again as this. Can you imagine? It would be one of the natural wonders of the world, I should think. As it stands now, there is much to admire inside. Stalactites and columns, curtains, and delicate crystal straws hollow in their cores and as thin as the stems of fine wineglasses. I know where there are ceilings covered in them, and they are astonishingly beautiful. And there are helectites as well—crystal straws, but twisted about as though gravity had changed as they formed, for they do not hang downward as the other formations do but contort into the most astounding shapes."

"Can one still become lost inside? Surely this map has eliminated that problem?" Erasmus asked.

"I wish that were so, Mr. Flattery, but I fear it is nothing like the truth. I sometimes think our efforts to chart the passages have done more harm than good in that matter. People who venture in armed with the survey are too confident, I think. They don't realize the real dangers, for there are some very precipitous climbs and descents required to get into the less frequented regions. Those who seek to open up new areas are the most often injured. But you can become lost even in the more frequented areas. It is more confusing than you might imagine. And I venture there are still many undiscovered passages, even in the parts that are fairly well known." He put his finger on the drawing. "You see this passage here? People walked by it for twenty years before it was discovered, for it is high up and difficult to see. I'm still not sure what caused anyone to notice it. But look! It opens up fully one quarter of the cave and eventually led us to find the third entrance: a tight little squeeze high up on a cliff. Twenty years that went undiscovered. Who knows how many such passages exist? No, if you go into the cave, Mr. Flattery, don't assume this survey will keep you safe. Only common sense will do that, though I am certain you have no lack of that."

Erasmus continued to examine the survey. Every so often there were ancillary drawings with lines pointing to a passage. "What are these?"

"Cross sections of the cave at that point." The man looked at

Randall. "It is a bit early yet to go far into the cave. It will likely be wet in places. Take good oiled cotton bags, Randall, and try to keep as much dry as you can. It is dangerous to go wet in the cave for long. I have seen men begin to lose their reason from this. They become lethargic and refuse to go on. I'm sure they would have died, too, had we not warmed them with our own heat."

"But surely the cave is not cold?" Erasmus said.

"No, Mr. Flattery, not overly, though the water is quite chill, especially this time of year. But the cave is not what you would call warm either and a man soaked through, unless he is very hardy, soon loses the natural heat of his body. Take my advice and keep as dry as you can. But perhaps it will not be so bad, and Randall has been in before and knows what to expect. You will be in good hands. Have no fear."

The meeting proper was convened then, Clarendon taking up the speaker's place at the front of a large room that had been fitted out with chairs for all the company.

"As many of you have already heard," the small man began, "the illustrious Erasmus Flattery, Fellow of the Empiricist Society, is among us this evening and has consented to speak on the subject of grafting to wild root stocks. I would venture to say that there is no greater authority on the subject. We are also fortunate to have visiting us Delford Simon, proprietor of Simon and Dean Wineries—a man well known to many of us, I'm sure. I would also welcome Deacon Rose of Wooton, a grower of great skill. Mr. Flattery, if you are ready. . . ."

Erasmus was so taken aback by the discovery that Deacon Rose was there that he did not start well. He found the priest seated in the middle of the audience, apparently in the company of two gentlemen not of the cloth.

It took a few moments for Erasmus to get over his surprise and warm to his subject, but then he managed to gain the attention of his audience, and held it for the duration of his speech. Discussion followed, and Erasmus had seldom found such a knowledgeable audience, even within the Society itself. Two hours went quickly by, and then the meeting broke up for the evening's real activity—the tasting of wines.

Erasmus was just swirling a particularly fine claret around in his mouth when the Farrellite priest found him.

"Well, Mr. Flattery, I did not imagine meeting you in Castlebough. I assume we have come pursuing the same matter?"

"You have come to take the waters as well?" Erasmus asked innocently.

"I was referring to our mutual friend, young Mr. Kehler," the priest said, his look of pious concern never slipping.

"Why would you think he was in Castlebough, Deacon Rose?"

The priest looked away for a moment, as though controlling his temper—not something Erasmus had seen in the man before.

"Perhaps we might speak more privately, Mr. Flattery?"

Erasmus took a second sip of his claret, considered a moment, and then nodded for the priest to lead the way. They went out into a walled garden awash in the fecund scents of early spring.

"Have you spoken to Mr. Kehler?" Rose asked. "Is he here?"

Erasmus looked at the man for a moment. "Since our last conversation, Deacon, I have learned that Mr. Kehler is not particularly destitute, as you suggested." Erasmus was about to ask how long Rose had watched his town home waiting for Kehler to appear but held back, to see what the priest would say.

Rose turned away stiffly, his eyes unfocused in the light streaming from the windows. "I will confess, Mr. Flattery, that I was less than forthcoming when last we spoke, but I assure you my concern for Mr. Kehler is quite genuine. He has taken something from our archives at Wooton that is of . . . great concern to us. I would even say that he is in some danger."

"From whom, Deacon?"

The priest hesitated, then turned his intelligent gaze on Erasmus. "You do not trust me, Mr. Flattery."

"I do not, that is true. Until you are willing to tell me more, I don't think that will change."

The priest stared down at the dark ground and nodded. "You were making inquiries this evening about the Cave of the Mirror Lake. . . . I assume that Mr. Kehler is seeking something there?"

Erasmus did not react—not even a shrug.

"If I camp before the entrance, I assume I will be able to speak with Mr. Kehler, for speak with him is all I wish to do."

Erasmus did not offer to confirm this.

The priest's manner changed, becoming suddenly very earnest. "You will not help me, then? Even though the young man's safety might depend on my intervention?"

"I'm afraid I can't," Erasmus said quietly, suddenly afraid that the man might be speaking the truth. Who had invaded Hayes' rooms and chased him through the streets? Could these men have been agents of the church? Or even of Eldrich himself? Could Eldrich know about Kehler's discovery?

"Are you going into the cave after Kehler? Tell me that, at least."

"I'm sorry, Deacon, but I will tell you nothing until you give me reason to."

The man reached out and put his hand gently on Erasmus' arm. "Let me accompany you, and then you can see yourself that I mean him no harm." Rose looked out over the garden wall to the stars and the hills. "I will tell you my fear, Mr. Flattery; I fear that I am already too late." He turned his gaze back to Erasmus. "When you spoke with Kehler, did he ask you about a man named Teller?"

Erasmus must not have hidden his surprise well.

"I see that he did. Perhaps he then told you what he found? If that is so, you realize why I must speak with him. It is true that I was not entirely candid with you on our first interview. I confess it, but certainly you can see that I could not be. You must see that? You lived in the house of Eldrich. I do not know what that might mean, but the mages and the church have long had an uneasy truce. We fear them, Mr. Flattery—even Eldrich in his waning years." Rose stopped, clearly unsettled to be saying these things aloud to someone outside the church. "Let me assure you, Mr. Flattery, in case you still have commerce with the mage, what happened was not of our doing. As soon as we became aware, we moved quickly to . . . cleanse our house of the disease. We have kept our pact all these long years and will continue to do so at any cost." The priest searched Erasmus' face, perhaps looking for some sign of understanding, but Erasmus was not willing to accept the position of emissary to Eldrich, or to refuse it. Better to let the priest wonder.

"Kehler came to you with questions that he hoped you might answer," the priest went on. "Did he tell you what he hoped to do?"

Erasmus did not answer, but the priest would not speak further.

"No," Erasmus said after a moment, "Kehler told me nothing, but I am hoping you will remedy that, Deacon. Why has he gone into the cave? What is he looking for?"

Deacon Rose turned and looked back at the house, then out

over the garden at the sky. "Something that might not even exist. Something that certainly should not exist."

"If you want my cooperation, Deacon, you will have to do better than that."

Rose continued to stare off at the stars, but he nodded vaguely. "Do you know, Mr. Flattery, that there is within the cave an area called the Fairy Galleries. It was named for its reputed resemblance to a mythical place—or perhaps the place was merely literary."

"'The Journey of Tomas,'" Erasmus said, realizing suddenly what the priest was saying.

"Yes. 'The Journey of Tomas.' It is an ancient lay, older than the Cary Minstrels' rendering, that is certain. The story of a man lost in a great cave who emerges into the starlight finally, almost starved, but he recognizes no constellations. When the sun rises, he finds he is in another land, similar but not the same as his own, and peopled by a different race. He lived there some time, learning their ways and their tongue. But finally he began to miss his wife and wonder about his small children, so he ventured back into the cave again. What happened there is a story unto itself, but eventually he emerged. And what did he find? His children grown, his wife dead and in the grave for many years, though he had been gone only two years by his reckoning. No one knew him, and his world was changed.

"After a brief time among his own people, he went back into the cave to seek the way back to Faery. There are different endings to the song: he finds his way back, he dies in the cave, or he almost dies when the people of Faery come and bear him through by their secret way. One may choose the ending one prefers—unlike life."

"What are you saying? That Kehler is seeking the way to Faery?" Erasmus laughed but this did not seem to affect the priest or his mood.

"The song is just a song, no more. I am only saying that men go seeking the objects of their desire. Perhaps even the creations of that desire. But what they find is invariably different than they imagined or hoped. This strange propensity in mankind is what makes us children—it is also what makes us great.

"What does Mr. Kehler seek? I am not absolutely certain, Mr. Flattery, though knowing him as I do, I would say he seeks knowledge. But what he will find, I fear, might be quite different."

Clarendon laughed as he and Erasmus walked through the village, returning from the gathering of vinophiles.

"'The Ballad of Tomas.' I do know it." He chuckled again. "Though I think most could say the same. You see, when the cave was discovered, it was given an entirely different name, and then some local worthy—a mayor, I think—got the idea to rename it for the cave in the old song. There is a fairly large lake within it, you see, and other features that are similar enough, though most large caves would have many of these. It draws the tourists, for in the summer many of the town's visitors tour the caves, the Cave of the Mirror Lake chief among them, for, you see, the plan worked." Clarendon laughed again. "This priest, what is he up to, do you think?"

"I wish I knew, Randall. I dearly wish I knew."

"Well, at least I think he spoke the truth when he said that men go seeking their desires and often find something quite unexpected. He failed to say, however, that these are among mankind's greatest discoveries—both for good and ill."

Chapter Eighteen

KEHLER held aloft the lantern, illuminating the opening. "I think we should go in tonight, at least some way, in case we're pursued."

"Do you think it's wise to go on in darkness?" Hayes asked.

"It's always night in the underworld, Samual."

Hayes could hear his companion's smile in the words. "Yes, of course, but . . ." He let the protest die. "All right, if you think it's best."

They climbed back up the path among the firs and found their guide unloading the horses. "We can make a camp here," the man said.

"We thought we'd go in tonight," Kehler said, not at all self-conscious.

The man stopped what he was doing. "Tonight? You might be better rested in the morning." He paused and looked at each of the gentlemen. "But suit yourselves." He set one of their bags on the ground. "I would caution you to be most careful in your explorations, gentlemen. You cannot imagine the difficulties of carrying a man back to the surface again. There are some tight places in the cave, and getting an injured man through such can be near to impossible. I have had to do it myself and never want to be so employed again. I urge you, be mindful as you go."

Kehler and Hayes divided their effects into sturdy canvas packs of the type used by foot soldiers.

"It seems an enormous amount of gear," Hayes said hefting his pack.

"We must have it, though. A spare lantern is a necessity, and lamp oil, and ropes. We must have food and a change of clothing, a compass, candles, and the survey. I have left everything out that I felt we could possibly do without. Feel fortunate that we do not have to carry water, for there is water enough in the cave." Kehler took a last look at their bags. "We will leave some food and a few other things just inside the cave to await our return, but the rest I'm afraid we must shoulder. Let me just fill the lantern, and we shall be ready."

A moment later Kehler resealed the fuel tin and hoisted his pack to his back. "Into the netherworld, my friend." He went to thank their guide, but the man was rolled in a blanket and already snoring.

They descended along the path to the cave mouth. At this elevation and among such massive trees the underwood was very sparse, and the earth was often carpeted in mosses. Hayes felt as though they were leaving a soft, green world for one hard, gray, and lifeless, for very little lived out of sight of the sun. He could not help feeling that the darkness emanated from this opening into the earth, exhaled like a dark breath each night. He didn't really want to go on, and hesitated at the very lip of the cave.

Kehler looked over at him. "It will be the discovery of a lifetime," he said simply. "And we shall write an account of it that will be seen by every reading man, woman, and child in all the nations around the Entide Sea. You will not want for money ever again, Hayes, I can assure you."

"It would come down to money," Hayes said peevishly. "Lead on, Kehler, I'm dreadfully tired of hiding from my creditors."

Kehler gave him a hint of a concerned smile, and went resolutely into the mouth of the cave. The lantern illuminated a floor of dried mud, caked and flaking, and convoluted walls worn by years of water erosion, now broken here and there and not so smooth as they were.

"You're sure this cave is . . . solid," Hayes said, his voice echoing in the small entrance chamber.

"There are some areas of breakdown marked on the survey, but for the most part the cave is utterly solid and not to be worried about. I can't believe you didn't read the pamphlet, Hayes."

"You read most of it to me," he reminded his friend.

Some enterprising individual in Castlebough had published a small pamphlet on the cave, and though its aim was to draw visitors out to see this natural wonder, there was some useful information as well. But even so, Hayes was not convinced that a survey and the information contained in some hack's pamphlet could really be considered adequate preparation for their expedition. But Kehler absolutely refused to take a local guide other than the man who brought them to the entrance. Whatever it was he hoped to find, Kehler was to be certain that he shared it with no one but Hayes—and Hayes was not sure that he would have been included if Kehler had felt he could have undertaken the matter alone. But apparently even the driven Kehler was not willing to go into the bowels of the earth on his own.

"You promised to tell me what you had learned once we were underground," Hayes said as they made their way into a narrowing passage.

"When we stop to rest," Kehler said. "You will not be disappointed, Samual."

No, but I will likely be too far along to turn back if I am.

The passage was high, disappearing from the lamplight at a dozen feet and varied in width as they went from three yards to places where the two could not walk abreast. The walls were uneven, appearing almost fluted in places, as though over the great expanse of geological time water had run here at different levels, and slowly eaten away at the softer whitestone so that the surfaces were uneven. The cave twisted unexpectedly, and then began to descend so that they were soon climbing down drops of four and five feet, like erratic stairs.

They went on like this for an hour or more, Kehler leading the way and holding the lantern for Hayes. They were young and hale, and even Hayes soon forgot his fears and began to enjoy meeting the challenge. They heard no sound but their own breathing and the scrape of their feet over stone, the sound of the packs rubbing against the walls of the cave as they squeezed through some narrower part. And then Kehler stopped, holding up his hand, obviously listening.

"Do you hear water running?"

Hayes listened. "There is something. . . . It must be water. Does your survey show it?"

"Yes, but I did not think to come upon it so soon. We are making better time than I guessed."

Heartened by this, they pushed on, hurrying where the cave would allow it. At one point the passage narrowed at its bottom, forcing them to climb higher, bridging their arms and legs to either side and picking their footholds with care. An hour later they were able to take to the floor again, but they had been slowed appreciably by this section.

The air changed, becoming suddenly damp and a bit refreshing, for they had been working hard and were both hot and sweating. In another twenty minutes they came to the lip of a drop, and there at the bottom lay a pool of water fed by a small falls. The water swirled in a swift whirlpool and then plunged down into the cave, sounding unnaturally loud in the hard world of stone.

Kehler handed the lamp to Hayes and peeled off his pack, setting it down with a theatrical groan. "I think we can easily climb down, but we should lower the lantern and the packs separately." He dug out one of their ropes, flaking it down onto the rock, and formed a loop at its midpoint. "When I get down, throw me the end, then tie the lantern to the loop. Feed it out to me, and I will endeavor to keep it clear of the rocks."

Carefully, but apparently without trepidation, Kehler climbed the thirteen or fourteen feet down to the edge of the pool.

"All right," he said, and Hayes threw him the other end.

The lantern was lowered down without mishap, and then the packs, one at a time. Hayes followed his friend, though with less confidence. Kehler held the lantern high and gave his friend instructions as to the best footholds. In a moment they were both standing beside the small pool, their relieved laughter echoing with the water sounds.

"Where does this go?" Hayes asked, waving a hand at the passage from which the water flowed.

"It goes a few hundred yards, and then chokes off, I think. Only a hole big enough for the stream."

They both drank and then sat for a moment. The chamber they were in was almost perfectly circular, rising fairly evenly to a dome overhead.

"It is remarkable, isn't it?" Hayes said, surprised by his reaction to the place.

Kehler agreed. "But we haven't come anywhere near the true wonders of the cave. There are chambers decorated with stalactites and curtains and flowing moonstone. There is a falls almost a hundred feet high and even a small lake, or so the survey shows."

"How far have we descended?"

"I don't think we've gone down a hundred feet yet, which leaves quite a lot of cave below us, for we started about three thousand feet above Blue Hawk Lake which lies at the cave's bottom. Unfortunately we will have to climb up again, for the entrances at the lake are under water until the dry summer months."

They sat quietly, watching the water swirl into the pool, a bit awed by what nature had carved around them.

Kehler filled the lamp again, checking his watch. "We may have to kill the flame when we stop to sleep," he said. "I'm not sure we have enough fuel to keep it alive for the entire time otherwise."

"But we have candles," Hayes said.

"Yes, though I hope we'll not need them. A lamp is so much more convenient and casts much more light. Imagine trying to keep a candle alight and make good time in here?"

There was a moment's silence, and perhaps sensing that Hayes was again about to ask the purpose of their expedition, Kehler jumped up and hefted his pack into place.

"Take the lantern and the lead, Hayes. I will follow blindly for a while."

They followed the course of the water, which ran swiftly down, its voice echoing in the dark tunnel. Where the passage narrowed, and there was no dry footing, they at first tried to keep their boots dry, climbing up and bridging again, but soon enough they had both slipped in one place or another and after that they simply plunged into the water, accepting the ruination of their footwear.

In half an hour they came to a short drop where the water course deviated into a fissure in the floor which left only a little room on one side where they might pass. They went carefully by this opening, afraid to slip into it, both imagining being swept down into a dark, water-filled tunnel devoid of both light and air.

"I did not care much for that!" Hayes said, slumping up against the cave wall once they were past.

"Nor did I. Fortunately we have clear sailing now for a while."

Kehler filled their single water bottle here, and then they set off again.

"In a little over an hour we should reach a splitting of the way," Kehler said. "We can go either left or right, for both ways join again. After that, I think we will be an hour from the great junction where four passages meet. Can you go on till then? Are you game?"

Hayes thought he was. Kehler took the lead now, pushing on as though driven to complete their journey that very night, though it looked more likely that they would require two days or even a bit more. It all depended on their ease of going. The passage was presently running along quite evenly, and they were making excellent time though that could quickly change. The next time they stopped, Hayes wanted to have a look at the survey. His memory of it was getting muddled already.

Hayes was not quite certain how he had gotten drawn into this, aside from the obvious reasons: money and bloody curiosity. He felt like he had betrayed Erasmus, slipping away without a word, but Kehler had insisted.

"It will be the discovery of our lifetime," Kehler had said, his eyes almost shining with his excitement. *"And your name will be attached to it forever."* Kehler realized how much his pride had been damaged by his fall in society. *Erasmus will never forgive me,* he thought. *I do not know exactly what Kehler expects to find, but with the similarities between his interests and Erasmus', I have little doubt that Erasmus will wish he were with us.* And there was also Erasmus' stated concern: that Kehler was pursuing matters that could be dangerous to him—matters that Hayes was pursuing as well.

The roof of the passage had begun to dip, forcing Hayes and Kehler to crouch as they went. But soon their packs were dragging on the rock, and they were forced to their knees. Packs were shed with some difficulty, and they proceeded, pushing the packs ahead as they went. The ceiling continued to drop until they were slithering along on their bellies, though the width of their tunnel remained six or seven feet.

"I hope it is not all like this," Hayes said, "or we shall be in here forever."

Ahead of him Kehler cursed. "Yes, I would say our pace has slowed to the proverbial crawl. Flames! I shall have no knees left at this rate!"

Hayes laughed, the sound echoing oddly in the darkness. They crawled on, saving their breath for their effort, though that did not stop an occasional curse. Hayes began to think of the tons of rock above him, and the tunnel seemed to press down, as though the roof of the cave were bending under the immeasurable weight. He struggled with a growing panic. What if the tunnel became smaller yet? What if they became trapped, unable to move? The thought caused him such anguish that he pushed it from his mind.

Concentrate on moving forward, he encouraged himself. He fought to lift his pack over an edge that snagged it, shoved it on in frustration, and then crawled after. He was not getting much light from the lantern, and Kehler, who could see perfectly, no doubt, was getting farther and farther ahead. At this rate Hayes thought he would soon be in complete darkness. To make matters worse, he was certain the tunnel was narrowing. And he had to struggle with his panic again.

He did not know how long they proceeded in this fashion, but it seemed hours. Hayes felt that his existence was shrinking as the tunnel became smaller. He was reduced to a crawling beast, fighting his fears, pushing his pack a foot, then dragging himself forward, pushing his pack . . . again and again.

And then the light appeared to grow; he thrust his pack through a hole into an open area and light flooded in. Hayes squeezed through and lay catching his breath. Kehler was sitting with his back against the rock wall, and he tried to smile.

"Do you know the hour? I have managed to smash my time-piece."

Hayes fished in a pocket and found his own watch unscathed, though he made note to place it securely in his pack.

"Two minutes beyond midnight."

Kehler nodded. "Six hours we have been at it. Three perhaps in this last section. Our progress is less than I expected."

"Perhaps this walking upright has its drawbacks after all. I'm sure our distant relatives, the ape men, would have managed much better than we."

Kehler produced the water bottle, and they both drank deeply. The survey was spread out in the lamplight, and the two bent over it.

"I would venture that we have just passed through the section known as the 'Slug's Race Course,' and I no longer wonder why it was so named. I wonder how far it is to this splitting of the ways?" He tapped the drawing. "Shall we go on, or call it a night?"

Hayes took a look around. He was feeling decidedly tired, but he was not certain that he could sleep. The claustrophobia of the last hours still touched him.

"I think we should go on. We have almost emptied the water bottle, and it would be good to be nearer water in the morning."

Kehler nodded. "You're right. Let's go to the place where the four ways meet. From there it can't be more than two hours to the resurgence."

They clambered on, relieved by the size of the passage, which was ten feet high and roughly round, though it quickly began to vary, and twist as it went. Their spirits rose, as often happens after an ordeal, and they talked as they went, buoyed by a sense of adventure.

In the world above, people slumbered, secure in their homes and the routine of their lives, while here, far beneath the surface, Hayes and Kehler went seeking secrets long hidden. Hayes thought that he felt more alive at that moment than he had in several years.

Sooner than expected, they found the **Y** in the tunnel and, for no particular reason, elected to take the left passage. In twenty minutes the passages joined again and they pressed on. A series of short drops, none more than ten feet, slowed them only a little, and an hour more brought them to the place where the four ways joined. Here they found a small alcove off the side of one passage and, calling it the "sleeping chamber," threw down their packs.

Hayes impressed Kehler by using the lantern as a stove. He removed the glass chimney and, using one of their tin cups and the lamp's handle, managed if not to boil water at least to heat it. Taking a small package from his pack, he brewed something resembling tea and this they shared quietly by the lamplight.

Kehler produced the survey again and hunched over it, examining it minutely. "If we take the southern passage, we will be forced to use ropes to negotiate some rather large drops, but there are no significant squeezes on this route. The northern way has a long crawl, perhaps longer than the one we have just survived."

"Let us go by the south, then, Kehler. I fear heights less than the tight spots."

Kehler looked over at him, his gaze resting on his friend with some concern. "I will tell you honestly, Hayes, that we have not really entered a tight passage yet. Some tunnels we might meet are just large enough to let a determined man pass and no more." Perhaps he saw the distress this caused, and he quickly added. "But I am smaller than you and will do most of the real exploration. Your job will be to pull me out by my ankles should I get stuck."

Hayes took the tea from his friend and sipped it. "You said you would tell me the story once we stopped."

Kehler laid his head back against the rock and closed his eyes. Hayes thought he would claim exhaustion and put the moment off again, but without opening his eyes Kehler began.

"In my time at Wooton I managed to gain the trust of a number of the priests who worked in the archives, although I will confess that I planned to abuse that trust right from the beginning. Like many historians in Farrland, I was of the belief that the church hid much of our history in their records. If they had so cheated us, I was prepared to do the same to them. I make no more excuse than that.

"The archives at Wooton house what is, perhaps, the most important collection in all Farrland. There are some documents there of astonishing age! Many of the priests who do their scholarly work there maintain exhausting hours, appearing to need no more than a few hours' sleep each day. This is part of the surrender of their will to the church, I think. I came to see it as a form of self-abasement, really. But it meant that the archives were open at all hours. I began to work long hours myself and gained the trust of a number of the priests this way, for I think they were impressed by my monklike capacity for work. I was not one of them, but I was, at least, like them in habits.

"I soon learned that there were rooms in the buildings that were not open to any but the most senior priests or scholars, and then only with consent from on high. The keys for most of the rooms were in the possession of the senior archivist, an ancient and kindly priest. I gained his trust by offering my services to him, for he did not get around as he once did. Through this action, I managed to gain occasional access to his keys. The poor man, he trusted me far too much, and I do regret this one betrayal, for I'm sure he has been retired in shame for what happened.

"I traced his keys one at a time, and then filed duplicates out of brass. It was a laborious process, I can tell you, and it did not always produce results, but eventually I had keys for most of the locked chambers. The first I entered documented the struggle of the church to influence government, and was astonishing enough, I'm sure, but it was not what interested me. I was a while finding what I looked for and, in fact, began to despair of ever discovering what I sought.

"And then fortune found me. I could only gain access to the rooms at certain times of the night, when those few priests who were in the archives were engaged elsewhere, and during vespers. I was expected to attend though occasionally I did not and was seldom missed, but everyone else attended, leaving the archives protected only by their ancient locks.

Kehler opened his eyes and fixed them on his friend. "I will tell you truthfully, Hayes, there is an archive at Wooton that deals almost exclusively with the Farrellite Church's struggle against the mages. It is an astonishing history! I hadn't time to read it all, of course, or even a hundredth part of it, but even so—the things I found! It was Althons, the mage King, who preserved the vestiges of the Farrellite Church after the war between the church and the mages. And the church leaders did not know why! It was as though the mages had some use for the church, perhaps far in the future, but would say nothing of it. The church fathers suspected that augury had led to this decision. The mages had seen something in one of their visions that had led them to spare the church, and the priests had no idea what it might be.

"But the information I sought was more elusive and took me months of subterfuge to find. All the while I expected discovery and expulsion—at the very least! And then one day I found a letter from Baumgere himself—a letter to the senior bishop of the Farrellite Church, no less. Although it was written with all apparent deference, and was clearly a response to a letter from the senior bishop, it contained a threat that was only very slightly veiled. 'I should not want to contemplate the reaction of the mages,' Baumgere wrote, 'were they to learn that you concealed their enemy all these years.' "

Kehler leaned forward and blew out the flame, plunging the chamber into a darkness such as Hayes had never known. There was not a trace of light. No shadow or area darker than another. Uniform blackness, and then odd visions, shades of color, seemed to appear before his eyes, though they were not light but only the eye's reaction to its absence. He heard his own breath indrawn. And then Kehler's voice came out of the blackness.

"I had learned about Teller by then, though at first I didn't make the connection. It was not until I found a record of an inquisition within the church carried out with utter secrecy that I began to realize what had happened. A hundred and sixty years ago the Farrellites found that the society the mages believed they had destroyed was still alive, and living like a parasite within the bosom of the church! The society of Teller had somehow survived. And where better to take refuge than within the defeated church? The church that no longer posed a threat to the mages; that did not dare to pose a threat! A priest speaking out from the pulpit against the mages would have been summarily excommunicated for endangering the church. And this was almost without question what Baumgere was referring to. He must have learned of it in his studies.

"Of course, by Baumgere's time, the society of Teller had been rooted out, though I was not able to learn what their fate had been. But still, the mages were not known to be just, and the fathers of the church were, with good reason, terrified that the mages might one day learn the truth. What if this had been their sole function, the reason the mages had allowed the church to survive? To destroy the vestiges of Teller's society? Would the mages have no more use for them if they were to find out? And Baumgere blackmailed them with this information—blackmailed his own church, though for what gain was unclear. No wonder he was denied absolution!

"So hearing Erasmus and Clarendon speak of Teller did not surprise me." Kehler paused a moment. "The priest came to the Caledon Hills seeking something, and he was clearly not doing so at the behest of his church. People would see him out roaming the hills with his deaf-mute servant, silent, as always, about his business. In any number of places there were excavations attributed to Baumgere. Then, when I had begun to lose hope, I found some of Baumgere's papers. Nothing like I'd hoped—no journal containing all the answers to my questions—but a few odd things that were likely deemed of no importance by whomever had filed Baumgere's papers away in this forgotten room. A deed to his home. A map of the vicinity to the west of Blue Hawk Lake marked here and there with intriguing circles and lines. A meticulous catalogue of everything he read. In a crate, I even found some of Baumgere's books—all of which were entered in the catalogue. And something that seemed very odd at the time—a number of cave surveys, all annotated in his wispy hand. It seemed from what he wrote that he had been engaged in carefully eliminating every section of each cave, though by what criteria could not be ascertained. On each survey there was a date and a brief entry; usually something like, 'nothing here' or 'not this one', but this cave—the Cavern of the Mirror Lake—this one he did not complete his work in. Something stopped him. Stopped him just when his hopes were rising, for on one section of the cave were written the words: 'Here, the way by darkness into light.' "

"And that means something to you?" Hayes said, surprised at the weight Kehler seemed to attribute to the inscription.

"I confess, at the time it meant nothing. But as I studied Baumgere's effects, these few scraps that proved the man had passed through this world, I was provided an answer. Among the books that Baumgere owned, I found that several contained the same lyric, and each was much underlined and written over, which was very anomalous, for he had not written in his books in any other place. It was an old lyric called the 'Ballad of Tomas' that interested him. You've likely heard it sung. . . ." Kehler then proceeded to sing, off key, a line or two.

"Remarkably, I actually do recognize it, which is saying a great deal as you entirely missed the tune, like a blind carpenter after a nail."

"Well, I make no claims as a singer. But the line, 'the way, by darkness, into light,' is from the ballad."

"I'm waiting for you to enlighten me," Hayes said.

"Well, clearly Baumgere had a romantic or poetical nature and a particular affection for that lyric. The way by darkness into light was the tunnel that Tomas used to reach Faery. The one tunnel in a vast cave. So you see, he used this line to mark the spot where he believed lay whatever it was he looked for. It is also a metaphor, obviously. Perhaps, given his religion, he would have interpreted it to mean the way to eternal life through death. Or the way to knowledge through struggle."

"Well," Hayes said, "I'm glad we have come down here on such concrete evidence. *'The way by darkness into light.'* Why didn't you just say so earlier? No more explanation would have been necessary. I would have plunged into darkness ready to do battle with all the creatures of the underworld, both real and metaphorical. Farrelle's flames, Kehler! Is that why we're crawling along on our bellies through utter darkness? Because Baumgere wrote that particularly edifying line on a cave survey?"

"There is more, Hayes, if you'll just bear with me."

"Well, I'm glad to hear that, but just for your information, I'm fixing you with a devastatingly skeptical look at this moment."

"I can actually feel it." Kehler paused only to draw breath. "I kept searching and began to take greater risks, going to the rooms when it was not really safe to do so. But by this time I was obsessed. I felt I was so close to such astonishing secrets. I kept digging, just as Baumgere had.

And then I heard from Skye, a rather cryptic note, for he was concerned that my correspondence might be monitored. I gathered, though, that he had found the Peliers which was news indeed. I assumed they were in the possession of the church. I spoke to one of the monks who was a resident expert on art and, fortunately, a man without a trace of suspicion in his rather narrow character. To my surprise I learned that there were Peliers in Wooton, stored away with a great deal of other art that is not on daily display.

"I managed to get access to these storage rooms as well, and was more than surprised by what I found, for there, carefully covered and leaning against a wall in a stack of other art, I found one of the Peliers that Skye described, and two other paintings as well.

"But if Skye had it, how could it have been found in Wooton as well?"

"An interesting question. I assume one or the other is a copy. Be that as it may, I found the painting of the crypt that you saw above Castlebough, the same painting that was owned by Baumgere, and a second painting of a man in priestly robes standing in a grape arbor. But his hair was too long, and he held a book that at first I thought was scripture, but upon closer examination turned out to be a book of the arcane, for it had upon it strange symbols and writing that I could not read—a book of the arts.

"Flames, Kehler! Pelier knew that Teller's people hid within the church?!" Hayes exclaimed increduously.

"I don't think you can say that he knew, but he had a vision that this was so. Perhaps he predicted it. Either way the church was forewarned, for Pelier lived before the discovery of the Tellerites within the church. The third painting was even more obscure. . . . It shows a gate pushed open, leading into what might be a courtyard or perhaps a garden. Inside stands a man, smiling oddly, almost gloating, and like the figure in the other painting, he holds a book inscribed with arcane symbols and a strange script. He also holds a leafed stem bearing a pair of small white blossoms. The background is difficult to discern, but the odd thing about this painting is that the man bears an uncanny resemblance to Erasmus."

"You aren't serious?! Erasmus Flattery?"

"None other."

"Martyr's balls, Kehler! Erasmus? Does the church know this? Do they realize it is Erasmus?"

"I would think they must, now. Deacon Rose will not have missed that when he visited Erasmus, and I am almost certain he will have known of the painting."

"But what does it mean?" Hayes asked, still trying to grasp the idea that someone had painted his friend, Erasmus, hundreds of years before he was born!

"I am not sure. As I said, the figure bears a striking resemblance to Erasmus—too near for it to be coincidence, I'm sure. I think it means that Erasmus knows more of the mages than he claims, or at least so I would surmise. So you see, it began with Baumgere being called to Compton Heath to listen to the Stranger's peculiar tongue. I don't know how he came across the Pelier that showed the stranger crossing the bridge, but he did, and from there a growing interest in the work of the artist would explain how he came across the Pelier that showed the crypt in Castlebough—and then the last painting that shows Erasmus."

"But that can have meant nothing to him. Erasmus was not even born when Baumgere was alive."

"No, that's true, but there is writing on the book that Erasmus held, and I haven't even the slightest idea of what it might mean. But then we're forgetting something. . . . We don't know that Baumgere knew anything about this last Pelier."

"But this still does not explain why we are here. What is it we hope to find?"

Kehler did not answer for a long moment, and Hayes was about to repeat his question when his friend finally spoke. "We are here because Baumgere searched for something in this cave. Something that had some connection to Teller and the remains of his society that was destroyed by the church. If you ask me to theorize, I will tell you this. I think the crypt Baumgere uncovered might have been the burying place of Teller himself, laid to rest by his followers, who then concealed the place. I think the painting of Erasmus indicates hidden knowledge—that is what Baumgere was looking for. Why he believed it to be here is not clear, but you must remember that Baumgere was a very accomplished scholar. He would not have been searching here if he did not have reason. I think he was seeking knowledge of the arts—knowledge that was hidden long ago, by the followers of Teller."

"But why was Erasmus the subject of a painting? What has he to do with this?"

Hayes could hear Kehler shake his head. "I don't know, Hayes. I don't know. Unless Erasmus was meant to find this knowledge . . . and somehow it has fallen to us. Or perhaps it meant that Erasmus would be the guardian of the arts, in some way. I can't say. All I know is that Baumgere believed what he sought was here."

They fell silent in the darkness. From somewhere Hayes could hear the slow drip of water punctuating the silence. Hayes' mind was racing to take in the story—a terribly incomplete story. What was Kehler keeping back? Something, Hayes was sure. Kehler would hardly have made such an expedition because of an obscure line of poetry scribbled on a survey. He was too thorough a scholar for that.

"It seems very slim evidence," Hayes said. "Hardly enough to bring us down into this particular netherworld. What is it you're not telling me?"

The silence was protracted this time.

"There was another letter," Kehler admitted with such reticence that Hayes suddenly felt apprehensive. The distant sound of water measured Kehler's reluctance.

"Yes . . ." Hayes softly prompted.

He heard his friend shift in the darkness, his clothing rasping against hard stone. "Atreche, the priest who refused Baumgere absolution wrote a last missive to the church. Baumgere had been searching the cave, looking for what, the priest did not know, but he had employed two young orphans in this endeavor—brothers ten and twelve years. Beyond the section of the cave known as the Fairy Galleries . . ." Kehler stopped and drew a long breath, "one of these boys met a very untimely end." He paused again. "The letter did not say how. The brothers were not from Castlebough, and so the boy was never missed. Baumgere kept it secret, somehow." Kehler cleared his throat, trying to force the emotion from his voice.

"The priest who refused Baumgere absolution, killed himself not far from one of the lower entrances to the cave, after performing last rites, it would seem."

"For the dead child."

"That is what I think."

"But why did he self-murder?" Hayes could hear Kehler's breathing in the darkness, short breaths. This was not a subject he liked to speak of.

"It is difficult to say, though he was responsible for putting the two boys into Baumgere's care. It would seem likely that he felt culpable. Perhaps he knew that Baumgere planned to use the boys in a dangerous endeavor."

"And this is where we are going, beyond the Fairy Galleries?"

"Yes."

"I can see why you didn't want to tell me this before. Why did Baumgere seek this knowledge?"

"The seeking after knowledge is, as you know, simply in man's nature—some men far more than others. But if there was some reason beyond that, it might be found in the story of Baumgere's hero—Tomas. He sought truth, and though he paid dearly for it, he also saw things no other had seen, and lived far beyond the years of men. That is enough reason to seek the knowledge of Teller."

"And this knowledge is guarded by the ghost of a dead boy?"

Kehler did not answer.

"Sacrificed for what gain, I wonder?"

No response from the darkness, only the slow drip, drip of water measuring the passing years in this sunless world.

Chapter Nineteen

THE countess was not sure what had aroused her. A sound? Had someone been whispering her name over and over. Almost a chant.

"A dream," she told herself. Even so, she got out of bed, agitated. It had seemed so real. Elauralelauralel. . . . She pulled a robe over her sleeping gown and went out into the hallway. Had Marianne called her? Perhaps called out in her sleep? She went to the door of her companion's sleeping chamber but decided that the voice had not been Marianne's and passed by.

Certainly it had not come from this floor. She went down the stairs and into the entryway, where she stood completely bemused, not quite sure what she was doing there.

"I am still half asleep," she muttered.

"Lady Chilton?"

This time there was no mistake. Someone had whispered her name. The handle of the door rattled.

It is Skye, she thought, and quickly drew the bolt, throwing open the door. On the threshold stood a small, round man, bowing awkwardly, his manner so sincere and so inept that she had to smile.

"He awaits you, m'lady," the man said, keeping his voice low. "You mustn't keep him waiting longer."

"Who? Who awaits me?" she said, still utterly confused, though, strangely, she did not feel frightened. "Skye?"

The little man bobbed his head, smiling encouragingly. He gestured behind, and she realized a carriage stood in the darkened street.

"But I am not even dressed."

"It does not matter. You must come as you are. Quickly," the man said. He extended a hand and she felt herself reach out and take it.

"But who are you?" she said, allowing herself to be lead down the few stairs.

"Walky, m'lady," he said, handing her up into the carriage. "There is a goose down for your comfort, m'lady. We've not far to go."

I'm dreaming, the countess realized and felt some relief wash through her. She almost laughed.

"Wake up," she said aloud, but still she remained in the carriage, moving through the streets of Castlebough. And it was cold! She reached over and pulled the goose down close around her. *I do hope I wake soon,* she thought. *This is most unsettling.* But then, if it was a dream in which she went to meet Skye, perhaps she should not try to wake, but keep this fantasy assignation.

Up they went through the town, the team laboring to pull the great carriage. It was a large coach she realized; large and quite old-fashioned. She could not remember Skye owning such a carriage.

It does not matter, she told herself, *it is a dream.* Certainly she felt as bemused as she did when dreaming. Nothing seemed quite real—not the little man who had come to her door, or the too-large coach, or even the moonlight which appeared too fair and bright.

Her thoughts seemed to drift, but when she pulled herself back to consciousness she still rode in the back of the carriage. Shaking her head did not clear it.

Should I not be frightened? Certainly she would be if she were awake, so that proved it was a dream. *I will shut my eyes and wake up in my bed,* she decided, and did exactly that, except that when she woke, she found the same small man leaning in the open door of the coach, shaking her gently.

"M'lady? We've arrived. Let me assist you." He handed her down onto the cobbles. They were beneath the roof of a large coach entrance, though the door lamps were not lit.

"He awaits you inside, m'lady, if you please."

"Who?"

"I thought you knew."

"Skye."

"Well, come along, and you will see."

"But who are you?"

"Walky, m'lady."

They went into the darkened house where, to her relief, a candle burned in a niche. Walky took it up and led her on. Down a wide hallway with old suits of armor standing guard, and weapons mounted on the walls. Martyrs and gargoyles were carved into the capitals of responds and looked down at her passing, alternately benevolent and ghoulish.

A dream, the countess told herself. Only a dream.

They passed through two massive doors into a rotunda.

"Here you are, m'lady. Wait but a moment."

And he was gone, taking the candle with him. Yet there was light. She looked up and realized she stood beneath a dome of stained glass. Through the clear panes, she could see stars and moonlight, which fell in a broken pattern on the stone floor around her, like weak sunlight falling through the forest.

Columns stood in a circle, like the great boles of trees supporting the canopy of the forest above. A dozen feet behind, lay a dark wall.

The countess waited in the center of this room, where the light was brightest and where she could see if anyone or anything approached.

Silence. Only the sound of her own breathing, her heart.

Awake, she willed herself. *I am becoming frightened. Awake!*

And then she heard the noise of someone moving, clothing rustling, but no footsteps.

"Who's there?" she snapped.

"Who indeed," came a voice from behind.

She whirled around and there, just near a pillar and slightly back of it, she saw a dark form.

"Who are you?"

"A question many have asked, my dear, though few have had an answer." The voice was musical, soft; not malevolent but nor was it kind. Mocking—it seemed to be mocking her.

"What . . . what do you want of me?"

"That is why you are here—so that I might decide." He came forth from the shadow, but still she could not make him out—as though the shadow moved with him. He began to walk slowly about her. "No, stay as you are," he commanded as she moved to keep him in view.

The countess was not sure why, but she did as she was bid. Very slowly he went, as though she were a mare to be bought—and bred, she feared.

"It is dark," she said. "I cannot see you."

"But I can see you. Perfectly."

Again she shook her head, trying to clear it, afraid that this fog that clouded her senses would bring her to grief. *I am in danger,* she told herself, but she did not feel it.

"Who are you, sir?"

"You don't know?"

"No. My mind is . . . it is in a fog."

"And would you have it cleared? You may be happier as you are."

"I would like my mind to be clear." She felt a stab of fear, and she drew a great breath, her senses returned. "*Eldrich*. . . !" she said.

"*Lord* Eldrich, Lady Chilton. You should respect your elders, at least."

She began to turn and shrink away from him, and suddenly she no longer controlled her muscles, but stood firmly rooted.

"Are you happy now?" he asked, his voice still gently mocking.

"I am far from happy. You abduct me from my home, and bring me here, wearing my night clothes. What gentleman would act so?"

"No gentleman, I would imagine. But I am a mage, the last of my kind, Lady Chilton. And you . . . well, you are not what men think."

"And what is that supposed to mean?"

"Perhaps you are not aware that it is the prerogative of a mage to speak in hints and riddles. Have you not read the histories?"

She did not answer, but stood, fighting to have command of her own muscles.

"Do not struggle, Lady Chilton. It is futile. Remove your robe," he said.

"I will not!"

He laughed. "What is it they always say in novels? 'I like a woman with spirit'?"

The countess realized that she was obeying his command. Her robe slipped to the floor from stiff fingers. Eldrich continued his circuit—he was beside her now.

He laughed again, as though genuinely amused. "I will tell you, Lady Chilton, you are the most amazing creation I have ever witnessed. I tip my hat to those responsible."

"My parents would be so pleased," she said, trying to control the anger she felt.

He laughed again. "Would they, indeed?" and this seemed to amuse him. "I am sorely tempted, Lady Chilton, even with what I know and as old as I am."

"Tempted by what?" she said, not liking the sound of this.

"By you, my dear."

"I will be the least cooperative partner you will ever have known."

"Oh, hardly," he said, clearly amused by this as well. "Some of the women I have known—" He took another step and came back into her line of vision, but still he was in shadow. "In days past people had more respect for mages." He almost sang a string of syllables, and perhaps moved his hand, and suddenly the countess felt such a wave of desire that her knees almost gave way beneath her. Not just a wave of desire, but desire for this man. It was an ache beyond enduring . . . and then, just as quickly it was gone.

"The most unwilling partner I've ever known? I don't think so." A hand reached out and moved the hair away from her cheek, pushing it back over her shoulder so that he could see her profile.

"I'm cold," she said quietly.

"Then come and sit by the fire," Eldrich said, and he turned and walked away.

The countess found that she could move again. The thought of running was quickly put aside. Clearly one could not run from a mage. Beyond the pillars a large hearth stood against the wall, and here a fire had burned to embers. As Eldrich came near, it flickered to life again, and then suddenly burst into flame—glorious, hot flames. The countess pulled on her robe and went toward the fire, trying to control her fear. Always best to show no fear—it gave the other person the impression that they were in control.

The mage had taken a seat in a high-backed chair, facing partly away from the fire. Only a cushioned footstool remained. She stood looking at it for a moment, and then remembered that he had said he was no gentleman.

Cold to the bone, she took the seat expected, though not without some anger. *I am almost sitting at his feet,* she thought. *And I'm sure he is enjoying it thoroughly.*

They sat in silence for a long moment. The countess could almost make out his features, but not quite, for he was still in shadow.

"Have you decided what you will do with me?" she asked suddenly, unable to bear his silent brooding on her a moment longer.

"It is not so simple as you might think. What is your purpose? That is what I must discover."

"My purpose? What in the world. . . ? I assure you that whatever my purpose might be, it has nothing to do with you, sir."

The mage did not respond. Silence stretched on until the countess could not stand it. She opened her mouth to speak.

"Be still," the mage said.

She realized that she sat with hands in her lap, like a schoolgirl, and she felt an anger burn up at this man before her.

"It is a great risk," the mage said softly.

"Pardon me?"

Eldrich rose suddenly and walked away from the fire out into the darkness. She could see him silhouetted in the light falling from above, though none of it seemed to reach him. He made no sound as he went. Slowly he paced in a small circle, like a man deep in contemplation, and occasionally he would stop and raise his head. The countess was sure that he looked at her at those moments. And then he began to mutter, words she had never heard, and a cold light moved across the floor in a precise line, following him as he walked.

Suddenly she was standing in the center of the rotunda, up on the balls of her feet, reaching toward the dome. Around her a pattern of lines and curves seemed to glow like the embers of a fire. She watched as they dimmed and died away, her mind so clouded that she could not remember how she got there, or what had happened.

"A work of astonishing craft," a musical voice said.

Suddenly she felt all her muscles relax, and she almost collapsed to the floor. The countess looked for the sound of the voice, and as her arms came about her in a natural gesture of protection, she realized she wore nothing at all.

"I cannot tell if they have underestimated me, or taken my measure exactly," Eldrich said, apparently speaking to himself. "Who in the world did this? Certainly not Medwar. It is the greatest mystery."

"If you have finished misusing me, perhaps I might have my clothes," the countess said bitterly.

"Are you cold?"

She realized that she was not. In fact, she was astonishingly warm. She almost glowed with warmth.

"Have you no concern for my modesty?"

"None. It is a strange vanity, I find."

The countess realized that her gown lay at her feet and she snatched it up. As she slid it over her head, she noticed that Eldrich stood, watching, and she tried to ignore him.

"Mr. Walky?" the mage said, and almost immediately footsteps echoed in the hall.

"Sir?"

"You may return her."

The little man came toward the countess, his manner very deferential, as though he would make up for his master's treatment of her.

The countess took a step and then stopped, turning to find the retreating form of Eldrich. "I do not think my friends will be much impressed with your manners when I tell them of our visit, Lord Eldrich."

The figure stopped. "I rather doubt you will tell them, Lady Chilton. The pleasures of the evening to you." He bowed deeply, and turned away.

"M'lady, you must come with me," the small man said.

"But who are you?"

"Walky, m'lady. Please, I'm to take you home."

"Are you not cold?"

Marianne found the countess seated by the large windows in the library. She was curled up in a chair, watching the morning light find its way into the small garden.

"Cold? No." The countess looked over at her friend and saw great concern on her face.

"You look perfectly awful," Marianne said disapprovingly. "I will tell you, Elaural, Skye is not worth this." She waved a hand at her friend. "Have you not slept at all?"

"It is very odd, Marianne. I woke here, yet I have no memory of coming down at all."

Marianne shook her head, her lips pressed tightly together in concern.

"And I think I had the most unsettling dreams, though I cannot quite recall them." She turned back to the garden for a moment, as though searching into her memory. "No. they are gone, though I have been left with the . . . feelings. And even those I cannot put a name to." She shivered involuntarily.

"You are cold."

"Not at all. Is it cool in here? I do not feel it."

"Perhaps you are coming down with a fever. The only time I recall walking in my sleep I was terribly fevered and delirious."

The countess smiled. "Well, I am neither fevered nor delirious. I feel perfectly hale, in fact." She stretched her arms over her head. "Is this unladylike?" she asked, her mood seeming to change.

"Entirely." Marianne rang for a servant and took a seat near the countess. "Is Skye coming to hear the results of your interview with Mr. Flattery?"

"I would think."

"But what did you learn? You are being a bit secretive about this."

"I learned only that Mr. Flattery agrees with Lord Skye. He thinks the writing on the Pelier is a script and language known to the mages. It also bears some resemblance to the writing on the Ruin of Farrow. He claims to know no more."

"And do you believe him?"

The countess shrugged.

"Now Elaural, I cannot imagine that he would keep anything from you if you exercised your charm on him."

"Then perhaps he really can't read it."

Marianne looked away. "I hope you will not perform such a service for Lord Skye again. I was rather shocked that he would ask it."

"I offered, Marianne."

"Well, he should have refused."

"For a woman who has rejected so many of our social values, I think you are rather old-fashioned occasionally."

Marianne shook her head in denial. "Oh, it is not this thing of gentlemen should or should not do this or that. But to ask you to be duplicitous . . . I will tell you, I thought it rather reprehensible."

"Well, I was not nearly so cunning. I was completely forthcoming with Mr. Flattery. I told him what I wanted of him and even that it was Skye had put me up to it. So you see, there was very little duplicity involved."

Marianne looked at her oddly. "Where is all this going, Elaural?" she said softly.

"Whatever do you mean?" the countess asked, though she was afraid she knew very well what was meant.

Chapter Twenty

CAPTAIN James looked into his brandy snifter, then back to his cards. "I think I shall have to resign," he said to his companion.

"Resign? And not give me a chance to retrieve my losses? Is that sporting?" Wilkes was a little inebriated, slurring his words noticeably, though he showed very little sign of his state beyond that.

"There is always tomorrow, Wilkes."

"So they say, though I've known men who've proved that wrong, not that they lived to brag about it."

James smiled. "Not an accomplishment that I personally aspire to." He tossed his cards down on the table and pulled out his timepiece. It was almost midnight, not late, really, though these past few years it had begun to seem so.

Wilkes sloshed more brandy into their snifters, and though his hand was not perfectly steady, his concentration was such that he did not spill a drop. "The King's health," he said, raising his glass.

"We've already drunk His Majesty's health twice this night."

"Well then, to our health. Damn the King."

"Ah, there's a toast for you."

Wilkes replaced his glass heavily on the table. "Can you imagine having such a woman pursuing you and choosing to sleep alone?" Wilkes said, shaking his head in disgust. "'Tis not fair."

It was the litany of the evening. Skye had gone off to the house in which he stayed, not even visiting the Countess of Chilton. James wondered if it was possible that the information from the countess' maid was not accurate. Wilkes had applied some of his abundant charm and a handful of coins to the problem and managed to learn much from the countess' servant. Most astonishing of all was that the countess was in love with the Earl of Skye who seemed hardly aware of her.

James shook his head. *Savants,* he thought. *They live too much in the rarified world of the intellect. Poor bastards.*

"I will relieve Lieutenant Darby tonight," James said. "I cannot sleep."

"Are you sure? 'Tis my watch."

"I'm sure." He stretched. "The excitement of taking all your money will not let me sleep. I must plan what I will do with such a fortune."

"Well, that's all right, then," Wilkes said, pulling a chair over and putting his feet up, clearly ready for leisure. "I'll relieve you at eight bells. You know where to find me if I'm needed. I'll tell you, if I were the earl, you'd know where to find me—in the sleeping chamber of a certain lady, make no mistake." He thought a moment. "How in Farrelle's name can he be considered such a great genius?"

"The laws of motion, the invention of the cannon, various arithmetical discoveries that I don't understand, the alloying of metals, improvements to the telescope. He even invented a better water closet. And that is only a partial list of his accomplishments. Perhaps the earl simply does not fancy the countess. He has certainly been with other women, by all accounts."

"Well, I think he's the greatest fool of a genius who ever lived!" Wilkes pronounced. "And I think this is all a fool's errand we're on. The man is a loyal subject of the King. There is no doubt of it. We should be at sea, James. Not stuck in this fool's town where the rich come with their pissing little complaints. Flames, but I hate this duty."

James shrugged and broke into a grin. "It is for the betterment of your character, Wilkes. And to keep you from trouble while you are landbound." He rose suddenly. "I must be off. Poor Darby will be asleep at the wheel by now. Till eight bells, then." He pulled on his great coat, checking the pocket for his gloves, for it was cool in the hills yet.

Darby was standing in the shadows of a small common across from the house where Skye stayed.

"All's well, sir," the lieutenant reported. "No lights, no one has come or gone. Where's Wilkes? I thought he had the next watch?"

"We've traded." James looked at the house across the street. "There has been a light in that window all evening?"

"Yes, sir, though there is no sign of movement within. A night light, I think."

James nodded. "All right, lieutenant. You're relieved."

"Pleasures of the evening to you, sir."

"And to you, Darby."

James took up his place in the shadow, leaning against the tree. He was mostly screened from the street by shrubbery, but he still worried about being seen. It was a small town, and it would soon get around if anyone realized that Lord Skye's house was being watched. But they could not let a room or even a house that afforded a view of the earl's home, so this was all they could do: stand in the dark and hope not to be seen.

There was little doubt in James' mind that they would eventually arouse suspicions in such a town—where everyone was interested in everyone else's business, for there was hardly another form of amusement.

James rocked from foot to foot, wishing that he could sit down at least. He would begin to pace soon, he could not help it. He was as impatient with this duty as Wilkes, though he did more to hide it. Unlike his friend, he had more information about what had gone on. Better Wilkes did not know. Sailors, even officers, were a superstitious lot, and any mention of mages would have driven Wilkes to the bottle with greater frequency than he visited it now. No, better to keep quiet about the admiral's real concerns.

Let this have nothing to do with Eldrich, James prayed silently, *or the arts in any way.*

He stared up at the windows and sighed unintentionally.

The truth was that he would have preferred to be as innocent of the truth as Wilkes and Darby. Unfortunately he had been one of the first to speak with Abel Ransom and the harlot. The worst of it was he believed they were telling the truth, and so did the Sea Lord.

Something damned odd was going on, that was certain.

"And what does the great Skye do that so interests you?" a woman's voice came from behind.

James whirled around. "What's that?" He could just make out the form of a woman standing in the shadows.

"I asked what the great Skye does that so interests you?" she said again, a little laughter in her voice. She did not seem the least uncomfortable standing here in the darkness with a strange man.

"I am merely taking the air, ma'am."

"As was your friend before you, and the gentleman before that. But that was you, wasn't it? Let me see, that would mean that Wilkes is in his cups and you have replaced him. Very dedicated of you, Captain James. The Admiralty will no doubt be grateful."

"I seem to be at a disadvantage, ma'am, for you know my name and business, but I do not know yours."

She took a step in his direction, enabling him to just make out her long coat and hat. She was dressed as a lady and certainly spoke like one.

"It is I who am at a disadvantage, sir, alone with you in the darkness. I'm sure if I cried out, no one would hear."

James did not quite know what to answer and she laughed at his awkwardness.

"You may call me Miss Fielding, Captain James, if you wish."

"Miss Fielding. What is it you want here?"

"Well, that is difficult to explain. I suppose the truth is that I wish answers to a few simple questions, but then you might take that wrongly."

He thought he heard her whisper, and in the shadow she seemed to be moving her hands, as though she wound a ball of invisible yarn.

"But I do think it would be a good idea if you were to come away from that tree. You're rather too close to the road and can be seen."

"I'm standing in complete darkness. No one can see me, I assure you."

"Well, that is not entirely true. I can see you perfectly. But indulge me, come back into the park a little farther. I give you my word that I will not harm you."

James heard himself snort. It was an old trick; send a woman to lure a man back into an alley and then—But this woman was a lady, not the usual sort to indulge in such behavior. What in the world was she doing here? Watching Skye as he was? The thought that she might be a servant of Eldrich occurred to him, and he froze in place. No, impossible, she was a barely more than a girl. Some admirer of Skye was more likely.

"I am happy here, I think," he said.

This answer did not please her, and she fell silent, perhaps wondering what she could say to convince him. "Were you among the gentlemen who invaded the rooms of Samual Hayes in Paradise Street?"

"I don't know to what you refer," he said evenly, deciding that this situation was not at all to his liking. She could not be so at ease and be alone. He glanced quickly back to the street, but it remained empty.

"In fact, you do. It is very difficult to lie to me, Captain James." She paused and he thought he heard her sigh. "What is said of the men who were surprised there?"

"What is it you want of me, Miss?" James countered.

He could almost feel her gaze on him in the darkness, as though she contemplated him. "I am not actually sure. You see, I fear you have information that might endanger me and what I do. I would rather that did not happen. What to do with you is what concerns me now."

She stepped forward suddenly, into the moonlight, and James saw that she was young, but faded, somehow, as though she had survived trials that had aged her terribly. He felt an unexpected wave of pity for her.

"Come away from the street, please. I do not have large, pugilistic men hidden in the shrubbery. If anything, I should be afraid of you. But I am willing to trust you if you will do the same."

"What is Skye to you?" James asked.

She sighed, looking off down the street and then toward the house. "It is a tale too long to be told now. Let me say that my purpose is not in conflict with your own. Please," she reached out and took his arm.

"I'm afraid, Miss Fielding, that I cannot cooperate," he took hold of her wrist. "But you will answer my questions, or you will find yourself in a situation not to your liking. What is Skye to you, and why do you care about the men found in Paradise Street?"

James heard her mumble something and reach out toward his face with her free hand. His vision clouded oddly, and he wavered. The park went suddenly dark and he felt himself falling. Someone caught him, someone soft who smelled of perfume.

"It was necessary," the woman said. "As you know there are limits to what I can do in a given situation."

James felt a cool hand on his forehead.

"I think it was a mistake," a masculine voice said. "We should do nothing more that might draw any attention. We have taken too many chances as it is. Far too many."

There were several people in the room, James thought. Mostly men. He could smell tobacco from their clothing and wine on their breath.

"What will we do with him now?" It was a third voice, another man. This one spoke very slowly.

There was no answer immediately, and James did not like the sound of that.

"Captain James?" the woman who had called herself Miss Fielding said. "You are conscious—it is obvious."

"I cannot see."

"You are in a darkened room, Captain James, but you are unharmed. There are four of you watching Skye, is that correct?"

"Yes," he answered though he had not meant to. Certainly this kind woman meant him no harm. There was no reason to keep secrets from her.

"Do you know why you have been assigned this duty? Was it the Sea Lord sent you?"

"Yes, Sir Joseph. He thinks that someone practices the arts openly once again."

A protracted silence. James heard the scraping of feet on wood as people shifted slightly.

"And who does he think this practitioner of the arts might be?"

"Eldrich," James said. "Though he has not ruled out . . . other possibilities."

"Meaning?"

"There is another mage of whom nothing is known."

Someone cursed under their breath.

"Who has set out to ruin Skye?" the old man asked. "Certainly Brookes did not do this on his own."

"Moncrief," James said without hesitation. "Moncrief hates Skye."

"And your only reason for being here is to watch Lord Skye?"

"No. . . . We are on the lookout for others."

"Who? Speak up, man."

"Two young men named Kehler and Hayes . . . and Erasmus Flattery."

No sound again. Someone cleared his throat.

"What has led Sir Joseph to believe the arts are involved?" Miss Fielding asked.

"I—I was not present, but it is said that the officers who searched for Samual Hayes surprised some others there before them, and these men leaped from the window, apparently coming to no harm."

"And who were these people?" the one with the old voice asked.

"No one knows."

"Well, we have that to be thankful for," a younger man said.

"Is there anything else that has made the Sea Lord suspicious?"

"A sailor and his girl saw two gentlemen bring a woman to the harbor. Without coercion or a word of protest she leaped into the water and drowned."

James heard the sounds of people shifting again. It occurred to him that he should not be answering questions as he was, but they seemed so kind, so trustworthy.

"It is worse than I'd hoped," the old man said, his voice trembling with fear or anger. "Far worse. Anthing we do now to disguise our involvement can only make matters worse."

James heard the woman draw in a sharp breath. Fear. He could sense fear in this room.

"What do we do with this one?"

"He is a danger to us," the old man said, his voice slow and devoid of warmth.

"It's too late to do anything about that. This goes up to the Sea Lord and Moncrief. Too late to put a stop to it with the likes of Captain James. No, send him back to his duty, that is all we can do."

"We could put him to work for us, at least," Miss Fielding said.

"No," the old man said. "It is out of the question. Eldrich would see our marks upon him in an instant. Even this is too much. If Eldrich finds him, he will know immediately."

"It is too late to worry about that. We must trust the vision now. But I was not intending to use those arts upon him. No, leave the good captain to me. Better he watches these others than we do it ourselves." She touched him; he was certain it must be her. A light hand on his head. "We are gathering here—all the players—and each will have a part. That is what our visions have taught us. Everyone will have a purpose. Perhaps even this poor sailor. Perhaps even these two boys who follow Skye so blindly."

Chapter Twenty-one

KEHLER climbed slowly down the drop, trying to stay clear of the spray from the falls, while Hayes leaned out as far as he dared, holding the lantern to try to give his companion light.

"It is not so difficult—if one could but see," Kehler called up.

They were in a large passage, almost round and fifty feet in diameter, that sloped down noticeably. Occasionally the floor almost leveled and then dropped a few feet, though never more than seven or eight and usually less.

Hayes leaned out a little farther, holding the lantern in a rapidly-tiring arm, and fought to ignore the muscles' complaints. He was stiff and sore as he could not remember being in years. His knees were tender from the long crawl, and his arms and shoulders ached so badly that it hurt terribly to carry his pack. Yet he did not really seem to mind. The cave was so incredible, so unlike anything he had ever seen, that he barely complained, and when he did, it was with a bit of laughter.

Suddenly there was a scraping of boots on stone, and Kehler shot down, landing and rolling backward.

"Are you hurt?" Hayes asked as his friend came to rest on his back.

"Oh, hardly," Kehler said with apparent disgust. "Ass over tea kettle, I think that particular drill is called. Very gymnastic, didn't you think?" He rolled over and pushed himself up stiffly, pulling off his pack and letting it fall to the rock. Bending over the stream of running water, he washed his now red face.

"Send me down the lantern," he said, "and your pack as well."

A moment later Hayes was standing beside his companion and they both hoisted their packs.

"I don't think it can be far now, though I am not so sure that the distances on our survey are really in proportion to reality. I think these passages were measured by men with vastly differing strides, that is what I believe."

They set off again, climbing down beside the falling stream, which followed its own meandering channel more or less in the center of the passage. Here and there they were forced to cross over to find dry rock on which to walk, and invariably this led to one of them soaking a boot yet again. They hardly cared now. Their clothing was soiled and torn, the leather of their boots scuffed and soaked through, and they were both in need of a bath, but it did not matter. It would not have been an adventure otherwise.

"One cannot adventure from one's easy chair," Kehler had said, and they had laughed, saying of the less difficult sections, "a veritable easy chair, that."

"I think the passage is opening a bit," Hayes offered, and in a few minutes he was proven right.

Suddenly they stepped out into a vast chamber, larger than any they had so far seen. Before them lay the dark waters of a lake. The lantern lit the far reaches of the cavern only dimly, but even so Hayes could see great stalactites and columns and formations called curtains, as well as moonstone, the flowing white substance from which the decorations in whitestone caves were formed.

The hollow sound of water tumbling into the lake seemed unnaturally loud and clear. Even though Hayes knew they were far from being the first to discover this place, it still seemed a deep wonder, hidden away, here, far beneath the surface of the world. *A lake,* at once familiar and strangely alien.

"The chamber of the mirror," Kehler said, taking up the lantern and going to the water's edge. Hayes joined him, and they both stared down at their murky reflections in the dark water. Two unkempt young men, their faces ruddy from exertion and adventure.

"I can't believe you forgot the shaving kit," Kehler said.

"Or the servants to tend our clothes and groom our wigs. Yours looks a bit shabby, I will tell you."

As if to reinforce the strangeness of the place, Hayes realized there was a bright blue skiff perched awkwardly on the rocks thirty feet away.

"Where in the world did that come from?"

Kehler laughed. "I thought that might surprise you. I'm relieved it's here. Some enterprising individuals brought it down here in pieces and built it in place, if you can believe it. In fact, there are two of them, one at the lake's far end, or so I hope. It is understood that we will take this to the far end, then use the other to return it, thus always keeping a skiff at either extreme of the lake."

Hayes lowered his pack to the cavern's floor and sat down on it, having realized that it was much softer than even the most malleable rock. "Do we go by boat, then?"

"Only a short way, and then I'm afraid it's back to our poor battered limbs—all four of them in places."

"Well, I thought it had become a bit easy. Don't want to grow soft, do we?"

They sat staring at the scene in wonder, pointing out the formations that caught their eye. Hayes trimmed the lantern wick and turned it up as high as he could, casting light out over the lake, though it did not reach the far shore.

"Pelier didn't paint this, I take it?" Hayes asked, and received a shake of the head in reply. He had begun to wonder if Kehler was right in his assertion that what lay ahead to be discovered would bring them fame and, even better, fortune. It seemed entirely possible that he was merely helping Kehler pursue his obsession, though he had to admit that so far it had been an experience well worth the effort, although he shuddered when he thought of the claustrophobia of the crawl. Occasionally he felt some anxiety when he remembered that he would have to pass back through that terrible passage.

"Do you still feel as confident of finding what we seek, now that you've seen the complexity of this cavern?"

Kehler nodded his head. "We must find it," he said quietly. Then he stood up quickly. "Well, help me with this skiff, and we will see if it still floats. I can't imagine who would leave it high and dry like this. The seams are bound to be open, at least a little."

They shifted the tiny craft down the rocks, careful not to scrape or bang it, for the boat was so lightly constructed that it would not stand misuse.

"I hardly think a boat this small will float the two of us," Hayes said, "it is barely as long as I am tall."

They loaded their two packs in, released the oars from their ties and stepped gingerly aboard. When they took their places on the seats at either end, the boat sank in the water until only a few inches of freeboard remained.

Hayes shipped the oars, careful not to make any movement that would unbalance them. "I hope a wind doesn't come up. Our ship will hardly stand any kind of sea."

He dug the oars into the still water and turned the cockleshell boat out into the subterranean lake. With Kehler in the bow holding the lantern aloft, and occasionally bailing, Hayes rowed fisherman style, facing the direction they traveled, and gazed in wonder at the cave.

The decorations were astounding and some of the columns and curtains were on a grand scale—thirty and forty feet tall from floor to ceiling—rising up like fantastic castles of ice. The dome of the chamber itself was lost in the darkness, though from the slope of the ceiling at the edges Hayes guessed it to be sixty feet.

Kehler waved the lantern at one of the largest columns. "Imagine how long it took for that to form. Thousand of years, certainly. Long before men came to Farrland, this great column might have already spanned from floor to ceiling."

"How old does that make the cavern, I wonder?" Hayes answered. They rowed on, their eyes feasting on the wonders of the chamber of the mirror: moonstone, like glacial milk, flowing over the surface of the parent rock, almost translucent, glistening in the lamplight.

"Surely it was worth all of our efforts and the ruin of our clothing to see this," Kehler said.

"Yes. I wish I were an artist, for I haven't the skill with words to describe it."

A small stream appeared from a side passage and added its water to the mirror. The lake opened up so that, for a time, they could see no shoreline, and small headlands began to appear, like the great capes of the world seen from afar. When the shore appeared again, they noted several passages of differing sizes in the walls, and, in one place, a ribbon of water fell from an opening in the ceiling. They rowed once around this in astonishment before continuing on.

Hayes could not believe the length of the chamber, but when they came to what they thought was the end, it proved to be only a narrowing. From either side a small peninsula jutted out, creating a pass no more than a dozen feet in breadth. On one headland a rock incisor was topped by a white column perhaps three feet across its base with a fine tracery of flowing drape running down from the sloping ceiling.

"Magical," Kehler whispered. "I feel like we have entered the kingdom of men who dwell beneath the mountain. A race that have chiseled and inscribed and sculpted for millennia, though now they are gone and their dark world lies abandoned."

They quickly crossed this final arm of the lake, which was more like a small bay, and found the second boat pulled up onto a shelf of stone. The stream disappeared into a passage here, and the sound of water falling could be heard.

They managed to land without tipping, and Kehler immediately began dragging the boat up behind them.

"We have to return that to the lake's end," Hayes reminded him

His friend stood up, his manner suddenly serious. "I have been thinking that we should leave this skiff here. Do you remember that Clarendon said Demon Rose was asking after me in Castlebough? And the guide who brought us here will certainly not keep our presence a secret, especially if he is offered a few coins. I don't want to suddenly find we have company on our quest."

"But is that safe?" Hayes asked, looking back out over the dark water. "What if we are injured or lost."

"With a little luck we'll be back before anyone becomes concerned. The Farrellites are not pleased with me, Samual. I can't imagine that Rose is going to come down here after me, but the church has long been skilled at using others. I don't think that it is a great risk to keep this boat here for the next day or two. The cave is not visited often until the lower entrances open in summer when the water level is lower. Anyone else venturing in here now would be after us, I fear."

Hayes nodded. He was tempted to admit that he had left a note for Erasmus, but decided against it. Kehler would likely be furious, afraid somehow that Erasmus would reveal this knowledge to Deacon Rose, though clearly that was unlikely.

"Let's eat a bite and then go on. At our present speed we might be at our destination yet this day. Is it past noon?"

Hayes found his watch. "Good guess. Twenty past."

They made a silent dinner on the shore of the lake. Hayes felt a little guilty that he had betrayed Kehler's trust by telling Erasmus, and at the same time he was annoyed that Kehler would not return one boat to the far shore. If some misfortune befell them, reaching them would be difficult in the extreme.

After their silent meal they took to the new passage, leaving the chamber of the mirror with great regret, and followed the underground river that drained the lake. The flow of water was strong here and had cut a deep channel in a soft vein of rock. The going was comparatively easy, and they made good time, saving their breath for their efforts.

Hayes wondered what Kehler was thinking. Was his mind completely focused on their goal, or was he really worried about the priest who apparently pursued him? Hayes could not shake the feeling that Kehler had not yet told him the whole story, as though afraid that he might not continue if he knew the truth. And Hayes was not sure that his friend wasn't right in this. What were they searching for? Kehler's belief that it was lost knowledge was, at best, a guess.

Whenever Hayes asked himself this question, he thought of a small boy, trapped in a tiny hole in the stone, impossibly far from any comfort—and that small boy was somehow Hayes.

The passage proceeded to drop and twist its way down, like a bowel, Hayes thought. After an hour the sound of falling water grew to the point where they would have needed to shout to be heard, had they talked.

Finally they were forced to wade into the rushing water, though the stream had widened and was barely two feet deep. They moved slowly, placing their feet with care, and finally came to the lip of a falls. A small dike of rocks, like jagged teeth, raked the water as it plunged out of sight. Warily they moved to the very edge, holding the lantern out so that they could look down. A chaos of white water disappeared down a large well, twenty feet across, but they could see no bottom. Hayes felt the pull of the water's movement, drawn mysteriously to the darkness.

The way, by darkness, into light.

"How far is it?" Hayes asked, stepping back, a little breathless.

"To the bottom? I forget what I read. A hundred and fifty feet? Something on that order. Farther than one would want to fall, that is certain."

"But where do we go?"

Kehler pointed out over the falls, and up the right-hand wall Hayes could see only a dark shadow on the stone.

"That is a passage?"

Kehler nodded.

"But how do we get there?" Hayes looked down again, a sudden feeling that the motion of frigid, coursing water flowed through him.

"It is not so hard as it looks, apparently. There is supposed to be good footing, and as they always say, the trick is not to look down. We will use the rope. I will try it first, if you like."

"No," Hayes said quickly. "You have gone first too often. I will take my turn." He felt a chill run through him as he spoke, a sudden weakening of both his will and his limbs. He glanced down again, wondering how many men had stared into their own, freshly-dug grave.

Kehler balanced the lantern on a high shelf, so that both of his hands were free, and then tied the rope around his waist, making a loop of one end and throwing this over a tooth of rock at the fall's edge. The other end was made fast around Hayes' middle, then Kehler fed the rope out slowly, snugging it around his own waist in the way of mountaineers.

"Have you climbed at all?" Kehler asked.

Hayes shook his head, looking out at the route he must take.

"Nor have I, but I have a friend who is something of a fanatic about it. He told me that the trick is to keep your body away from the rock wall. You must maintain your weight over your feet. Do you see what I mean? If you lean into the cliff like this, you force your feet out and they can slip much more easily. Are you ready?"

"No. But I shall not become so with time. Weight out over my feet," he repeated, and went to the edge. His leather soles would be impossibly slippery, he realized, and elected to remove his boots and go on in stocking feet.

Balancing on the corner of the falls, Hayes looked down for the briefest second and felt his balance waver. Automatically he grabbed the wall for balance.

"Flames," he heard himself whisper.

"Easy on, Hayes," Kehler said.

Gathering his resolve, Hayes stared out at the rock and tried to pick his route to the opening. He stepped out onto a foothold and found to his relief that it was quite large and the wall was not as vertical as it looked.

The sound of the falls changed as he moved, and he could hear the frightening cascade falling into the dark well beneath him. He tried not to think about what a slip would mean. Another step onto a smaller foothold.

"Keep your weight out, Hayes," Kehler reminded him, and he tried to comply, though he felt that he was leaning out dangerously far and feared the weight of his pack might suddenly drag him back.

He searched for another place to move his foot, and for handholds, reaching out and testing the rock, which all seemed sound, if a bit too smooth. He took a larger step this time, up and out to his left, pulling on a good handhold. And there he stood, looking for a way to go on. A small platform a foot or so square was not far off, but he certainly could not reach it in one step, and perhaps not even in two.

"Can you see the route?" Kehler called over the sound of the falls.

Hayes shook his head. "There are no handholds and the footholds seem too small—barely toeholds, in fact." He felt panic begin to grow in him, and he glanced back. He seemed already to have come impossibly far. The safety of the lip of the falls seemed too far away, he was not sure he could get back without falling.

Hayes felt his leg begin to quiver, perched as he was on such a tiny hold, the muscles rigid. Suddenly the rock all looked impossibly smooth and slippery. The sound of tumbling water seemed to grow louder, reverberating inside his chest, as though making him part of it.

"Hayes? Either come back or go on, but don't stand there! Your leg is trembling, I can see it. Come back and let me try."

"Martyr's blood, there is nowhere for me to go." Hayes looked back but could not see the footholds he had used to get this far. His fingers began to cramp where he clung to the stone, and he realized that in a few seconds he would fall.

"Take hold of yourself, Hayes!" Kehler said, his voice rising.

Hayes saw Kehler sit down in the rushing water and brace his feet against the rock, readying himself for the coming fall.

I cannot fall, Hayes said to himself. *If I fall, even if the rope holds me, I don't know how I will ever get back up again. I must not fall!*

He looked desperately at the small platform that seemed so far away. There were two impossibly small toeholds between where he was and the comparative safety of the platform, but he could see nowhere for his hands. If he could only land on the toeholds lightly and pass on, perhaps. . . .

"Give me slack, Kehler," he called out, and felt the rope release its pressure.

Realizing that his shaking legs were about to fail, Hayes focused on the possible holds, forced his legs to be still, and then stepped quickly onward. One toehold came under foot, and he brought his other foot onto it, feeling the tiny ledge with only three of his toes. His hands found no purchase and he could use them only for balance. He moved again, setting his left foot on a hold equally precarious. He brought his other foot inside this, and passed on, almost leaping onto the platform.

It seemed a dance floor when he stood there. Impossibly large. He felt he could perform a jig there without fear of falling.

"Well done!" Kehler called out.

Hayes stood, catching his breath, nodding to acknowledge his friend's support, unable to speak.

He glanced up at the opening. Ten feet to go, but the way looked comparatively easy—almost a staircase.

"Are you all right there?" Kehler called.

"Yes. . . . Yes. I'll go on in a moment. The way looks easier now." He felt himself smile with relief.

A moment of rest and relative security helped him immeasurably, and his confidence was somewhat restored by what he had done. He caught his breath, and then examined the rock before him.

"I'm ready to go on," Hayes alerted his friend, and then went deliberately out, picking his footing carefully, feeling the cold rock beneath his stocking feet. Three or four minutes of intense concentration, thinking of nothing but where to place his feet and hands, and how to move, and he pulled himself up into the passageway. The light was not good here, but he felt around and found a place for his pack. Kehler sent the lantern over, and to his dismay discovered that he now had very poor light for climbing.

After a moment of standing and shivering, he found a candle in his pack which he could not light with a flint, and so the lantern was sent out over the falls again, swinging on the rope. Kehler lit his candle and sent the lantern back yet again. They managed to bash it into the rock as it came near to Hayes, but miraculously the glass chimney did not shatter.

Holding the stub of the candle in his mouth so that the flame wavered six inches before his face, Kehler stepped out onto the stone.

Hayes had tied himself to a horn of rock and kept a tight rein on his companion, but even so he worried. He was not sure that he could hold Kehler should he fall.

Fortunately, Kehler seemed more confident than Hayes had, no doubt helped by seeing that the climb could be done, but he was shivering visibly from having sat down in the icy waters. Even at a distance Hayes could see his hands shaking as he tried to grip the rock.

"Keep the rope snug," Kehler called out suddenly, his words distorted by the candle in his mouth. He had come to the place where Hayes had nearly lost his nerve altogether. Here he paused, too, though perhaps more to draw on his physical reserves. He shifted his weight to one side and accidently stubbed out the candle against the rock.

"Martyr's blood!" he swore around the candle, then spit it out, letting it fall into the void below.

"Can you see at all?" Hayes called out over the chaos of the waterfall.

"Barely, and if I stand here and let my eyes adjust to the darkness, I shall certainly fall. I'm trembling like a leaf in the wind as it is." A silence ensued in which Hayes could feel the fear growing.

"Hayes? Can you tie the rope off? I can't go on without light. You'll have to tie the rope off and hold the light out so I can see. Can you do that?"

Hayes did not like the sound of that. If he tied the rope as it was, Kehler would create slack when he moved on. If he did fall, he would hit the end of this slack and almost certainly part the rope.

"I'm not so sure this is a good idea, Kehler. Can't you see at all?"

"No. I must have light, and quickly. My legs are shaking so violently that I'm sure to fall at any moment. Please, Hayes, do as I ask!"

Reluctantly Hayes tied the rope over the horn of rock, but kept his own line about his waist so that he could lean out as far as possible with the light in his hand.

He swept up the light and crawled to the very lip of the passage. Taking hold of the rope in his free hand, he leaned out over the abyss and stretched the lantern out precariously. The sound of water was suddenly very loud.

"Flames!" he heard himself say. "Bloody blood and flames."

Feeling utterly helpless, he watched his friend who stood shaking on the rock. Hayes was almost certain that Kehler would fall, when suddenly he reached out with a hand, and then swung his foot onto a toehold. Just as he positioned his weight over his foot he slipped, and for a second clung to the rock with his hands, flailing for a foothold, and then, mercifully, he was back on the rock, gasping like a consumptive, though it was from fear.

Hayes could hear him muttering, cursing under his breath.

"Keep your body away from the rock, Kehler, or that will happen again."

He saw his companion nod, then push himself out a bit, though still not far enough, Hayes thought. Kehler took a second to collect himself and then moved on, with exaggerated care this time. Another step, and then he was on the platform.

"'Tis child's play from there," Hayes called out. "A regular easy chair of a climb, I would call it."

Kehler could not even manage a smile in response. His face was drawn and white, his whole manner grim, though more determined now. A moment more and he joined a relieved Hayes in the mouth of the passage.

"Are you shaking from fright or cold?"

"Both, I confess," Kehler said. "I must find some dry clothes immediately.

Hayes had to help his friend into dry clothes, for his hands were not functioning properly, and he also made Kehler take his coat which was warm from his own body's heat. Using his previous trick, he made something resembling tea over the lantern flame and this seemed to help. Even so it was a good hour before Kehler was warmed sufficiently.

They ate there, on their balcony overlooking the falls, and drank a second cup of the warmed tea.

"I think we must go on," Kehler said. He had stopped trembling and regained some of the color in his face, though he hardly looked well. Hayes was sure that Kehler needed a night's sleep in a warm bed, and then a day's rest. But nothing even remotely like that was possible here. They could either go on or go back: those were their choices.

Hayes helped his friend shoulder his pack, and then raised his own. Taking the lantern, he set off, keeping his pace moderate. The passage they were in now suffered from a low ceiling, and in places they had to crouch, but it was ten feet wide and Hayes was relieved when it did not seem inclined to shrink any more.

"We are going up," Hayes said suddenly. After descending since entering the cave, they were suddenly ascending.

"Yes, this part of the cave drains down this passage when the water is high, and down into several other passages the rest of the year. It is almost a separate sytem. As far as anyone knows, this is the only link between the two sections of the cave, and another entrance has yet to be found. We are into the remote parts of the cave now. Few venture beyond the falls, for that traverse we just managed stops all but the brave and the foolish."

"We are the latter, I take it?"

"Well, I certainly was not feeling terribly brave, hanging out there over the falls. I could think of nothing but falling into that pit, and being swept down into the deep channels below the mountain. I think I shall have nightmares of it for the rest of my days."

A trickle of water ran in this passage, and occasionally they would find small pools of perfectly clear water. In one place they were forced to climb up a fifteen-foot face, but this hardly slowed them after what they had just managed.

"I should think that any fear you have of Deacon Rose sending his minions after you should be put to rest now. They would have to walk across the lake of the mirror and brave the traverse above the falls. I think we can safely say we are beyond their reach now."

Kehler nodded, but he did not respond. Obviously he was not as confident as his friend, which surprised him a little.

Chapter Twenty-two

ERASMUS awoke to a sound, not sure what it was. A scratching at the door and sniffing.

The dream, he thought. *The wolf at the door.* He rolled over and closed his eyes, bringing up a mental picture of the countess: something to drive the feelings of the dream away.

A soft knock.

Erasmus sat up.

A knock again.

Who in this round world? he thought, but got quickly out of bed. Perhaps it was someone with word of Hayes and Kehler. Blood and flames, he hoped they had not met with misadventure.

He threw on a robe and unbolted the door, opening it a crack. There in the dim hallway stood a small, round man, unfamiliar at first, but there was something about him. . . .

"Martyr's blood! Mr. Walky?"

"Ah, you've not forgotten me, my young lion," the man whispered. "Now, let me in, if you please."

Erasmus threw open the door, and Walky entered the room, almost an apparition in the starlight.

"I have never been more surprised by a visitor in my life," Erasmus began, both overjoyed to see the man, and apprehensive. Why, after all these years, would Eldrich's servant appear? Perhaps the question was written clearly on his face.

"I have come to fetch you," Walky said, a bit of apology in his voice.

"Ah." Erasmus felt something like dread growing in him. "What does he want, Mr. Walky?" he asked, his mouth quickly drying.

The little man shrugged. "Only the mage knows," he said, and tried to smile reassuringly. "Dress quickly, he has not grown in patience since your last meeting."

Erasmus nodded and began to pull on clothes.

A carriage awaited them in the street, drawn up in the shadow of a building.

After traveling a block in silence, Erasmus spoke. "You are well, I hope?" though it was not the question he wanted to ask.

"Yes, of course. How could I not be?"

The old man, who must be very old now, hardly seemed to have aged. His hair, what little there was of it, had been white those twenty years ago, and in the poor light his face did not appear more creased. Twenty years. . . .

"Do you still teach the young gentlemen?" Erasmus asked, trying to think of some way of hinting toward the events of the past, perhaps to see if Walky shied away from the subject.

"There have been no young gentlemen since your day, sir. I tend the garden now, and do the mage's bidding."

The slow clatter of iron-shod wheels and horses' hooves echoed among the houses—the hard sounds unable to penetrate stone.

"I don't think he means you harm, sir," Walky said suddenly, his manner reassuring.

"No? No, I suppose he wouldn't."

The carriage rattled on, climbing slowly up the switchback road. Erasmus shut his eyes for a moment and saw his last meeting with Eldrich, and Percy. Exerting all his considerable will, he tried to force the image from his mind. *Percy. . . .*

"We are almost there, sir," Walky said, pulling Erasmus from his thoughts. "Mr. Flattery? I know you have grown and become a man among men. . . . But to the earl, the greatest man in Farrland does not impress him overly. It would be best to remember that. He has no tolerance for pride among men."

Good old Walky. Even after all these years he was concerned

for his charges. Had this concern only manifested itself a little more effectively all those years ago. . . .

They pulled up under the roof of a carriage entrance, and a silent footman lowered the step.

"Where are we?"

"You don't know? This is the house of the priest, Baumgere. He is waiting here."

Walky led Erasmus into the old mansion, and as they passed through the dimly lit entrance way, Erasmus realized another man emerged just behind them, led out to the waiting carriage.

It could not have been, Erasmus thought. It must have been a trick of starlight, for he thought he had seen a head of silver hair—like Skye—but it could not have been.

They made their way down hallways lit only occasionally by candles and finally into a rotunda, beneath a dome of stained glass, Erasmus thought, for a pattern seemed to fall upon the floor, like the imprint of wet leaves on a walkway.

When he looked down again, he realized that Walky had retreated back through the door. The room was almost entirely dark, and Erasmus felt his apprehension grow.

"You have nothing to fear," came the voice that he would never forget—musical yet entirely lacking in human warmth. Not the voice of a man at all.

"Lord Eldrich?"

"Yes, come forward, man. If I'd meant you harm I would have done it long ago."

But you did, Erasmus thought. He stepped forward, his hand out before him like a blind man. A fire flared up across the room, causing him to step back. He thought he heard a chuckle in the darkness.

Remembering Walky's warning, he went forward quickly. He found Lord Eldrich sprawled in a chair near the hearth. Erasmus had forgotten how tall the mage was.

He had also forgotten the man's presence. There was not a lord who could equal it. Eldrich was a man who knew his place, utterly. There was no mistake. Nor was there any mistaking what Eldrich thought of others: mere men, hardly worth his time.

"Sit down, Erasmus," Eldrich said, his voice almost soft, though still devoid of warmth. "So this is what became of you. . . ." He fixed a disinterested gaze on his former charge.

Erasmus could just make out the man, his dark hair framing a thin face, always terribly white as though he did not care for the sun. Thin lips, and a sharp nose - almost raptorlike, Erasmus thought. A hunting falcon, with all-seeing eyes and no remorse.

"It has been how long?"

"About twenty years, sir."

"Really. Time . . . it speaks to me so little. Servants die. I hear rumors that there is a new King. Friends . . . they've been gone these many years now." He shook his head a little sadly, a little confused, as though not sure how these things had come to pass. "And you have grown to manhood, and some prominence, I understand. Walky takes great pride in your accomplishments." He smiled, though it was not a smile of affection—more of amusement, Erasmus thought. Eldrich appeared to regard him for a moment, his gaze not hostile though neither was it friendly.

"What is it that I might do for you, Lord Eldrich?" Erasmus asked, suddenly losing his patience, annoyed that this man would treat him so.

Eldrich's smile was derisive. "You play your part, Erasmus, do not be concerned. I want to know if you have been contacted by certain people that are of interest to me."

"Which people?"

"Well, that is difficult to answer, for I do not know their names. You see, they have gone to great lengths to be sure that I do not know of their existence—but they have not been entirely successful. And now they are growing positively bold. Desperate even. So much so that I expect they have approached you. The only one I can describe is a woman—slim, hair of reddish-blonde, but faded. 'Drained' was the word one used to describe her. She uses divers names."

"I have no knowledge of such a woman." Erasmus was surprised to find Eldrich at all interested in the affairs of men.

The mage shifted in his chair, turning his head sharply, looking into the darkness. *Thought overlain by sadness.* That was what Erasmus saw, if one even dared to imagine what a mage felt. What they might think was an utter mystery.

"You had seen this text on the Pelier before meeting the countess, I collect?"

Erasmus was surprised. Did Eldrich keep such close track of him? Had he done so all these years? "A friend, Samual Hayes, had shown it to me. A friend of his had unearthed it in the Farrellite archives in Wooton and sent it on to him."

This seemed to focus Eldrich's attention. "You know these young men."

Erasmus nodded.

"And they are here, in Castlebough?"

"Yes. Or rather they were. They appear to have gone down into one of the caves, searching for what I cannot say."

"The Mirror Lake Cave."

"Yes."

Eldrich rose from his chair and paced out into the dappled darkness of the rotunda, pausing as though forgetting where he went or why. He turned back to Erasmus.

"Have the priests come seeking this young man? What is his name?"

"Kehler. There is a priest here—a Deacon Rose—who is pursuing him. The priest told me that Kehler is in some danger, though he would not say more. He also told me that if I were ever to see you, sir, to assure you that the Farrellites have kept faith with the mages. He seemed very concerned that this be understood."

"And well he should be," Eldrich said, and then walked another three paces, a hand to his brow, Erasmus thought, though it was hard to tell in the poor light.

The mage stopped in the rotunda center and looked up at the dome overhead, standing a moment with his arms thrown oddly out, and then he came back and stood by the fire.

"You have been busy these past years, Erasmus. No doubt you have heard of Teller in your researches?"

"I—I have."

"Do you know what became of the society the man thrust upon the world?"

"I believe it was destroyed. Five mages conspired to trap them and put an end to their efforts."

"An end was put to more than their efforts," Eldrich said emphatically, "though it was not an easy thing, for the followers of Teller had grown cunning and knew how to avoid coming to the attention of the mages. And the years have not made them less skilled in this matter, that is certain. But they think I am near to my end, my powers waning, and that is making them rash. They also sense what is coming, and they grow desperate."

"Are you saying that the Tellerites still exist?"

"Do you not listen when I speak?" Eldrich said, his temper flaring. He walked away again, out into the center of the rotunda. After a moment of pacing he turned and gazed intently at Erasmus.

"Erasmus?"

He felt himself falling through darkness, and then he struck something hard, though he felt no pain.

"Erasmus?"

He opened his eyes and saw what appeared to be low flame rippling before his eyes. His vision began to clear and he realized that it was not flame, though it was fading so quickly he could not put a name to it.

"You can get up now. You're perfectly whole."

Erasmus realized that Walky stood over him, holding something draped over his arm.

"I have your clothes, sir."

Erasmus sat up suddenly, his mind still not clear. "What has he done to me?"

"Only looked into you a little; to be sure that you had not been contacted and your memory fogged."

"What?"

"Come along, sir. I can help you if you aren't able. Daylight is not far off. We should get you back, sir."

Erasmus realized that there was a little gray seeping down from the dome above. He felt a bit of light was finding its way into his brain as well.

"What part am I to play in this, Walky?"

Even in the poor light he could see the man shrug his round shoulders. "Only the mage knows," he said.

Chapter Twenty-three

SKYE pulled on a plain white waistcoat, checked the hour on his timepiece, and slipped it into a pocket. Still a few minutes left. He walked over to the window and stared out over the town of Castlebough down to the lake which glittered hypnotically in the sun. The note from the countess had hardly been warm—it had been rather curt, in truth. Unusual, he thought, then shrugged. There was no understanding women, especially this countess. She seemed alternately overanimated, almost girlish, in his company, or sullen and petulant. He simply did not understand.

Perhaps the fact that she turned the head of every man in Farrland had made her a bit odd, but then this was something that was lost on him. Oh, she was an attractive woman, there was no doubt of that, but there were others he found far more lovely, and they did not act so strangely around him. As though he'd made them some promise that he had not kept.

His eye came slowly back from the lake, just visible over the slate roofs of the houses. Skye wondered what the countess had learned from Flattery; certainly her note gave no clue. Perhaps Flattery had been unpleasant to her and that explained her manner—she was angry at Flattery, not him.

His eye came to rest on the small park across the street from the house he let. Nannies watched over playing children and gossiped among themselves as they did handcrafts, apparently without devoting any part of their awareness to the activity.

On one of the benches a man sat reading a book, one of the men who always seemed to be in the park—leaving only when Skye left his house. Agents of the Farr government, he was sure, and felt the fear that seemed always to tighten around his bowel.

"They would have arrested me by now," he muttered. Certainly they had no evidence. Their attempt to compromise him had failed, thanks to an unknown woman and her friends. He thought of her often, fearing that she had somehow fallen into the hands of the Admiralty. Who in this round world was she, and how had she gotten wind of Moncrief's plot? Meeting her had been one of the oddest experiences of his life. Thank Farrelle she had been there or he would likely be in the gaol, now.

"They cannot touch you," Skye said, squaring his shoulders. They had tried and failed. And now he was on his guard. The King was still an admirer. Moncrief would get what he deserved for this travesty, in time. Let him sweat a while.

The man in the park appeared not to notice when Skye emerged onto the street, but Skye knew he was there. Half a block behind, perhaps on the street's opposite side, but he was there.

Put him from your mind, he told himself. *There is nothing the man can do now but follow.* Follow rather impotently.

As it was a fine day, he decided to walk the short distance to the house where the countess was staying.

So absorbed in thought was the countess that she had lost all awareness of her surroundings. She sat on a small terrace, the warming sun touching her, protected from the small breeze by a stone wall. Though there was increasing warmth in the sun, the air still bore the cold of the recent winter, which lingered in the shaded valleys and on hilltops.

"The pleasures of the day to you, Lady Chilton," Skye said, startling the countess from her thoughts.

She rose immediately and curtsied, wondering if her manner was as guarded as it felt. Skye, of course, showed no sensitivity to her mood, as she had come to expect. "Please, Lord Skye, sit. Be at your ease." She took her own seat and faced him, silent for a moment, wondering if he would ask about her meeting with Erasmus or if he would pretend that visiting her was more important than anything she might have learned. When he did not speak, she began to feel foolish.

"Your paintings are ready. Shall I have them taken to your carriage?"

"I walked, in fact, Lady Chilton."

"Then I shall have them delivered to your place of residence, if you will but give directions to my servants."

He nodded his thanks.

"You would like to hear of my meeting with Erasmus Flattery," she said.

"You have met with him already?" he said as though the thought had not occurred to him. As if he had come here merely to stare at her in anticipation.

"Mr. Flattery was kind enough to visit me." She met his eye suddenly. "I had not realized he was a man of such charm." Her gaze dropped to her hands. "I showed him your paintings. He divined immediately that I was your agent . . . I'm not sure how." She looked up at him as though he might explain, but he only shrugged. "I managed to charm a few things from him, all the same. He admitted that the script on the Pelier, or rather the copy, was likely known to the mages and might even be similar to the script on the Ruin of Farrow, as you expected." She looked up to see Skye's reaction to this news, and though he sat perfectly still, she could see the excitement on his face. "He claimed not to be able to read the script, however." She felt herself shrug. She had almost blurted out the truth. Anything to please him. A shudder of revulsion ran through her at what she would do to attract this man.

"But can he? Did you sense he was telling the truth?" Skye had leaned forward in his seat, staring at her intently.

She shrugged again, feeling that she looked at him a bit hopelessly, trying to hide the excitement she felt in his presence. If he would only look at her so for the proper reasons. . . .

Skye turned suddenly in his seat, and stared off at the view. "But if it is the script of the mages . . . ? How could Pelier have known?"

"He did not merely adapt it from the script on the Ruin, I collect?"

"No, I don't think so. Flattery would know better than I, but no, I think it has come from some other source. Perhaps from 'inspiration' as Pelier claimed." Skye ran his right hand back into his thick silver hair, as she had noted he did when deep in thought.

"But why does this interest you so?" she asked softly.

Skye looked down on her as though surprised by the question. "It is difficult to explain."

"I have no pressing appointments. Take all day if you like. In fact, I think I will be free tomorrow, as well, if a story could take so long."

He seemed to measure her for a moment, with that gaze that never looked upon her warmly. Then he shifted in his chair, as though to speak with her more intimately, but still he said nothing. The countess remained silent, waiting, afraid to push now. The slightest misstep and he would decide to say nothing—all chance of intimacy would be gone.

Twice he turned his attention to her, and drew a breath as though to speak, but both times his resolve failed or he could not find the words, and he looked away.

"I shall swear myself to silence, if that is a concern," the countess said softly, hardly daring to utter a word.

Then she saw his face change, the tension draining from it, and he nodded unconvincingly. "The story of the Stranger of Compton Heath has intrigued me since the day I first heard it, and the more I learned the more fascinated I became. You see, I don't believe it was merely a local myth, as do many, nor do I think it was a hoax. The priest, Baumgere, met the Stranger, and I think there can hardly have been a shrewder man than this priest. No, his knowledge of languages was far too deep for anyone to deceive him. The Stranger unquestionably spoke a tongue that Baumgere had not encountered before.

"So where did this Stranger come from? Some unexplored part of the world is the accepted explanation, and one can hardly imagine a more convincing answer, but I have reason for doubt. You see, there have been other such occurrences in history, all thought to be hoaxes for one reason or another, and likely some were. Of course one would have to ask what purpose they served other than gaining the impostor some brief notoriety. But some are of such a nature that I wonder if, indeed, they were hoaxes.

"A boy was discovered in Doorn, nearly frozen on a winter's day, and he soon succumbed to his ordeal. But he, too, spoke a strange tongue and was dressed oddly and found his surroundings unfamiliar. He seemed altogether foreign to the people who found him.

"Seventy years ago a woman dwelt in the mountains of Entonne, a hermit who was said to sing songs in an unknown tongue and had knowledge of healing that others did not. She was a little mad, some thought, for she always claimed that she had been spirited here from another place—a place one could not reach by land or sea. And a boy of about twelve appeared near Tremont Abbey. A shepherd and his son found the child, wandering the hills, frightened, speaking a language the man had never heard. They took him to a physician in the town, and as happened at Compton Heath, a carriage came late at night, and the boy was never seen again."

"And last, and strangest of all, the case of the Milbrook children. You must know it? The three children and the nanny all disappeared from a room while others were outside. It was a great mystery seventy-five years ago, and rewards were offered for the nanny, who was thought to have abducted the poor children. But they were never found, nor could anyone ever explain how they had disappeared from the room without anyone seeing. The laughter of the children stopped, and the parents thought they had fallen asleep, or listened raptly to a story. But when they opened the door later, there were no children to be found. Gone. Impossibly gone." He fell silent.

"They could not have disappeared into the air," the countess said, strangely affected by this story of lost children.

"Not into the air, no." Skye paused, thinking. "In ancient times there was a belief among a group of scholars—they called themselves the 'lunarians,' for it was their habit to meet at the full moon—thus the terms 'fool's moon' and 'lunatic' were born—and they had many strange ideas about the nature of the world and the heavens, and have been much scorned by men of learning ever since. But even so, they were some of the earliest to believe that the earth was a sphere, and even calculated its circumference very close to our present value. They also believed that the netherworld was a real place. They believed it lay within our world, which they hypothesized was hollow at its center. To this end they explored some very deep caves and even tried to enter a marginally active volcano, with near disastrous results. This belief that another world lay within was part of a larger cosmology—if one can call it that—a hypothesis that there were other worlds, 'infinitely distant yet near at hand.' It was their belief that these worlds were, at times, so close that people could pass from one to another, and that sometimes, though not by design, they did." He gave her an odd defensive look as though he expected her to laugh, but when she did not he continued.

"It sounds foolish, I know, but where did the Stranger of Compton Heath come from? And where did the Milbrook children go? Somewhere. Somewhere that is not explained by our present description of the heavens. I am a practitioner of natural philosophy, and it is my belief that we will one day come to understand the laws of nature in all of their vast intricacy. I am also an empiricist and believe only in knowledge that can be confirmed by empirical methods—but what if our perception of the world is . . . incomplete? What if there are worlds, 'infinitely distant, yet near at hand' that we cannot detect by any method yet devised? If this were possible, then our entire view of the cosmos would be ludicrously narrow. If such a thing were possible, then we must begin rewriting the few natural laws we have recorded—my own laws of gravity among them."

He stopped, gazing at her, judging the effect of what he'd said.

"It is . . . astonishing. I hardly know what to say. If such a thing could be proven, it would stand all orthodox theory on its head. Are there others who share this view?"

"This is the worst of it," he said, his face twisting in anguish. "The only men who give voice to such beliefs are charlatans and fools. Not real empiricists at all, but buffoons who believe in fairies and spirits. Table knockers who claim to receive messages from the dead, who conduct spirit readings and perform trumped-up 'rituals' at midnight on the solstice." He shook his head, his face turning a bright red. "That is why I keep my interest to myself and tell no one. I would become a laughing stock. I cannot think what cruelty I would meet. No, you are the first I have told."

"I am honored that you would trust me with this confidence, but what will you do? Will you keep such thoughts to yourself forever?"

"Yes, unless I can find proof. That is where this priest comes in. He met the Stranger in Compton Heath and, I believe, spent his life trying to discover where the man had come from. He had access to all the books and documents collected by the Farrellite Church, and I believe he found evidence there. Some information that brought him here to Castlebough where he spent the rest of his life in this pursuit. I had hoped to find this information—I still hope to find it." His manner changed, and he blinked several times quickly, turning slightly away from her.

The countess could not miss his distress. "What is it?" she blurted out, unable to stop herself.

"Nothing, I . . . I have not been sleeping well. My thoughts will not leave me alone. I sometimes think that they will drive me . . . to utter distraction."

"If you will permit me to say," the countess pitched her voice to its warmest most compassionate tone, "I think you spend too much time alone with your own thoughts, and though this may produce much for the good of the world, I cannot think it is best for the Earl of Skye, and it is he that I am concerned with. You should spend more time in society—oh, it need not be with the crowds, which I know you dislike. But with your friends who care for you."

He nodded, pulling himself up, almost reanimating himself after looking so dejected. "I'm sure what you say it true."

"I have been invited to a dinner this evening—at the home of one of Castlebough's leading families. I thought I might accept. Would you care to accompany me? It could be the beginning of your new policy."

"This evening? I—I would dearly love to, but I have foolishly committed myself elsewhere. I am sorry."

"Oh, well, not to worry. I only thought. . . ."

A clock chimed in the village, and he rose suddenly. "You must forgive me, Lady Chilton, but I am called elsewhere. I cannot thank you enough for your efforts with Mr. Flattery—and for listening to my rambling. You are too kind."

When Skye had gone, the countess stood on the terrace staring at the door. He had run out on her. After what she had offered, intimacy, friendship . . . more. After what she had done for him, pumping poor Erasmus Flattery, she expected at least a little gratitude. At the very least, politeness.

"I have never been treated so . . ." She could not find a word, nor could she find words to express the pain and confusion she felt. "Perhaps he is mad."

"It is unsigned," Marianne said. "Your admirer does not want to be known—he even keeps the identity of the painter he engaged secret so that you will not find him out. You think it's Skye, no doubt?" Marianne and the countess stood looking at a painting, which had been delivered to their abode without so much as a card. It was a portrait of the countess sitting upon a divan, and Marianne had already said she thought the artist was more than a little in love with his subject.

"I don't know who it is from, though I am almost certain that it is not from the earl." She hoped her voice remained neutral, but Marianne cast a quick glance her way all the same.

"Well, whoever it is, they are likely in Castlebough. I can't imagine that anyone would find you here to deliver such a gift, but would simply send it to your Avonel home."

"I suppose."

"Well, it is a painter of some skill, and therefore he will not be unknown. We'll take it along to dinner tonight. It will be the parlor game—name the artist."

"Oh, that would be unkind!" the countess protested.

"Nonsense. If the man has not the courage to declare himself, then he deserves nothing less. I wouldn't be surprised to find he's married, for Farrelle's sake. But if we can find the artist, we will know his employer soon enough. No, no. Do not protest."

Chapter Twenty-four

THE house was perhaps the oldest house of any size in Castlebough, and was suitably dark in its decor, with small windows, and floors of ancient tile and deeply polished walnut. Erasmus did not want to be there. In fact, he was becoming a little frantic with inactivity. At least everything was ready for their departure early the next morning, or so Clarendon claimed. They would set out in search of Kehler and Hayes at last.

The two men had come to dinner at the Baron of Glenock's home, and though Erasmus was not usually overly enthusiastic about such events, the baron was a member of Clarendon's vintners group, and as such had applied pressure to the little man to bring Erasmus along. If he was honest with himself, Erasmus had to admit that his real reason for attending was the possibility of meeting the countess again.

Now that she's learned what she wanted from you, the countess will likely not pay you the slightest attention, he thought. *But I will hang back and if she does not appear to recognize me, I won't make a fool of myself by pursuing her.*

He was not quite sure why he was doing this. Certainly she was not interested in him. The Countess of Chilton was likely desired by every man of station in Farrland and beyond. Still, she had taken his hand at her door, and kissed his cheek, and for a few seconds he had felt that something passed between them. Something. . . .

The servant opened the doors to the great hall, and there Erasmus found the thirty or so dinner guests gathered in a half circle, their attention entirely taken up with something. Flames, was this how the countess was treated? People simply collected about her and stared?

"Well, it isn't a Sir Geofry Sandler, that is certain," someone offered. "The subject appears to be alive."

There was general laughter.

"Vita Corning," someone else suggested.

"No, it was done by a man, clearly. You can see the artist was enamored of his subject."

"Exactly! Vita Corning."

This brought much knowing laughter.

Erasmus came up to the edge of the group unnoticed.

"Obviously a Warton," a man said emphatically.

"Oh, don't be perfectly ridiculous. It was done by someone with talent."

Erasmus Flattery found a shoulder he could peer over and there, at the center of this gathering stood a framed painting on an easel. A painting of the Countess of Chilton which, he thought, came near to conveying the mysterious allure of the woman's beauty. Erasmus found himself staring at it raptly for a moment and then realized the head full of curls before the painting must belong to the countess herself. Suddenly he was nervous with anticipation. Would she acknowledge him? Would there be the slightest hint of what had transpired between them?

"It is a self-portrait, and the countess is hiding her talent from us?"

Such fawning was too much even for this gathering and was met with various sounds, none of which could be described as overly kind.

"There aren't a dozen good portraitists around the Entide Sea. Certainly it can't be too hard to find the artist when there are so few to choose among."

This comment was met with general agreement.

"Mr. Kent?" the countess said, "I can't believe you won't venture an opinion. Are you protecting one of your brothers in art?"

Erasmus noticed Averil Kent hanging back behind the others, looking a little sheepish, he thought.

"I fear that my own areas of interest don't include portraiture, Lady Chilton, so I am of little use in this matter."

Erasmus looked back to the painting again. The pattern of the fabric that covered the divan was striking. New world warblers of bright yellow on leafed branches of some unknown tree, likely an oak, also not an old world variety.

Erasmus leaned nearer to Kent and said quietly, "Do you know the pattern in the divan? Is that *Quercus lyrata,* do you think?"

Kent hesitated, looking back at the painting. "Perhaps *stellata,* though I'm not sure."

Erasmus nodded. *Well,* he thought, *you have not fooled quite everyone, Mr. Kent.* A quick jealousy flamed up in him, but he forced it down, smiling at his own folly. It was likely that neither the talented Kent nor the supposedly "renowned" Erasmus Flattery would stand a chance in the competition for the favors of the countess. Hardly worth a fit of jealousy.

Another painter was suggested, this one prompting even more laughter. The countess looked over her shoulder to see the originator of this suggestion and noticed Erasmus. The smile was replaced by a wavering look of uncertainty which Erasmus did not understand. She nodded just perceptibly and then turned back to the painting.

He found the uncertainty of that look infected him, worked its way into his blood and left him ill with doubt. He forced his attention back to the painting.

Perhaps it was just the moment, but Erasmus thought the painter had captured something of that uncertainty in his portrait. The countess gazed out from the canvas with a look at once intelligent and extremely guarded, though almost masked by the beauty and by the ease with which she inhabited that near-perfect form. It was, Erasmus had to admit, a brilliant portrait.

He glanced over at Kent. The man's manner spoke very clearly to Erasmus: the painter was overwhelmed by both a sense of hopelessness, and of fervent hope. Hopelessness because his head told him that he stood no chance with the countess, yet hopeful because his heart believed that this offering of his art would make her realize the depth of his feeling for her. Somehow, Erasmus realized, Kent had convinced himself that the countess would look at the painting and recognize that such depth of true feeling could come from no one but Kent himself and this would open her eyes to him and what he offered. In a world where all men desired her, only Kent's feelings were true and noble.

You poor bastard, Erasmus thought. He wondered if the countess had done anything at all to encourage the painter. Clearly she knew who he was, but was there anything more to it than that?

Erasmus turned his attention back to the painting, reminding himself that looking at Kent might be more like staring into a mirror than he could bear. Best not to let a foolish obsession with the countess take hold of him, especially when it was so unlikely.

He turned away from the group, but when he did, a vision of the countess standing near to him at the door of her home appeared in his mind. Her manner, so earnest and vulnerable, pierced right to his heart. He must have looked near to falling, for Kent reached out and took hold of his shoulder.

"Are you well, Mr. Flattery?"

"Yes, perfectly." He looked over at Kent and tried to smile, for they were brothers in misery.

To his astonishment Erasmus found that he had been seated near to the head of the long table, and next to the countess. The baron sat at the table's head getting quietly drunk in his own jolly way, and his wife sat to his right. To his left was the Countess of Chilton, and next to her, Erasmus.

The baron looked like a man who had discovered that he'd died and gone to heaven. Servants continually delivered him exquisite food and drink, while to his left sat the most beautiful woman he had ever seen. He was too blissful even to talk but merely sat there filling his face and glowing. Erasmus thought he had never seen a man who so much resembled a baby—though a giant one. He wondered if the baron would have to be burped after the meal.

Kent, sadly, sat near the table's farthest end and looked like a man exiled to the provinces.

"Did you see my mystery portrait?" the countess asked when the baroness' attention was elsewhere. "From a secret admirer, apparently. Have you a guess as to the man's identity?"

Erasmus hesitated. Would she be impressed if he were to name the artist? The thought of poor Kent hanging back behind the crowd made him hesitate. "I . . . no, I don't know who it could be."

"Now, Mr. Flattery, I saw you hesitate. Do you know? Tell me."

Erasmus shook his head, leaning a little closer. "I could be wrong, and if I am not, I would rather not embarrass the man, who is, in fact, a gentleman of some sensitivity."

The countess pulled back to examine him for a second. "Was it you who had the painting done?" she said so that no other might hear. "Is that what you're telling me?"

She did not look displeased, he realized, and he felt the urge to lie, to at least give the impression that it had been him. "Me. Oh, no, Lady Chilton. Not me. Though if I had such talent, I cannot think of a subject I would rather undertake."

"Ah, live by the name, die by the name. Though I am not sure I believe you." She lifted her wineglass and smiled at him. "To flattering portraits—can one ever have too many?"

Erasmus laughed. "I have been waiting to have just one."

"Is this a private conversation?" the baroness asked.

"Not at all, Lady Bingham. We were just speculating again about my portrait."

A deep, even breathing caught their attention and they turned to find the baron asleep in his chair.

The baroness looked more amused than embarrassed. "It is the effect of the wine. Half a bottle and he cannot stay awake. Once, at a ball, he leaned against a pillar, and, I swear, he went to sleep on his feet. I roused him, somewhat, when he began to slide to the floor and managed to steer him into our carriage, though I don't think he was awake the entire time. Walked out to the carriage in his sleep, I am convinced of it. And the next day he had no memory of what had transpired. Denies it still." She shook her head, rolling her eyes a little.

"It is interesting that you would say that," the countess said, her tone more serious. "I awoke this morning in the parlor downstairs, dressed in my sleeping gown and a robe. I have not the slightest memory of rising or descending the stairs, nor do I know how long I was there before I awoke. It was the oddest thing, and I've never done anything like it before."

Erasmus stopped eating. "Why, last night I awoke while in the midst of undressing. I was sitting on my bed taking off my shirt. The odd thing is that I had gone to bed earlier, and I have no memory of rising and dressing, and wonder what in the world I was doing."

The baroness laughed. "There is an epidemic of sleepwalking apparently. Perhaps there are some at this table eating in their sleep, even conversing. Somehow, I sense that there are."

With the baron asleep, Erasmus received much of the countess' attention that evening, and he could not remember being happier. And it seemed to him that the countess took pleasure from his company.

Far too quickly, the evening was over and Erasmus found himself stalling near the door, hoping to at least say good night to the countess. Clarendon came up. "We have the kind offer of a ride home, Mr. Flattery."

"Well, that is very thoughtful. . . ." Erasmus began, trying to hide his annoyance, but he did not finish, for the countess appeared in the entry hall. He almost cursed aloud. How could he escape Clarendon and his untimely kindness?

"Ah, Mr. Flattery." It was the countess. "You have not forgotten your promise to escort me home, I hope?"

"Forgotten? Of course not. May I present, Randall Spencer Emanual Clarendon, Lady Chilton."

Clarendon bowed deeply, and the countess looked immensely charmed. "Mr. Clarendon, it is a great pleasure. Are you a resident of this lovely village or a visitor, like the rest of us?"

"I have a house here, Lady Chilton, though I confess I retreat to warmer climes once the snow begins to fall."

"Well, perhaps we shall meet again, then, as I will be here a bit longer. I'm rather charmed with Castlebough, I must admit. The pleasures of the evening to you, Mr. Clarendon."

A moment later Erasmus was handing the countess up into her carriage and then taking his place beside her, certain he was the envy of every man present. And there they were riding through moonlit Castlebough, and he was not really sure what he had done to be so fortunate.

They rolled on in silence for a moment, leaving Erasmus to wonder what would happen when they came to the door of the countess' home. The town was so small, however, that they arrived at the house before Erasmus had decided upon which tack he would sail.

"Would you like to come in and meet Marianne Edden, Mr.

Flattery? She is always sitting up at this hour, and though she could not be convinced to go to dinner, she will require a complete report of the evening's events."

"I would be delighted."

Erasmus felt both let down and relieved. If there was another present, then there would be no question of how the evening would proceed. At least he would not be able to make a fool of himself if he misread the situation completely.

Servants took his hat and Lady Chilton's cloak and he was ushered into a small withdrawing room where he was left alone. A fire burned in the hearth, but Erasmus found he was drawn to the window which looked out over the valley below. In the distance he could see the lake, silvered by moonlight and starlight, shimmering in the distance. A breeze moved in the branches of the pines, and even inside, he thought he could smell their sweet scent.

He heard a noise behind and turned to find the countess seating herself by the fire, gazing at him intently, as though there were some weighty question she was about to pose.

"It is unprecedented, but Marianne seems to have retired for the evening," she said. "I wonder if she is entirely well?" A servant poured wine and slipped away silently.

Erasmus came and sat by the fire. The countess was subdued, perhaps tired, or burdened with something, with some knowledge. He wondered if it was Skye. She had pumped Erasmus for the great empiricist, so there was clearly some connection between them. Like everyone else, Skye was probably enamored of her.

And what are my accomplishments compared with his? Erasmus thought.

"Have you heard this odd tale of the man they call the Stranger of Compton Heath?" the countess asked suddenly, looking up at him as though she expected ridicule.

Erasmus nodded. "I have. Yes. Most peculiar."

"Where in the world do you think he came from?"

Erasmus shrugged. "It is a mystery, though I will say that I think it was no ruse, and there seem to have been other cases."

"You give it credence, then?"

"Certainly I can neither prove nor disprove the story. I am convinced that the man did appear, and that he was genuinely lost and confused. Whether he was merely a lunatic, as some have suggested—I cannot say." Erasmus paused. "I know a man who interviewed the doctor who was first called to see this stranger. He, at least, believed the doctor's story, and he also believed the Stranger was no fraud, nor was he mad."

"You have an interest in this matter?" she asked, surprised and perhaps relieved.

"The people of Compton Heath believed a mage came and took the stranger away."

"And you are interested in the mages. . . ."

He nodded and sipped his wine.

"Do you ever feel that we are at an end of a chapter of history, Mr. Flattery, and that the world as it existed before was so much more alive with marvels? I almost feel this stranger was somehow left from that period. Like lizards are the tiny remnants of the great beasts that disappeared. And now we are left with this world of reason that we are building, and it will be an infinitely ordered and predictable world devoid of such wonders as mages and strangers who have come from we know not where. Not to mention wondrous beasts. Do you know that there were said to be white deer in these hills long ago?"

Erasmus nodded. "Yes. I have seen the hide of one. They were true and real, just as this man who appeared in Compton Heath was real, but I would not be too concerned. I think there are wonders enough in this world, to last our lifetimes at least." Erasmus could not help himself, he had to ask. "How did Skye respond to my verdict on the script?"

He wanted to see her reaction to Skye coming up in the conversation.

She did not brighten at the sound of the man's name. In fact, she turned away slightly to stare into the fire. Erasmus was not sure how to interpret this.

"It is always difficult to say with the earl. . . . Can you read the writing?" she said suddenly. "I ask this only of my own curiosity. I will say nothing."

Erasmus sipped his wine, then rose from his chair, almost without meaning to. For a moment he stood with his arm resting on the high mantle. "During my time in the house of Eldrich I was under the tutelage of a man—Walky was his name. He taught all the things that schoolboys are to learn—Old Farr, Entonne, arithmetic, grammar, history. Nothing that other boys in far more common circumstances did not learn. But old Walky was beginning to suffer the disabilities that plague the old. Not that he wasn't strong and healthy—he seemed to have these qualities in abundance—but his mind was not what it once had been. His memory was in decline. Often he would call us by the names of former students, or he would begin to teach us things that he had not meant to. On more than one occasion he asked us to repeat things that we had not been taught. Arcane things. He even occasionally addressed us in a language we could not name." He heard the countess draw in a quick breath. She stared at him in fascination, but almost, he thought, he saw some pity there.

"He once left a book on a shelf of the room in which we commonly pursued our studies. It sat there for two days before I realized that it was not a book in any common language. When I first opened it, I slammed it closed immediately. Although we never met Eldrich, as small boys we lived in mortal dread of the mage. I was certain that I would suffer some terrible magical retribution for merely opening the book. But I did not. Two days later I looked again. By the fourth day, Percy—the other boy my age who lived there—Percy and I were sure that Walky had forgotten the book altogether and we took it to our room to examine.

"We were more frightened than you can imagine, but we were also utterly fascinated, and as small boys often are, we were heedless to the effects of our action.

"The book was completely undecipherable to us. Filled with strange writing and odd diagrams." Erasmus stopped unable to continue the story.

"What happened?" the countess asked, her voice nearly a whisper.

"We were discovered . . . and punished," Erasmus said, keeping his tone carefully neutral.

"Oh," the countess said, not quite sure what this might have entailed. "And the writing?"

"I believe it was the same script found in the painting."

"And how were you made to suffer for this transgresson?"

"We . . ." Erasmus felt himself try to swallow in a suddenly dry mouth. "We were punished," he said again.

"And you will not say more?"

He shook his head.

"And this is what I have driven you to tell me?" she said, rising from her chair. She took both his hands. "I'm sorry, Erasmus. I am truly sorry. I have no business delving into your secrets. Things that disturb you. I did not bring you here to pry secrets from you, for myself or anyone else."

"Why did you bring me here?"

She paused looking up into his face, measuring, perhaps. "Because I owe you an apology. I misused you when I invited you here so that I could pry for—"

"For Skye," he finished the sentence for her. "What is Skye to you?" he asked suddenly, though he had no right to.

"Oh, do not talk to me of Skye," she said, looking down. "No, it is a terrible thing to use another for one's own ends. To play with their hopes, with their feelings, and then to dash them without regard. It is shameful. No one should be treated thus."

Erasmus was about to protest, when she looked up again, meeting his gaze, her eyes glistening. He could not help himself; he bent and kissed her. At once, he thought he had made a terrible mistake, for she responded not at all. And then suddenly her lips softened and met his.

When they pulled apart, she looked at him in surprise and wonder.

"Mr. Flattery, you forget yourself."

"Yes," he said, hardly able to catch his breath, and kissed her again.

Erasmus would have been convinced he was dreaming, if he had ever known a dream so fair, so overwhelming of the senses. He pulled a divan up before the fire, and here began a slow exploration. Each lace released was a revelation, each kiss more wondrous than the last. Erasmus felt that he had fallen into another world, a world of the senses, where one's thoughts were driven out and replaced with wonder and pleasure. A world in which he was the stranger.

Chapter Twenty-five

HAYES dropped his pack to the cave floor and stretched his back. "Not what I imagined," he said to Kehler.

Kehler shed his own pack and dug out the cave survey, unfolding it near to their lamp.

In the poor light Hayes could just make out the Fairy Galleries above them. The formation of the room did give the impression of a gallery above, and here he could see elaborate decorations. Stalagmites like melting candles projecting up from the floor, a myriad of crystal straws hanging from the ceiling, shimmering even in the poor light. Hayes thought that if he sang the perfect tone, the entire ceiling would resonate in brittle harmony.

"We are in the right chamber," Kehler said after a moment. "Disappointed?"

"Not at all. It is magnificent. Beautiful, really, but not what I expected. Where do we go from here?"

"Up." Kehler pointed up into the gallery. "There is a good-sized passage there. But we should eat first, then I, for one, need at least a few hours sleep before we go on. They were losing the rhythm of the sun, and sleeping when they felt the need, eating when hungry. Hayes still wound his watch and consulted it occasionally to see just how long they had been down here, but it no longer dictated their schedule.

Hayes had learned to put his battered jacket down for a seat and then lean against his pack which insulated from the cold hard rock. They sat thus, their packs propped against a wall, the lantern between them, and ate their meal, unsure if it was supper, dinner, or even breakfast.

They ate quietly, then warmed more water over the flame to make their "netherworld tea." Afterward, they put out the flame in order to preserve their precious supply of oil.

In the darkness, questions would not leave Hayes alone. He wondered why he had come. Yes, Kehler had promised him there was a discovery to be made that would pay them handsomely, and that reason was as valid now as it had been at the beginning. But even so, there were moments when the risks, or at least the fears, outweighed the possible gains. And the fears were real and tangible, while the rewards were yet to materialize, if they ever would.

Worry could not keep exhaustion at bay indefinitely, and finally Hayes slipped into an unsettled sleep.

Fleeting dreams haunted him, like images floating swiftly past—clouds borne on the wind. And then he settled into a single dream. A woman's voice was calling him, echoing from far off, like someone whispering into a well. He crawled down a passage that was almost entirely dark. Again the voice called him, and he struggled on, pushing himself through places so tight that he knew he would never return.

"Hayes?"

He woke to the sounds of Kehler striking his flint. A moment later a piece of paper caught and he saw fingers pick it up and tease the lamp wick, reminding him of the squares of light on Paradise Street. An age ago that seemed.

The wick adopted the flame, and a sad light illuminated their chamber.

"Ah, you're awake."

"Only partly."

"Time to go on," Kehler said, though there was no excitement or anticipation in his voice, which was uncharacteristically subdued.

Hayes heard himself sigh. "I suppose."

While Hayes packed by lamplight, Kehler retreated down a passage to fill their water bottle. When he returned he seemed to fuss unduly with his pack.

"I'm ready to have you reveal this great mystery," Hayes said, forcing his tone to be light. "Lead on, my friend."

"Yes. Let us hope . . . " Kehler muttered, shouldering his pack and setting off, an uncomfortable silence falling between them.

Climbing up to the gallery proved easier than they'd thought, and once there, as the survey showed, there was but one passage leading on. As Kehler went ahead, Hayes used a candle to mark a letter H in wax beside the entrance. Then, with a little trepidation, he followed his companion in. Thoughts of the death of a small boy haunted him. What kind of beast had this priest been to use children so?

The passage curved gradually to the right, and maintained a fairly constant angle down. To Hayes' relief it also maintained its size, more or less, so that he only occasionally had to duck his head, something he was becoming adept at, having nearly rendered himself senseless several times early on.

When half of the hour had passed, they met a second passage and followed this. It ran along almost level toward the west.

"How far have we to go?" Hayes asked. Kehler always seemed to put the cave survey away before he had given Hayes a chance to examine it thoroughly—an annoying habit, Hayes found.

"Not far," Kehler called back, though he did not seem terribly excited. An hour later they came to a small chamber, perhaps twenty feet long, but quite high and a dozen feet across.

"Where now?" Hayes asked, stretching his back and shoulders.

Kehler pointed down into a dark corner. "It goes there," he said.

They dropped their packs, glad to be rid of them at last, at least for a while. Kehler busied himself with filling the lamp, giving Hayes the impression that there was something he was avoiding saying. Just as Hayes was about to ask what this might be, Kehler shook the oil tin.

"We haven't long to find what we seek. If we're here longer than half a day, I fear we shall have to find our way out by candlelight."

"Then we should be about our business," Hayes said, the moment passing.

The hole in the corner turned out to be about three feet around and they crawled in on bruised knees and blistered hands, Kehler ahead with the lantern, his shadow thrown back toward Hayes, and moving oddly on the floor and stone walls, like some lumbering beast of the underworld.

Hayes found this view of his friend disturbing, as though he had somehow found entrance to a world not meant for men. His knees were swollen and scraped, but he'd learned that if he could force himself beyond the initial torment, it would subside somewhat and become almost tolerable.

For a hundred yards he followed the shadow of the creature that led him, and then, to his relief, the passage opened up a little and they could actually stand if they were careful to duck their heads now and then. Not much farther on, the passage turned abruptly to the right and died in a small pool.

"What is this?" he said coming up beside Kehler.

"A pool," Kehler said, stating the obvious.

"But where does the passage go?" Hayes slumped down on his pack, his gaze darting about the walls, searching.

Kehler was staring at the pool. "The survey ends here," he mumbled.

"What? Ends? Are you telling me we've come all this way to find this?"

"No. We've come seeking something more, I'm just not quite sure where it is, though I have an idea." He spread the now-tattered survey of the cave out on the floor. "If you look here, you'll see what I mean." He put his finger on the Fairy Galleries, and the passage leading away from it toward the west. It came to a pool and stopped—clearly where they were now.

"I thought you knew of another passage. Some secret way that Baumgere had found."

"Well, there is one, I'm sure of it. 'The way, by darkness, into light' Baumgere wrote, and something else. In one of his several versions of the 'Ballad of Tomas' he had marked a pasage with an exclamation point and the phrase. 'How could I have missed this?' " Kehler sat back and looked at him. "In the song Tomas was looking at his reflection in the Mirror Lake—or, in some versions, a pool—

when he slipped and fell. Strong currents swept him away, and when he surfaced, he was in another world. Or at least in passages that led to that world."

Hayes looked at him, stunned. "What are you telling me? That if we leap into this pool we will surface in some other place? Kehler, did you bring me all the way down here to play a cruel jest on me?"

Kehler shook his head. "No. I think Baumgere followed the instructions in the lyric and discovered another part of the cave. He passed through this pool."

Hayes stared at the calm, impenetrable surface of the water and then back to Kehler as though the man had lost his mind. "You aren't talking sense," he said firmly.

Kehler began pulling off his boots and hose. "Perhaps not. But I have come this far, I will not go back out of fear of looking foolish." Kehler stepped gingerly into the pool, and in six strides had reached the wall.

Hayes laughed. "Well, it does not seem to have worked, Kehler. You're still very much here." He could not help it; the entire situation was so absurd. They had put such effort into getting here, and for what?

Kehler bent down, his face near to the surface, staring intently into the dark water.

"Do you see your reflection?" Hayes asked, still laughing. "One mustn't dive in unless one sees a reflection!"

Kehler came out of the pool scowling at his friend. "Well, I am willing to try it."

"What? You'll smash your rather addled brain on the bottom."

"No, look. This is what I think." He fetched pen and ink from his pack and turned the survey over, drawing quickly on the back. "Imagine that this pool is but a low spot in a passage—we've seen plenty of those—and water collects here." He pointed up to the shimmering wall, which was clearly wet and dripping. "So a pool forms, but if one crawls through it, there is a passage on the other side."

Hayes felt his jaw drop open. "You can't be serious! Crawl through a passage filled with water? What if there isn't another side? What if one becomes jammed? Farrelle's blood, Kehler, you would be dead in a moment. A moment! This is too much of a risk. Think, man. Even if you're right, the water level now might be quite different from the time of Baumgere. It could be a hundred feet to air. It could be a mile."

Kehler looked from his drawing to the pool as though somehow gauging its capacity for treachery. "I'm willing to try it."

"You *are* mad. Whatever might be down here, it can't be worth dying over. Seriously, Kehler. Give it up. So we don't find this great mystery and gain fame and wealth. I would rather have my life."

Kehler stood and began to shuck his clothes. "Let us just do an experiment."

"Kehler, I will not let you go into some water-filled passage. You're clearly not rational enough to make sane decisions." Hayes put himself between the pool and his friend.

"I promise, I will not go in. Let us just see if there is a passage, as I guess. That would prove something. If it is merely a wall of rock . . . I will give it up, and we can go back, or search elsewhere."

"You give me your word that you will do nothing rash?"

"My solemn word. I have no more desire to drown than you. Be sure of that."

"Then what exactly are you going to do?"

"I'm going lie down in this absurdly cold water and see if I can sound the passage with my foot. I promise, I will keep my head above water the entire time. Now get out of my way, Hayes. I'm freezing, here, and would like to get this over with."

Hayes moved reluctantly aside, and Kehler went resolutely into the water. He sat down near the wall, cursing the cold, and pushed his foot forward.

"You see! There is a hole—just as I said." He almost lay in the water, now, only his head and shoulders showing, more than half his body disappearing under the stone wall.

"Is there another side?" Hayes asked, amazed. "Can you feel it?"

Kehler pushed himself in so that only his face was dry. "No. . . . No, I can't feel anything. It does not seem to get too much tighter, though, which is something." He pulled himself back out, shivering.

"Look, I'm in here, freezing as it is. Let me just duck in for a moment. You come in and be prepared to drag me out by my feet. Come on, Hayes, I'm turning to ice."

Hayes stripped off his boots and hose and went into the water, which was colder than he'd imagined.

Kehler took a number of deep breaths, then ducked himself

under, flailing forward, his head and shoulders disappearing. In a second he was gone to the waist, then the knees, his absurdly white body being drawn into the dark waters.

Hayes reached down to take hold of a foot, but Kehler shook him off, pushing even farther in.

"Kehler!" Hayes called. "Don't be a fool!"

But Kehler was gone. Hayes knelt down and reached in under the rock as far as he could, but there was no Kehler there to grab.

"Bloody blood and flames! *Keh-ler!*"

What to do? Had Kehler found the other side? Or was he starving for air, and pressing on foolishly, too far in to return.

"You bloody fool! What if it's a hundred feet through! What if there's no other side at all?" He forced himself to be still, listening. The water in the pool had gone calm suddenly, as though Kehler was no longer moving.

"Damn you!" Hayes said, and took three long breaths, but as he was about to duck under in search of his companion, a hand grabbed him about the ankle, and Kehler pushed past, shooting out of the water, gasping, spitting up water and coughing horribly.

"Farrelle's balls, Kehler, you've scarred me half out of my wits." Hayes began to pound his friend on the back.

Kehler nodded, drawing in long breaths, unable to speak. His coughing subsided.

"It's there," he managed after a moment. "Not far. Ten, twelve feet."

"You've gone right through?"

Kehler nodded.

"And there is a passage beyond? A passage with air?"

"Yes." He looked up at Hayes. "I had only the poorest light filtering through the water from our lamp, but I could see. . . . There is a room, at least."

"How tight is it?"

"A foot and the half, I think. Not bad. One takes a deep breath and then pulls oneself through. It is not as difficult as you might imagine. It just takes some nerve."

"I should say so! Come get out of this water and dry." He took Kehler's arm and helped him out of the water. "Even if we can get through, we'll be positively soaked. And what of our lantern and gear?"

Kehler pulled on his clothing, huddling close to the tiny flame of their lantern. "I've brought the oiled bags recommended by our guide. They'll keep our clothing at least somewhat dry for the few seconds we will be underwater. We'll extinguish the lantern and wrap it in our clothes. We've got candles as well."

"I'm not sure I can do this," Hayes said, imagining himself stuck in the small passage and dark waters.

"It is not really so difficult," Kehler said. "If one does not let one's imagination get the upper hand. You can hold your breath and crawl a dozen feet. That's all this is. One just has to ignore the water."

"And the possibility of getting stuck and drowning in a teacup."

Kehler smiled. "As I said, one must not allow the imagination a free hand."

Kehler took a candle out of his pack and lit it from the lamp. Dripping a little wax onto a ledge in the rock, he set the candle out of harm's way, then blew out the lantern to let it cool.

By the light of a single candle they began packing their things into the oiled bags.

"It will take more than one trip to bring all this," Hayes said.

"I will make all the crossings necessary, Hayes. You just get yourself through."

Hayes felt fear taking hold of him. A vague panic that was more than just mental. His stomach and bowel complained audibly, and his motions had become stiff and vaguely disconnected, as though he watched but had only imperfect control over his limbs. The stress and strain of their two days in this strange place wore on him, and their lack of sleep did not help. "I don't want to do this," he said suddenly.

Kehler sat down and looked at him. "You don't have to, Hayes. You have done much coming so far. I would hardly have dared it without you. Stay here, if you will. But I can't come this far and abandon it." He looked over at the pool. "Though I will say again that the danger is more imagined than real. I don't think you could get stuck in so large a passage. But suit yourself. . . ." He smiled. "I will still share whatever profit might come of it."

Hayes felt terribly craven, balking at this final test, but he did not swim, and the thought of dying without air—*without air to breathe*—frightened him more than anything he could name.

Kehler tested the lantern again, found it had cooled sufficiently, and in the confined passage began removing his clothes. He wrapped the lantern in these and put the bundle into an oiled cotton bag. This he sealed with a cord and then placed it inside a second bag.

"Wish me luck," he said, shivering a little.

"You have a flint and paper to light the lantern?"

Kehler nodded.

"Then good luck."

Kehler slipped into the water awkwardly, caught his breath and ducked under, propelling himself into the submerged passage. Hayes saw his feet kick and disappear, the water surging back and forth in the pool, and then after a moment it was still.

"Farrelle preserve him," he whispered to the now much emptier passage.

He waited for some sign that his friend was safe on the other side, but there was none.

"Mustn't let the imagination range freely," he muttered.

The candlelight fell upon the dark pool as it undulated slowly—like oil, Hayes thought. And then the faintest glow, like iridescence in the night sea, filtered through the watery tunnel.

Hayes felt himself relax a little.

"Oh, Farrelle's bloody ghost!" he said, and began wrapping food in a shirt and stuffing it all into one of the oiled bags. By the time Kehler reappeared, he had two bags ready and had begun to pull off his shirt.

"Hayes. . . . Are you considering a bath? I must tell you, it is past due."

"I'm sure I can't sit here with my guttering little candle while you go off to make the discovery of our age. I can't guarantee that I can do this more than once in and once to come back."

"No matter. Bring yourself. That will be enough. I'm used to it now. Except for the bloody cold. But be quick. The quicker we're through and dry, the better."

Hayes stumbled into the pool, the cold nearly taking his breath away. He stuck an arm into the hole beneath the rock, testing the way forward. At least there was some light to go toward.

"All right, Samual," he said aloud. "In we go." He took a deep breath and plunged in, clawing along the rock ceiling, panic gripping him immediately. He battered his heels and knees against the rock as he went, and immediately he became desperate for air.

He could not be sure how far he had gone. He cracked his head and then his elbow against hard stone. He was about to turn back, sure that it was much farther than Kehler had guessed, when he realized his face was in air and light.

"Thank Farrelle!" he muttered, scrambling out of the water, huddling near the lamp rather pathetically.

A moment later Kehler appeared, tossing a bag to Hayes and then a second. "Get your clothes on. I'll be back in a moment." He ducked under and disappeared back into the tunnel.

As Hayes pulled on his damp clothing, Kehler reappeared, carrying two more bags.

"One more trip, I think. Empty those bags. . . . Ah, good. Thank you." He disappeared again, clearly anxious to get the ordeal over with.

Kehler appeared again a moment later bearing the last bags and both their empty packs. He came unsteadily out of the water, grabbing up his clothing in trembling hands and pulling it on awkwardly. The two of them sat there, shivering, water streaming from their hair and eyes.

Kehler laughed. "You look like a half-drowned hound."

Hayes laughed as well. "You look much the same."

"It wasn't so bad, really—was it?"

"Yes, it was," Hayes said, and laughed. "Martyr's balls, but I don't look forward to going back."

Kehler shrugged. "It will be easier next time."

"Did you snuff the candle?"

"No. I didn't think. It's still burning. Well, we can't afford to lose any, but . . . I don't think either of us is ready to go back for the sake of saving a candle. Let's go on before we're too cold."

They repacked their bags, drank a cup of netherworld tea, and set off down the passage which soon became large enough for them to walk upright.

In no time the passage changed. Openings began to appear on one side, most small but some seemed almost large enough for a man. The rock was riddled with them, as though it had been attacked by enormous, boring worms. Fifty feet farther the larger passage ended.

Kehler and Hayes stood looking around, and then at each other.

"There must be a hundred openings here," Hayes said. "And look at them! They are tiny!"

"Just the size of a child," Kehler said dully.

They stood staring at the endless number of openings. Openings that seemed like speechless mouths. Mouths that knew how to keep secrets.

Chapter Twenty-six

SIR John Dalrymple was not asleep when the knock came. Indeed, he could not remember when he had last slept well. In concession to the idea of sleep he had gone through the motions of going to bed, where he then lay in the darkness listening for the sound of nightingales, which he thought he had heard earlier.

His first reaction was to ignore the banging, but when it seemed apparent that whomever it was would not soon stop, he roused himself slowly. A sudden fear struck him and he threw his robe on. *Bryce,* he thought, and hurried to light a lamp.

His accommodations were an odd arrangement, over a carriage house attached to a larger home. A stairway led from his room down to a door into the courtyard or a second door into the main house, where he could take his meals. It was more comfortable than an inn, and relatively inexpensive.

He opened the tiny window in the door and found his fears made real.

"Mr. Bryce! I was asleep. I do apologize," he said, wondering why he apologized for sleeping in the middle of the night!

The man said nothing, but stood waiting impatiently for the door to be opened.

Still without speaking, he led the way up the stairs, forcing Sir

John to hurry after, trying to light the way, struggling for breath almost immediately. When they entered the upper room, Bryce turned on him.

"There are agents of the Admiralty, here in Castlebough, watching Skye," Bryce said.

"Ah. I should have thought Moncrief would have been warned off. . . ." He looked at Bryce, wondering why it was of particular concern. If Bryce was not out to bring down Moncrief, as Sir John had once believed, then what were his intentions? "I assume you haven't wakened me just to give me this news?"

"No," Bryce continued to stand, frustrating Sir John who felt a great need to sit. "I have a task for you, of course. I must speak with this Admiralty man—Captain James is his name—it is an absolute necessity. You will have to arrange it."

"I suppose it would be out of the question for you to simply approach the captain yourself."

Bryce glared at him. The man had no sense of humor at all.

"I thought not. You would like this meeting arranged as soon as possible, I collect?"

Bryce nodded.

"Let me dress, then. I won't be a moment."

Kent was more than embarrassed by what he was doing—he was ashamed. The gate seemed to be barred, but the wall was not high, and there was a convenient barrel meant to catch rain.

He hoped there were no dogs nearby, for though he was as silent as possible, he was only quiet by human standards. In a moment he was over and in a lane between the house and garden wall. He stole along in the faint light of the stars, feeling before him as he went, listening for the sounds of discovery.

If he were caught doing this it would mean his ruin. *"Fool,"* he hissed without meaning to. He had barely missed ruin once that evening, and he was still not out of the woods on that one. Not in his wildest dreams had he imagined the countess displaying his painting to everyone and starting a game to see who could name the artist. What a buffoon he would look if someone discovered the truth!

But that was nothing compared to what he would suffer if he were discovered now.

"Go back," he urged, but he was past listening to the voice of wisdom. Kent seemed to be divided in half. Part of him, the sensible part, was aghast at his actions but unable to do anything to stop them. He was being ruled by something else. Not his heart, he hoped, for he had always hoped his heart was more noble.

It is a madness, he thought. *I will be fighting duels next, and I have not spent as much as an hour in her company.*

He came to the corner of the house and peeked out to see what was there. A terrace, doors and windows, all closed. There seemed to be light coming from one room. For a moment he stood in the shadow, certain that he was alone, hoping that somehow his common sense would gain the upper hand—to no avail.

He bent low and went under the first window, and then came to the one from which light escaped. It was slightly ajar, and as he came to it heard unmistakably a woman moan. For a second Kent froze in place, almost reeling. It was his absolute worst fear. It could not be the countess. She had left with Erasmus Flattery, for Farrelle's sake. The man was brilliant, no doubt, but he was hardly an object of fascination to the women of Avonel. No, this must be some maid and her buck. The sounds of love became more insistent.

Ever so slowly Kent raised his head. Before the fireplace a man and woman lay on a divan. A trill of laughter, then a moan. Then suddenly the woman rose, astride her lover, her face hidden by dark tendrils of hair. She moved over her partner more urgently now. With a quick motion she threw her head back, revealing her face, her naked torso.

Kent closed his eyes and let his head rest against the window ledge. It was she. As he stayed thus, he listened to her cry out, unable to contain her pleasure.

He opened his eyes again, watching her move over her lover. Drawing up the man's hands she pressed them tight to her breasts.

When her climax came, she collapsed over her lover, burying him in the dark avalanche of her hair.

"Mr. Flattery!" she teased, her voice filled with pleasure. "You have taken liberties with me, sir! As penance you shall be flogged . . . with my hair—fifty lashes. And you shall have to stay and pleasure me until the light of day."

Kent heard the unmistakable sound of Erasmus Flattery's laughter. The countess rose up again, and Kent did not even attempt to hide, she was so beautiful. The firelight played upon her perfect form, turning her skin the color of copper.

Kent was sure he had never felt such exquisite agony, and at the same time his heart was pounding at what he had just seen. The Countess of Chilton in the act of love. He had heard her cries of pleasure, and though it was not he in her arms, as it should have been, it was more than most men would ever know. At least he had seen her lost to passion. To his obsessed and confused mind, it seemed almost like intimacy.

Sir John waited in the small lobby of the White Hart Inn, having bribed the night clerk to tip him when Captain James came in. Not that it was likely he would mistake the man, but he knew that a bluff must be supported by something—in this case knowing the man's name and business, and very likely knowing who had sent him as well.

In his mind, he turned the possibilities over again. Moncrief and Brookes had set out to bring Skye to ruin, but surely his miraculous escape must have made them realize that this endeavor should be abandoned. So why had they men watching Skye still?

One thing was certain. The Admiralty did not continue to monitor the activities of Lord Skye without the Sea Lord's approval, though he may have distanced himself from the endeavor. Perhaps the real question was: Who in the Admiralty's intelligence department was utterly loyal to the Sea Lord, and therefore would not reveal their activities to the government? Likely Admiral Matheson, he reasoned. The man was brilliant, and utterly trustworthy. It almost had to be Matheson.

The door opened, and a tired, unshaven man appeared. He was not dressed in uniform, though his bearing was unmistakable. Sir John looked over at the clerk who nodded.

"Captain James?"

The man stopped as Sir John rose from his chair.

"Sir?"

"Sir John Dalrymple. Foreign Ministry. I've been asked to have a word with you by a mutual friend," he said offering his hand.

The officer's eyes narrowed as he took Sir John's hand.

"Have we met, sir? You are very familiar."

"It is likely. I'm in and out of the Admiralty offices regularly, for we have much business in common. Admiral Matheson is a particular friend, as is the Sea Lord himself."

"Ah, yes, of course." The man's eyes opened fully and he smiled. James looked tired enough to collapse where he stood, though he still held his shoulders square, even if his head seemed to bow a little.

"Can we speak more privately, Captain James? I shall not take but a moment of your time."

James retrieved a key from the clerk. "Will you come up?"

"If you don't mind, I have something to deliver to you. My lodgings are not far."

James looked at him suspiciously.

"I know it seems a bit odd, but . . . " he cast his gaze around the room, "I would like to be certain we speak in privacy. I am fulfilling the instructions of your superior. Do you understand?"

James hardly seemed less mystified, but he nodded. They stepped out into the night, and proceeded down the street and around the corner. Bryce had instructed him to bring James four blocks to a certain dark corner.

"Where are we going, Sir John?"

"But two blocks more. Not far. I do apologize for the mystery, and the lateness of the hour."

He found the carriage drawn up in the shadow of a darkened house, but it was not Bryce's carriage. It was hard to see in the dark, but it was a large, old-fashioned looking coach, drawn by a four horse team.

He thought James might balk as they approached the carriage, yet he did not seem in the least concerned.

"The carriage waits for you," Sir John said, the exact phrase Bryce had told him to use, and James nodded as though acknowledging an order.

Stopping twenty feet off, Sir John saw the door swing open and James climb unconcernedly aboard, as if it was not the most unsettling thing. The carriage moved off without a word from the driver, who hunched on the seat above, bent over his reins like a very old man.

Well, Sir John thought, *my involvement with Mr. Bryce becomes more and more strange.* He rather hoped no ill befell Captain James.

His head filled with questions, Sir John set out for his rooms, but soon realized that he would not sleep this night and so continued along the street, wandering about the town like a man deranged.

Chapter Twenty-seven

It was a journey of several hours from Castlebough to the cave mouth, so Erasmus and Clarendon had left at first light. They rode a horse and a pony, while behind them followed a servant leading a packhorse that bore their gear.

On some level Erasmus was aware that the countryside they passed through was beautiful, but his attention was fixed on memories of the previous night which he turned over and over in his mind.

If I live to a hundred years, I shall never know a night to be its equal, he thought.

The countess had made him no promises. In fact, her manner had left him uncertain as to their future, and this offset the incredible bliss that he felt—but only a little. Never had he imagined that he would win the favors of such a woman. Not that he had been entirely unsuccessful in his pursuit of the fairer sex, but still . . . *the Countess of Chilton.*

And here he was, entirely against his will, setting off into a cave in search of two foolish young men—and whatever it was that they had found. How he wanted to be back in Castlebough in the company of the countess. She had not quite understood why he was undertaking this expedition, and he did not really feel he could explain it all to her. Not that he completely understood himself. What, exactly, did Kehler expect to find in this cave? Certainly whatever it was it had the Farrellite Church concerned, and this as much as anything drew Erasmus.

"You look alternately troubled, then happy beyond one's dreams, Mr. Flattery," Clarendon said suddenly. There hadn't been much conversation since leaving the road for the simple reason that the trail through the trees forced them to ride in single file, but they were crossing a wide meadow now and Clarendon had dropped back to ride beside his companion.

"I am worried about these young gentlemen," Erasmus said, not commenting on his alternate mood.

Clarendon smiled at him. "They do not seem like impetuous young men, Mr. Flattery. I'm certain we shall find them perfectly well; at the worst they might suffer a bit from disappointment."

"You don't think they'll find whatever it is they're seeking?"

Clarendon shook his head. "The cave has been explored by some very dedicated men over the years, men who were a bit obsessed by their endeavor, and nothing but natural miracles have been reported. These men had a great deal more experience than your young friends, as clever as they might be. No, I think they will be disappointed, but nevertheless, we shall go in and find them if that is what you wish."

"My concern, Randall, is that Kehler had some information that the more experienced explorers did not, and that might lead them into unknown dangers."

"But Hayes would never say what this information was?"

Erasmus shook his head.

"Though certainly it related to Baumgere's search. Perhaps they will find the source of the priest's wealth. From what you have said, Mr. Hayes, at least, would not be hurt by such a find."

They rode into the trees again where the narrowness of the path allowed no further conversation.

The trail went up and after an hour of climbing they came to an indentation in the mountainside. Here, in a hollow, they found two men sitting on moss-covered rocks and talking quietly. It took Erasmus a moment to realize that the older of the two was Deacon Rose, for he had abandoned his priestly robes in favor of a huntsman's garb.

"Ah, Mr. Flattery, you have come at last," the priest said, rising from his seat. "I was beginning to think you had changed your mind."

"Changed my mind?" Erasmus said, "I don't remember making a decision to meet you, Deacon Rose."

"Nor do I suggest you did, but nevertheless, here you are, and if I cannot accompany you, then I shall merely follow. I assume you will not stop a man from going into the cave if that is his wish?"

Erasmus swung a leg over his horse's back and dropped to the soft ground. For a moment he stood staring at the priest, and then he glanced up at Clarendon, who remained on his pony. The small man raised his eyebrows, his mustache almost twitching.

Erasmus was not sure how he should respond. Certainly he wasn't prepared to stop the priest from entering the cave. What was he to do? Tie up Rose and his companion?

Yet he did not trust *Demon Rose,* as Kehler named him. The man was not telling the truth about what he knew, that was certain, and his intentions toward Kehler were not clear. The church bred a certain kind of arrogance in its priests, and they did not hold much respect for the sovereign rights of mere citizens.

"I might be more inclined to take you with us, Deacon, if you were to tell me what you, and what Kehler, expect to find here."

The priest stood looking at Erasmus for a moment, considering, then he inclined his head to one side. "Let us speak more privately, Mr. Flattery."

Erasmus handed the reins to Clarendon's servant and motioned for his companion to follow. They walked beyond the hearing of Rose's guide, into the dappled sunlight of the pines, and a view opened up before them. Far below they could see a lake, and for the first time Erasmus noticed the fragrance of the trees.

"I am sworn to secrecy, Mr. Flattery, and a priest does not break such an oath easily, but I feel that your request is eminently reasonable, so I will break my covenant this time." The man stopped and drew a breath, considering where to begin. "I am not absolutely certain what Kehler discovered in Wooton, and I say this in complete truth. He disappeared before we could question him and discover the extent of his betrayal—which is what it was," he said, showing a little pain. "A betrayal of trust." He paused again. "I have been sent here to be sure that this betrayal does not bring my church into conflict with Lord Eldrich. In this matter I am hoping for your assistance, Mr. Flattery. It is my greatest hope to stop Mr. Kehler in his endeavor before he draws the attention of the mage."

"But what is his endeavor?" Erasmus said quickly, his impatience taking control.

Rose nodded, realizing perhaps that he could no longer answer Erasmus with vagaries. "It is likely that what Kehler found in Wooton was a painting by Pelier; a painting and perhaps a letter from the priest who refused last rites to Baumgere."

Erasmus could see that Rose suddenly had Clarendon's full attention.

"Mr. Kehler likely learned that Baumgere spent a great deal of time searching the cave. And the painting . . . the painting showed someone offering knowledge. Not just knowledge but knowledge of the arts of the mages. Forbidden knowledge, Mr. Flattery. I'm sure that is what Baumgere sought, and what, in turn, Mr. Kehler hopes to find."

"The other night you suggested this all had something to do with Teller," Erasmus said.

"The priest nodded again. "It is possible."

"He hid records in the cave. Is that what you think?"

"I don't know, Mr. Flattery. Pelier's painting, like all of his work, is open to interpretation. But it seems likely that Mr. Kehler believes something is hidden here, and likely Baumgere did as well, though he never found it."

"And if that is so, why are you here?" Erasmus asked. "Even if Kehler finds some records or texts, it is, as you suggest, Mr. Kehler who will bear the brunt of Eldrich's anger, if the mage even finds out."

"I am here because we have a pact with the mage. If Mr. Kehler has found his information in our archives, it is more than likely that Eldrich will hold us accountable. But if I can convince Kehler to abandon this quest, then perhaps I can avert the intervention of Eldrich. And if Kehler finds what he seeks, I will see it myself and be the first to report it to the mage, unless you yourself do it before me. In either case you will be a witness, Mr. Flattery, and Eldrich will know that we have not broken our pact with him. Nor will we, Mr. Flattery. Let me assure you."

Erasmus looked over at Clarendon but could not read the man's reaction.

"I will not be a burden to you, Mr. Flattery. I work almost daily in the fields and barns of our monastery, and it has long been my great joy to explore the meadows and woods, walking many miles in a day. I will not slow you or need your help as we go."

Clarendon had planted his feet far apart, hands on his hips. "You will let us consider what you have said in private, Deacon Rose." It was said with remarkable firmness, from a man who did not reach the priest's shoulder.

Erasmus followed Clarendon away a few steps.

"What do you make of this, Randall?"

"As much as I hate to admit it, I think it would be better if he accompanied us, Mr. Flattery. I will feel more comfortable if he is under our watchful eye. I still do not trust him, though what he has said has me suddenly anxious. Could this matter interest Eldrich? Are those young men doing something incredibly foolish?"

Erasmus shook his head. "I don't know, Randall. I'm not such an authority on the mage as some people think. It seems unlikely to me that Eldrich has any notion of what two rather anonymous young gentlemen are up to. But if Baumgere searched here for some hidden records of the Tellerites, then it is a matter of great concern. Hayes and Kehler might not realize how much this would interest Eldrich, and how he might react to such a discovery. Rose is right in this. Better to inform the mage of what is found and then say nothing to anyone. I can't imagine what Hayes and Kehler think they will do with this knowledge."

"Then we will take the priest and watch him closely," Clarendon said. "Are we agreed?"

Erasmus nodded. "Reluctantly, yes."

An hour was lost while they prepared themselves to enter the cave. It was decided to take two lanterns and keep one carefully packed for use in case the first should be damaged or lost. They also split an enormous bundle of candles into three smaller packages.

"We must have light and more in reserve," Clarendon said. "A hundred feet into this cave we enter a world that is beyond the reach of starlight or sun. It is a blackness you have likely never experienced before. Without light we shall come to harm, gentlemen, have no doubt of it. Light. It is about to become the most precious commodity we have. A day into the cave and you would pay gold for it. Mark my words, you would give everything you own for a spark."

After resting for a moment and eating a little, they shouldered their packs and set off down the path to the cave mouth. The opening was hung with moss and vines which covered the hard rock that extended back into the darkness. The entrance to the underworld—though it was not guarded by wolves as the myths said.

They lit their lantern in the sunlight, and then, with Clarendon in the lead, set off into the darkness. Thirty feet into the cavern, Erasmus turned and looked back at the irregular patch of green framed by the cave mouth. Sunlight tumbled through the trees onto a bed of moss and lit the swaying ferns. Erasmus thought the world looked incomparably fair and verdant. He turned back and hurried after his companions who made their way resolutely downward into a land devoid of sunlight and rain and the whispering of wind in the pines.

Chapter Twenty-eight

KELLS tapped a glass paperweight against the table.

Knock . . . knock . . . knock. Pause. Then repeated again. He was unaware of it, Anna knew, as were most of the others, but it had begun to drive her to distraction.

Knock . . . knock . . . knock. Pause.

"Skye remains on the surface," Kells said at last. "And if he is to open the gate, as Anna has seen, then we might be advised to stay on the surface as well."

"But it is a vision," Banks said in frustration, "and therefore requires interpretation. I think the gate *is* open . . . *now*. Look who has gone down into the cavern: both these young men Skye employed; the priest; and Flattery and Clarendon as well. They have hardly undertaken such a thing for amusement."

"I think Banks is right," Anna said. "It feels . . . true to me. The gate is open, and we sit here idly arguing. If Flattery has gone down into the cave, then it is all but certain, I think."

"But he went in the company of a priest, and not just any priest—Deacon Rose. If Erasmus Flattery still serves Eldrich . . . well, *there* is an unholy alliance for you."

"But if Flattery still served Eldrich," Anna said, "would he expend all of his energies seeking knowledge of the mages, as we all know he does?"

"Over the centuries," Halsey said, "many have served the purposes of the mages and not known. Erasmus Flattery could very easily be one of these." The old man shifted in his chair, lost in thought. He was always uncomfortable, never quite free of pain, Anna knew. If she hadn't resented him so at that moment she was certain she would pity him his suffering.

"I fear, though, that Anna and Banks are right," Halsey said slowly. "The gate is open." He moved carefully in his chair, his eyes pressed tightly closed—the only sign of pain he showed. "I think the question is, how much risk are we willing to take? All other discussion is mere distraction. Do we go down into the cave not knowing if Erasmus Flattery still serves Eldrich? And do we go, knowing full well both the loyalties and intent of Deacon Rose?" He looked at the others around the table, holding the gaze of each of them for a moment.

Knock . . . knock . . . knock . . . pause.

Anna took a deep breath, knowing the full significance of the decision they made. "I believe Erasmus Flattery does not serve Eldrich, but pursues the knowledge of the mages of his own accord. As such, he is our natural ally. The priest is another matter. He will destroy us if he can. We cannot be misled by any lie or subterfuge he might employ. It is his sworn duty to destroy us, and therefore we must . . . do what the situation requires. And I believe we can."

Halsey stared at her for a moment, just a hint of emotion there, then turned to the others. "Kells?"

"I can't dispute Anna's vision if she feels this is the time. . . . I agree that the risk is Flattery. We simply do not know with any certainty what his loyalties are. And even if he hated Eldrich more than any man alive, that still would not mean that he did not serve the mage. Halsey is right in this; many have unwittingly served the mages." He looked down at the paperweight, hefting it as though he tapped it against an invisible surface. "But if the gate has been opened and the knowledge of Anna's vision is in the cave . . . we have little choice, I think. But—"

"Exactly so!" Banks interrupted. "There is no choice. That's what I—"

"Mr. Banks . . . !" Halsey said. "Let Kells finish. Please!"

Banks nodded, hanging his head a little. Anna felt pity for him—it was so frustrating at times.

"I was going to say that Anna must be prepared to be far more

. . . merciless than she has ever been." He looked up at Anna. "Do you understand? This priest—in fact, all of these people—their mere existence could threaten us. Eldrich must never know what has been found. Never. Or he will train others."

Anna nodded, looking down. She was hardly able to find her voice. "I—I knew it might come to this. Deacon Rose, I believe, is well within my abilities. Erasmus Flattery is a risk. We all know it. If Eldrich trained him. . . ."

"He has no familiar," Banks said firmly. "Flattery would have a familiar."

"It is not impossible to hide such a thing," Halsey said.

"I will do what is required to protect us. I must," Anna said. No one answered, and unable to bear the doubt-filled silence, she went on. "And there is something else. . . . Something we never discuss, for we hardly dare hope such things. In my vision the man had a blossom." She looked at Halsey. "If there is seed, then we should hold nothing back. I say risk everything for the seed."

Halsey did not respond, but only held her gaze a moment. "Then you will go down into the cave," he said quietly. "But if this knowledge you have seen is real—if you find it—then I charge you to let none of these others return to the surface, for if anyone escapes with knowledge . . . Eldrich will find us. Do not think this is just the irrational fear of an old man. Eldrich will find us, and his revenge upon us will be terrible."

Chapter Twenty-nine

HOLDING the lantern as near to his face as he dared, Kehler pressed his finger to the rock and lifted it away, examining the ball of his finger for residue.

"Chalk, I think. Look." He held his finger out to Hayes.

"Taste it," Hayes suggested.

Kehler considered this for a second, decided there was likely no harm in trying and thrust the finger into his mouth. "Eagh!" He spat on the cavern floor. "No doubt of it. Chalk mixed with mud, I think."

"Baumgere, I suppose?"

Kehler nodded. "Unless someone else has been here before us. It would make sense to mark what you'd done. The place is a labyrinth. It would be easy to forget which passages you'd explored. We should mark them as well."

"But chalk is hardly permanent. Wouldn't it have made more sense to use something that would last?"

"Perhaps, but would you carry a pot of paint in here? It has been many years since Baumgere was here, so the marks have almost gone, but perhaps in the short time he was searching—maybe only a few months, or even weeks—the chalk would have been adequate." Kehler paused for a second. "Or maybe he didn't want to leave permanent marks. He may even have erased them himself."

They looked back at the faint smudge on the rock. Several such marks had been found, each above an opening, though they were illegible, now, if they ever had been writing. Unfortunately no signs could be seen above many of the passages and Hayes and Kehler didn't know if this meant these passages had not been explored or if the chalk had simply worn away over the years.

Hayes looked down the length of the passage. There must have been forty openings in the short distance he could see. "Would you not approach this with some kind of order?" he asked. "I would certainly start at one end and work my way to the other."

"Yes, certainly. Meaning?"

"Well, if we can find the last passage that Baumgere explored we would save ourselves a great deal of effort. Do you see what I'm saying? Even if the last passage on which we can discern a mark is not the last he explored, we could still be eliminating some of them."

"Yes, that would make sense." Kehler moved to the next passage and began searching the rock around the opening.

After several hours of effort, they finally chose the passage they believed was the last that still bore a mark, and this eliminated perhaps fifteen openings—less than half the possibilities, though Kehler was quick to point out that any number of passages could possess branches, making the number potentially greater—perhaps much greater.

They sat to eat and rest, for both of them were greatly fatigued, as well as stiff and sore. The exploration of caves was not as painless as they liked to pretend.

Kehler fell into a deep sleep in the middle of their meal, and Hayes blew out the lamp and shut his eyes. It was important to preserve fuel. Strangely, he could not sleep, though he was as deeply fatigued as he could remember being.

He lay in the dark, feeling the immeasurable tons of rock above him, imagining the layer of soil, and then the thin cover of vegetation. Above them the night would be unfolding. Somehow he was sure a soft breeze swayed through the branches and the sweet fragrance of the forest filled the night. Overhead stars sparkled in a clear sky.

The fantasy would not hold, however, for even in the darkness Hayes could feel the cave around him. It had a certain smell, not unpleasant, but, still, for him it would always be associated with darkness and the damp and the constant weight of the rock above.

Kehler began to snore softly, and Hayes pulled his collar closer around him, suddenly cold. He tried not to think of the trek out; the abyss above the falls, the climbs, the sections where they would be forced to crawl. The cave entrance seemed impossibly far away, as unreachable as the past.

At last he fell into a troubled sleep and began to dream that he was lost in the tunnels of an endless cave, wandering through an eerie semidarkness, constantly coming to branchings and not knowing which way to turn. Occasionally he would see lights in the distance and think that he was rescued, but run as he might he could never catch the bearers of the light, and he would be left alone again, hearing only the distant fall of footsteps, and what sounded like muttering.

He lay in the darkness listening to an even breathing.

This is no nightmare, he realized. *I am awake.*

Even though he had no idea how long he'd slept, he decided to light the lamp and rouse his companion. They had much work to do and had not meant to sleep at all.

They began with the initial unmarked tunnel, Kehler insisting that the first would be his. The opening was small, almost round, and quite smooth. Kehler pushed himself into this, his legs kicking awkwardly for a moment, and then he disappeared, drawing the light in after him. Hayes was left in the darkness with only the sounds of Kehler's progress for company. Every so often he would call into the opening, checking on his friend, and he and Hayes would share a few words, then he would find his pack in the blackness and sit down, embarrassed by how dejected and alone he felt. Perhaps three quarters of an hour passed and suddenly a faint glow emananted from the passage Kehler had disappeared into. Hayes became confused as the light grew, for it almost seemed to him that the glow came from the opening next to the one Kehler had entered.

Anxiety gripped him; the next exploration would be his, and Hayes was not looking forward to it.

A few moments later the light grew from a glow to its anemic best, and the lantern swung out into the open. Hayes forced himself up and took it from his friend's hand. "I must be in a muddle," he said, "for I would have sworn you entered this next opening down."

Kehler's head and shoulders appeared. "You're not as addled as you think. I began in the next passage, but it joins this one and then peters out to nothing. I was able to turn around in the join and come out this way."

Kehler stood up stiffly and let out a long breath. "Well, it wasn't so bad. Shall I do another?"

"No, it's my turn. There is oil enough in the lamp? Then I shall be tortured next."

He sloughed off his coat, and took up the lantern. The next passage was no larger than the first two, but more importantly it was not smaller, and Hayes reached the lantern in and, with great reluctance, crawled in behind.

Once in the tube for his full length Hayes stopped. He looked down the narrow tunnel which bent away from him and went up slightly. What he could see did not seem terribly frightening. Tight but no worse than he had done. It was what lay beyond that preyed upon his imagination. Could it become so tight that he would not be able to go either forward or back?

With great effort Hayes pushed back the fear and forced himself to go on. From previous experience he knew that his shoulders were made narrowest if he put one arm forward and one back and slithered along on his side or stomach, depending on the shape of the passage. He would move the lantern ahead a few inches then drag himself along, scrabbling for purchase with his feet, regulating his breathing so that he did not panic, for panic was the great enemy. He would have been better to have been born with a less active imagination as it only made things worse. He could imagine the most gruesome scenarios: getting stuck in the passage; breaking the lamp and setting himself on fire in a place where he could barely move, let alone put himself out; and on and on. He shut his eyes and tried to will the images away. Best to think of nothing but moving ahead the next few inches, of moving the lantern carefully, being sure to set it where it would not fall and shatter the chimney.

To his great relief the passage did not grow tighter, nor did he set himself ablaze, so after thirty feet he began to relax a little. Suddenly the passage opened into a small room perhaps four feet square and here he sat up and rested for a few minutes, drawing deep ragged breaths.

From this room the tunnel continued on at an angle from an upper corner and he studied it for a moment, thinking it might be hard to get started unless there were some good holds inside that he could use to pull himself up. For a second he considered merely going back and telling Kehler that the passage ended, but he realized that he would not feel right about telling such a lie—and what if the secret they sought were here? No sense coming all this way and not making as thorough a search as they were able.

As he reached for the lantern to go on, he realized that a small bit of metal lay on the floor. He picked it up and found he held a copper rivet, perhaps from a belt or even a boot. This was not an unexplored passage! Someone had been here before. He looked up at the opening. If it was true that Baumgere did not find what he sought, then there was little reason to go on. Hayes felt his spirits lift.

Resolving to at least look into the tunnel, he thrust the lantern into the passage and peered in. Wedging himself in the opening, he managed to crawl in six feet, but it definitely tightened down to the size of a man's head in another length.

His energy restored by this, he crawled back out to the main passage and found Kehler wrapped in a blanket, fast asleep.

"Well, I'm glad I didn't need to call for help," he said as he shook his friend awake. "Look at this." He held the rivet out for Kehler to examine.

"You found it in there?"

"Yes. The passage burrows in for thirty feet or so to a small room. From there the passage doesn't go seven feet before shrinking down to mole size. But the rivet was on the floor."

"Farrelle's ghost. So Baumgere had explored this far."

"Assuming it was Baumgere."

Kehler nodded continuing to stare at the bit of copper. "It is unfortunate that we are still poking into passages that our good fallen-priest already eliminated, but I can see no other method of going about this. Can you?"

Hayes shook his head.

Kehler forced himself up. "Well, my turn for the fire." He lifted the lantern and shook it slightly, listening to the sound of fuel in the reservoir. Before he entered the next opening he took a candle and marked those that they had explored with an X in wax. A moment latter he had wriggled into the rock, leaving Hayes to listen to his progress and watch the light fade to darkness.

Hayes wrapped himself in Kehler's blanket and settled on the two packs. It was hard to stay awake, but he wanted to be sure to hear his friend should he call out.

And so it went for several hours as they eliminated one passage after another. Exhaustion caught up with them and they slept. As they became more and more fatigued, Hayes found it harder to stay warm when he was not exerting himself and lay shivering in the darkness, sleeping fitfully and shifting his position often. Each time he slept, the dream returned, though he never managed to catch up with the lights and their bearers, but wandered alone in the underworld, hollow with hunger and thirst and yearning, never able to find his way out.

A rasping wakened him, and Hayes opened his eyes to a slight glow coming from the opening his friend had crawled into some unknown time ago. Hayes threw aside the blanket and stumbled as he went. From out of the hole he could hear muttering and the harsh rasp of breath. Hayes stuck his head in the hole and called out.

The sounds stopped and Hayes called out again.

"Am I almost out?" came Kehler's reply though it was half grunted as he began to move again.

"I think so. I can hear you clearly."

"Farrelle be praised."

It was another quarter of the hour before Kehler's feet appeared and Hayes took hold and dragged his exhausted friend out. Kehler wavered as he found his feet and Hayes grabbed hold of him lest he fall.

"Sit down, Kehler."

"No, let me stand," he steadied himself on the rock wall. "Let me feel the space around me." He moved his arm and worked his cramped shoulders, gasping as though he had been under water.

"Flames," he said between breathes. "Bloody blood and flames. What a hellhole."

"What did you find?"

"Find? Nothing only two hundred feet of passage so tight I thought I should never get out again. Farrelle's flames, I hope they're not all like that." He lowered himself to the rock and leaned his back against the wall. "How long was I gone?"

Hayes produced his timepiece. "Three hours and a bit, I think."

"Well. . . . We will be here some time if they all take such effort. Flames, I wish we knew which tunnels Baumgere eliminated. We could save ourselves days. We haven't brought nearly enough food, I fear."

"We'll have to ration, that's all."

"Yes, but all this effort has made me hungry all the time."

"Well, it is about mealtime anyway—noon in the world above." Hayes began to rummage in his pack for food. "Let's eat something, and then I'll take my turn."

Before they ate, Kehler took up a candle and made a prominent X above the opening he had just explored, as though to be absolutely sure not to have to enter it again.

They ate and drank and spoke of small things of the world above. Laughed at old stories of wilder days, and did everything they could to put the matter they pursued from their minds. Hayes had never really been convinced that they would find fame and fortune from this mad endeavor, but had accompanied his friend partly out of loyalty, partly from curiosity, and perhaps in part for lack of anything better to do. His creditors were unlikely to find him here. But now that the true cost of the exploration was becoming apparent, he wondered if it would not be more sensible to give it up. It was difficult for him to imagine that they would find anything that would make this terrible crawling into the bowels of the earth worthwhile.

"Can you bear to do another?" Kehler asked after they had both avoided the issue as long as possible.

Hayes felt the darkness reach out and touch him, the infinite cold stored in stone seeping into his beating heart. "We can't quit now," he heard himself say. He tried to control his fear. "I, for one, need the fortune you promised." With the utmost care he filled the lantern, knowing that they could ill afford to spill a drop.

Hayes stretched his stiff muscles, took up the lantern, and went to meet the next passage. His courage failed him as he stood looking into the dark mouth that was about to consume him, but then he forced himself to go on. Leaning down, he stretched as far as he could, setting the lantern in the passage. He was surprised at how unresponsive his muscles were, as though he had driven them beyond exhaustion and now they no longer answered to his commands as they should.

He crawled awkwardly into the unyielding rock, feeling it bite into his battered knees and the heels of his hands. When his hip contacted the rock, Hayes stopped for a moment and let the pain subside.

"I feel like an old man," he muttered to himself.

"What's that?" he heard Kehler call out.

"Nothing but curses. Put on the tea, I shan't be but a moment."

He reached out and moved the lantern ahead, dragging himself after it, battering his shoulder cruelly into the rock. On he went, trying not to think about what lay ahead. He didn't even look up the passage except to move the lantern, for it hurt too much to wrench his neck around any more than he had to. A few moments passed before he began to warm from the exertion and then he broke out in a sweat that did not feel natural, as though he were falling ill as well.

The passage tightened down around him, and he contorted himself around to find a way forward, trying to maneuver his shoulder and hip around irregularities in the rock. For a moment Hayes jammed his shoulder back against a swelling and forced himself to relax, breathing deeply. He was so tired that he could hardly force himself to move.

He closed his eyes and concentrated on breathing. He knew he wasn't seriously stuck here, it was more the fatigue, he hardly had the strength it required to get himself free.

"I can go back," he reassured himself. *"Go back."* His voice sounded so overwhelmed with fatigue and laden with sadness that he almost thought he listened to another, and this frightened him almost more than anything. He shook himself, not sure if he had begun to fall asleep.

Forcing himself to back up a little, he managed to release his shoulder and then wriggle around to get past the projection that impeded him.

The cold sweat did not abate, as though it were not a bodily fluid at all but cold fear that flowed out of his pores.

He reached out to move the lantern, forcing himself to raise his head so as not to burn his fingers yet again, and he recoiled in horror, smashing himself hard into the stone, and hearing himself cry out. The lantern toppled, leaking oil, and immediately caught fire. And there he stuck, gasping for breath, cowering back against the stone, unable to bear the sight. Beyond the flames lay a human skull, a tiny wisp of hair still clinging to it like a spider's web. One skeletal hand reaching out toward him, toward the world of light.

Oh, bloody flames. Farrelle save me. . . . It is a child. A poor, forsaken child."

Without thought as to what would happen, he reached quickly into the flame, putting the lantern upright, his sleeve catching fire.

"Nooo!" He battered his wrist against the stone in desperation and managed to put the sleeve out before he went up in flame himself, though his hand stung insufferably from burns. He coughed from the smoke and backed away from the lantern that still sat in the center of a ball of flame.

"Flames! Let me go. It is a child. Baumgere's child. Farrelle grant him peace."

The leaked oil burned away, and though he was nearly blind from the sting of the smoke, Hayes forced himself to move forward again, and reached out gingerly and touched the lantern's handle. Still too hot. He would have to wait.

He could see the entire skeleton now, spread out behind the skull, so small and shrunken he wondered how the child could ever have become jammed in such a passage, but he was sure that was what had happened, for it narrowed to almost nothing around the child's remains.

After the handle had cooled, he lifted the lantern with his burned hand and began a slow retreat, not taking his eyes from the horror, as though afraid it might follow.

The crawl out was painfully slow, inching along like a slug, finding his way through the narrow parts, until he emerged in the passage again. He lay on the floor while Kehler bent over him and took up the scorched lantern.

"Did you call me? I awoke to a sound, but I was not sure if it was a dream." He looked at his friend who sat up now and covered his face with his unburned hand. "Hayes? Are you all right?"

Hayes shook his head, though he kept his hand over his face, as though he could shut out the horror. "I found the child . . . Baumgere's child."

He felt Kehler's hand on his shoulder. "Wedged in the tunnel?"

Hayes nodded. "Though the skeleton is so small it is impossible to imagine how. Flames, Kehler, the man was a monster! Only a child, and he sent him into that hell. What terror the poor boy must have known. The priest was right to refuse that man absolution. I pray he is burning still."

Kehler sat on the floor beside his friend, saying nothing, but hoping perhaps that just being near would mean something. Hayes could not remember shedding tears since childhood, but he felt the sting of them now. The poor child. . . . What a horrible death. Trapped in a nightmare that had but one escape. No one deserved such a death. Except perhaps Baumgere himself.

Hayes felt a rage burn up in him toward this man. It was lucky for Baumgere that he was long dead, for Hayes was certain he would seek him out, otherwise. Refusal of absolution might seem like a terrible punishment to a Farrellite, but Hayes had a more earthly retribution in mind.

Chapter Thirty

ERASMUS stood by the lake of the mirror, holding his lantern aloft to illuminate the scene. It was haunting, as well as unreal in some way—the strange beauty of another world.

Behind him he could hear the others talking, the sound of their voices carrying down the passage like a strange mumbling in another tongue. He half expected some unknown creature of the underworld to appear.

Erasmus and his companions had soon realized that one lantern was not sufficient for three men, for the leader had to have light, and most of the time this left the last man in near-darkness. It was too dangerous to proceed in this way, so they had lit a second lantern, though they put it out whenever they stopped to rest or eat.

Erasmus shed his pack and began climbing over the nearest rock, searching, and it was just then that the others appeared, the strange rumble of their words turning into common Farr the second they emerged into the chamber.

"There should be a boat here," Clarendon called out to Erasmus. "Can you see it?"

"No. I fear it has been carried away, or Hayes and Kehler have not returned it."

"Can't we climb around?" Rose asked as Erasmus joined them.

Clarendon sat down on his pack, shaking his head, and looking a little angry. "No. That is why the boats were built. It is impossible to pass except over the water. Damn their imprudence. If they are in any trouble, we shall be of no use whatsoever."

"If one can't pass over the water we must pass through it," Erasmus said, peeling off his coat. "How far is it to the end?"

"Three hundred feet, perhaps a bit more," Clarendon said, rising as though he would protest Erasmus' proposal. "But the water is quite deep, and one cannot always find holds along the walls. It is too dangerous, Mr. Flattery. Far too dangerous."

Erasmus pulled off a boot. "But not for one who can swim, Randall, which, fortunately, I can."

"But three hundred feet, Mr. Flattery . . . !" Clarendon said, forcing Erasmus to laugh.

"I don't know exactly how far I can swim, for I haven't measured in some years, but in my youth I swam upwards of five miles at a stretch, so I think I can stay afloat for three hundred feet, even at this advanced age. The problem shall be that when I get to the lake's far end, I will have no light." He stopped pulling off his clothes and considered this. "If we put a candle in a tin bowl I shall try to carry it with me."

This was done, and with some trepidation Erasmus slipped into the icy waters. He tried floating the bowl before him but in ten feet he'd put the flame out. After returning to have it lit again he swam on his back and held the bowl and candle clear of the water. If he went slowly enough and was careful not to blow out the flame with his own breath, he might just make it to the far end.

But this was not to be, most of the way there the flame snuffed out again, and Erasmus decided to carry on, hoping the weak light from the lamps would be enough.

He was shivering when he finally came to the lake's end, and was beginning to imagine all kinds of creatures that might live in such a lake, when a faint curve, too consistent to be natural caught his eye.

He scrambled out of the water, stubbing a toe brutally, and found the two skiffs side by side in the darkness. Without further damage to either himself or the boat he managed to launch one of the craft, and shivering like it was the worst winter, he set his oars to work. In a moment he was back with his companions and pulling on clothes over his wet limbs.

"What lies at the far end?" the priest asked.

"I can't say, for I could hardly see," Erasmus answered, beating his arms across his chest and slapping his shoulders to try to gain warmth.

"Just a small shelf of rock not unlike this, though not so large. Perhaps there was an opening to a passage." Clarendon blew out the flame in one lantern. "I think we should make a meal here and then rest. We have been pressing hard, and this place is as comfortable as any we shall see for some time."

"How far into the cave have you been, Mr. Clarendon?" the priest asked.

"Some way beyond this, to a falls. Once we pass that, it will be as new to me as to you." He began taking food from his pack.

The three men made themselves as comfortable as they could and shared out their food: dried apples and cheese; bread that would soon be too stale to eat; and a bitter smoked meat.

As at their other rest stops, a silence fell over the group and Erasmus was sure that this was because attempts at polite conversation failed and the real questions that lay between them would not be asked—or if they were, would not be answered. Something about the harsh reality of the cave made social discourse seem utterly false—almost an offense to their situation.

So they ate in silence, all three of them speculating, Erasmus was sure. He wondered why Rose was really here. Was it truly fear of Eldrich? But certainly the priest suspected that Erasmus himself was a servant of the mage. There was some other explanation for the priest's presence, or at least he had not told the entire truth.

Erasmus thought the air in the chamber became more and more charged with unasked questions, like the atmosphere before a storm. He was not sure how long this charge could continue to build before it would be released. And he feared that what would be released would not be answers.

Erasmus looked at his two companions. Perhaps it was something about the cave—it was so harsh and unyielding that those who ventured into it could maintain few illusions—but Erasmus had begun to wonder about both Rose and Clarendon. It was obvious that he should not trust the priest, despite the man's very real charm, but now he even looked suspiciously at the savant. It was all so convenient, the way Clarendon found Erasmus at the Ruin, how he just happened to be an authority on Baumgere, and knew about the cave as well—had even explored it himself. Clarendon had refused to allow Erasmus to come down here alone, and it was not some younger man that he sent to guide him. No, he professed to be such an admirer of Erasmus that he must accompany him personally.

Too much coincidence, Erasmus decided, and this was a man who professed not to believe in coincidence.

Clarendon and then Rose drifted into sleep, their soft breathing comforting and somewhat familiar in this harsh place. Erasmus blew out the lantern and then closed his eyes, and though he achieved a state near to sleep, he never quite lost consciousness. His thoughts began to drift, random memories surfacing. He thought of the countess, and a warmth and excitement welled up in him. The idea of taking up a lantern and leaving this place came over him, rushing back to the surface, to this astonishing woman. How had he been so blessed as to have her bestow her favors on him?

But even thoughts of his night with the countess could not keep his focus, and other memories surfaced. His last days in the house of Eldrich, the terrible imprudence of young boys, and the carelessness of his teacher. Walky. What had ever become of the man? Certainly he would not still be alive? But somehow Erasmus felt that he was. There was some odd memory of Walky just at the edge of his consciousness, but he could not quite bring it into the light.

The countess again, stroking him, whispering in his ear, her eyes in the firelight. It was impossible that a woman should have such beautiful eyes. A sudden fear that he would never look into them again felt like a chasm opening beneath him—as though there were suddenly nothing solid in his world.

Percy, his loyal follower, easily influenced by his only friend in the lonely world of the mage's house. Percy . . . gone.

He slipped into something like sleep then, memory blending with dream. The countess sweeping her hair slowly across his chest. A tall man in the dark, and then a flame licked up

A spark in the darkness, and Erasmus realized he was watching

Clarendon relight the lamp, watching the flame shiver into existence, created from nothing—the miracle of fire. The priest stirred, and without saying anything the three men began to ready themselves to go on.

"Mr. Flattery and I should go first with our packs," Clarendon said hoisting a pack into the tiny boat, "and that will leave only the deacon and one pack for you to bring next trip."

They lit the second lantern for the priest and gingerly Erasmus dipped the oars, pulling the skiff out onto the black water, the blades leaving tiny whirlpools at the surface.

When they were twenty feet out, Clarendon touched Erasmus' arm. "Hold our position," he said quietly, then he sat up and looked back at the Farrellite priest. "Deacon Rose?"

Erasmus turned the boat sideways so that he could see the priest, not quite sure what Clarendon wanted to say.

"I think it's time that we had the truth out in the open."

Erasmus saw that the little man had Rose's attention now.

"You believe that there are followers of Teller still alive, is that not true?"

Rose clearly did not like what was happening, but he kept his temper in check, for there was nothing he could do—a moat divided them. "I don't know what you're saying, Mr. Clarendon. I have come here out of concern for a prize student."

"No, you have come here because you fear he is a follower of Teller, and your church will have no practitioners of the arts remaining when Eldrich is gone. That is why you are here. Now it is time that we spoke plainly, Deacon Rose, or we shall simply leave you here until we return, and unless you can swim like Mr. Flattery, you . . ."

"No!" The priest put out his hands. "No. I must come with you."

Clarendon looked at Erasmus who nodded slightly, giving him permission to continue. He was more than a little impressed with the small man's boldness.

"The only way you will join us, sir, is by satisfying us with the truth. Not before. Now tell me why you are pursuing Mr. Kehler, and be quick about it. I'm tired of your prevarication—speak now and take no time to concoct a lie."

Rose paced quickly to one side, his hands to his face.

"Row on, Erasmus, the priest cannot be trusted."

"No! You will need me if Kehler has made the discovery he hopes. I don't know if Kehler is a follower of Teller. I pray that he isn't. Nor do I know if there are such people still alive, but Mr. Clarendon is right. It is not impossible. I have been sent by my church to be certain that this heresy no longer exists, and to be sure that Eldrich does not turn his anger on us. I am sworn to preserve the church, Mr. Flattery, that is my function." He ignored Clarendon now, and addressed Erasmus as though appealing to his common sense.

Clarendon, however was not finished, or apparently satisfied. "You were trained to deal with just such a situation, is that not so? I know the church has ways of dealing with the arts—how else could you have rooted out the Tellerites from among you own?"

Rose nodded his head stiffly. "Yes! Yes, I have been trained to perform this function. We must protect ourselves. If Eldrich were to find out that a student found his way here with information from our archive—It would not matter that we were innocent of any crime, the mage's anger would be turned on us. I cannot allow that, Mr. Flattery, I cannot."

"And what will you do when you find Kehler and Hayes?"

The priest did not answer.

"I don't care for his hesitation," Clarendon said quietly.

"I will obey the orders of my church," Clarendon said quickly.

"That is not an answer, Deacon."

"I will perform a ritual that will determine their . . . *culpability*, and if they are simply innocent young men driven to folly by their curiosity, then I will not harm them."

"But if they are not deemed innocent, you will destroy them if you can," Clarendon called out. "Is that not so?" The priest did not answer. *"Is that not so?!"* he shouted, the words reverberating in the cavern.

"I—I have no choice. If Eldrich is to discover that we have let such a thing occur. . . . And think what Eldrich will do. His justice will be less compassionate than mine."

"And you believe I will be the witness you'll need to convince Eldrich you act in good faith?" Erasmus asked so quietly that he could see the priest strain to hear.

"Yes, Mr. Flattery, you will be my witness."

"But what if I am a follower of Teller, or what if Mr. Clarendon is?"

The priest shook his head. "Eldrich watches over you, Mr. Flattery; that is what I believe. It is almost certain that followers of Teller, if such exist, would be interested in you. Eldrich would want to know if they ever approached you. No, I do not fear that you can betray Eldrich."

"But Mr. Clarendon?"

The priest shrugged. "Mr. Clarendon is another matter."

Erasmus turned and looked at the small man in the boat with him.

Clarendon's face seemed to sag, his mustache drooping. "Do you suspect me, Mr. Flattery?" his voice very hard, almost hurt.

"I'm sorry, Randall, but I am beginning to suspect everyone, even myself."

"You think you are a tool of Eldrich?"

"It is not impossible, though I have not seen the mage since I was a child. But you change the subject, Randall. You said you do not believe in coincidences, yet there have been any number in our brief friendship."

"I said I didn't believe in coincidences, Mr. Flattery, meaning that I believed there are other reasons, other forces at work. There is a design, that is what I believe."

"And everything will work out for the best?"

Clarendon shook his head, almost sadly. "No, I feel that is very unlikely, for the design depends on men, and men are too often weak when they should stand firm and foolish when they have the greatest need of wisdom. And here we sit, accusing each other, while who knows what awaits discovery inside this cave, or what difficulties our young friends might have found."

"And who began these accusations?" the priest called from the shore. The boat had begun to drift back toward the priest, and Erasmus backed the oars to keep his distance.

"I began the accusations, priest, but I did not begin the lies," Clarendon said, his kind manner disappearing and disdain taking its place.

"Do you plan to test us all, Deacon Rose? Is that your intention?" Erasmus asked.

The priest did not answer. "Do not go alone with this man into the cave, Mr. Flattery. I cannot tell you if he is one of them or not, but we should always be on our guard."

"Ah," Clarendon said, "just like a priest to try to sow the seeds of distrust and dissension. He will turn us against each other, Mr. Flattery. It is their way."

Erasmus did not respond but turned back to the priest. "If you were to perform this trial on Mr. Clarendon, what would result if you found him to be what you most fear?"

Again the priest hesitated.

"I would not survive," Clarendon said, no doubt in his voice. "Is that not so?"

Still the priest did not answer.

"Well, Randall, what of it? Are you a follower of Teller? Speak carefully now, for if you deny it, I might well take you at your word and let the priest perform his trial."

Clarendon's mustache twitched, and Erasmus was not sure if it was from anger. The dwarf met his eyes for a long moment, and then he shook his head. "I am no follower of Teller, nor a member of any such society. No, I am merely a small man of enlarged curiosity, and concerned about these young men. And a friend to you, Mr. Flattery, though you don't seem to believe it."

These words sounded genuine to Erasmus and he felt guilty that he had betrayed this man's trust. It seemed to him that Clarendon had known enough betrayal in his life.

"I . . . I'm sorry, Randall, I'm just confused by all of this. I don't know who to trust any more."

Clarendon nodded. "I understand what you're saying, Mr. Flattery. It is one of life's greatest quandaries—who do we trust. But I vote we do not trust this priest."

"Mr. Flattery?" Rose called out upon hearing this. "There is more. You cannot know what we will find in this cave. If the Tellerites hid something here, it might be protected by the arts. Young Kehler and Hayes, if they are innocent as you think, could be in real danger. Unless you know more than you claim, I do not think you will be able to help them. In fact, you might suffer the same fate. I can detect such things and protect us from them. If you go on alone, you might not be able to return for me if you require my help. Do not leave me here."

Clarendon looked at Erasmus, raising his eyebrows.

"Is this possible?" Erasmus asked him.

The small man shrugged. "Let us row on and discuss it out of earshot."

Erasmus nodded, and called back to Rose. "We will consider what you've said." With that he dug in his oars and set them off across the underground lake.

Neither Clarendon nor Erasmus spoke for some time, nor did they seem to notice the wonders around them, but both brooded on what had been said. It was not until they'd passed through the strait between two small peninsulas that Clarendon spoke.

"What did you make of all that?"

"I don't know, Randall, I really don't. I'm getting the feeling that Rose expects to find . . . something significant in this cave. Perhaps the church has suspected for some time that something is hidden here. And I'm afraid of what he might try to do to our young friends. Whether they are followers of Teller or not matters not to me. I am no minion of Eldrich, and I don't believe it is the place of either the church or the mage to pass judgment on them. Unfortunately, we shall not stop Eldrich if he finds out, and I fear that this priest would not hesitate to inform the mage if he believed it would deflect Eldrich's anger from the church. For that reason I am reluctant to bring him with us. Even if he does no direct harm to our young friends, he might well do greater harm by informing Eldrich."

Clarendon considered for a moment. "But what if his claims are true? Could the followers of Teller have left some kind of charm or spell that could cause us harm? Is that possible, do you think?"

Erasmus nodded. "From the little I know, I would say that it is, though such things fade with time. Still, a well-wrought work of the mage's art can last many decades, perhaps even longer. It is possible. If Hayes and Kehler have encountered such a thing, I don't know what we shall do."

"So, though we may need him, we cannot trust him," Clarendon said.

"That seems to be true."

They came to the end of the lake and brought their boat gently to the shore. They disembarked and unloaded their packs, neither making comment on their dilemma.

The dwarf sat on his pack. "If we could only bind him to his word. . . ." He considered a moment. "We could make him swear an oath to Farrelle."

Erasmus shook his head. "If it came to protecting his church, I think our good Deacon would burn for eternity before he'd put it in danger."

"Then you're saying we cannot trust him to live by his word, so we should go on," Clarendon declared, not sounding so sure of himself, despite his earlier opposition to the priest. "I suppose that if we found need of his services we could come back for him—though he may no longer be waiting."

Erasmus nodded. "We are, of course, doing the same thing as our young friends, and making it difficult if not impossible for anyone to follow. We must hope we don't require rescue."

Having exhausted the argument they sat, still unwilling to make the decision to go on. Suddenly there was a splash and a distant call for help that echoed eerily in the cavern.

"What in Farrelle's name?" Erasmus leaped up and pushed the tiny boat back into the water, climbing quickly aboard. Clarendon set the lantern on the aft seat as Erasmus dropped the oars into their sockets and then swept out into the lake. Another half-muffled call for help and then his name, followed by more frantic thrashing of the water.

Erasmus pulled his little skiff through the narrow pass and quickly found Rose, in the water, clinging to the wall of the cavern. Just as Erasmus spotted him, the priest's grip slipped and he went under, flailing ineffectually. He managed to get a hand on the stone but only pushed himself away from the wall. Erasmus thought he would have to leap in and rescue the man, but somehow the priest's flailing kept him on the surface until Erasmus came near.

But just out of reach Erasmus brought his skiff to a stop.

"Listen to me now. If you upset the boat, we will both be in the water. Take hold of the transom gently, and do not try to pull yourself up. Just hold your head out of the water, and I will tow you to shore. Do you hear me?"

The priest nodded desperately, trying to take a grip on his own fear. Erasmus backed the oars and brought the stern up to Rose. To his relief the priest did as he was instructed.

Erasmus towed the priest back to the place from which he had started and they were joined by Clarendon who had launched the second skiff.

Rose crawled wretchedly up on the rock, looking like a half-drowned dog. "I will swear not to harm Hayes and Kehler," he said between coughing. "I will swear by my church, and my sacred oath." He tried to catch his breath. "But if you do not take me with you, I will be forced to try to make my way across the lake again, for I will not be left behind. I will not."

Erasmus glanced over at Clarendon, who looked on with some concern. The little man nodded and Erasmus stepped ashore to assist the priest, not at all sure they were making the right choice.

Chapter Thirty-one

OVER the years Eldrich had used entrails, bones, mirrors, cards, even tea leaves, but water and its variations remained his favorite medium. He was not a master of augury, though in the present world he was almost certainly without equal. This did not, however, allow him to forget that compared to practitioners of the past he was not particularly skilled.

The mage also knew the folly of making all one's decisions based on augury—even in the hands of a master, it was, at best, an inexact art. No, one must focus on the so-called "real world," the here and now. But even so, he could not resist the occasional attempt to see into the future, though lately these attempts were more than occasional.

Everything is so clouded, he worried. *Nothing is clear.*

He knew that events were building to a crisis, but the closer this point came, the less certain were the signs. But perhaps one more attempt. . . .

He had collected a double-handful of white cherry blossoms, and crouched before the pond, waiting for a cloud to reveal the moon. Starlight would do, if it were pure, but if there was a moon, one had to use it. He heard the sounds of his familiar in the copse nearby. It watched him, a little apprehensive though it did not understand what he was about to do.

Instinct, Eldrich thought. *It is a creature of almost pure instinct.*

He looked up at the sky. The moon illuminated a cloud so regular in shape that it looked like a white, translucent stone worn smooth by the endless flow of years. The night resonated inside of him: the movement of the stars and planets. The mage could feel the earth hurtling through the cosmos. He could actually feel it.

For a second he shut his eyes, and experienced himself falling, tumbling through the darkness among the stars.

He looked down into the pond and watched the reflection of the moon emerge from behind its pebble cloud, and at that precise instant he cast the cherry blossoms into the air and watched them fall upon the water. They rippled the surface, creating patterns, and Eldrich focused on them, opening himself to the cosmos for a split second, letting the great void flow into him through this pattern on the water. And a second was all he could bear.

He shut his eyes, reeling back from the water's edge, staggering. He felt his wolf pass near him, felt its uneasiness. He staggered a step or two and dropped to his knees, trying to grasp the kernel of knowledge, nurture it.

A woman riding an armored steed, her hair flowing back, a sword raised. But the steed was a massive wolf, its fur tipped with silver, its eyes impossibly light, like the cloud illuminated by the moon. His vision changed, and he saw a skeleton aflame and heard a long, horrifying scream. And then he gazed into a long tunnel of utter darkness, and saw a single point of light. A spinning star, blue-white and cold as winter.

And then it, too, was gone, and he was spent utterly, gasping, on hands and knees. The world spinning around, hurtling through the cosmos, though no man seemed aware of it. No man.

An hour later Eldrich was still not himself. He sprawled in a chair by the fire, eating a bowl of soup. Practicing the arts always left him warm, except for augury, and that invariably left him shaking and devoid of body heat, as though he had fallen into a winter river. It sapped his strength for some time, leaving him tired and lethargic.

It is the cold, dark void among the stars, he told himself. *It enters into one, and is not easily driven out.*

"Lord Eldrich?" his servant said, concern in his voice. He had been saying something, and the mage had not answered.

"Yes, Walky, I'm listening. There is something stationed before the cave. . . ."

"A great wolfhound, sir."

"Indeed. . . ." This news actually focused his mind for a few seconds. "And is it natural, do you think?"

"I don't know, sir. It has only been reported to me. All I can answer for certain, sir, is that it is there."

"It can't be Erasmus' " he mused aloud. "Can it?" he asked the old man who stood so solicitously nearby.

Walky shook his head, clearly troubled. "I wouldn't think so, Lord Eldrich. I . . . I hope it isn't."

"Yes. I hope it isn't as well." Silence. He stirred his soup absent-mindedly, watching the vegetables surface, then drown in the broth.

"The problem is that it seems it will not allow anyone to enter the cave."

"Ah. I am . . . rather tired this evening. My mind. . . . Has anyone tried to kill it?"

Walky shook his head.

"So whoever reported it believed it unnatural?" Eldrich looked back down into his bowl. "Well, I will deal with it, then."

He stared down into his bowl again and suddenly thrust thumb and forefinger in, bringing them out dripping, but holding a piece of meat. Setting the bowl aside he rose wearily and went to the window, pulling it open. He stood there, facing the night, and made an odd sound, somewhere between the call of an owl and a whistle, though low and long. And then he waited, seemingly with infinite patience.

Walky stayed where he was, not moving, which he believed was the wisest course. He was not exactly afraid of Eldrich's familiar, but the beast was unpredictable, as unpredictable as its master, and Walky was never sure that either of them would continue to treat him as a valued servant simply because they had done so for many decades. He simply wasn't sure.

Perhaps a quarter of the hour passed before Walky heard the sounds of the wolf as it came over the wall and into the garden. It was panting a little as though it had been on the hunt when the summons came. Unlike Walky, it never looked particularly concerned when it had kept its master waiting. There was a bond between mage and wolf that Walky could not fathom—something far more than man and . . . "pet" hardly seemed the right word.

Eldrich stroked the beast behind its ears somewhat roughly, and spoke low in the tongue of the mages. Walky could not quite hear the words. The wolf took the morsel in a gulp, hardly noticing, it seemed. A moment more of this show of affection, and then the wolf bounded away, leaving its master watching, his hand still raised as though not finished with its stroking.

Eldrich lowered his hand to the windowsill, and supported himself, still fatigued from his efforts. It was certainly not his place to say, but Walky believed the mage indulged in this practice too often. The servant was certain that there were more questions resulting from augury than answers. No, it was all right to See now and again, every few years or even once in a year, but very few weeks went by that the mage did not practice the art in some form. And what did it bring him? Too many possibilities, too many by half.

No, it was not worth the effort.

Walky looked at the mage, still standing before the open window leaning on the frame like an elderly man. It was a sign of desperation, Walky knew. This task Eldrich had been left. . . . Walky feared it was almost beyond him. All the centuries of augury had missed the most important truths, and now there was only one mage left to deal with the situation. The last mage of all, or so he hoped.

Eldrich cleared his throat and Walky put aside his musings, attentive to his master's needs.

"I am sorry about Erasmus, Walky."

The little man felt a wave of sadness settle over him, like leaves upon the earth. "I know you are, sir."

Chapter Thirty-two

THE countess shaded herself with a parasol and sat in the stern of the boat, smiling somewhat enigmatically. Kent was trying to smile as well, but the soft look of remembered pleasure on the countess' face made it difficult. He could hardly take his eyes from her all the same, and occasionally he would notice that a look of anxiety would transform her beautiful face, as completely as a cloud would turn the blue waters of the lake to gray. He wondered what matter pressed on her so, and despite his own pain at what he had seen through the window, he felt a desire to comfort her.

As he looked at her sitting so primly in the stern seat, dressed impeccably as always, he could not erase the memory of her in the act of love. It almost seemed to him that this had been some other woman, abandoning herself to pleasure. His jealousy toward Erasmus—and the fact that Erasmus had experienced this side of her nature—was driving him a little mad. He dipped his oars and drove the boat on a little more briskly.

Marianne sat in the bow puffing on a pipe, reading from time to time from her work in progress, and then disparaging what she had written. She was taking one of her periodic breaks to contemplate—though whether she was thinking about her book, meditating upon her own genius, or considering the beauty of the scene, Kent could not tell.

He dipped the oars and moved the boat again, hardly aware of the beauty of the hills behind the countess.

"Mr. Kent? Do you think my depiction of Frederick's response is realistic? I am asking you to speak as a man?"

"How else could I speak, Miss Edden?"

She blew out a smoke-filled laugh. "As an artist, for certainly the artist has a way of seeing the world that transcends their own situation. Good artists, anyway."

Kent tried to remember what she had just read. The character, Frederick, was hopelessly in love with a woman who thought him her dearest friend in the world—though she had given her heart elsewhere, and very unwisely, too. It was not an original situation, but Marianne's description of the man's feelings was so exact, so unusual. Before he could answer, the novelist prompted him by reading from her manuscript.

" 'While in her presence he felt as though he had been cast loose from his world. All the ties that bound him were severed, and he could no longer even imagine what his place had been. Suddenly he could not speak to children without feelings of terrible awkwardness and inadequacy, as though afraid all the while that he was making an absolute fool of himself. As though the judgment of children mattered. And this in a man who had lunched amicably with the King and had courtly flirtations with some of the most notable beauties in the capital. He floated in the sea of faces, adrift, adrift, adrift—and no one reached out a hand to him.' "

Kent nodded, unable to escape the thought that Marianne was not only describing him but trying to tell him something as well. Perhaps it was only his own reaction to his present predicament that made him feel so, but he blushed all the same.

The countess, mercifully, did not seem to notice, or at least pretended not to.

"I don't know, Marianne," the countess said. "I think Frederick far too strong a character to react this way. I simply can't believe it."

"But that is the point," the novelist protested. "The most successful, most assured people can suffer this same undoing. I have seen it. Certainly you have seen it. And perhaps those around Frederick who don't know him well do not notice—though he feels even children can see through him. Which is my point entirely. It is all internal and 'real,' if we can even use the term, only to him. Objective 'reality' hardly figures in our perception of the real at all. In this sense, the world of a novel is as real as this world we inhabit. If you believe it—it is real."

Kent looked off at the distant shore. He had long trained his mind in the habit of examining his surroundings, puzzling over how one would paint this or that. Today he was fascinated by the apparent haze of green surrounding certain trees, though this was only the forming leaves breaking free of their buds. Yet, from this distance it appeared that a rarefied green cloud hung in the branches.

Despite this attempt to fall back on old habits, Kent did feel cut loose from the stable grounds of his own life. *That is what comes of hopes and desires and absurd expectations,* he told himself. *Why in the round world did I ever imagine that this woman would be interested in me?*

But another part of him kept asking, *Erasmus?* She had taken up with Erasmus Flattery? Not some wealthy noble at all, but a man of substance. A man who could not even bother to dress in fashion. Even Kent qualified on at least one of these counts. Why not him? Was he not talented? Did he not have a certain charm and wit? Kent believed that he could be as handsome as Erasmus, even if he did not have the presence, for it was true that Erasmus commanded not just respect but attention, without seeming to make any effort.

"You are staring at the shore with an intensity that makes me think you are ready to quit the sea, Mr. Kent," the countess said.

"Oh, not at all, Lady Chilton. I apologize. It is a terrible habit of mine. I see something that catches my eye, the play of light, the shadow and light behind a hill, the color of the birch tree branches, and immediately I find myself trying to decide how I would capture that on canvas."

"Do you know what I think, Mr. Kent?" Marianne said, causing Kent to crane his neck around in her direction. "I think that if you ever applied your abundant talent to painting people so insightfully, you would be the foremost portraitist of our day. Wouldn't you think, Elaural?"

The countess' face revealed nothing, though Kent felt as though the boat had begun to sink around him and him alone. "I think that Mr. Kent would be successful at whatever he chose to do with his art, but what he does now is perfectly suited to him. But really, Marianne, can we not speak of anything but art? I, who have no talent whatsoever, am beginning to feel a bit inferior. Have you no gossip for a poor unaccomplished person such as myself?"

"Well, let me see. Erasmus Flattery and that astonishing Mr. Clarendon have gone down into this great cave everyone speaks of, which I'm told is not a little dangerous at this time of year because of the spring flooding raising the water inside. No one is quite sure why—unless you know, my dear?" she asked playfully.

"Mr. Flattery does not confide in me, I assure you," the countess said quickly.

"Someone has let the house of this man Baumgere, and no one seems to know who it is. There are even rumors that it is the crown prince, here to take the waters. Lord Skye was seen yesterday in the company of the Waldmans' very blonde daughter. What was her name?"

"Miss Trollop, I think."

This made Marianne laugh. "And what else have I learned? These navy men who are about are said to be trying to catch an Entonne spy, though the one officer seems to be more interested in this same Miss . . . what was her name again?"

"My, she does get around, doesn't she?"

"I do love small towns. Imagine what they're saying about us," she said with some delight. "Think, Mr. Kent, in the minds of the people of Castlebough you might be involved in a love triangle with the Countess of Chilton and that strange novelist. What was her name again?"

"Busybody," the countess offered.

"There, you see—the perfect name for a woman trapped by her own desires."

"Who is in Baumgere's house, do you think?" Kent asked suddenly.

"Someone who might be interested in the works of Averil Kent, perhaps?" Marianne teased.

"No, seriously."

"Well, I don't know. I have seen the man they say is his servant, but he is no one to me."

"Well, if you know all the doings of Castlebough," Kent said. "Why is Sir John Dalrymple here, and who is the man he is with? Bryce, I believe he calls himself."

"Ah, now that is a question. The town seems split on the matter. Sir John is either here to assist the navy men in capturing a spy, or he is here begging money from this man Bryce, to whom he defers, even when he means to give the impression that he does not. Who this man Bryce is, is another matter. A wealthy merchant, I have heard. A smuggler, which I think more likely. A dealer in fine jewels—also a possibility, but not nearly so interesting. Or a rogue who has made his fortune marrying wealthy women, and then pushing them off balconies. And I must say he is terribly attractive, don't you think, Elaural?"

"I don't know to whom you refer, my dear."

"Ah, too much time looking at stars," Marianne said wistfully. "But Mr. Kent; it was a surprise to find you in Castlebough, especially after you have visited the countess so recently."

"Mr. Kent often travels to paint, Marianne. Now please—stick to the gossip."

"What else have I heard?" she mused. "Another group have gone down into this cave everyone seems to be visiting—though this group had in its numbers a young woman. They apparently were prepared to be gone several days."

"A woman went into the same cave as Erasmus?" The countess leaned to one side so that she could see Marianne past Kent, and the jealousy in her voice stung him. The painter felt, suddenly, as though he were not even there.

Marianne blew out a long stream of smoke that curled around Kent, causing him to choke. "That is what I've heard. What's in this cave, do you think?"

"I . . ." The countess paused, looking terribly troubled. "Erasmus told me, and you absolutely mustn't repeat this, that he was going into the cave to look for two young friends who he feared did not understand the danger of what they did. He expected to be gone three or four days."

"Well, it is all very odd," Marianne said. "Why should we not repeat this? If Mr. Flattery has friends in trouble in the cave, should we not alert the town? Should not a rescue attempt be mounted?"

"I only know that he asked me to say nothing. He was not certain that these young men were in difficulty, but only went to be sure they were safe. It all seems a bit odd now, and it is quite a coincidence that these others have gone into the same cave. It is not safe at this time of year, you say?"

"That is what the locals claim. It is often visited during the summer, for it is a natural wonder, after all, but the local people stay out of it in winter and spring, for the water levels rise and fall without warning, and the lower entrances, which are on the shore of the lake are under water. I hope all and sundry are safe in there. Who were these foolish young men?"

The countess shrugged. "I don't know. Friends of Erasmus' . . . Kayes and Heller, I think he named them." She looked to Kent, who shook his head. He didn't know either.

"If he is not out in a day or two," Kent offered solicitously, "I will talk to the local people about mounting a search."

The countess tried to smile at him, but looked away, and Kent felt it was a rather pathetic offer he had made, but it was all he could think of. Hardly enough to have her throw herself into his arms with gratitude.

What was Erasmus up to, he wondered?

Chapter Thirty-three

HAYES managed to pull himself together, considering what he'd found, and that he'd almost set himself afire in a space so tight he was still amazed he had managed to escape largely unscathed. He felt lucky to be alive.

Kehler bathed his hand in fresh water and bound it in a strip of linen torn from their cleanest shirt. Hayes drank some water and sat on his pack, still coughing from the smoke that had seared his lungs.

Kehler stayed close, saying little, perhaps feeling a little guilty at having exposed his friend to such horror.

Slowly Hayes began to recover from the fear and the shock, and the coughing subsided. Kehler made him a cup of their lukewarm tea, which in Hayes' state actually tasted good.

"I noticed something while you were gone," Kehler said. "Can you get up?" He lit a candle and led his friend down the passage.

"It was so quiet while you were inside, and I began to believe I was hearing something. I thought it might be my mind playing tricks, unable to bear the silence, perhaps, but I came down here, listening with all my attention. First I would think I heard it, then it would be gone again. A regular sound I can only describe as tinkling, almost metallic, but very even when I could hear it." He held up a hand. "Stop here and listen."

Hayes did as he was told, straining to hear sounds beyond their own breathing.

"Nothing?"

Hayes shook his head.

"Step along three paces. Now?"

Hayes listened again, trying to calm his ragged breathing.

"Something, perhaps. . . . Flames, it is so faint that I'm not sure."

"Exactly. Now come down here." He led them along another few feet and then bent down before a low opening. Inclining his head Kehler shut his eyes, his face tense with concentration. "Do you hear?" he whispered.

"Something, yes. Yes. There is a sound. Is it water, do you think?"

Kehler shrugged. "Likely. But watch." He brought the candle close to the opening, moving it slowly and then holding it still, his hand wavering just a little.

Ever so slightly the flame bent away from the opening, as though affected by air currents, and then it swayed the other way.

"What do you make of that?"

Hayes held out his hand, trying to feel the air movement. "I almost think I can feel something."

Kehler nodded.

"But does it mean anything? Is this passage more likely to contain what we seek, or is it less likely?"

Kehler shook his head. "I don't know, but it is the only one with any feature to distinguish it from the others. For that reason alone, I'm in favor of exploring it next. At worst, we'll simply have eliminated one more possibility."

Hayes agreed, as it was Kehler's turn to go next anyway. The two made a short meal, and Kehler cleaned and filled the lamp before he set out.

Hayes pulled their packs down before the opening Kehler intended to explore and wrapped himself in his coat and blankets. "You'll have to shout your loudest if you need me," he said, "I can't possibly stay awake."

He watched his friend crawl into the opening, dragging his feet in behind him, and when the light was gone he fell almost immediately to sleep.

Occasionally he would awake with a start, escaping a dream in which he was trapped in the stone, or in which the skeleton reached out for him. On one of these occasions he awoke calling for help, and then realized that he was not the one that was calling out.

"Blood and flames!" He thrust aside the blanket and got up stiffly, hunting around for a candle and the materials to light it. It took him a moment floundering around in the darkness with his one hand in pain and only half-useful, and then a flame was slowly born. All the while he heard the regular muffled shouts of his companion.

Careful not to blow out the flame, he went to the opening Kehler had entered.

"Kehler!" he shouted, but all he heard in return was an increase in the calling, not a word was clear.

"Martyr's balls," Hayes swore. "He must be lodged." With great trepidation he knelt down on the hard stone and started into the opening, still so fatigued that he could not imagine how he would make it more than a dozen feet, or what he would do when he reached his friend.

He was forced to rest every few feet, lying in the near darkness, his fingers cramping from holding the candle and unable to bring his other hand forward. When he rested, he would call out to let Kehler know he was coming, but if Kehler was as little reassured by this as Hayes was confident that he could help, the poor man must have been near to despair.

After he crawled beyond what he thought was the limit of his endurance, Kehler's voice was suddenly quite clear, almost near at hand.

"Hayes?"

"Kehler? Are you lodged, man?"

"Bloody martyr's blood! I thought you would never wake. I've been stuck for hours. Flames, man. . . ." But then he seemed to run out of words.

"I'm coming along as quickly as I can. Try to relax. If you could get in, you can get out. Don't worry." Hayes tried to sound confident, but he'd seen the skeleton and knew what it meant.

Finally, in the dull light of his candle, he saw the worn soles of Kehler's boots, a few feet away. As he drew up behind his friend, the lantern glow could be made out, though Kehler's body blocked it almost entirely, the passage was so small.

Hayes reached out and tapped the bottom of his friend's boot.

"Praise be," Kehler said, sounding genuinely relieved. "I am so desperate that I have had a religious conversion; may Farrelle be praised. I'm being punished for my theft of church property."

Hayes laughed. "Only you could find humor in this," he said.

"Hayes?" There was no humor in his friend's tone now. "I'm really in a jam, and I have worn myself to exhaustion trying to get free. I don't want to end up another skeleton in this particular hell."

"We'll get you out, Kehler, don't worry. Let's look at it logically. Where are you jammed?"

"My hips, if you can believe it. I got my shoulders through after some effort, but then I jammed my hips."

Hayes held out his candle trying to discover how his friend was stuck. "Don't move your feet, Kehler, you'll put out my candle." After wrenching his neck around for a moment so that he could look ahead, he had to lower his head to the stone to let the muscles rest. "Try to describe how you're jammed in there."

"Well, there are two ridges in the rock," Kehler began, focusing his attention on different parts of his anatomy. "They run across the ceiling in two bands about four inches apart. My left hip is jammed between them, and my right is stuck as well. If I could move one of them forward or back even two inches, I could go ahead."

"Go forward!?" Hayes said in disbelief. "You want to back out, Kehler, not get farther in. We want to get out of this place."

"But you don't understand. . . . The passage is opening up beyond this. I can see it. The largest section of passage we've found since our arrival. All we have to do is get through the squeeze, and we can go on. Flames, we can almost crawl on hands and knees in the next bit."

Hayes could hardly believe what he was hearing, but then the thought of having some space around him drew him in a way that he could not explain. Only feet away there was room to breathe freely.

"I can't really see why your right hip is stuck. It might be in a small pocket in the rock and you're just too exhausted to get it free. Let me see if I can pull it back, and you try to help me." Hayes poured some wax on the stone and stuck the butt of the candle in the soft wax, hoping it would stay upright. He gripped Kehler's ankle with his forward hand and, bracing himself, pulled as hard as he could. After about fifteen seconds of effort he had to relax.

Flailing for purchase with his free foot, Kehler managed to put the candle out, leaving Hayes in almost complete darkness and beginning to feel panicked himself.

"Kehler? I have another idea. I'm going to put my head against the sole of your left boot and pull on your right foot at the same time. Push on my head as best you can. Is that clear? We'll push your right hip forward and your left back at the same time. Are you ready?"

"No. Rest a moment more."

Hayes put his head down on the stone and tried to think of the world above. A world of sunshine, but he could not hold the image there in the darkness.

Kehler was silent so long that Hayes began to wonder if he had fallen asleep from exhaustion.

"Kehler?"

"Just a moment more."

"Are you all right?"

Silence, and then a very small voice came from the darkness. "What if this doesn't work?"

"Then I'll bring a rope in here and tie it to your foot, and then crawl back out where I can get some purchase. I'm sure all we need to do is get your lower hip to come back a few inches and you'll be out."

"All right. I'm ready."

Hayes grabbed his friend's foot and moved forward until he felt the boot sole contact his head. He expanded his shoulders against the stone and braced his feet as best he could.

He pulled with his hand and pushed his head against his friend's boot, feeling the pressure on his neck, not to mention the pain.

Nothing.

"Blood and flames!" he heard his friend curse and then suddenly the pressure went off his head.

"*Oh, flames . . .*" Kehler managed, "I'm bloody well through." His voice broke on the last word and for a moment the two of them lay gasping.

"Hayes?" Kehler said, his voice thick. "Well done." Kehler dragged himself slowly forward and light poured into the narrow passage. Suddenly Hayes realized Kehler's face was nearly filling the opening ahead. "Can you make it through? There's room to breathe here. Look, I've actually turned around."

Hayes crawled forward, running his hand over the rock where

his friend had stuck. Seeing how his friend had lodged was of great help, and with Kehler pulling him, Hayes was through in a moment.

They could actually sit up, the passage was so tall—perhaps two feet and a half in diameter.

They slumped there like two survivors of battle, not a breath of energy left to carry them on, or even to speak. Kehler managed to raise his hand and clap his friend on the shoulder, but beyond that they didn't move for half of the next hour.

Finally Kehler made shift to go on. "I have to move to get some warmth, or I shall begin to shiver."

"Do you think we should?" Hayes asked. "Should we not go back and eat and get some sleep, gather our strength a little?"

"Let's just see how far this goes. If it narrows down again, I agree; we should go back for now. But if it simply ends in fifty feet. . . . I don't want to come back in here just to find that."

"Neither do I."

Kehler started out on hands and knees, but around the next bend they were walking upright, though ducking now and then.

"This is more like it," Kehler said, unable to hide his excitement. They both knew this was likely to lead to nothing, but even so, it was the first time they'd found a passage that opened up and it lifted their spirits immeasurably.

Another bend and the passage began to angle up. Kehler stopped them at one point, holding up his hand for silence. "There. Do you hear it?"

"Yes. Without question. It is water running, isn't it?"

"I think so." They hurried on.

Around another bend and then they climbed natural stairs up a slope, the passage opening up to a dozen feet. They crested the top with Kehler a few steps ahead. When Hayes came up, watching his footing, Kehler put out a hand and stopped him, gesturing forward.

"*Martyr's blood,*" Hayes whispered, the words barely audible.

Ten paces before them, at the top of three man-made steps, stood the arch of a small doorway built of white stones. The two stared dumbly, Kehler lowering himself to a ridge of stone as though he could not bear to stand a second more.

Hayes took a step forward, but his friend reached out a hand to restrain him. "No. Stay back. Do you see the flowers inscribed on the keystone?"

"Teller. . . . Is that not what Clarendon said? Two vale roses and an unknown blossom."

"Yes. This is their chamber, but we might not be able to enter."

"What?! We have come all this way through such hardship, and we must stay outside?" Hayes felt his temper rise, and he was too exhausted to control it.

"I said we *might* not be able to enter. There could be charms protecting it."

"Charms? Spells, you mean?"

Kehler nodded.

"And do you have any idea how to deal with them?"

Kehler shook his head. "None at all."

Hayes laughed, he could not help himself. "Well, this has been the most futile endeavor I have ever been tricked into pursuing. Why did you not tell me this before? Is there anything else you are keeping back? You might as well tell me now."

Kehler made an odd face, almost a grimace, and shrugged foolishly.

"And there shall be no fame or fortune either, I'm sure." Hayes shook his head, half angry, half overcome with the absurdity. He could hardly believe that his good, solid friend Kehler tricked him so infamously.

"We should have brought Erasmus," Hayes said suddenly.

But Kehler shook his head. "No. I fear your friend would get word back to Eldrich, and then no one would ever learn of our discovery—whatever might lie beyond this door. No, Hayes, we must keep this from Erasmus."

"Well, I don't think we need fear Erasmus, who is the most decent of men." Hayes wondered if he sounded as guilty as he felt. Had Erasmus already begun searching for them?

"The most decent of men, yes, but he served Eldrich, and mages are not known for letting men go. Not only do I suspect Erasmus of knowing far more than he claims, but I'm distrustful of his loyalties. We absolutely must be sure that Eldrich learns nothing of this until such time as we reveal all. We will publish our findings and make it impossible for Eldrich to bury what we've found. Knowledge should not be kept in the hands of the few, who use it to suppress the many. If nothing else, I became convinced of that while I lived with the priests."

"So what do we do now?"

Kehler considered a moment. "It is my belief that one of us should attempt to pass through the door. I will do it as I'm the one who began all this. I am not certain what you should do, Hayes. I don't know if you will be safe, or if you should go back out the main passage. I don't even know if you will be safe there."

Claustrophobia gripped Hayes at the thought of going back into that passage. No, they had come this far, going back did not seem an option. Not yet, anyway.

"I'll come with you."

Kehler considered this a moment. "You realize that might be foolish?"

Hayes laughed. "This entire endeavor has been foolish."

Kehler nodded, and Hayes gave him a hand up. Neither said a word, but only went forward, a bit tentatively, perhaps, but they went on.

They put their feet upon the first step and Hayes realized it was marble, not the stone of the cave at all. They paused briefly at the door, as though their nerve had failed, and then Kehler forced himself to go through, with Hayes close on his heels.

By the poor light of their lantern they could see a hall before them. And then a bright light flared, blinding them utterly, felling them like trees in a storm.

Chapter Thirty-four

SINCE the incident at the lake, conversation had almost ceased. Deacon Rose was helpful and solicitous, never complaining about the arduous nature of their undertaking. Not that Erasmus or Clarendon were given to complaining, but they did not act as though the trials of the body were of no consequence, which was the impression given by Rose.

The priest would often make small talk at their meals and stops, displaying the kind of modest, self-effacing charm that he had exhibited when he first visited Erasmus. There was little doubt in Erasmus' mind that if the good deacon had not chosen the cloth, he would have made a very successful courtier.

Erasmus noticed that Clarendon did not respond to this display of charm, keeping his responses carefully neutral. Obviously he had reservations about taking the priest along, though Erasmus was not sure the savant would have chosen to let the priest drown as an alternative. Still, Clarendon was not happy, there was no question of that, and Rose could not have missed it.

They were wading along a waterway now, occasionally climbing down small waterfalls, so that they were wet and cold. According to Clarendon's survey, there was a falls not far ahead of them, which marked the farthest point Clarendon had penetrated into the cave in the past. The small man had claimed that it hadn't been worth the risk to go farther, which Erasmus found a bit ominous, for it was apparent that Clarendon was not a timid man.

They slipped and splashed their way down the slope, the water running cold and swift around their knees, boots ruined and their feet near to numb.

Erasmus was aware of a growing sound, though it was difficult to describe for it did not vary, nor did it have any particular defining characteristics. He was only certain that it came from ahead.

"How difficult is it to pass beyond the falls?" Erasmus asked Clarendon.

"I have never done it, nor have I seen it done, but it is said to be an intimidating traverse. Not really so hard if it were but two feet off the ground, but it is over a falls that plunges down into an abyss. It is more a test of nerve than skill, I think, but it is a great test of nerve, and not all have passed it. Several men have been lost there. Not two years ago a man fell and dragged his rope partner with him." Clarendon shook his head. "The danger is real, but I think we can pass it. I will go first and set a rope for safety."

"No, Randall," Erasmus said, "you have put yourself forward to explore all the tightest places. Let me lead the way across the falls. Don't forget, I can swim."

"Well, that is up to you, but when you see this falls, Mr. Flattery, you'll realize that even such skill in the water as you possess will be of no use."

They carried on for some time, and finally the roar of the falls drowned out all other sounds, and then they were at its lip, staring down into the darkness.

"There is no hope for swimming there," Clarendon said. "Do you still intend to go first?"

Erasmus nodded, gazing out at the rock face he would have to cross. "Where is the route, do you know?"

Clarendon pointed out the path that had been described to him, explaining as best he could how he thought it could be negotiated successfully.

"Deacon Rose," Clarendon said, "it is you who will have to hold the rope, for I am not large enough for this service. I will instruct you."

"I have traveled in the mountains, Mr. Clarendon, and have held the rope for many a man. Do not be concerned, Mr. Flattery. I shall not let you down, nor will the greater powers, I am sure, for I will pray as you go."

A rope was produced, and Erasmus prepared to start. Both Clarendon and Rose advised him to climb in stockinged feet, for boots would be too slippery on this rock which was wet from constant spray.

When Rose gave him the signal, Erasmus stepped out over the roaring falls, glancing down once, and then focusing his attention on the route he would take across the stone. Rock dug painfully into his feet, soft from a lifetime of wearing boots, and his hands were already battered from the climbing and crawling that they had done. But he tried to put the pain out of his mind—the climb would require his entire focus. Clarendon called to him encouragingly over the sound of the falls, and gave instructions which Erasmus did his best to follow.

He knew that what Clarendon said was true; if he had been only a few feet off the ground, this would have been child's play, but with an almost certain, horrible death only a slip away, suddenly it was as difficult a climb as he could imagine. Rose held him steadfastly on the rope, but ropes often parted, and there was the story of the man falling and dragging his partner with him.

"You are past halfway, Mr. Flattery," Clarendon called. "Not much farther, now. Reach up with your left hand—is that a hold there? Do you see? Good. Now I would try to move so that your right hand is where your left hand is now. You're doing well."

Erasmus glanced ahead. It did not look so simple from here, at least not when one was out over a yawning gorge.

"Do you see what looks like a small platform ahead? You cannot stop to rest before this, for the holds and steps between are not large. Do you see?"

Erasmus was not sure that he did. All the holds that had seemed so large when he had stood looking from the top of the falls, appeared, upon closer inspection, to be very small indeed.

"Do not hesitate too long, Mr. Flattery. Better to do it before you begin to tire."

It was likely good advice, Erasmus thought, for already he was feeling his muscles knot—from being too tense, he was sure. He took a long breath and stepped out, moving as quickly as he dared. Then he was on the platform and forced himself on without stopping, as though the safety of the other side called to him. A moment later he was crouched in the mouth of the passage, catching his breath, which he was sure had been taken by fear and not exertion.

"It was not so bad," he called back. "Not with a strong man on the rope and another to give instructions. Who will be next?"

"Mr. Clarendon; and we will safety him from both sides," Rose said. "No, Mr. Clarendon, I insist. I will come last, for I have had the most experience in climbing, I think, and you can both take the rope from the far side. Can we send the packs and one lantern across first?"

This was done, and a few moments later Clarendon prepared to go. He would benefit from light from both behind and ahead now, as well as men holding his rope from either side. Rose tied the smaller man into the center of the rope and took up his position, sitting in the flow of the water, his feet braced against a rock.

Erasmus had done as Clarendon said, and found a spire of rock inside the new passage. He threw a loop over it and tied himself onto the tail so that he could sit just in the opening and take the rope around his waist.

Thus protected from either end of the rope, Clarendon set his stocking feet out on the path just navigated by Erasmus.

It was Erasmus' turn to call out encouragement and instruction. He concentrated on Clarendon and his efforts almost as much as Clarendon did himself, and because of this did not notice Rose moving across the falls.

"Erasmus?" Rose called out suddenly. "Hold fast!"

The priest had moved to the far wall, and with no more warning, he gave the rope a yank and pulled a flailing Clarendon off the rock. Erasmus was dragged forward almost a foot before the rope around his waist came taut. And there hung Clarendon, out over the terrible void, his feet dangling in the rushing water, the spray thick around him, and he cursed the priest without respite.

Erasmus tried to pull in on the rope and succeeded in raising Clarendon up a little, but Rose held the end tight and Erasmus was afraid the rope might break.

"Now who will be forced to tell the truth?" Rose called, more than a little triumphant.

"Rose!" Erasmus shouted. "You gave your word. You swore an oath."

"I swore I would not harm Kehler and his companion, but I said nothing of Clarendon. I think your friend is a follower of Teller, Mr.

Flattery, and a danger to us both. Eldrich is his sworn enemy, and that means that you, too, are his rival. Is it not so, Mr. Clarendon?"

The man dangling over the falls, said nothing but began to twist about as though he could free himself.

"Well, I will have the truth, whether you will cooperate or no, Mr. Clarendon, for I have ways of dealing with your kind."

Erasmus thought the priest began to mumble, but the sound of the falls swept any words away. Clarendon had taken hold of Erasmus' side of the rope and begun to pull himself toward the rock. But the priest was too strong for the little man. Erasmus could see Clarendon's face was white with rage and fear.

Raising one hand, the priest closed his eyes, continuing to mumble as he made odd geometric gestures in the air. And as he did so, suddenly Clarendon produced a knife and cut the rope connecting him to the priest.

Clarendon swung hard into the rock below Erasmus, and as quickly as he could, Erasmus began to pull in on the rope.

"Randall? Randall, are you hurt?" Erasmus was surprised at how light the man felt.

"Mr. Flattery!" Rose shouted over the sound of water. "Do not go on with that man. He is your enemy. You cannot trust him."

Randall scrambled over the edge of the precipice, so enraged that he did not seem at all frightened. He was on his feet in an instant, shaking his fist at the priest.

"Cannot trust me!? Farrelle's blood, but I have never met a more deceitful man. And I have met all manner of men. Come near to me again, priest, and I will see that you never lie again."

Without warning Randall turned, lifted the priest's pack, and flung it into the abyss. The little man shouldered his own pack and snatched up the lantern.

"Come," he said to Erasmus, "I will not assist his crossing. Let him stay where he is, or plunge into the netherworld where he belongs."

Without waiting for Erasmus, Clarendon went stomping up the tunnel, carrying the light with him. Erasmus stayed for a moment, staring at the priest, who stood there meeting his gaze, holding up a lantern. Despite being soaked from head to foot, the priest still retained his pride. Certainly he did not look repentant. He stood at the top of the falls like a proud man falsely accused.

"You are in danger, Mr. Flattery," he said evenly, shaking his head a bit sadly.

"Mr. Flattery!" Clarendon called.

Digging quickly into his bag, Erasmus found a bundle of candles and some food. He tied these together and tossed them to the priest.

"Make your way to the surface," Erasmus called, and then turned and went after Clarendon. Every step he took into the tunnel he could feel the priest standing behind him—could feel the reproach in his silence.

Chapter Thirty-five

I went to hear Asquith play, and I don't know by what magic this was accomplished, but I cried inconsolably for my lost childhood, and for the harsh and dread-filled place the world had become.

The Countess of Chilton

KENT could hardly believe what he was doing. He brushed at his frock coat, which was spotted with loose dirt and dead leaves. Lifting his glass, he pointed it toward the lit window and through the foliage could just make out figures moving—or so he thought.

He looked around quickly, listening for any sound. By starlight he had scrambled up a steep embankment and now stood in the farthest reaches of someone's garden. He did not have quite the view of the countess' house that he had hoped, but it was much safer than what he had done the night he saw her with Erasmus.

Flames—if he'd been caught! He would have been forced to move abroad and change his name. What a fool he was acting. And this—sneaking into someone's garden with his field glass—was almost as bad. Claiming to be looking at stars would hardly be believed—there were a hundred more accessible places in Castlebough that were not someone's private domain.

He focused back on the windows of the countess' house. Perhaps that was someone sitting by the fire—but whom? Kent looked around a little desperately. This would never do. He needed either a better vantage—difficult because the house of the countess backed onto a slope—or he would have to return to his place below the windows. And if he did that, it was only a matter of time until he was discovered.

But what was she doing? Had Erasmus returned? Was she visited by Lord Skye, and had that fool realized that the most beautiful woman in Farrland was mad for him? He shook his head. If he could only trade places with Skye for one evening.

Almost desperate, Kent decided to abandon all caution and return to the window.

This is insanity, he thought. *Utter insanity.*

Having made the decision, Kent decided not to go down the embankment again. Instead he went quickly toward the house and the street. There were lights in the windows, but the chances of anyone being in the garden at this hour were probably slim—it was not a warm summer evening, after all.

Emboldened by the passion that gripped him, Kent marched up through the garden, past the house and out the gate. In a moment he was at the corner of the countess' street, and here he stopped in the shadow of a tree that hung over a garden wall. Before the countess' house, a coach and four stood at the curb, and a small man was handing the countess up into the large carriage.

Instinctively, Kent stepped back around the corner as the carriage passed by, the night too dark for Kent to see into the coach.

The street, Kent knew, snaked back and forth up the hillside, and after a moment of watching to be sure what the coach would do, Kent went quickly across the street and up a narrow stair between the houses. The faint starlight barely penetrated here, and Kent stumbled more than once, striking his shins cruelly on stone.

At the stairhead he stopped, staying to the shadow, and waited for the coach to pass. When he was sure it would continue up and not stop at a house, he went on, taking the next stair. Here he fell again and lost his glass, wasting several moments searching in utter darkness. When he emerged on the street, the carriage had already passed and he sprang across the paving stones and onto the next stair.

If the stairs had only been uniform in height and depth, but there were landings that sloped up and every stair was a different size, forcing Kent to feel his way up like a blind man. Again the carriage had passed when he reached the street, and this time it was even farther ahead.

Kent was almost certain he would not catch it now, for he was struggling to breathe as it was. As quickly as he could, he plunged into the shadow of the next stair, and here was helped by lights in the windows. He sprinted up the steps, his breath coming in terrible gasps.

He met the carriage this time, and waited for it to pass before setting his feet to the next flight.

On he went, upward, the carriage gaining each time it passed, and then finally it did not appear on the street at all. Kent stood in the middle of the thoroughfare looking both ways, wondering what could have happened. He was certain he had not fallen so far behind. Had it stopped back around the corner where he could not see it?

Thinking there was no other explanation, Kent hurried down the street. But at the corner he found no coach, nor was there a gateway large enough to allow it to enter.

Where am I, he wondered, trying to recall the lay of the town, and how many flights he'd raced up. "There must be another road here," he said, thinking aloud. "A carriage cannot simply disappear."

He set off down the slope and in a moment discovered a small lane running out of the town, following the contour of the hillside. It was too dark to see if there were marks of the coach's passage in the soft earth, but he could not imagine where else the coach could have gone, and began to trot along the lane.

To his right, through the trees lining the lane, Kent caught glimpses of the lake shimmering far below. To his left lay a wood, broken occasionally by small glades. The town had not escaped its confines to take root here, despite the likely vistas, and tall grass grew down the center of the lane indicating how little use it saw.

After half of a long hour Kent was beginning to wonder if the carriage had actually come this way, and contemplated turning back, but then a familiar odor assailed his nostrils telling him that horses had passed this way, and recently too. The painter pressed on with renewed energy.

A few moments more and he passed through an open gate, and the lane suddenly sloped down toward a level bench. At the bottom of the hill he could see a large home illuminated by the stars. Near to the entrance a carriage stood, its lamps burning dully.

He slowed his pace and tried to keep to the grass to muffle the sound of his approach. Whose home this was Kent did not know.

There hardly seemed to be an entertainment in progress—the house was all but unlit, and only one carriage waited.

Remembering what he had seen the last time he'd spied on the countess, Kent went forward torn between dread and excitement. Erasmus was supposed to be in the cave, so she could not be visiting him.

Kent was not sure how he would respond if he were to discover the countess had another lover—that she bestowed her favors so liberally and yet treated him no differently than she treated her friend Marianne.

Staying to the shadows as much as possible, Kent stayed high on the slope along the edge of the wood. Once he was convinced there was no movement in the lit windows, Kent decided to circle the house at a distance.

Certainly if the countess came here at such an hour, it must be for an assignation. What other explanation could there be? He felt a flash of anger toward her.

This is why men she can't even remember meeting fight duels over her, Kent thought. *Look at me. Look at what I do.* But still, he carried on, despite the fear that dueling with strangers would come next.

Kent slipped around the side of the house, keeping to the shadows wherever possible. The grounds had obviously not been tended in years. The hedges were overgrown, flowerbeds choked with weeds, lawns gone to seed, and fallen branches and leaves lay rotting everywhere.

As the far side of the house came into view, Kent saw the dull orange of a flame—an oil lamp burning inside a ground floor window, or perhaps a fire in a hearth. A little farther along he realized that the light came from inside a row of leaded-glass doors. Here there were people, he was almost certain, though there was much furniture and it was difficult to make out the shapes in such poor light.

Slipping partway down the hill, Kent stood in the shadow of a bush, peering down over an open section of lawn with his field glass. Something moved inside—a man, he was almost certain.

"Mr. Kent?"

The painter whirled around, raising his glass like a cudgel—but the man before him was familiar, even in the poor light.

"Sir John?"

"Yes," the man whispered. "Keep your voice down and come back from the house. I fear you will give us away if you stay here."

Kent hesitated, embarrassment was rapidly replacing fright. What in the round world was Sir John Dalrymple doing here? Was he spying on the countess as well? Not knowing what else to do, Kent followed Sir John until they were some distance from the house and hidden by the corner of a garden wall.

Here, in the pale light, they crouched down, looking out only occasionally to see that they were alone.

"I would ask what you do here, Mr. Kent," Sir John whispered, "but fear you will say it is not my business, and rightly so. But perhaps the fact that we are here, watching this same house, might indicate common purpose, or so I hope."

Kent tried to read the man's face but the light was so poor. He could not even begin to guess why Sir John was here, other than for the same reason as Kent.

"I am here out of concern for a friend," Kent said.

Sir John nodded as though this made sense somehow. "Well, you are more noble than I, Mr. Kent, for I am here out of concern for myself. You followed the woman who arrived in the coach?"

Kent nodded.

"Who is she, pray?"

Does he really not know, Kent wondered? "The Countess of Chilton," Kent said, unable to think of a reason to lie—or perhaps to see Sir John's reaction.

"Of course," Sir John said, glancing down at the house.

"But whose home is this?" Kent asked.

"You don't know? It was the house built by Baumgere, the infamous priest. But who is staying here now, I cannot say." He paused, and Kent sensed that he was trying to decide what else to say, or how to say it. "I have a man who passes me information. . . . Invaluable information, I will tell you, but he is a complete mystery to me. I cannot say where he is from or name the source of his knowledge, and this troubles me, Kent." Sir John nodded his head toward the house. "I have reason to believe the man comes here, to this house, so I am here hoping to discover who it is that he meets. One wants to be sure one is not unwittingly embroiled in the plot of a foreign power."

"This is the man I met on the road to Castlebough—Bryce?"

Sir John nodded.

"And what has he to do with the countess?" Kent said quickly, afraid that jealousy was obvious in his voice. Had not Marianne Edden named the man handsome? Yet the countess had claimed not to know whom she meant.

"I. . . ." Sir John stopped, shaking his head, the motion so small it was almost indiscernible. "Bryce is interested in Skye, for some reason, but I don't think Lord Skye is here."

"Who is, then? Did you follow Bryce here?"

"One does not follow Bryce, Mr. Kent. At least that is what I believe. No, it was luck only that had me see Bryce's carriage come down this lane. And so I am here, watching, not quite sure what I hope to see."

Sir John leaned out to look around the corner of the wall, and held his hand up quickly, stopping Kent from speaking.

Kent moved so that he could see past Sir John, and there, in the center of the ill-tended lawn, a man and a woman walked under starlight. Even at this distance he knew it was the countess, but the man was a mystery to him. Certainly not Skye. Nor was it Erasmus. Was this Bryce, then? And what had he to do with the countess?

"Is that your man?" Kent whispered, keeping his voice as low as possible. But even as he asked the question, he was sure that the answer would be no. The man on the lawn, was tall, with a stiff posture and movement. *A king in pain,* Kent thought immediately, though he didn't know why—but that was what the man seemed to him.

Sir John shook his head.

Just as Kent started to raise his glass, a large dog appeared at the edge of the lawn. It hesitated a moment and then loped across the open space toward the people.

Kent was certain the woman froze with fear, but the man held out his hand and the beast, which he realized now was massive, circled them once. It didn't do this warily, Kent thought, but out of independence.

Sir John pulled back behind the wall again, drawing Kent back as well. Kent was not sure what had come over Sir John; he seemed to be suffering from some sudden ailment, and Kent feared it might be the man's heart. Sir John could not seem to catch his breath, and Kent was sure he could see sweat running in rivulets down the man's face.

"Is that beast a dog, Kent?" Sir John managed, "or is it a wolf?"

It seemed an odd question, but Kent leaned out to look again. The animal had deserted the people and went back toward the trees, its head down, and neck stretched out. Definitely not a dog, and then he realized what Sir John meant and almost threw himself back behind the wall.

"*Eldrich,*" he said, realizing the only reason that a wolf could cause such fear. "Is that what you think? It is Eldrich?"

Sir John could not speak but nodded his head, his breath coming in quick little gasps. "Farrelle . . . save us," he managed. "I had . . . no idea."

He grabbed the front of Kent's frock coat and levered himself to his feet, stumbling toward the wood. "*Flee,*" he hissed, and Kent hesitated only a second, before following the terrified man into the utter darkness beneath the trees.

By the time they found their way back to the lane, they were bruised and their clothing torn and soiled, for the starlight penetrated into the wood only rarely.

Sir John had finally regained his breath, to Kent's relief, but the painter was now so concerned for the countess that he almost went back, despite his fear of the mage.

"Don't even think about it, Kent," Sir John said, sensing what was in the painter's mind as he looked back over his shoulder. "There is nothing you can do. Even if the countess needed rescue, you could not accomplish it. He is a mage. I can't quite believe we have escaped unharmed. Just be thankful for that, and do nothing foolish."

They went on, listening for the sound of horse and carriage, or the howl of a wolf.

At last they stopped so that Sir John could catch his breath. He seemed only slightly less terrified, even though they appeared to have escaped.

"Are you recovering, Sir John?"

"Recovering? My breathing, yes, but I shall never recover from the shock. I had no idea what I involved myself in, Kent. Eldrich!" He shook his head in disbelief. "Bryce is an agent of the mage. What shall I do? Whatever shall I do? I have been promoting the interests of a mage, unknowingly. And what does Eldrich want with Skye?"

Sir John seemed to realize that he was ranting, and stared up at Kent, immense fear and regret apparent in his manner. The man looked so cowed, almost cringing where he sat.

He suddenly grabbed the painter by the arm. "Kent, you must promise me that none of this will go any further. I had no idea what I did, I swear. And at no time did I ever subvert the interests of my country. I swear to you, Kent." He looked down at the ground, almost ready to collapse, Kent thought. "How will I ever get free of this? *Eldrich!* He will never release me. What am I to do, Kent? Whatever am I to do?"

But Kent neither knew nor cared what Sir John should do. Why was the countess in the company of Eldrich? What was their involvement? That was all that concerned him. Was she in danger? Was she his agent? His mistress?

Kent sat on the step of a deep-set door, so that a shadow hid him from the street. It was the farthest point on the street from which he could still see the countess' home. Never in his life had he felt so utterly powerless, so unsure of what to do. Was the countess in danger? Or was it much simpler than that: she was the most beautiful woman in Farrland, and the histories were clear that mages were not immune to such things. He pressed his fingers to his eyes, which burned from lack of sleep.

But somehow he could not shake the feeling that the countess was in danger. No doubt his feelings for her held sway here—but even so he would wait and see.

The thought of waking Marianne Edden crossed his mind, but she was likely the countess' ally in all things, and would not be so sympathetic to Kent. He believed she thought he was a bit obsessed anyway.

What he wanted to do was ask the countess herself, so he waited, trying to imagine how he would approach her, what he would say.

It was too dark to read his timepiece, but Kent was sure that daylight couldn't be far off. He wondered what he had landed in the middle of, here in this odd little village in the Caledon Hills. Skye had a copy of a painting by Pelier which showed the structure Baumgere had uncovered above the town—though the painting, if it was a true copy, must have been done many years before Baumgere made his discovery. Erasmus Flattery, a man who had served Eldrich, had become an intimate of the Countess of Chilton, though Kent had thought she was in love with Skye. Eldrich was here! Not on his estate, which he was said never to leave.

And what was this about Erasmus going into the cave? And others had followed, apparently. And Sir John? What was this man involved in? He could not remember having seen a man so overcome by terror. Sir John was entangled in all of this somehow, and he was a senior member of the Farr government!

Kent had not the slightest idea of what went on.

The sound of horses and a carriage rattling over the cobbles echoed down the empty street. Kent pulled himself back into his shadow, trying to wrap it around him like a cloak.

The same carriage Kent had seen take the countess away, stopped before her door. A small, round man handed the countess down, and she slipped quickly inside. The carriage came Kent's way, and he regretted hiding on the street, now. He drew his knees up, pressing back against the door. Without thinking, he hid his face, not looking at the carriage as it passed. When its sound was barely audible, Kent forced himself to move. With absurd caution he stepped out onto the avenue, but the carriage was gone and the street deserted.

Kent crossed to the countess' door at a run, but when he raised his hand to knock, he hesitated. Despite all his thought, he still did not know what to say. If the countess was involved with Eldrich in some way, she would likely report him to the mage, and Kent certainly didn't want that.

For a moment he stood there before the door, unable to decide, and then he went immediately around the side of the house. He would see what he would see, and then decide what to do.

The faintest light came from the window he had crouched beneath before, and the thought of what he had seen then both propelled him on and made him want to turn away. As quietly as he could, he went to this window and peered in, showing as little of his face as he could.

The countess sat before a fire that had burned to embers. She sat rigidly straight in her chair, unmoving. There was something unsettling about her manner. Thinking that it was perhaps the greatest folly, Kent tapped on the window. There was no response. He tapped louder. Still the countess did not stir.

She must have heard, he thought. Pressing his face to the glass, he was sure that something was greatly amiss. He tried the door but found it locked, and it would not give way to pressure. He was becoming a little frantic, when he noticed a casement window slightly ajar. With a small blade he worked it open and went in as quietly as he could.

The room was dark, and it took Kent a moment to find the door that led into the hallway. When he entered the small sitting room, the countess still remained unmoving before the hearth.

"Lady Chilton?" he whispered, but she did not seem to hear.

Kent went nearer. "Lady Chilton?" Her eyes were opened, but it was as if she were deep in sleep.

Kent put a hand tentatively on her shoulder. He realized that she wore only a sleeping gown beneath her cloak.

What has been done to her, he wondered. She seemed to have been mesmerized. Was this the way a person acted when they had been bespelled?

He shook her ever so gently. "Lady Chilton? It is Averil Kent. Lady Chilton? Please. . . ."

To his relief the countess took a quick breath, as though surprised, and then seemed to relax.

"Mr. Kent?" she said, startled.

"Yes. Do not be afraid. You're all right now."

She pulled away from him a little as her wits returned. "What has happened? What am I doing here? What are *you* doing here?"

"I will explain everything, though be at ease, Lady Chilton, I mean no harm." Kent pulled a chair nearer so that they could speak without waking the house.

"I was passing earlier this evening, returning to my rooms, when I saw you entering a large carriage. You were dressed as you are now, and seemed . . . I cannot describe it, but you were not yourself. Almost as though you walked in your sleep."

"Mr. Kent!" the countess exclaimed, obviously disturbed, "you are not serious?"

Kent nodded. "I'm afraid I am. This is what I saw. You entered the carriage and your manner was so . . . unworldly, that I confess I followed you. Out of concern for your wellbeing.

"I chased the carriage, running up the stairs through the village, and finally out along a lane to the manor house that this priest, Baumgere, built." He paused to gauge her reaction and was touched by her look of distress. "The house seemed deserted, but as I circled, keeping my distance, I saw you on the lawn. You were standing with a tall man I didn't know. And as I watched, what I thought at first was a large dog came out of the wood. But as it crossed the lawn, I realized that it was not a dog at all, but a wolf. A massive wolf."

The countess stared at him, uncomprehending.

"It is well known that a great wolf prowls the estate of Lord Eldrich. . . ."

The countess pulled away from him completely, as though what he said were so offensive that he could never be forgiven. Her beautiful face contorted in fear and rage. "What are you saying? That I was whisked away to see Eldrich in my sleep?" Then the fury gave way to sudden comprehension. "Farrelle save us, Kent. . . . I woke here once before, having walked in my sleep, or so I assumed. Is it possible that I have been taken away before? Abducted from my house and have no memory of it." She pulled her cloak close around her, crossing her arms over her breasts. "What has been done to me as I walked in my sleep?" she said so quietly Kent could barely hear. "What does a mage want with me?"

Kent shook his head, not wanting to say what he thought.

"What should I do?" she asked suddenly, and though she did not really seem to be asking this of Kent, he felt he must answer.

"You must flee," he said immediately. "Leave Castlebough. Leave Farrland, even. To Entonne, perhaps, or Doorn. Get as far from Eldrich as you can. He has hardly been away from his estate these thirty years past, I can't think that he will pursue you."

The countess rose from the chair and paced to the window, stopping to look warily out, as though she feared the mage was watching. "But what does he want of me, Kent?" she asked, turning away from the window. "Erasmus told me that Eldrich cares little for men and their concerns. That he will use them to his own ends without remorse." She stared at Kent, a sudden realization striking her. "Has Erasmus something to do with this? He served Eldrich. . . . And look at all that goes on here. Skye has his copies of the Peliers and pursues Erasmus to have the script translated. This man Baumgere found some great secret in Castlebough, or so everyone believes. It is all connected. It must be." She looked at Kent to confirm her fears.

"I think you are right, Lady Chilton." Kent was tempted to tell her about Sir John, to prove somehow that he cared for her well-being by revealing his secrets to her, but something stopped him. The fear Sir John had exhibited: it was one thing for Kent to risk himself, but to expose another, especially one so convinced of his peril, was unforgivable.

"But what goes on in this sleepy little town?" she asked.

Kent shook his head.

"I can't help but think Erasmus knows something more. . . . And then there is Skye. I will speak with him this very morning."

"Do you think that's wise?" Kent blurted out, jealousy overruling all reason.

"Why do you say that?"

"Only because I think you should not waste a moment. We should be off this morning. Within the hour. Who knows what plans Eldrich might have for you. You said yourself, the mages were always ruthless—Eldrich will be no different."

The countess looked at him oddly. "Tell me honestly, Mr. Kent. Were you watching my house?"

Averil felt fear at being discovered, but strangely he felt great indignation as well. As though the accusation was not entirely true. "Lady Chilton," he said, his voice shaking a little, "I assure you that witnessing your abduction was entirely coincidental."

She continued to fix him with that measuring gaze. "Then I apologize, Mr. Kent," the countess said, although she did not sound at all convinced. "I have had such odd things happen with men. You understand. . . ."

Kent nodded.

"It is almost light. I'm going to wake Marianne, and then send a note to Lord Skye. I hope you'll stay, Mr. Kent. I would like them to hear your story."

"Of course," the painter answered. Left alone, he banked the coals in the hearth and built a fire, conjuring the flames with a bellows. He was not happy with the countess' decision to call on Skye, or to bring Marianne Edden into this matter. What he wanted most was for her to flee, with Kent as her protector. If they were together for a month in Entonne, he was certain she would begin to feel differently toward him. She would begin to see things which perhaps weren't readily apparent in a quiet man like Kent.

Perhaps half of the hour later a servant delivered coffee and freshly baked pastries, and another fifteen minutes saw the countess return in the company of Marianne Edden.

The novelist greeted him rather perfunctorily, as though she suddenly did not approve of this poor painter. Kent found her entirely changed toward him. Servants brought more coffee and food to break their fast and for a while there was no conversation.

As the servants closed the door, Marianne fixed Kent with a look that could hardly be called warm. "You were out for a stroll, Mr. Kent, when you saw the countess taken away?"

"Yes, I could not sleep," Kent said, not liking where her questioning might be going.

"And do you recognize this?" Marianne asked. Reaching over to one of the trays the servants had brought, she snatched away a cloth, and there lay Kent's field glass. "A servant retrieved it from the rear garden."

Kent felt himself color. "Ah, that's where I left it. Yes, it is mine. Like many, I'm an amateur empiricist myself. I was looking at the heavens."

Marianne's scowl left little doubt that she didn't believe him. "And how did you come to be in the house when the doors were locked?"

"I confess, I came in a window left ajar."

"You stole into our house like a prowler and found the countess sleepwalking in little more than her sleeping gown? Mr. Kent, this is most irregular. What could have led you to take such liberties, I can't imagine."

"I know it seems very irregular, Marianne, but if you had seen Lady Chilton, you would understand. Her manner was so very odd—like a string puppet. I hesitated, not sure what to do, and quite unsettled by what I had seen. I almost knocked on the front door, but for some reason did not. Concern for Lady Chilton made me a bit reckless, I fear. I realize it is unconscionable, but I slipped around the back and peered in the windows. And there I found the countess, seated, unmoving, before the fire as though she had been shocked into immobility. I knocked on the window and she did not respond—even when I knocked quite loudly, she did not notice. Frightened, I tried the doors, which were bolted, and then in desperation I found the open window and let myself in. I woke the countess here, before the fire, and the rest I'm sure Lady Chilton has told you."

Marianne began to speak, but the countess interrupted. "Bet that as it may, Marianne, the truth seems to be that I was outside the house this evening and completely unaware of it. I believe Mr. Kent is telling the truth there."

Kent did not much like the implication that he was not telling the truth elsewhere—even though this was the case.

"And you believe this story that it was a mage?" Marianne said, a little incredulous. The countess hesitated. "Marianne, I awoke here, wearing my cloak over my sleeping gown. But that is not the oddest thing. My feet were dirty and stained as though I had walked across wet grass. As Mr. Kent said, he saw me on an expanse of lawn."

"But you could have just as easily have walked out onto our own lawn."

"Marianne. What reason would Mr. Kent have for making up such a story?"

"To have you flee with him. With him! To Entonne, and who knows where. Men have been driven to even more foolish stories, and plans. I have been witness to it, and more than once, too." The novelist scowled at Kent.

"Mr. Kent," the countess said, a little warmth and vulnerability entering her voice. "Please tell me truthfully. . . . Did you see me taken away in a carriage? Truthfully, now."

"Lady Chilton, I swear that I did."

"And were you spying on the countess with your glass, Mr. Kent?" the novelist asked pointedly. "Now answer that truthfully as well."

Kent hesitated, feeling somehow that if he was not honest he would not be believed at all. "I did not actually spy on the countess with my glass," Kent said. "But I will tell you honestly, Miss Edden, that I did consider it."

"Kent!" the countess said, such disappointment in her tone that it made the painter utterly ashamed, "I thought you were my true friend."

"I am," he said quickly. "I just . . . I forgot myself. I . . . I have no excuse." He hung his head, unsure of what to say. An apology seemed terribly inadequate.

"Well, Mr. Kent," Marianne said. "I think you should leave us for the time being. It has been a disturbing morning, make no mistake, and we need some time to consider what has happened."

Kent went out into the newly risen morning, a bit dazed. He had been caught spying on the Countess of Chilton. He was ruined. There would be no redemption for such an act. But what had he seen! He stood on the street for a moment, unsure how to proceed.

Eldrich. The mage had taken the countess from her home, and she was not aware of it. Kent shook his head. She had not believed him. Or, more correctly, Marianne Edden had undermined her confidence in him. If only he hadn't left his cursed glass in the garden! What madness had led him to confess?

"What will I do now?" he asked aloud.

Somehow he had to convince the countess that what he said was true. Sir John was his only hope. Kent set off down the street with great urgency. But would the man help him? Kent could hardly remember seeing a man so frightened. But what other hope had he?

He almost ran through the sleepy streets. There was no other way to support his claims, for they did sound like the result of madness—a particular kind of madness that occurred around the countess with disturbing regularity.

"I will be ruined," Kent whispered, though the world did not seem overly concerned. "Utterly ruined."

He located Sir John's residence, and fortunately found the man awake.

"Kent, you look worried out of your mind, man." Sir John bade him sit, and a cup of coffee was put into his hand.

"I went to see the countess," Kent blurted out.

Sir John's eyes widened. "You didn't mention me, I hope?"

"No. Not a word. But I found her sitting in her parlor, completely dazed. Her eyes were open, but she seemed asleep. Unwilling to raise the entire household, I slipped in the window and roused her. I related what I'd seen, not mentioning you, of course. But then Marianne Edden woke and she didn't believe my tale. She was certain that I had fabricated the story to convince the countess to run away with me." Kent shook his head, feeling himself color a little. "You know how men are with the countess. . . . I think she was inclined to believe me until Miss Edden arrived—and then the idea of what I had seen so unsettled her that she preferred to believe only that she had been sleepwalking, out into her garden." Kent spilled his coffee as he set it down. "I am ruined if I cannot convince them of the truth, Sir John. They thought I had been spying on the countess. Can you imagine? Spying. And then, of course, I slipped into her home unasked. Concocting this fantastic story to frighten her into running off with me. Flames, there will be no place where such infamy will not follow me." He tried to pick up his coffee, but his hand shook so that he spilled more into the saucer, and he set it back down quickly.

"And now you've come to ask me to support your story," Sir John said.

Kent looked up, his hopes rising.

"But don't you see, Kent, the countess is an object of interest to Eldrich? Think what that means. The mage might very quickly discover your interference. He must speak with the countess, after all. As noble as it was to try to warn her, it was more foolish, still. Eldrich will not tolerate interference in his affairs." Sir John let out a long breath. "I will tell you, Kent, you have greater things to worry about than your reputation."

"But what of the countess?" Kent said, realizing that he was pleading. "Who knows what Eldrich . . . intends with her? She has no knowledge of their meetings."

Sir John leaned forward in his chair. "Kent, listen to me. I realize you have feelings for the countess, and no doubt this situation she is in seems monstrous, but there is absolutely nothing you can do but draw the rage of Eldrich, and I will not have that fate visited upon me."

"You will not help me . . ." Kent said in disbelief.

Sir John drew himself up, his look defensive. "I will not. And I beg you to think what you do. You might as well dive into an ocean storm as try to stop Eldrich. Come to your senses, man, a mage is a force of nature."

Chapter Thirty-six

HAYES and Kehler scrambled up quickly as the light faded to a pale glow. It was not lamplight, but a cool white light, like the pure light of stars, that emanated from beyond the opening.

Kehler stood before Hayes, partially blocking his view. Neither of them moved for a moment, and then Hayes stepped up so he could see past his friend. A long corridor perhaps a dozen feet in width, extended before them. Feeling no ill effects, Hayes pressed his friend forward, and they stepped through the door into the hall.

It seemed not to be a cave at all, but the entranceway to a great palace. The walls were straight and plumb, decorated with intricate carvings. Ten feet above the floor, a border carved like a twisting vine ran the length of the hall, and into this blossoms and unfamiliar characters had been worked.

The light emanated from above, and when Hayes looked up, he thought that he looked into a star-filled sky. A sky of infinite depth.

Kehler followed his gaze up and stood transfixed for a long moment.

"How many men living in this day can say they have witnessed the arts of the mages?" Kehler asked.

"But were they mages?" Hayes said.

They walked slowly down the wide hall, the sound of running

water clear now. To either side, sections of the wall were covered in text of the same unfamiliar characters found in the border.

The hallway was long, a hundred feet or more to an arch at the far end. Hayes' initial impression of stepping into a palace, he realized now, was wrong. This felt like a temple, though none that he was familiar with; still, there was no doubt in his mind that this was a place of worship.

"Who built it?" Hayes asked.

"I don't know," his companion said, shaking his head.

"But you think it was Teller?"

"Perhaps. I can't say. In my reading I have come to the conclusion that there was a division in opinion among the mages—a period of internal strife. Not that they were ever particularly united except in their war against the church. But this schism was something greater than their normal individualism. Perhaps this chamber had significance to one of these groups, or perhaps it was a chamber known to all the mages."

To their right a tall doorway opened onto a stair. Hayes leaned in and found the stairway curved up and to the right in a long arc.

He leaned back and looked down the passage toward the end. "Up or on?" he asked.

"Let's explore as we go," Kehler said, and started up the stair.

Once on the stair they returned to the poor light of the lantern. As in the hallway below, the walls were decorated here and there with text and floral designs. Twice they stopped to rest. The stair was so long and they were utterly fatigued. Even the excitement of their discovery could not overcome that altogether. They were considering giving up this climb when they came abruptly to the stair's end. A large character of the type they had seen carved on the walls was the single decoration on the blank surface that ended the stairs.

"What does this mean?" Hayes asked.

"It means that however this chamber was built, the people who used it, or intended to use it, did not enter it as we did."

"You think this is a door?"

"Perhaps not a door, but an entrance all the same. Or perhaps it was merely meant to be an entrance one day. I would guess that the surface of the world lies not far beyond this wall."

Hayes stepped forward, pressing his hands against the stone, moving them across it as though its secret would be revealed to him by such an inspection.

"Remarkable. What does this character mean, I wonder?"

Kehler shook his head. "I don't know. . . ."

Hayes looked at him sharply. *So why had they risked their lives to find this chamber?* "Does anyone?"

"Eldrich, almost certainly. Perhaps Erasmus Flattery. Maybe Deacon Rose and a few others within the church."

"But what good will it do us?"

"Us? We have little to do with this matter, Hayes. It is about the hoarding of knowledge—worse by far than the hoarding of riches. Reformers talk incessantly about leveling society, doing away with the advantages of the wealthy and the aristocrats. But there is no leveler like knowledge. Who knows what is concealed here? It could be the great discovery of our age. For centuries the arts were in the hands of a select few—but what if that could be changed? What if you could suddenly heal the sick as no physician ever can? Imagine what that would mean."

"But how do we know there is any such knowledge recorded here? Knowledge that can be used."

Kehler shook his head. "All we know is that Baumgere was willing to sacrifice a great deal to find this chamber, and that the church did everything in their power to hide it. The Farrellites have long been the greatest hoarders of knowledge. They would keep the population in utter ignorance if they could. Better if men could not even read. Whatever is hidden here has long been suspected by the church—suspected and kept secret. That is enough for me. It must be brought out. Out into the light."

They turned and descended the stair, the sound of water growing as they went—a sound that had not been heard by men in this place for many years.

When they came to the foot of the stairs and into the cool light, Kehler blew out the flame in their lantern and set it aside.

They continued down the long hallway, and found small niches on either side into which faces were carved in high relief. Both men and women were represented here. Around each niche, text in the same script was arranged. They stopped and looked carefully at each face, as though they might find there someone they knew. The faces were sensitively rendered, Hayes thought—noble and sad. More than one wore a circlet around its brow, often surmounted by a brilliant stone set into the sculpture. And then he realized that each face bore a stone. One in a woman's ear lobe. Another on a pendant around a man's neck. All different colors and brilliance, some so unusual that Hayes could not even guess what they were.

"Who are they, I wonder?" Kehler said softly.

Hayes stared at one face, unable to tear his gaze away. "See how sad they look. What could have made them so?"

Kehler shook his head, though he looked almost as troubled as the faces he contemplated.

They carried on past the sorrowful faces, most of them older, it seemed, but one or two quite young—the age of Kehler and Hayes.

"Either the artist who sculpted here was a genius," Kehler said quietly, "or these faces are touched with the mages' art, for I feel I almost know their stories. Do you feel it? The faces are so evocative. I look at them, and some knowledge seems to be just at the edge of my consciousness." He stopped before one—the long face of a man in his middle years. "Look at this one . . . noble and tragic. See how his brow is almost knit, as though he wrestles with a terrible burden. He is a man who has been much disappointed, and remained alone throughout his life—no wife or children, clearly. He dedicated himself to some cause, and paid a terrible price. Look at the depth of his thought. Those brooding eyes. Here is a tragic hero if ever there was one. A man who made choices that cost him dearly—yet he could make no others.

"And do you see this woman? How old is she? Thirty-five, do you think? What is that look? Is it pride? Not quite. Pride is too close to vanity. But even so, she has struggled against some terrible fate, and not surrendered. I cannot say that she triumphed, but she did not surrender." Kehler looked at his companion. "Do I sound like I'm raving?"

"Raving? No, I feel the same thing. These faces are touched by a great art, though I don't think it is an art of the mages, but merely the result of genius and inspiration." Hayes reached out tentatively and touched the face of the woman, brushing his fingers over her cheek—almost a gesture of affection. Lonely, was what Hayes thought when he looked at her. Hidden down here for how long? Centuries? Lost to the world—to all mankind. A portrait of loneliness.

They walked on, every few strides passing two more faces, none joyous, none even content.

And then a great hall opened before them. They stood in the archway and stared into the chamber—as long as the hallway they had just walked, but five times the width. Hayes didn't know where to look first. The ancient white walls were covered in neat, linear rows of script, the characters as high as his hand was long—thousands of them, for the walls were tall, thirty or forty feet, Hayes was certain.

Gingerly they stepped into the room, as though they were trespassers in fear of being caught, or in fear of spells left for intruders, but even the mysterious light did not alter.

In the center of the room, against one wall, stood a raised terrace of smooth stone, and it was from this that the sound of running water emanated, as it likely had for uncounted years.

Ten paces into the room they turned in a complete circle, overwhelmed by the wonder of their discovery.

"I feel like I am suddenly surrounded by mystery," Hayes said.

"You have always been surrounded by mystery," Kehler said, a hint of a smile appearing. "But perhaps we have reached to the heart of this one."

Hayes went to one wall and ran his hands over the letters, which were raised in relief, not inscribed. The script he thought exceedingly fair and yet curious, for it didn't seem to resemble the common or even the ancient scripts used around the Entide Sea. But it was almost definitely the same script that Kehler had included in his letter.

Hayes realized that he felt a little disoriented, finding himself in this vast chamber of light after the dark little tunnels he had navigated.

They crossed the room and mounted three steps to the raised terrace. Here the water flowed from the mouth of a wolf head set upon the shoulders of a man. A stream of water fell into a small font, and then apparently ran under the platform to appear again at its base, finally flowing in a narrow channel to the far side of the chamber where it disappeared into the floor.

Above the fount, life-sized torsos of a man and woman grew out of the rock, the man wearing the mask of a fantastic crested bird, the woman a mask of a hawk or falcon, Hayes was not sure which. To either side of the figures text was inscribed inside a floral border.

"Look," Kehler said, staring down at the floor. "These lines lead to seven points, and at each point a circle is scribed and a different colored stone laid into the floor." He stood by one of these stones. "This one seems to have stars cut into it, though if these are constellations, they are unfamiliar to me. And that one has more written characters. This central stone has no markings at all."

The last was black and glistened.

"What material is that?" Hayes asked.

"It appears to be glass," Kehler said, bending down and touching it. He stood up, looking around. "Does this not feel like an altar to you? The center of the temple?"

Hayes nodded, though he could not begin to guess at the purpose of such an altar. His eye kept being drawn back to the man and woman above the font, their faces hidden by masks. When he had first looked, he thought they held hands, but now he realized their wrists joined into one and ended in the claw of a bird. Both their free hands were slightly extended as though in supplication, but the woman held a long-stemmed blossom in her hand.

"Everything I see here seems to have some meaning that is just beyond my grasp," Hayes said suddenly. "I have never felt so much that I walked in a dream. Do you know what I'm saying? Like you, I felt that the stories of those men and women whose faces we saw were just on the edge of my consciousness. And I feel much like that here. As though I can almost understand the significance of these figures, of this font. Of these stones set into the floor. Look at the way this man and woman hold out their hands. . . . I am touched by this, in some way that I cannot explain, as though my heart understands, but my head is not quite able to grasp it."

Kehler nodded. Hayes realized that his friend was close to tears. He had persisted in his efforts for so long, taken such risks, and now he was so overwhelmed by what they had found that he could no longer control his reaction.

He sat down on the step, hanging his head so that Hayes could not see, and if his shoulders shook a little, Hayes did not think it was unwarranted. Hayes was not far from tears himself, though largely because they had survived the ordeal of the cave. Tears for the child he had found and the horror of crawling through those dark tunnels. And he hadn't taken the risks in Wooton that Kehler had. Demon Rose did not pursue him.

Kehler rose suddenly, not looking at his companion, and went on, his attention apparently drawn to the script on the far wall.

Hayes kept his distance, continuing to float through this peculiar dream, in which everything seemed to have ephemeral meaning, yet nothing was familiar.

Kehler walked along one wall, Hayes the other, running his fingers over the words as though he could absorb their meaning thus. He closed his eyes, hoping words would form in his mind, and felt yet again that the meaning was so close, but he could not quite grasp it—like a memory trying to surface.

The two met before the final archway, and gazed through, wondering what would be revealed to them here. But this room had no light of its own and what lay within was not clear. Hayes waited for Kehler to go first, for he found himself curiously reticent to enter. When his friend made no move, Hayes gathered his nerve and stepped through the arch.

His eyes quickly adjusted and he found himself in an oval room, its ceiling vaulted and carved to look like a beamed ceiling of intricate design.

In the center of the chamber stood a crypt of white stone, its cover sculpted to resemble a recumbent knight in full armor. His hands closed over the hilt of a sword, the point of which rested at his feet, and he held the stem of a small blossom entwined in his fingers.

Kehler had come in behind him and stood staring at the face of this knight. Like the faces carved in the hall, this man's countenance was marked with sorrow, his heavy brows and strong mouth speaking nothing else.

"And who is this they have laid here in such solitary state?" Kehler asked, quoting a well known line.

Hayes turned away from the melancholy knight and realized there was yet another face sculpted into the wall behind him, but as he stepped closer, he realized that it had been left incomplete.

"Look at this," he said. "Everything we've seen was finished to the smallest detail, but this is hardly begun."

The face was unquestionably that of a woman, or would be when it was complete. The curve of her hair was clear, but the eye sockets remained unfinished and she stared blindly out at them. The nose would be relatively fine, and the lips full. The chin was small, but even so the face was strong. Hayes felt there was a personality trapped in the stone that struggled to emerge, to take form before them.

"It is like looking through frosted glass or fog. The features are not quite clear." Kehler squinted as though somehow that action would bring the face into focus. "Very odd. As you say, nothing else we have seen was left unfinished." He turned to examine the rest of the chamber. Text covered the back wall, and this, Hayes was almost certain, would tell the story of the man who lay in the crypt.

On the wall at the foot of the knight a second head was carved, this one a man and quite complete. Hayes moved closer, drawn to these mysterious individuals, as though they held the key to understanding the purpose of this chamber.

"Farrelle's blood . . . !" he said under his breath.

Kehler came up beside him, and stopped, putting a hand to the wall for balance. "It is Erasmus. . . . Isn't it?"

"So I thought, but now that I have stared at it a moment, I am not so sure. The likeness is not perfect, but it is so close that it can hardly be coincidence."

"Like the Pelier. . . ." Kehler said.

Hayes sat down, suddenly utterly exhausted. He put his back against the wall, drew up his knees, and buried his face on his arm. *What in this round world? Erasmus Flattery?*

A moment later he opened his eyes and found Kehler sitting opposite him, slumped against the crypt, his eyes fixed on the face that so resembled the man they knew.

"I came here," Kehler said, his voice trembling with fatigue and awe, "unsure what to expect, with little more than the maps and the painting of Pelier to feed my imagination, and what I have found is utterly unexpected. I thought I knew something before we arrived here. I thought I had delved into the secrets held by the church and knew things that others did not even suspect. And now I realize I am utterly ignorant. I know less of these matters than a child knows of the greater world. I. . . ." He shook his head in bewilderment. "What have we stumbled upon, Hayes? Is it nothing more than an elaborate tomb? Is it the key to some secrets of the mages themselves? The recording hall of Teller's society? Or something else altogether? Something we cannot even imagine. Why is there a likeness of Erasmus Flattery here, in this chamber that must be . . . centuries old? What in the round world have we found?"

Hayes looked up at the face again. The likeness showed a younger Erasmus, or so it seemed to Hayes—a man in his early twenties. But was it Erasmus? The hair was curlier, and the features finer, but then clearly the artist had not been working from knowledge of the model.

"It must have been done from a vision," Hayes said, struck by sudden insight.

Kehler nodded. "Yes. That would explain it. But whatever does it mean?"

"I think that Erasmus is not so innocent of the ways of the mages as he claims. Perhaps the rumors are true, and he is a mage himself. Does he even know of this chamber, I wonder?"

Hayes shook his head. "I suspect he has never seen it, but considering our discoveries, I would not be overly surprised to find that he knew of its existence. We might even be performing the task of finding it for him."

Kehler had obviously never considered this, and looked sharply at his friend. "Do you think so?"

"Anything is possible. We are dealing with mages, with men who, it was said, could look into the future. Perhaps their vision was not perfect, or utterly clear, but they could see some things. Perhaps they even saw us."

Saying this, Hayes lowered himself to the hard stone and, using his arm as a pillow, surrendered to the sweet sleep that overwhelmed him.

Chapter Thirty-seven

SHE stood before a small niche that time and water running over stone had etched into the rock. A crystal stalactite, thrice the thickness of a stem of grass, hung there, and on it a drop of water laboriously formed. *Like a swelling womb,* Anna thought. She could see a reflection of the lantern's flame flicker in the droplet, like a tiny, rapidly beating heart.

For a long moment the drop continued to swell, and then, with what appeared to be a final inhalation, it let go its hold and fell into the world. She watched the droplet distend as it plummeted toward the natural basin below.

Opening her mind at that instant, Anna stared into the water. The droplet created a hollow where it struck the surface, and in the depression she saw stars spinning.

And then she reeled away from the basin, clutching her head in pain. Hands took hold of her, lowering her gently to the floor of the cavern, which spun around her so that she spread her arms to keep her balance. She wept.

Gentle hands supported her, and after a moment the world resumed its normal ways; the spinning slowed and then stopped altogether. No one spoke for some time, and she kept her eyes tightly closed, trying to shut out the cold, the terrible feeling that she balanced on the edge of a precipice, and all around her was a dark, cold void.

"Anna?" It was Banks. She could hear the concern in his voice, though it was partly worry that she would lose the vision if she did not speak it soon. It happened sometimes. She would cling to the vision, but it would be driven out by the feelings of terror and anguish that augury engendered.

"I have it, still," she said, and no more, not quite ready to move. She knew that this attempt at augury would slow their progress by several hours, but it couldn't be helped. There were times when a vision announced itself, and she had learned to listen at such moments, listen very carefully.

"They are here, ahead of us. I saw them; a priest, a man, and a dwarf, climbing above a raging torrent. But there is more. Two men sleep, and an armed knight watches over them. And in a window I could see a man, Erasmus Flattery it seemed, and he looked in on this scene with great sadness. Behind him there was the shadow of another. Someone very large and powerful, I thought. On the wall I could see writing. . . ." She paused, pressing her eyes closed, focusing her mind. Trying to create a complete picture of the vision. "Landor," she said. "There are more words, but. . . . *Curre d' Emone,*" she said suddenly, words coming clear to her.

Those around her waited as she tried to recall more, but finally she shook her head. "That . . . that is all."

"*Curre d' Emone,*" Banks said. "Heart of the world."

"Landor's gate," Kells said, his voice echoing like falling water.

"It is only a story," Banks said, the disdain in his voice less than convincing.

"All stories have roots," Anna said, pulling her hand free of Banks'. "However remote and disconnected, they have roots."

She forced herself to her feet, swaying terribly, her head suddenly light. But she did not fall.

"We must make haste. We must drive ourselves until we are there. I fear Halsey was right—the shadow behind Erasmus Flattery must have been Eldrich. I can think of no other explanation."

"But if Erasmus is an agent of Eldrich, then we are already too late," Kells said, looking genuinely frightened.

Anna shook her head, trying to work the knots from her shoulders and back. "But I sensed that Erasmus was not knowingly the mage's agent. That feeling was very strong. We might influence him yet. I must try. But we must make all haste. With such a thing to be discovered, Eldrich cannot be far off."

Chapter Thirty-eight

CLARENDON kept staring at the survey, which he had spread in the lamplight on the cavern floor.

" 'Beyond the Fairy Galleries.' This is the only passage that is shown, but clearly there must be another that hasn't been recorded." He nodded at the pool of water which ended the passage. "Perhaps we have passed some little bolt hole. Such things can be almost impossible to see, sometimes."

Clarendon made an effort to sound his usual self, but even Erasmus, who had not known him long, could tell that he was still affected by the incident with Rose. Erasmus was not sure if Clarendon was still enraged at the priest (very likely) or if he was a little chagrined by his own reaction. After all, he had placed Deacon Rose in more than a little danger when he threw the man's belongings into the void.

Despite his own hostility toward the priest, Erasmus was concerned about the deacon's well-being. If Rose were injured, or worse, on his journey to the surface, Erasmus would feel more than a little responsible. Perhaps he should have done more for the man, but then Clarendon had caught him utterly by surprise when he threw the priest's pack into the falls. Erasmus would never have allowed Randall to do that if he had realized what he intended.

Turning his mind from this, he began to search the immediate area, examining the rock, looking for an odd shadow that hid a small opening. They had already noticed a few of these as they traveled through the cave. And then he spotted a tiny bit of flowing moonstone which was too gray-white to be real.

"Well, look at this." Erasmus dug a fingernail into the wax. "I don't think that this has been here too long. Certainly only days and not years." And then he realized that the letter H had been etched on the rock in wax.

Clarendon stared at the marking, his mustache twitching. "Our friends were here, that is certain. Perhaps they didn't know precisely where the passage was, but had to look for it themselves. At least it seems they arrived at this point unharmed. It gives me hope."

Starting at the pool, they began searching back up the passage, Clarendon holding the lantern and Erasmus investigating every niche and concavity in the rock. A short time later they arrived back at the Fairy Galleries.

"We have missed something," Clarendon said.

But Erasmus shook his head. "No. I don't think so. Not in that passage at least. Let's look at the survey again."

They made their way back to the pool, where they spread out the survey and stared at it as though it were a puzzle with a hidden solution, some trick that they couldn't quite see.

"I might be a fool," Clarendon said at last, "but I can't see anything here that answers. Perhaps there is an undiscovered passage back in the Fairy Galleries, but certainly there is nothing in this section. What did your young man's letter say?"

" 'Beyond the Fairy Galleries. . . .' And that he would mark his route with the letter H."

They slumped down on the rock, both of them lost in thought.

"I can answer your question," a voice said softly.

For the briefest second Clarendon looked puzzled and then he was on his feet. "I warned you to go back!" he shouted down the passage.

Deacon Rose stepped forward, a dark form on the edge of the light. Erasmus found this apparition unsettling.

"That is true, Mr. Clarendon, but without me you will not go forward, that is certain."

"Will we never be free of you, priest?!" the small man shouted, and Erasmus rose up to calm him.

"Don't be so hasty, Randall," Erasmus said, putting a hand gently on his shoulder. "I'm willing to hear the Deacon out."

Clarendon shook off Erasmus' hand, glaring at him, clearly not intimidated by size. "Have you not heard enough lies? Enough promises? He put me in the gravest danger, swinging out over the falls because of his obsession. I don't believe there are followers of Teller still among us, and I have looked into these matters, Mr. Flattery. Studied the life of Baumgere, and much else besides. . . ."

The priest interrupted quickly. "Yet you are curiously reticent to allow me to perform a trial that would prove you, and these young men you pursue, innocent," Rose said, his voice as reasonable as ever.

"Because I do not trust you!" Clarendon said with feeling. "Because the church of Farrelle has always judged in haste and with little regard for the truth. I know your history, priest. I will not have you sit in judgment of me."

Rose came forward a step, and Erasmus could see that he bowed his head, almost like a penitent. "I cannot dispute what you say, Mr. Clarendon, for there is truth in it. Some truth at least, and despite what you think, some members of my church do care for truth. I count myself one of these. That is why I'm here. I believe that there might well be Tellerites still among us, but I will see no innocent men or women persecuted. However, if there are Tellerites, as I fear there are, their purpose will not be innocent.

"They desire the power of the mages, and you do not even begin to understand what that means. You claim to know history, Mr. Clarendon; look at the history of the mages. They did not even know the meaning of the word justice. If they did not bring ruin to men, it was not because they were just or fair, but because their energies were taken up with other matters. But the followers of Teller, who hope to replace the mages after Eldrich is gone—what are their intentions?

"I believe there is a reason the mages have dwindled to one. It is not an accident. They mean to leave no trace of their arts behind when the last of them is gone. But we will have new mages to take their place, and who can be sure that they will maintain the same indifference to the affairs of men? Are you willing to take a risk that these mages will leave men in peace? I am not."

"You have already persecuted the Tellerites without mercy," Clarendon said, his voice calmer now, but the tone of accusation hardly reduced. "What will be their intentions toward the church if they rise to power now? It is no wonder you are apprehensive. You have reason to be. It is not men who need fear, but priests."

"Can you be sure?" Rose asked. "Can you, Erasmus? You know something of mages, I think. You know how little they care for mankind. Shall we have new men of power rise up, when we know so little of their intentions, or their morality? I, for one, fear it."

"It doesn't matter what he says," Clarendon countered, appealing to Erasmus as the priest had just done, as though it were Erasmus who sat in judgment. "He is a priest and has already proven that he can't be trusted. I believe he is a danger, not just to me, but to Hayes and Kehler, and perhaps even to you, Mr. Flattery."

"But you have overlooked something, Mr. Clarendon. I know the way on. I saw what Kehler saw in Wooton, though at the time I did not quite realize what it meant. But I have located the way and could simply go on without you. I could confront your young friends, and there would be nothing you could do. But, you see, I am trying to make amends for what you believe was an act of bad faith. I will show you the way, and you can accompany me. We will find Kehler and his friend, and you can assure yourself that I will not harm them. I believe now that you are no follower of Teller, Mr. Clarendon, and I apologize, both for doubting you, and for my actions. I'm sure it was terrifying, though I will say I would never have done it if I had not had utter faith in the rope to hold your weight. Despite what you might think, I did not intend to endanger your life."

"Why?" Erasmus said suddenly. "Why do you suddenly wish to make amends for what you did to Randall?"

"Because it is a long and dangerous journey out of the cave alone," Clarendon growled.

"No more dangerous than traversing above the falls alone with no one to hold the rope," the priest answered. "Because I'm now convinced that you are not followers of Teller. Because if any discovery is made, I hope to be able to convince you of its danger, should it become known. If we find your young friends, there will be four of you and but one of me. If my powers of persuasion are not up to the task, you will override me and do what you will. I am only asking to be heard. That is little enough for showing you the way on, for I can guarantee that you will not find it without me."

"We should search on," Clarendon said. "I'm not ready to admit we cannot find the way."

"By all means," Rose agreed. "I will await your decision." He sat down, his limbs sprawling like a man entirely exhausted, and no longer caring about appearances.

"Have you food left?" Erasmus asked the priest as they passed him to return to the Fairy Galleries.

"Very kind of you to ask, Mr. Flattery. I have a little and am used to fasting anyway. What I need is sleep." The priest rolled onto his side on the cold rock and shut his eyes. Erasmus though he would be asleep in seconds. He was almost that exhausted himself.

They left the priest, warmed only by the small flame of his candle, and went back up the passage carrying their lantern and the survey.

When they were sure they had passed beyond the priest's hearing, Clarendon turned to Erasmus. "I will never trust that man. I am suspicious of him even now. It is foolish even to leave him alone with our packs."

Erasmus nodded. "I agree with you, Randall. I'm not quite sure what Rose is up to, but he can't be trusted. Yet what has he gained by coming to us? Do you think he is after the contents of our packs? He intends to go on without us somehow? Perhaps one of us should wait here in the darkness to see what he will do."

Clarendon shook his head. "But he knows we don't trust him. He might even imagine that we would do such a thing. No, there is something else. Could the way on be in this passage and we have missed it?"

"We searched every crevice. . . ." Erasmus stopped in his tracks.

"Mr. Flattery?"

"What if it is through the pool?"

"What are you saying?"

"Imagine the pool extending beneath the wall, and then the passage opening up again beyond. Do you see what I mean? The pool could merely be a low spot in the passage where water accumulates."

Clarendon spun around and bolted down the passage. Because the tunnel was small, Erasmus was soon left behind, following the dull glow of the lantern, stumbling in the growing darkness. Once he hit his head so hard that he fell to his knees clutching his scalp in pain.

He heard Clarendon cursing beyond him, and tried to hurry on, but he was leary now of doing himself further injury. Light began to grow before him, and in a moment he found Clarendon crouched down in the pool reaching frantically under the wall. The priest was nowhere to be seen.

"I saw him, Mr. Flattery. The blackguard was disappearing under the wall as I came. I was not swift enough. May he drown for his lies and his false heart."

Erasmus waded in beside his friend and reached in under the wall as far as he could. The passage was narrow and completely water-filled as far as he could tell.

"I will chance it," Erasmus said quickly. "But we must think about how we will take our lantern through. How could he have light beyond?"

Clarendon pointed back at their gear, which was spread across the cave floor. "He had a lantern still and has taken a tin of our lamp oil."

Erasmus lumbered, dripping, from the pool, and to his dismay discovered that many things had been taken. From one of the packs a large section of canvas had been jaggedly cut.

"Here. He has wrapped everything in clothing and canvas and hopes that will be proof against water for as long as he is submerged. We will do the same." He found two candles and lit them, then blew out the flame in the lantern.

As soon as they felt the lantern had cooled sufficiently, they wrapped it as best they could and took up the bundles they would carry on with them. Erasmus tied one end of their rope about his wrist with a knot that he could easily release and went into the pool where he knelt in the cold water.

"As soon as I have found air, I will pull the rope through. Hold fast to the end. If all is clear, I will tug it sharply three times." He took three deep breaths and forced himself into the tunnel beneath the wall. The idea of being submerged was not particularly unsettling to Erasmus, but he was worried about how far he might have to go before he found air again. If Rose could make it, then Erasmus was certain he would manage—though he feared finding Rose drowned in the tunnel. The priest obviously didn't lack courage, but he'd already proven himself a poor swimmer.

Clarendon was more of a concern, but then Erasmus had seldom met a man with greater tenacity. If Rose and Erasmus could go through, then so would Randall Spencer Emanual Clarendon—have no doubt of it.

The dark waters seemed to cling to him as Erasmus clawed at the rock, pulling himself along as quickly as possible toward the air he hoped was near. Air. . . . The urge to breathe began to take hold of him. If he went much farther and did not emerge, he might have gone too far to return.

Suddenly his survival seemed to depend on turning back immediately.

Go on, he told himself. *The priest did it, and he could not swim.*

And then as he reached forward to grab the rock, his hand broke the surface. A few seconds more and he sat upright in a pale, glowing pool, light coming from the candles on the other side. Rose was nowhere to be seen.

Erasmus scrambled out of the freezing water, shaking. The knots on the roll of canvas defied his cold fingers for a moment, but then he got them opened and pulled out his clothes and the lantern, only dampened from their brief submersion. He pulled on his shirt and breeches, drying his hand before striking the flint and lighting the lantern.

In a few moments he had hauled their remaining pack through the siphon, and then he stood knee-deep in the pool waiting for Clarendon, ready to offer assistance.

The water began to surge around him and in only a few seconds he had Clarendon by the hand and pulled him out into the air and light.

"Flames. . . !" the little man sputtered, trying to catch his breath. "I thought I should never come to the end of it. Farrelle preserve us, but that is my own version of the netherworld: dark and airless and unbearably close." He shivered uncontrollably.

Afraid of what the priest might be up to, they went quickly on, following wet footprints on the rock.

In less than half of an hour they came upon a section of cavern where innumerable openings gaped to one side. Here they found two packs, all but empty.

"I don't think we are far behind now," Clarendon said. "It is only a question of which tunnel they've entered."

Erasmus bent down and put his hand to the rock before the nearest opening, then reached inside. "I'm not sure if this is damp, but it is the most obvious choice." He bent down and peered into it, listening for sounds of a man crawling. "Flames, it is tight."

"And that is where I prove my worth, Mr. Flattery." Clarendon was still not dry from his encounter with the pool. His fringe of white hair was plastered to his scalp and his clothing still damp. But despite this his determination did not seem diminished.

"Let me go ahead," he insisted, "I fear for our young friends. I will take one end of the rope, and if this is the right passage I will signal you to follow. Just as we did at the siphon."

A moment later the man's small feet were disappearing into the opening, and Erasmus was left in candlelight, wondering what they had found. Worrying about Kehler and Hayes and Clarendon. And this treacherous priest.

Hayes was drawing carefully on the slightly mushy paper. Despite being meticulously protected in oilcloth, their writing supplies were damp, to say the least. Each line of ink spread out as it was laid down so that it looked like the efforts of a child, and any attempts at precision or elegance were futile.

In the hours since they had wakened, Hayes had come to realize that the inscriptions on the walls were much more complicated and diverse than he had originally thought. The walls were not simply covered in text, but also boasted diagrams, art, what might be a chart of the heavens, stylized figures, even a map. There were characters that Kehler was convinced were numbers arrayed in complex formulae. On the wall opposite the font, seven large intersecting circles were cut into the stone and surrounded by stars. Hayes was almost convinced that the lines scribed on the central circle depicted the Entide Sea, though Kehler was less convinced.

"Perhaps these represent our globe, but each view is a partial rotation beyond the last. Seven views of our world," Hayes had offered, but it was mere speculation, though in such a place one could not contain the desire to speculate, and they did so endlessly.

He stood by the font looking at the sculpture above. The avian masks of the man and woman looked less exotic and more macabre as time went on. The font and raised floor still felt like an altar to him, and he had a strange foreboding that the rituals that might be performed here would be dark and strange.

They had been so overwhelmed by exhaustion and by the magnitude of their discovery when they arrived that they had not noticed two urns that stood to either side of the font. These were made of white marble and sculpted to resemble blossoms—like the one the woman held, although the urns were much larger.

"What do you make of these?" he asked Kehler who was sitting on the top step leading to the terrace.

He looked up from his work, a slightly dazed look on his face. His pen paused in midair. "What's that?"

"These urns. What do you make of them? Do you see, they were made to resemble the blossom held by this lady."

Kehler put the end of his pen to his front teeth. "You're right, I think." He rose stiffly and stood by his friend. "The top almost looks like it might have been made to lift off," he said reaching forward. He jerked his hand back abruptly. "Flames! What was that?" Kehler looked over at his friend, his eyes wide. "Do as I did," he said.

"But what happened?"

"Nothing too serious, apparently; but try."

Hayes put his hand gingerly forward, and then he, too, jerked it back. "What in this round. . . ?"

Kehler shrugged. "I don't know. It wasn't quite pain, nor was it really heat. More like a tingling and numbness, but it was unbearable. I don't think I could possibly hold my hand there." He reached out again.

Hayes snatched his hand away. "I'm not sure that's wise. It is certainly not natural, whatever it is. I'm not certain we should toy with it." He looked up suddenly. "Did you hear a noise?"

They both stood perfectly still, straining to hear.

"I hear nothing," Kehler said. "What did it sound like?"

"Footsteps, I think—or scuffling, as though someone walked or crawled." He shook his head. "I'm sure it was just imagination."

The rope fed out slowly, water squeezing from the strands as it ran through Erasmus' hands. Occasionally it would stop altogether, worrying Erasmus, but he was afraid to shout into the tunnel for fear of alerting Rose, who might not realize his pursuers were so close.

Randall might have an indomitable spirit, but Erasmus feared that he would be no match for Rose physically. He hoped Rose was in such a rush to find Hayes and Kehler that he wouldn't wait to see if they followed, otherwise poor Randall could be in trouble. Erasmus had even begun to wonder if the priest would use violence. Clarendon had been right in the end; Rose was utterly deceitful.

"Hurry, Randall," he whispered. "Hurry."

May we catch the priest before he can perform his knavery.

The rope began to move again, like a languid snake. Erasmus realized that this rope would have to be carefully dried or rot would set in, for it still remained for them to make their way out and cross again above the falls.

Suddenly two feet of rope slipped quickly through his hands, and he dropped it lest he blister. But then it lay limp for a moment, Erasmus' concern growing. And then it began to run quickly as though it were being taken in, hand over hand. Three distinct tugs followed, and Erasmus sighed. In his mind he had an image of Rose waiting at the tunnel's end, and overpowering poor Randall, and then luring Erasmus to follow.

Erasmus had stiffened up considerably while he waited, and he got down on his belly to slither into the opening with some discomfort. His still-damp clothing seemed to stick to the rock and the effort it took to drag himself forward was enormous.

Randall had taken their lantern, so Erasmus carried a candle, which made this hand ineffective at pulling him forward. He soon had hot wax pouring on his fingers and after ten minutes dropped the candle and accidentally snuffed it out. He lay in complete darkness in the tightest passage he had yet encountered.

Large enough for Randall, he thought, *but what of me? Perhaps I cannot make my way through.*

He forced himself to go on, against growing panic, as though he were making a terrible mistake. The entire endeavor suddenly seemed a terrible mistake. But then a hint of light came down the tunnel ahead, or more accurately a hint of gray. The passage almost materialized.

"Mr. Flattery?" came Clarendon's voice.

"Randall? Am I almost through?"

"Very nearly, Mr. Flattery, though it is a bit tight right at the end. I assume if the others managed, you will as well. But hurry. I fear we might be too late."

Erasmus forced himself to push on, heartened by the thought of light and space, and a moment later he twisted himself through the constriction at the tunnel's end.

The passage was still small but seemed like a ballroom to Erasmus. He sat for a moment, taking long breaths, each one seeming to increase his sense of relief. Clarendon stood impatiently by, fidgeting.

"All right, Randall. Let's go on and see if our friends are here."

As quickly as they could, they set off along the passage, crawling on battered knees and blistered hands. To their relief the passage opened up, and Clarendon helped Erasmus to his feet.

"Do you hear a tinkling sound?" Clarendon asked.

"Running water, I'm almost certain."

A pale light seemed to illuminate the tunnel beyond the reach of their lantern's flame, though it was so faint they could not be sure. But as they went forward, the light grew. Not the light of lanterns or candles, but a pure white light—more like the light of the moon than the sun. Supporting each other, they increased their pace and a moment later came to a natural stair, its rounded steps ascending a low slope.

Erasmus looked up. "A doorway," he said, and the two of them stopped to stare in wonder.

"And there is Teller's symbol," Erasmus said, pointing to the three blossoms raised in relief on the keystone."

"I . . . I'm not so certain, Mr. Flattery. These blossoms are all the same, I think. There are no roses."

Erasmus went forward, up onto the man-made steps, and then he nodded his agreement.

They went up and through the door, dousing their lantern, and found themselves in a long, high ceilinged hallway bathed in what appeared to be starlight or moonlight. And then they heard laughter.

Chapter Thirty-nine

HALSEY sat working by the light of a poor lamp, bent close to the page so that he could see. His pen scratched across the paper rhythmically, and behind him a log moved in the fire, followed by a crescendo of sparks. There were no other sounds; both the house and the town were asleep.

Then, distinctly, someone cleared his throat. Halsey raised his head, registered what he'd heard, and then whirled around. A tall man stood by the hearth, hanging a poker back on its hook.

"Who are you?"

"I thought such an authority on the arcane would need not ask."

Halsey raised a hand to his face, so slowly it seemed almost to have moved without his knowledge. He felt a strange disconnection with his limbs, with the world. A nightmare unfolded before him. "*Eldrich*. . . ." He whispered the name as though he named a fiend.

"Ah, you are an authority, I see," the man said mockingly. Eldrich shifted his position, though he made no movement that would imply fear or even concern for his situation.

"I warn you," Halsey said, "I am not without resources," but he could hardly catch his breath, and still felt as though gravity did not quite hold him.

A smile flickered on the mage's face. "I stand forewarned. You don't mind if I sit?" he asked, sitting.

Despite the strong sense of unreality, Halsey could not help himself—he stared at the man in utter fascination. *He was in the presence of a mage.* Certainly it meant the end of everything he had hoped to accomplish in his life—but even so he was utterly fascinated.

"How is it that you found me?" Halsey managed, his voice still quavering a little.

The mage shrugged.

But there could be only one answer. "*Skye. . . .*"

Eldrich stared at the man, saying nothing.

"And Erasmus was meant to lure us as well?"

Eldrich continued to stare, his look of mild amusement not varying.

"You have trapped me, can you not at least answer my questions before . . . before you do whatever it is you intend?"

The two men regarded each other for a moment, and then Eldrich spoke. "Augury is a strange art—its subtleties almost impossible to teach. . . . Skye, you see, is my creature. I created him, in a way—created him to serve only one purpose. He was the grain of sand around which your vision formed."

Halsey was not even sure he understood. Eldrich had created Anna's vision? Was that possible?

The fire cracked, shooting sparks onto the floor, and the mage swept them, rather lazily, back into the coals with the toe of his boot. "After he appeared in your vision, I arranged to put Skye in danger. You, very gallantly, rescued him." He tilted his head as though to say: 'It was not so difficult.' "Though I will confess, I thought you might approach Erasmus first." He stared hard at Halsey. "This young woman—your mage in waiting—she has gone down into the cave with the others?"

Halsey said nothing, feeling like a belligerent child faced with an infinitely more powerful adult.

Eldrich glanced down into the fire, as though considering what he might do with this wayward child.

"I will confess to you," he said, his manner so offhand he could have been addressing a friend, "until two years ago I was beginning to think my augury was false—that you did not exist—but I had a feeling. Intuition perhaps, and a mage should always trust his intuition." He glanced up at Halsey. "And here you are." He tried to force some triumph into this declaration, but it rang hollow, and he looked suddenly tired and sad, almost melancholic.

Halsey said nothing, but sat and stared, aware that his threat had been hollow, knowing that Eldrich knew it, too. Anna . . . her impetuosity had been their undoing, though he knew she should not be blamed entirely. He had sanctioned many of her actions, however reluctantly. He shook his head. It was the oddest moment, his flash of fear had disappeared and now he felt only inevitability. He could not change what was to happen, but could only wait.

"But why am I here?" Eldrich said suddenly. He looked at Halsey expectantly, as though the question were not merely rhetorical. "Do you have any idea what is to be found in that cave?"

It was said one could not lie to a mage, and even Anna could usually discern truth from lie. "No, I haven't."

Eldrich raised his eyebrows, a distinctly human response. "They search for nothing?"

"They hope to find a chamber left by Teller's people."

Eldrich's face darkened at the mention of this name. He stared at Halsey for some time, his gaze unsettling. "I wish them luck," he said finally.

Halsey shook his head, suddenly finding his emotions. Angry at being toyed with. "I think I have little to add to this conversation. You trapped my brothers at the abbey. Trapped and murdered them."

"Me? I was not even born. Nor were you, I think. That is history, Mr. Halsey. And history is but memory—ever unreliable memory. . . ." The mage paused, staring at his captive, for that is what Halsey was, and he knew it.

"Do you know what Medwar said about history? It is fiction without dialogue." Eldrich smiled wanly.

"What will you do with me?" Halsey asked, unwilling to listen to jests from his likely executioner.

"To a large degree, that depends on you, Mr. Halsey."

"I will not betray my fellows. I have ways of averting that."

A smile pulled at the corners of Eldrich's mouth. "I have no doubt that you do, but let me ask only that you hear me out, Mr. Halsey, for there is a tale I would tell you, and at the end. . . . Well, I think we will have more to discuss when I have finished."

"You cannot win me over. Even a mage is not that persuasive."

"I ask only that you hear me out, Mr. Halsey. The story, I think, is more persuasive than I could ever be." Eldrich rose from his seat and paced across the hearth, gazing down at the floor, seemingly unaware of the Tellerite.

Flames, he does not fear me in the least, Halsey thought. *Do we truly know so little of them?*

"It began with Lucklow in his middle years," Eldrich said, his musical voice even more melancholy. "He was skilled at augury, much more so than I. Much more so than you, Mr. Halsey. . . ."

Chapter Forty

WALKY rode up behind the cab of the carriage as though he were a footman. He had an unerring sense for the times when his master needed to be left alone, and this was one of them. He looked around at the night. Moonlight found its way through the trees in splashes highlighting a world drained of color. There were no coach lamps flickering fitfully, for the carriage of a mage did not require them. Driver and team traveled unerringly to their destination on even the blackest of nights.

Walky had served the mage for a very long time now, over seventy years, and he had never seen Lord Eldrich so troubled as he had been these last weeks. This constant reversion to augury was one sign, but to Walky there were others as well.

The mage revealed almost nothing of his thoughts, let alone his concerns, but Walky hadn't remained in his service for so long without reason. He was sensitive to his master's moods, and Eldrich's mood was dark and very troubled.

This entire affair was unsettling. Eldrich had returned from his encounter with the old man who followed Teller, and shut himself up alone for twelve hours. Walky had heard him pacing, back and forth across the room—forth and back like a caged wolf.

And now there was this young woman and her companions who

had gone down into the cave, to perform all manner of mischief, no doubt.

The cave itself was a matter of the greatest concern, or, more precisely, what was hidden there. And then there was Erasmus. Even though Walky knew that he was still alive, he grieved for his former student all the same.

The knowledge that all of this was necessary hardly made it easier to bear, but it was all the comfort he had.

We all die, he thought. *Even the mage will pass through eventually.*

The carriage rocked to one side, and Walky took hold quickly. He saw a bird glide through a shaft of moonlight, making no more noise than a passing cloud—or a mage. An owl, Walky realized. Eldrich's great wolf howled somewhere out in the darkness—an unmistakable if not a common sound, for the beast was usually as silent as its master. Perhaps it howled the despair the master felt, Walky did not know. Nor would he likely ever know. He served the mage, and one did not ask questions of a mage.

The driver brought up his team, and as Walky peered into the darkness, he realized that the lane had ended. He climbed down from his perch, not nearly as quickly as he once had, and opened the door, lowering the carriage steps.

Lord Eldrich did not emerge, and Walky stood patiently by, never thinking to speak. The driver readied two saddle horses that had been tethered behind, and when he spoke softly to Walky to let him know the mounts were ready, the springs of the carriage rocked, and Eldrich stepped out. Without a word, he mounted a horse, and with the help of the driver his servant did the same.

Walky was almost sure they were on a path, though he could not see it. On occasion, when the need arose, the mage cast a spell over him that allowed him to see in the darkness. *Owl sight,* the mage called it, though Walky suspected that this was Eldrich's idea of humor. In any case, owl sight seemed to bathe the world in soft starlight. There was only the slightest shade of color to even the brightest objects, but even so one could see perfectly. Tonight, of course, Walky did not have to see. He could follow the mage, who could see perfectly, he was sure—and it would never occur to Eldrich to give his servant sight merely out of consideration. The mage did not think in such terms.

Walky, of course, didn't feel the slightest resentment over this. When he needed to see in the darkness, he was given sight. When he needed to know, he was informed. It was the life he had chosen, and he could not even imagine another.

Erasmus would never have been able to adapt to it, even if that had been the reason he'd come to live with Eldrich. No, Erasmus had questioned everything, and resented anyone who kept knowledge from him. From what the old man could tell, that had not changed.

Walky wondered if this was one of the reasons that Erasmus was where he was this night. But, no, even the mage couldn't be so petty. After all, Erasmus had been only a boy in those days. He could hardly be blamed for his actions, he had been so young.

Leaves brushed across his face, and he bent down quickly.

Ahead of him, Eldrich emerged into an area of moonlight so that Walky could see his slightly bent form almost clearly. The mage, with his head bowed, riding through a wood by night. There was an image to frighten children, and for good reason. Eldrich did not care much for men, at any age.

Although Walky had long ago accustomed himself to following blindly wherever his master led, whatever he did, this night the servant felt a vague uneasiness growing in him. What was it they did this night? Had it to do with some larger purpose? And if so, what?

They were somewhere above the great cave into which Erasmus had disappeared, Walky was sure. Erasmus and the others—the followers of Teller. He began to feel nausea creeping over him.

Walky knew that Eldrich would act without the slightest compassion toward those who opposed him, but Erasmus was in this same cave, had helped draw the followers of Teller there, in fact.

Has that been his purpose all along? Walky wondered. *Poor child. Poor sad child. . . . Better to have burned.*

Chapter Forty-one

"ERASMUS!" Hayes rubbed his eyes as though he might wipe away the image of his friend. Surely he could not be here.

Kehler turned quickly on Hayes, the accusation clear.

"I—I left a note for Erasmus in case we didn't return. I thought our friends might like to know where we'd perished."

"And it was a wise precaution," Clarendon said, almost crossly. Then he waved his hand about the chamber. "But what in this round world have you found?"

Kehler didn't look quite as furious as Hayes expected. In fact, he looked almost relieved to see the others.

"We aren't quite sure, Mr. Clarendon," Kehler said. "It is what Baumgere sought, or so I surmise, but beyond that I cannot say. The mark above the door seems to be Teller's, but that is about the only token we recognize."

"And even there you are mistaken," Clarendon said. "For the blossoms over the door were not vale roses. They were not roses at all." He stared at the sculptures above the font, his eyes darting here and there and then back again.

Hayes caught Erasmus' eye. "Do you have any idea what this place might be?"

Erasmus looked down, shaking his head. "I think only Eldrich might have that answer, Hayes." He looked up. "I assume you've seen no sign of Deacon Rose?"

"Deacon Rose!?" Kehler said.

Erasmus nodded. "Yes. I'm afraid he learned of our expedition into the cave and, suspecting our purpose, confronted us at the entrance. We thought it better to bring him, and keep him under our eye, than let him wander free, but he slipped away and got ahead of us at the pool. Now we don't know where he's gotten to."

Kehler slumped down on the stair of the terrace, suddenly limp with resignation. Twice he raised his hands and tried to speak but couldn't manage to find words. Finally he said; "But that is why I kept this so secret. Rose is a Farrellite 'inquisitor.' A priest trained to deal with matters that have to do with the arts of the mages. Men just like him burned the Tellerites who were discovered within the church—burned them for heresy. You cannot imagine how powerful he is. And his dedication is beyond all. The church will do anything to see that the arts do not live beyond the years of the last mage. They believe, once Eldrich is gone, that the church will rise again—and they will have no practitioners of the arts to deprive them of their rightful place. This man Rose, he is more than just a fanatic. He would burn for eternity before he would fail in his duty. He would sacrifice any number of innocent people." Kehler looked up at Erasmus, his face drawn with exhaustion and fear. "I cannot think what he will do to me if ever he finds me," he said, losing his voice suddenly. "I can't think."

"He believes you are a follower of Teller," Clarendon said, watching the young man's reaction carefully.

Kehler's hands flew up as though they were on strings. "I am undone," he said.

"Can we not simply stand guard at the mouth of the passage?" Hayes asked. "No one could pass through there without us knowing."

"And then what will we do?" Kehler asked, his voice filled with accusation.

"I don't know, Kehler, for I cannot begin to imagine what this man can do to us. Can we simply keep him from exiting the tunnel? After all, a man in that passage is hardly at an advantage."

"You don't understand. Deacon Rose has been trained in the arts of the mages," Kehler said.

"No, he is trained in the lesser arts only," Erasmus said emphatically. Everyone turned to him, a bit surprised. "The church has long had some knowledge of the lesser arts. They can detect certain things—people who practice the arts for instance, or have a talent for them. They have practiced augury with partial success. Perhaps they can even protect themselves from the charms of a person who has some small knowledge of the arts—but that is all. The mages would never have allowed the priests to retain more power than that. I'm sure this priest is every bit as fanatical as you say, Kehler, but he is not nearly so powerful as you think. Fear, I suspect, is his greatest weapon."

"How do you know?" Kehler asked, still utterly despondent.

"Because I did learn a few things in my time with Eldrich. We must be wary of the priest, certainly, but here are four of us and only one of him. He cannot overpower us." Erasmus looked around him, shaking his head in disbelief and wonder at what they'd found.

"What do you make of this, Erasmus?" Hayes asked, placing a hand on Kehler's shoulder. He felt a bit guilty about Erasmus' arrival, but he was also greatly relieved.

Erasmus did not answer, but turned in a slow circle. "It is a miracle that such a thing exists. And even more so that you found it." He shook his head again. "What lies through the doorway?"

"A crypt, or so it seems; and something you should see."

Erasmus and Clarendon mounted the steps onto the terrace, slowing to look at the font and the sculpture above before going on toward the chamber's end.

Inside the doorway they stopped, Kehler and Hayes hanging back, watching their friend's response. Clarendon reached out and touched the supine figure of the knight, resting his hand there as though it were the grave of a friend he had finally come to visit.

"Who was this?" Clarendon asked softly, his voice oddly filled with emotion.

But Erasmus shook his head. "Look at the arms on the breastplate. These are not Teller's signs."

"No, but who has been honored so?"

"Landor," Erasmus said, though the word came out reluctantly. His three companions stared at him, the question unspoken.

Erasmus pointed at the text on the wall behind the crypt. "I have seen that name before . . . in a book in the house of Eldrich."

"But who was Landor?"

"The first, perhaps the most powerful of the mages, or so say the myths. I don't know more than that." Erasmus turned to the sculpted face of the woman, gasping in wonder. Perhaps, like Hayes and Kehler he felt that he should know her. Reluctantly he turned away and crossed behind the crypt to examine the text, his jaw tight, but his eyes glistening as though tears tried to form.

When he came to the end wall, Erasmus stopped so abruptly that Clarendon, who followed, was almost knocked off his feet.

"*Blood and flames,*" Erasmus breathed, and said nothing more.

Clarendon stared at the face and then up at Erasmus. "But it is you, Erasmus," he said, stepping back quickly, as though he should not stand too close to this man. His eyes darted back and forth, from the face in stone to Erasmus.

"Is it me?" Erasmus asked, his tone a little desperate, as though asking to be reassured that it could not be. "Is it?"

They sat on the steps of the raised terrace in the perpetual starlight of the chamber, eating some of the food that Kehler and Hayes had brought through the tiny passage.

The conversation was quiet, punctuated by long pauses as they contemplated the meaning of what they'd found.

"Erasmus?" Hayes said. "It seems that you can read—some of this, at least. Will you not give us some idea of what is written here?"

Erasmus looked up at his young friend, and then turned his gaze to the writing on the wall. For a moment he said nothing, and Hayes was almost certain he would again deny having any knowledge.

"The language," Erasmus said, his voice quiet and solemn, as though he were in a place of worship, "is one of the root languages of Farr and Entonne. It is called Darian, in that tongue. Scholars today have small fragments of it, though these have never been translated. I cannot read it fluently, and most of what is written here is as much a mystery to me as it is to you. I could read the name 'Landor' which was inscribed in the crypt." He glanced back toward the chamber where his likeness was carved. "The text begins in that corner and runs right to left for the first line, then left to right, and so on, back and forth, I don't know the first word, though it would appear to be the word or name of this chamber. The first line appears to say, '. . . was built to mark,' or perhaps it is, 'to solemnize the meeting of the two worlds, Tearalan and Darr.' Do you see the circles opposite us? Each is marked with a name. The one most central is Tearalan, the circle next to the right is Darr. The first word of the next sentence is Landor. Perhaps, 'Landor discovered this gateway in . . .' I think it is a date, but I cannot tell you what it might be. 'Honor and high praise to the great mage who opened the way. Let his name be remembered always. Let his . . .' perhaps 'praise.' 'let his praises be sung by all who come after.' " For a moment he fell silent, his eyes scanning the script. "It appears to be a history. Seven mages passed through the gate, Landor and six who followed him. 'The land was fair, and they named it . . .' It is a form of Landor—perhaps 'Landoria' would be our equivalent. 'The tide followed them, sweeping through the land, and the arts grew in strength as the tide rose.' I know only two words of the next line. . . . I cannot make sense of it. Then, 'The King's Blood was spread upon the earth, and took root and blossomed. Thus ended the first years of the . . .' More words I do not know." For a few moments he said nothing at all. "I have forgotten so much. There are words I think I should know, but they escape me. It would seem that this chamber was built as a monument to Landor and to the others who were his followers or supporters. It marks the place where these first mages arrived."

"But from where?" Hayes asked, unable to contain his question.

Erasmus shrugged. "From Darr, apparently."

"Faery," Clarendon said. He gestured to the intersecting worlds on the opposite wall. "From a world beyond." He looked at Kehler. "Don't you think?"

Kehler shrugged. "There was so much to be learned in the archives of the Farrellites. Perhaps if I'd had more time. . . . I came seeking Baumgere's secret, never knowing what it was."

Erasmus cleared his throat and began to recite:

"And Tomas plunged into the mirror lake,
And emerged he knew not where
A land unnatural and unknown to man
And he wandered out by star and moon
To a land both fell and fair."

"The Journey of Tomas," Hayes said.

Erasmus nodded. "I spoke with Deacon Rose before we came

searching after you, and he reminded me of the tale. He said that whatever you were seeking, what you might find could be very different—as unexpected as Tomas' journey into a strange land."

"He seems to have known something, Mr. Flattery," Clarendon said. "Does it not seem so? Did we not plunge into a pool and emerge beyond? Does it not say here we are at the gate to another world?"

"Baumgere had several different versions of the lyric for the ballad," Kehler said. "That is how we found our way through the pool—he had written a note on one of the texts. Rose must have seen it as well."

Erasmus nodded. "He likely spoke of the ballad to see my reaction."

"We have not yet taken you up the stair," Hayes said. "You passed it as you entered. It spirals up and ends in a wall. And there a single large character has been carved. Perhaps it is the gate you spoke of—Landor's Gate."

"Perhaps," Erasmus said, though he did not seem at all inclined to go see this wonder. "Whatever the purpose of this chamber, Kehler, I doubt that we shall ever comprehend it. And I can tell you without a shade of doubt that we will never be able to use it as the mages did—even if we could read every word written here. It takes a man's lifetime to become a mage. Seven decades. Not three years, as some people seem to think."

"It does not matter if we understand," Clarendon said. His eyes still glowed with wonder. "We have found it. A miracle, as Mr. Flattery said. And we shall copy every word and reproduce every diagram, and this wonder will not be lost to man again."

"I don't think you understand the implications of this discovery, Mr. Clarendon," came a voice from the hall's end.

They all looked up to find Deacon Rose standing in the archway at the chamber's entrance. He raised his hands, palms out. "I carry no weapon, as you can see. And Mr. Flattery is right in what he says: I do not have the powers of a mage. You need not fear me. But I do hope you will listen to me, for I have some knowledge of things arcane, and more knowledge about our last mage, for he is of particular interest to my church."

Hayes looked over at his friend, who really did look as though he confronted a demon. To his right, Clarendon clenched his fists as though struggling within himself to not assault the man.

Rose didn't come forward, and though he was some distance away, his voice carried easily in the stone chamber. "I'm sure that if Eldrich does not know of the existence of this chamber, he certainly suspects that it exists. Even I have read a reference to it, though I believed at the time it was merely myth. Landor's Gate. *Poart Landorianné.*

"If you think you will publish what you have found here and not draw a reprisal from Lord Eldrich, you do not know much of the world. Nor do you understand the powers of the mage. I know your intentions are noble, Mr. Kehler. You wish to see knowledge spread to every quarter of society. I know you believe that my church hoards knowledge to keep its power, and I will freely admit that sometimes this has been true. But it is not as simple a matter as you make it out to be. Eldrich will make you pay a terrible price for what you have done here. This is a sacred place, if I can use such a term, for that is how the mages viewed it. Just being here is enough to earn you Eldrich's wrath. You had best pray to Farrelle that the mage never learns of our transgressions . . . as unlikely as that might be. I fear it is too late for all of us." He stepped out of the doorway, and for a moment he forgot what he was saying, and stared in awe at the chamber. But then he shook his head quickly and looked back to the others.

"I tried to stop you, Mr. Kehler, but you eluded me. And Mr. Flattery, Mr. Clarendon . . . once you had led me to the Fairy Galleries and I realized where Mr. Kehler must be, I tried to slip away, hoping you would not follow. I tell you honestly that I hoped to spare you this. . . ."

Clarendon stood suddenly, unable to contain himself any longer, but Erasmus took hold of his arm. "Be at peace, Randall. In this the Deacon does not lie. If Eldrich learns that we have defiled this place with our presence—and I can hardly imagine that he will not learn of it—he . . ." Erasmus stopped suddenly, his look very odd. "The price he exacts will be more than you will ever wish to pay, I assure you."

Hayes was truly alarmed. "Then what should we do?" he asked, a bit embarrassed at the apprehension in his tone.

"Leave this place," the priest said. "Destroy every scrap of paper you have written on. Leave this place and never speak of it to anyone—not even to each other. Let is be as though we found nothing. Never write a word of it in your most secret journals. Do not even think of it. And if we are fortunate and Eldrich does not already know of our discovery, we might escape his notice." He was agitated now, and began to pace across the chamber. "You cannot conceive of the powers of a mage. He might even now be aware of our trespass. Mr. Flattery is here, and though I believe that you are no minion of Eldrich, sir, still, you might be surprised at how much he knows of your endeavors. We should leave now—not tarry an instant more." He pointed up at the figure above the font, though Hayes thought he almost seemed to avert his eyes. There was a look near to horror on the priest's face. "We have seen too much. Things we were never meant to see."

Clarendon could be restrained no longer. "And when we leave this place with nothing to show for it, this priest will offer us up to Eldrich. When the mage is gone, the church will want to be sure that no word of this place escapes. Who knows what might be learned here? But the Farrellites will bury that knowledge. They will bury it, and we will be buried as well, frightened into silence, or betrayed to Eldrich. If we were not civilized men, we would leave your bones here, priest, for you are the danger to us. You and your desire to appease Eldrich." Clarendon stopped suddenly, his anger so great that it drove out his thoughts.

"Randall is right," Erasmus said, his tone so quiet and reasonable that it hardly seemed to belong to the same debate. "We always come back to this problem of trust, Deacon. If you go to Eldrich, the rest of us will suffer for our discovery."

Rose nodded, stopping his pacing. He looked up at Erasmus. "There is an answer to this, Mr. Flattery. You must go to Eldrich and tell him what has been found. Make him realize that no one understood what their discovery would mean. Plead our case. Eldrich would not likely accept our promise of silence, but the mages have ways of making people forget. It is our only chance, I think, unless you are willing to trust my silence—and I am sure you're not."

The others looked hopefully at Erasmus. Here, from this unlikely source, came an offered solution. But Erasmus did not look so hopeful.

He shook his head. "I am willing to try to take our case to Eldrich, though I will tell you honestly that there is no reason to believe the mage will even speak with me. He has forgotten me, I think, and was barely aware of me even as I lived in his house. I would not pin my hopes on this. Even if Eldrich heard me out, there is no guarantee of leniency or even justice, no matter how eloquently I plead our case."

No one spoke. Even Clarendon's anger seemed to give way to despondency. The little man sat down hard on the steps, glancing once at Erasmus and then quickly away.

"We have already desecrated this place," Erasmus said after a while. "It is too late to change that. We're all exhausted and our thinking no longer clear. Let's stay some hours and rest and then decide." He looked up at the priest. "Deacon Rose? I'm afraid we will have to ask you to make your bed in the chamber at the far end of this hall. We will sleep before the door. I mean you no harm, but we would like to decide our course together, if you don't mind."

The priest looked up at Erasmus, and then nodded once. He would not cross the terrace where the others sat so casually, but instead stepped over the small stream which flowed across the chamber.

The others followed the priest, staying a few steps away, as though he were a condemned man, and no one wanted to stand so close to anyone about to meet death.

Rose hesitated as he went into the poorly lit chamber. On the threshold he paused, leaning in to look, as though he feared foul play, but then Hayes thought the small room with its crypt had such a religious feel—though not of the priest's religion—that Rose hesitated entering.

When he did cross the threshold, he went slowly, still unsure, taking in everything without urgency. He passed behind the crypt, pausing to examine the unfinished face of the stone woman. He gazed for a moment at the text on the back wall, and Kehler caught Hayes' eye, his question obvious: *Can the priest read this?*

But Deacon Rose moved on, stopping abruptly when he came to the face that resembled Erasmus. He looked sharply back at Erasmus, but to Hayes' great surprise he asked no question. Backing away, he slumped down against the wall, his eyes still on the face that so resembled their companion.

Yes, Hayes thought, *how long ago was that face sculpted? And what does it mean?*

To Walky, Eldrich seemed to be listening, though he knew it was not the sense of hearing that was being used. But that was how he thought of it, for Walky had seen this before. Eldrich walked among the trees that grew in this small depression in the hillside, and then stopped, his head bowed as though completely given over to concentration—sensing things that other men were unaware of, things the mage could not explain, even if he were inclined to explanation.

An unseasonably warm wind, fresh from Entonne, hissed through the hills, sweeping away the clouds and leaving the sky unnaturally clear. Stars stood out, cruelly bright, and Walky could not remember seeing such a clear moon.

All around, tree branches waved in circles, and the new leaves fluttered softly. Gusts seemed to fall from above, pressing the underworld flat against the hill, and all the while Walky thought *the emotions of the world are in this wind.* A world disturbed by the presence of Eldrich and by his intentions. The emotions of the world; whirling up, ebbing, rising in sudden agitation, moaning and shaking the trees, then falling to despairing silence. He could feel the concern, the distress. The knowledge that the natural course of events was about to be interrupted.

And Walky had begun to feel much as the earth did, though he had some idea of what was to come.

Poor child, he thought. He so wanted to speak. To intercede.

Apparently unaffected by the concerns of the earth, Eldrich stopped near to the bole of a beech tree, its silver bark almost aglow in the moonlight. The wind blew his dark hair and tugged at his coat as though seeking his attention, but he was not to be distracted from his task.

"Sir?" Walky heard himself say, so quietly that the wind certainly drowned him out.

"Sir?"

Eldrich's eyes snapped open and he glared at his servant. *"Mr. Walky!"* he said, using the honorific and a tone Walky had heard only once before.

And the servant fell silent, realizing that his entreaties would have no effect. He swallowed hard, not because he had earned the displeasure of the mage, but because someone needed him and he had failed.

But he is a mage, and I am merely a servant, he thought. Even knowing this did not take the shame away.

Eldrich turned his back to his servant, a deliberate gesture. For a moment he did nothing but move his head very slightly as though listening. Walky knew the mage's eyes were closed. Then the man turned, his stiff movements a bit odd in the poor light.

Eldrich's eyes opened, and he moved a few paces to one side, stopping to look up at the stars. Walky saw the wolf glide across the edge of the clearing, as swift and silent as the shadow of a bird. A deep howl came from far off, like a beast in pain, but Eldrich paid no attention.

He crouched down before a flat rock that emerged like the back of a whale from the moss and ferns of the forest floor. Lifting his hand, palm down, the hand hovered above this stone for a moment, and then suddenly struck the rock with great force. Walky was sure he saw sparks fly from the impact, and he stepped back, startled. The wind muttered through the trees, disturbed.

The mage spoke in a low voice, addressing his words to the earth, it seemed, and he ran his hand over the stone in a pattern, over and over. Lines began to appear on the stone, lines of glowing silver, like moonlight or starlight.

Walky shut his eyes, knowing what was to come. He reached out and placed his hand against the bole of a tree. A tear escaped from one eye and, as it ran down his cheek, the breeze marked its path with a welcome coolness.

A troubled sleep was all Hayes could manage. He felt so guilty that his note to Erasmus had led the priest to them that he slept sitting in the doorway of the crypt to be sure the priest could not slip away. Every half of the hour, or so it seemed, he would wake, cock open one eye and find the priest had not moved. Around him the others slept, Kehler most fitfully. Twice he leaned over and shook his friend out of a nightmare, and both times Kehler awoke with a moan, putting his hands over his eyes briefly.

Later Hayes woke to muffled voices, far off, almost beyond the dream, and lay listening in the enchanted starlight. He closed his eyes after a moment, hearing only the sounds of his companions sleeping, and the constant voice of the water as it sang to itself.

Sometime later he woke again, certain he heard a woman's voice; and then he fell into a sleep and saw a beautiful woman. She seemed to be making her way toward him through a tunnel in a thick mist, reaching out blindly as though she might find him by touch.

Later still, Hayes woke to find Erasmus standing on the terrace, staring up at the figures above the font. For a moment he watched, but when Erasmus made no move, Hayes fell back asleep without meaning to.

When he woke again, it was to a hand on his shoulder. Erasmus stood over him, and some of the others were already awake, trying to shake sleep from their minds.

"I've heard something. From back in the tunnel," Erasmus said. "Wake the priest."

"I'm awake," Rose said, emerging from behind the crypt.

Clarendon was on his feet, rubbing his eyes like a tired child.

Erasmus met the priest at the doorway. "Has someone followed us into the cave?" he asked.

"Not to my knowledge." Rose met Erasmus' gaze as he said this, and Hayes felt he was either the consummate actor or was telling the truth.

Erasmus shook his head. "I don't know who it is or what their intention might be, but we had best meet them at the entrance in case they do not wish us well."

"Is it Eldrich?" Hayes asked, unable to stop himself from voicing his fear.

"I don't think so, Hayes. The mage is not one for crawling through tunnels."

Erasmus set off across the chamber, and Hayes thought Erasmus looked both tired and very grim. Sensing his mood, everyone fell in behind, not even asking what he'd heard.

"Stay off the terrace," Erasmus said, stepping over the stream, "something is very odd here. I can feel it."

Hayes looked at Kehler who shrugged, his eyes a bit wide.

They passed quickly into the long hallway, the stone faces watching their process with infinite sadness. At the arch leading back into the cave Erasmus stopped abruptly, and Hayes pressed forward so he could peer over Kehler's shoulder. There, at the bottom of the slope leading up to the three stairs, stood a woman dressed in the clothing of a man, and just then, behind her, a young man appeared.

They stood staring up at Erasmus and the others, like poachers caught in the act of trespass.

"I saw her . . . in a dream," Hayes said, certain this could be no other, though she was begrimed and exhausted.

She extended her hand, still looking a bit intimidated, and opened her mouth to speak, but suddenly she looked around her, frightened, and sank toward the floor.

Hayes felt something deep inside him, something disturbing that he did not recognize, like an internal vibration that gripped his heart. And then the walls before him blurred, and he lost his balance for no reason that he could discern. The woman and man down the slope both reeled as though they'd been struck.

"Come up!" Erasmus shouted, and then staggered down the steps, falling to his knees and crawling on. A terrible rumbling came through the rock, and Hayes felt himself fall atop someone. He lay there as the world lurched and vibrated around him.

An earth tremor, he finally realized, and then the world fell into chaos. A deafening roar and the sound of crashing stone seemed to strike him like a blow. And then a choking dust blinding him, filling his lungs and mouth. Light disappeared, and he lay in the pile of his companions, like a frightened animal whose only defense was to remain still and hope to avoid the notice of the terror.

And then it was still. Still and dark.

Hayes didn't move, but lay coughing and fighting for air, as did the others around him, he realized. Not knowing quite why, he began to crawl back into the hallway, or so he hoped.

"Mr. Flattery?" a small voice managed: Clarendon. *"Mr. Flattery?!"*

The fear in Clarendon's voice was obvious, but Hayes crawled on, his own terror greater. Suddenly his head exploded, and he fell limp and dazed.

A wall, he thought, *I struck a wall.*

He fought for air, trying to breathe through the fabric of his sleeve. And then a dull light began to grow. Dust. The air was filled with dust which swirled and swept past him as though on a wind.

Sitting up, Hayes realized he had only crawled diagonally across the hallway, until he had struck his head. The others were spread about him, only Clarendon standing. He was bent over someone, thumping him hard on the back.

"Breathe, man," the dwarf was saying. "Breathe!"

And then the air was clear. Hayes continued to cough, pressing a hand to his scalp where the wound was slowly seeping blood.

The woman who had appeared at his door, rose to her knees suddenly, turning toward the archway.

"No . . ." he heard her say, her voice low and still filled with anguish and disbelief. "The others. . . ."

"Are we all here?" someone asked. "Are we all in one piece?" It was Deacon Rose, taking charge.

The priest stood, steadying himself on the wall. "Mr. Flattery? Thank Farrelle. Mr. Kehler? Are you well?" He nodded toward Clarendon, ticking him off mentally. "Mr. Hayes, you are injured."

"Not so badly, I think. Just a scratch."

A man Hayes had never seen sat up, coughing, and covering his mouth with both hands, but there was no dust left in the air. The light had returned to normal as well, if such a light could be called normal.

Hayes propped himself against the wall, and realized that he heard crying. The woman was sobbing into the shoulder of the young man who accompanied her. Hayes felt a strange surge of jealousy.

Clarendon helped Erasmus to his feet, though Erasmus bent over as though in pain, and clutched one hand to his back.

Scrambling up, Kehler pushed past the others and into the archway. He stared into the darkness for a moment, and then turned back to his companions, a look of utter hopelessness on his face.

"The tunnel . . ." he said through a dry mouth. "It collapsed. We're sealed in—utterly." He looked around a bit wildly. "Do you hear me? Do you hear . . . ?"

Chapter Forty-two

HAYES put his hand to one of the smaller rocks and tried rather gingerly to move it.

"I shouldn't do that if I were you," Deacon Rose cautioned.

Hayes took his hand away. The passage beyond the entrance to the chamber was completely choked with rubble.

"But has the passage collapsed back ten feet or two hundred? That's the question," Kehler said.

Hayes nodded. It was the question. Was there any hope of them tunneling out?

Erasmus stood staring at the collapsed section of cave, though his eyes did not seem focused.

"Mr. Flattery?" Kehler asked.

Erasmus started slightly, as though he'd been wakened. "No amount of effort will allow you to make a tunnel through this. It was not a natural tremor that we felt and was certainly meant to collapse the main passage well beyond this. We weren't meant to escape."

The woman and man who had arrived as the passage collapsed stood near to each other, grief etched on their faces.

"It was Eldrich, wasn't it? He meant to murder us?" she said, a building rage kept in check by grief. "All of my people . . . we were lured down here for this." She put a hand to her face and tears appeared from closed eyes.

"I fear you're right," Erasmus said softly.

"But why us?" Hayes asked, surprised by the sorrow in his voice.

"We trespassed in a sacred place," Deacon Rose said. "As I warned you." He nodded to the woman. "And these people—followers of Teller—I would not be surprised to find Eldrich had been planning to trap them for years. Everyone had a part: you, Mr. Kehler, with your insatiable curiosity. Even Mr. Flattery. I have no doubt the Tellerites have been watching him for years. Wondering if they should approach him. Now they know."

The woman glared at Erasmus.

"I knew nothing of it," Erasmus said, "if it is even true. But you see, I am trapped as well. If I am an accomplice, I am an unwilling one."

The woman turned her back on the scene of ruin, standing for a moment looking down the long hallway. "It is not nearly so simple," she said. "You will note that not everyone perished. Some of us have been left alive, at least for the time being, in this place. Seven of us, to be precise. This was no accident." She began walking slowly down the hallway, staring at the sad stone faces as she passed, her companion in tow.

"What is she suggesting, Mr. Flattery?" Clarendon asked.

"I'm not sure," Erasmus said. "Seven was a number of great significance to the mages." He hesitated, not wanting to give voice to his thoughts. "I can't say more than that."

But Hayes was afraid that Erasmus could say a great deal more.

Hayes followed Erasmus into the chamber, where they found the woman and her companion staring in rapt wonder, their grief temporarily displaced by awe.

"Is this what you sought?" Erasmus asked quietly.

The woman glanced at him and then back to the wonders before her. She shook her head, as though the power of language had been temporarily lost.

The man at her side looked at Erasmus. "Until Anna had a vision, we didn't know what might lie here. Even then we did not believe it. You are Mr. Flattery, I collect?

"Erasmus Flattery, yes."

"Josiah Banks. And this is Miss Fielding. Miss Anna Fielding."

Hayes saw that Rose had come up and stood staring at the two new arrivals, his manner less than welcoming. "So I finally see you with my own eyes," he said.

"And who might you be, sir?" Banks asked.

"This is Deacon Rose," Kehler said. "But don't let this modest title deceive you. He is the Farrellite Church's Grand Inquisitor."

Banks fell very silent, his look and manner changing. Hayes thought that this was the way a man would react when introduced to an infamous murderer. Shock, and then fear, and finally a perverse interest.

"You must be terribly disappointed, Deacon," the woman called Anna said. "It seems Eldrich has done your work for you." She did not seem at all concerned that this man spent his life seeking to find and eliminate people such as her. In fact, she looked away as though dismissing him from her thoughts.

"If we are trapped here together, with no hope of escape," Clarendon said, "then let us put aside out differences."

She looked at him sharply. "Differences? Here is a man sworn to discover people such as myself, and then do you know what he is to do, sir? Burn them for heresy. And this is not just some travesty of the past, it has been done in living memory. Perhaps our good Grand Inquisitor has done it himself." She turned and looked at the priest. "What say you, Deacon? How many have you burned for their alleged sins?"

Rose met her gaze, and then he slowly shook his head, looking down. "No, Miss Fielding, I have been spared such horrors. But Mr. Clarendon is right. We are trapped here. Why make our last hours a misery? I shall overlook your heresy if you will forgive me my loyalty to the word of Farelle."

"I cannot forgive you your prejudice, sir, for we have no quarrel with your church, and yet you burned my brethren out of cowardice and jealousy. Afraid of the mages, and even more afraid that we might rise up one day and challenge the church, though this had never been our intention. I am surprised that you will so easily let me live even though we are trapped and doomed to die here. Is this not dereliction of duty, Deacon? And more important, how can you deprive yourself of such pleasure?"

"You do not know me, child," Rose said, his voice trembling just a little, "so you do not realize what injustice you do me. But my offer stands. We cannot live long in this place. Starvation awaits us all. There might be some comfort, yet, in the word of Farrelle. For any who wish it, I will offer what comfort this knowledge will bring."

Anna had drawn herself up, her manner hard and imperious. "I will die with a curse for Farrelle on my lips," she said. "Farrelle and his church. That will be comfort enough for me."

The priest looked at her and then turned away. He retreated back into the hallway, and a moment later they heard a musical chant begin. A rite for the dead, Hayes was certain. For some reason the singing touched him—its warmth and strange sadness oddly uplifting.

A look of horror crossed the face of the woman called Anna, but her companion drew her on into the chamber. "It will do no harm," he said to her soothingly, and she let herself be led away.

As they walked slowly along the length of the hall, all the others watched their reactions with great interest. Neither of the newcomers spoke, but occasionally they shook their heads, and both seemed overwhelmed by what had been discovered.

The terrace, with its font and sculpture, stopped them for several moments. They circled it at a distance, as though fearing to set foot there.

"The *nance,*" she whispered.

"What?" Kehler asked.

"The *nance,*" she said, but offered no more.

They stepped over the stream and continued down the hall.

"Do you know what this place was?" Clarendon asked after a moment. "Does it have a purpose?"

The newcomers gazed at the small man, a look like alarm on their faces, neither of them offering an answer.

"There is no point to secrecy now," Kehler said, his curiosity clearly driving him. "We will take anything you tell us to the grave, there is no doubt of that."

"You really don't know what you've discovered?" the young man asked.

"Mr. Flattery can make some sense of the writing, though not all of it. That is all we know."

The woman nodded. "I need some time to read and think," she said.

"But is it really Landor's Gate?" Kehler said, though Hayes was certain his friend asked the question just to see their reaction to the name.

Both the man and woman looked utterly unsettled to hear the name of Landor. "We . . . we need time," she said again.

They moved on, turning their backs to the others. Occasionally the two would share a look, as though they had both noticed something of significance, but they continued in their silence.

Finally they came to the crypt, and at the door they paused.

Anna stared up at the symbol inscribed above the archway and then put her hands to her face. She glanced once at her companion, who seemed as moved as she. And then Anna made an odd motion with her hand before her face and then over her heart. She mumbled something that Hayes could not catch, though he was certain that the words were from no language that he knew. She made a fluid bowing motion and then crossed the arch into the crypt. Banks did the same, and followed.

A soft light grew in the small chamber as she stepped inside, which had not happened on any occasion when the others had entered. Kehler began to follow her, but she looked at him so sharply that he drew back. Everyone stood in the opening, watching.

She made the same bowing motion before the crypt itself, mumbling again. She gazed at the face carved there for a long time, as though she memorized every feature. Once she reached out her hand to touch the stone of the crypt, but it looked to Hayes that she lost her nerve, and her hand fell limply to her side.

For a few moments she paused, apparently reading the text, and then began to move slowly to the left. The unfinished face of the woman drew her attention for some time, and she and Banks whispered together as they examined it.

They moved on, passing the text, and then stopped at the second face cut from stone. They both glanced back at Erasmus, and then spoke quietly to each other.

"Can you read what it says?" Kehler asked.

The woman turned to him and put a finger to her lips, and he fell silent.

They stayed in the crypt, reluctant to leave, for some time, and when they finally did emerge they came only a few paces into the main chamber, before Anna sat down on the stone, as though what she had seen had taken away her strength.

For some moments she leaned her forehead against Bank's shoulder, but finally she straightened up, composing herself purposefully.

"What is this place?" Kehler asked, voicing the question for all present. Everyone stood a few paces off, their body language odd, Hayes thought, for they were all turned slightly away, as though not to intrude on their privacy.

She glanced at Banks.

"It is a chamber in memorium," she said, clearing her throat. "A historical archive. A chamber of great power located at a nexus of the world's forces. It is a solemn place, almost a shrine. And it is a gate as well. A gate to places no man has traveled in . . . a very long time. It is a commemorative monument—to those who first opened the way, and ventured here as explorers. A monument to Landor—to the seven who made the gate and its key. And it is a place of arcane rites and sacrifice. And that is why we are here," she said forcing her voice to be very even. "We are a sacrifice."

The newcomers to the dungeon, as Hayes thought of it, explored every corner of their subterranean cell, but even when they were done they offered no explanation. Hayes found he did not really care so much what the purpose of the chamber was unless this knowledge would help them escape.

Hayes also realized that he did not yet believe that they were trapped here. It was probably nothing more than a refusal of the mind to accept the horror of their situation, but he could not believe it. He was utterly sure that the stairway that led nowhere was significant. Why had it been built? Surely because it once opened to the world, or at least was intended to be opened. There could be no other explanation. Perhaps there were only a few feet of rock separating the head of the stairs from the light and air beyond. Perhaps there was only a foot. Hayes believed this was their best chance—use some of the fallen rock and try to batter their way through.

Hayes and Kehler sat on the stairs of the terrace, what Anna had called the *nance,* defying the superstition that the others were developing, which seemed foolish to them.

Anna and Banks emerged into the main chamber. They'd been up the stair for a second time. Hayes had been half afraid that they would perform some spell that would open a doorway and let them escape, so he was a little relieved to see them—and a bit embarrassed that he would worry about such a thing.

Noticing them on the stairs, Banks came forward. "Mr. Hayes, Mr. Kehler: you must not set foot on the *nance.* One must perform certain ablutions when venturing there."

Hayes rose immediately, stepping down to the floor, but Kehler remained on the stair.

"Then you must teach me," Kehler said, rising but showing no signs of moving away, "or I will go on defiling your sacred *nance.*" He half-turned as though he would step up onto the terrace proper.

Banks held up his hand. "No. . . ." But he stopped. It was clear that he was not about to teach Kehler the proper rites.

Banks almost turned away, but then reconsidered. "Mr. Kehler, you might be letting yourself in for some bad fortune by acting with such disrespect. This chamber is bespelled in a manner that we cannot even begin to comprehend. That is hallowed ground you stand upon. It is neither prudent nor wise to treat it with disrespect."

Anna turned back to watch this confrontation, her gaze rather hard, as though she did not much care if Kehler brought disaster upon himself—if there could be a greater disaster than being trapped here.

Kehler continued to stare at Banks. "You want me to cooperate, Mr. Banks, yet we have no cooperation from you. Enlighten me. Tell me what you know about this chamber, and you will find that I am a most convivial companion. As was said earlier, we all lie in the same grave. There is no reason to keep secrets now."

"There are oaths that have been taken," Banks said.

Some of the others had drawn closer to hear this conversation. "I have taken oaths as well," Deacon Rose said, "but as it seems I will live out my last few days here, I would have my curiosity satisfied. I will answer your questions, Mr. Banks, if you will answer mine. In fact, I will go further. . . . I will tell you my story first if you will reciprocate by telling yours. Perhaps we all have a story to tell.

Mr. Flattery certainly has a tale we would all like to hear. And Mr. Clarendon is a most interesting individual. I would even like to hear what Kehler found in the archives, though I suspect I know. What say you?" he asked, turning to the others.

No one spoke immediately, and Hayes thought their reluctance very curious.

"I will tell my story," Kehler said after a moment. "Why should I not? It takes some time to starve to death, I think, and we have little to do to pass the time. I will bare my soul if others will do the same. In fact, I will tell my tale even if others will not speak. Perhaps, when I am done, others will be more inclined to follow."

"You see," Rose said, turning back to Banks and Anna. "I will break my oath, for I'm sure it can do no harm here, and Farrelle will forgive me this, I think, considering the circumstances." He tried a weak smile on the two who were supposed to be his sworn enemies.

"Will you not come down, sir?" Banks said, his tone so very sincere that Kehler relented.

"You have been up the long stair twice now," Kehler asked, as though sensing this was the time to ask. "Was it meant to go to the surface? Can we break through, do you think?"

Again the Tellerites only stared back at him, saying nothing, but then perhaps Banks realized that Kehler would not cooperate if he received nothing in return. "It is not so simple, I fear. Much of what is written here suffers from ambiguity, to say the least. The mages were famous for it, as though they were always afraid that their writings would come into the possession of people who should not have them. Such as yourself, Mr. Kehler, or me for example. But the stair. . . . it could have had a number of purposes, I fear." He reached out and clasped Kehler's arm. "Thank you for coming down."

They gathered near the door to the vault—Landor's crypt—and sprawled on the hard stone. Clarendon had assessed their tiny food supply and realized that, even if rationed to the point of absurdity, it would not last three days. After that it was only a matter of time.

There had been a rather macabre discussion of how long people could live without food, and the longest anyone had heard of, that seemed believable, was nineteen days. Ten or twelve days seemed more likely given their exhausted state. Hayes had been hungry since they'd entered the cave. If he believed they were truly trapped, the prospect of starving to death would no doubt terrify him.

He stretched out full length on the stone, propping his head on his hand, and waited, not sure who would begin this confession. Certainly not him, for he had nothing to tell. He looked over at Anna, marveling at how different she looked dressed in the clothes of a boy—not like the elegant and somewhat threatening lady who had appeared in his dream. Her manner and her appearance were in contrast, for she looked tired, even pallid, but in her movements she was no more exhausted than the rest—perhaps less so.

She noticed him looking at her, and Hayes suddenly felt he must ask a question to justify his staring. "What did you mean when you said we were a sacrifice?"

She returned his gaze briefly and then looked away. "It would appear that Eldrich has been aware of us for many years. We were utterly wrong in many of our assumptions, and the mage long schemed to trap us." She glanced at Erasmus. "He used Mr. Flattery and another to draw us out into the open. . . ." She faltered not quite answering Hayes' question.

"I think that Miss Fielding is right," Erasmus said. "Eldrich wanted to lure us down here, and not just any seven people. That means that you, too, were required, Deacon, though I cannot imagine why."

That left everyone thinking. And then Kehler looked around the circle. "Who will begin?"

"It started with me, or so I begin to perceive," Erasmus said, "so I will start." He sat with his back to the wall, his legs stretched out and crossed. Hayes had known Erasmus for many years and during all that time Erasmus had made few concessions to fashion, but even so he had always retained an inexplicable dignity—never looking even faintly ridiculous the way many scholars did. Even now, with his beard and hair unkempt, clothing dirty and torn to rags, Erasmus retained a certain disheveled distinction—like a prince in exile. He could not say the same for Kehler, or likely himself.

"It seems that everyone knows of my time with Eldrich," Erasmus began, looking up, his manner almost defensive, "though no one suspects the real truth of it, I'm sure. I will apologize in advance to Hayes if the story I am about to tell is a little different from the one he heard previously." He stopped, took a long breath, and looked over the heads of the others, his eyes focusing on another place and time. "I was sent to the home of Eldrich when I was aged ten years. It is true that I don't know the reason for this, though something my mother once said left me believing that it was at the request, perhaps even insistence, of the mage himself.

"I was given a room to share with another boy of about my own age: Percy. We were schooled together, and we were as close as brothers for those three years." Erasmus looked a bit distressed at the thought of this other boy, or so Hayes thought. "An elderly servant named Walky was our schoolmaster. He was a forgetful, kindly old man, and the closest thing to a friend we had in that strange house, so despite his eccentricities we loved him dearly. I will not bore you with all the details, but let us just say that Walky had obviously taught boys before, and he kept confusing our lessons with the things he had taught in the past. The subjects he had taught previously it seemed, were not always so mundane as our own lessons."

"Are you saying that Eldrich trained others, but it has been kept secret?" Anna asked, her surprise obvious.

"I have asked myself that very question many thousands of times, Miss Fielding. I have spent entire nights trying to puzzle it through, and I've never reached a conclusion."

"I have an answer," Rose said, "or so I think. The mages commonly had young men in their service, and almost all of them were taught some small part of the arts. Most, however, never rose beyond being servants and their knowledge was not great. This man Walky would be one of them. But many a failed apprentice to a mage was sent back to his family—and if he learned anything out of the ordinary in his time at the mage's house, he could not remember it. Some, it seems, remembered nothing at all."

"So Mr. Flattery has had his memories obliterated? Is that what you're saying?" Kehler asked, his curiosity so great that he actually spoke to Demon Rose.

"But I remember everything perfectly," Erasmus said. "Not every tiny detail, perhaps, for it was long ago, but there is no time unaccounted for in all my years there."

"Let Mr. Flattery finish his story," Clarendon said before anyone else could speak.

Erasmus looked a little unsettled by this discussion, as though his part were suddenly suspect. "As I said, Walky began to confuse our lessons. At the time I didn't think we were meant to be taught anything but the normal subjects for schoolboys. Now I am not so sure. . . . It seems Eldrich does nothing without purpose. We learned a script and some few words in another language, Darian it was called. Although we suspected Walky was not to teach us these things, we never questioned him. In truth, we were fascinated. We had never been told why we were there, and Percy developed the theory that we were meant to be trained as servants to the mage—not just servants, but to assist Eldrich with his pursuit of the arts. I think we both secretly wondered if we were to be mages ourselves, a thought that was rather terrifying, and attractive at the same time. We were only boys, after all, and had no real idea of what this might mean.

"And then, after we had been there almost a year, Walky left a book in the room we used for our studies. It was an intriguing looking book, its title, so worn it was barely legible, in the script we had learned, though the words meant nothing to us. *Alendrore Primia.*"

"The primer," Anna whispered.

"You know it?" Erasmus said.

"No . . . I've never seen it," she said, apparently still reluctant to speak.

"A rough, incomplete copy exists," Banks said. "Made by Teller from memory. It is the first book in the training of a mage: the *Primer of Alendrore.*"

Erasmus nodded. "For the first few days the book sat there, we were afraid to touch it, though it was seldom out of mind. When we realized beyond a doubt that the book had slipped from Walky's mind, we worked up the nerve to open it. You can't even begin to imagine the thrill this gave us—forbidden knowledge, after all. And it was a book full of wonders; diagrams of things arcane, written in an ornate, highly ambiguous language that filled us with awe—like a voice from the past, but the voice of a mage.

"It was not a slim volume, and the first section was devoted to language. After a fortnight we smuggled the book out of the room and hid it in the loft above the stables. Here we pored over it by the hour, though in the good weather we took it to the wood that surrounded much of the hill on which Eldrich's house stood.

"After the section on language, which we learned with a diligence that would have impressed Walky—but then the text was so impressive to us that we dared not approach it in our typical schoolboy manner—came a section of lyrics and poems. All extremely ambiguous, but fascinating all the same, for they seemed to speak of a distant and mysterious history, and like the sculptures in the hall, these poems seemed to evoke something more. That odd feeling that one knew more than was actually presented.

"The second year went on. It became clear to me that we were not mages in training, for most of our work was in the most mundane of subjects. But even so, we learned our lessons, including those that we were never meant to have learned—or so we thought.

"As we progressed into the primer, we mastered some very simple charms—tests I believe they were. Tests to determine our talent for the arts. Some of these might make good parlor tricks. There is one which employs a candle and a rose that is impressive, for instance."

Hayes noticed that the priest nodded his head when he heard this.

"Much of this first book had to do with the control of fire, which was very exciting to boys who, of course, love nothing better than to play with fire. I think that was the plan of it, for whoever wrote this book knew his readers well. Without Walky to guide us, though, our progress was slow, and we were constantly afraid that we'd be discovered. If we performed the simple enchantments we found in the book, would Eldrich sense it? We debated this endlessly, and then with the imprudence common to young boys, we went ahead. I cannot tell you how thrilling it was to bend the flame of a candle this way and that, to make the smoke behave in a manner completely unnatural. We could hardly have been happier, and for the first time stopped dreaming of returning home.

"During all of this time we never met the mage, and, in fact, were warned to keep our distance should we accidentally happen upon him. Once, while I was idling on a window seat, I did see a man I took to be Eldrich walking in the garden. He looked up at me suddenly—this is the story I told to Hayes—and I felt so utterly sure he knew about our book. That he could sense terrible guilt within me. I fled back to our room and put such a terror into poor Percy that he almost fainted from fright. But Eldrich did not appear, nor did Walky suddenly wonder where his book had gone.

"I wonder now if it was merely the overactive imagination of a boy, or if Eldrich put that fear in my heart, for I will tell you I have never known such overwhelming terror. Astonishing to think that a man of such power would take pleasure in terrifying a small boy, but I am not sure he didn't. Be that as it may, we went back to our book in a week or so. It was near the end of my third year there when we came to the method of lighting fire—a skill we thought useful beyond our ability to express. I was the dominant partner in this alliance, and in the manner of children, coerced Percy into first trying anything that seemed at all dubious to me. It is a tradition of sacrifice practiced by children the world over, I'm sure," Erasmus said, but the irony was tinged with sadness and regret. "In this case I could not imagine what this small act of cowardice would lead to. Percy performed the spell as it was described in the book, exacting in the preparation, or so we thought." He stopped and took a deep breath. "But the small fire that we thought to start did not materialize. I was standing several feet away, mindful of my own safety, as usual. We were in a small clearing in the wood, and Percy stood in the center of a geometric design we'd marked out on the ground.

"We had experienced failure before, and worked through the explanations in the book to find our error, and this is what I thought we would do again. I went to step forward, opening the book as I did so. And suddenly Percy screamed . . . and a column of flame erupted around him. I felt as though I was thrown back, and when I regained my feet, I saw Percy staggering toward me, engulfed in flame, such a wail of agony erupting from his throat that I can hear it still.

"As quickly as I could, I quelled the flame with my coat, and Percy lay on the ground, horribly burned, howling from the pain. Before I could even consider going for help, Eldrich arrived with Walky only a few paces behind him.

"The mage stopped, surveying the scene—the geometric markings on the ground, the book—and then he thrust me aside and whispered something over Percy, who seemed suddenly released from his agony. Wrapping the child in his coat, Eldrich bore him up, saying only, 'Bring the book, Walky.'

"I followed behind, terrified for my friend, overcome with guilt and shame. Walky sent me to our room, though not unkindly. I saw no one until the next day when Walky arrived to have me pack my belongings. 'But what word of Percy?' I asked. 'Don't you be worrying about Percy. You have other matters more pressing,' was all Walky would say. 'Where are you sending me?' I asked. 'Home, child,' he said. And that is what happened." Erasmus put a hand to his brow, hiding his eyes for a moment, and then, self consciously, moved the hand to his chin. In that moment Hayes thought that Erasmus looked utterly dejected and anguished, for clearly this was one of those great shames of childhood that some men bore. "That afternoon I was put in a carriage and taken home. To this day I cannot tell you what happened to Percy, though I fear the worst. Slowly I recovered from the horror, if not the guilt of what had happened, for I blamed myself. I was the leader of our small league, and I had let Percy do something so foolish. I realize now that I was only a child acting as children do, but only my head believes this—my heart knows differently.

"As I grew to be a young man, I found that the events of my childhood haunted me. If Deacon Rose is right and many who serve in the house of a mage can remember nothing afterward, then I can only think I was being punished by being left with my memory intact. But my curiosity had not been burned away by our terrible fire. I began to believe that for both myself and Percy, who I believe died of his burns, I would seek the knowledge of the mages. I would learn all the things that we were meant to learn as boys. Perhaps I would even find out if Eldrich could have healed my boyhood friend—something that would have given me great relief—for I could see that even the terrible mage was not unaffected by Percy's suffering." He opened his hands as though displaying something. "And this has led me here . . . and it seems now I will be truly punished at last."

There was no immediate response to Erasmus' story. No one asked the questions that had occurred as he spoke. Hayes wanted to comfort his friend, for it was certainly true that Erasmus had merely acted as children often do, but he could not deny Erasmus was being punished—for Eldrich was a mage and mages were vindictive. History bore this out over and over again. If Erasmus had not been meant to see the book, then he might well have earned the mage's anger. But if Eldrich had merely used Erasmus to lure the Tellerites out of hiding, as had been suggested, then why was Erasmus trapped here as well? Did Eldrich use people so callously?

"You should not censure yourself for what happened, Mr. Flattery," Rose said at last. "You were a child and could not understand the possible consequences of your actions. We do not allow children to play with knives or rapiers, for their inexperience makes mishaps likely. The book should never have fallen into your hands. If it was an accident, then the one to bear the blame would be this man, Walky, not you. Guilt is a consuming emotion, and it clings to us like no other. I sometimes think that we are more able to stop loving another more easily than we shed our guilt, though very often I have found men's guilt to be unwarranted. And that, I believe is the case here, Mr. Flattery. You were a child, and you have made penance enough over the years. And who knows, this young boy, Percy, might live a perfectly whole life, cured of his affliction, or less affected by it than you think. I would advise you to give up this atonement. Let your last days be free of this torment—this feeling that you deserve to be punished."

Anna looked at Erasmus. "I think you were merely playing a part in Eldrich's plan, Mr. Flattery," she said, her tone unusually warm. "You and your boyhood friend, used without remorse to trap me and my companions, and if you are innocent of any alliance with Eldrich, as you claim, then I am sorry for it. But the mages have always been so, even to the last, it seems."

Erasmus looked at them gratefully, a bit of relief on his haggard face, as though telling his tale had provided some small comfort. "What day is it, do you think?" he asked.

Banks and Kehler produced watches that did not agree, and Clarendon did the same, his timepiece committed to its own theory. It turned out that there was no concordance, and only an estimate could be made.

"Whatever day it is, and whatever hour, I think I must sleep," Clarendon said, and the others agreed. Only Anna did not seem so inclined.

She leaned closer to Banks, but Hayes could just hear. "I shall have all the sleep I want soon enough," she said, and rose, leaving the rest of them to find their own places to rest.

Hayes watched her walk toward the *nance*. She stood looking up at it for a moment, then began to whisper, making odd motions with one hand in the air. She bent down, almost reverently, and kissed the floor of the *nance*, and then, casting a quick glance back at the others, she went up the stair and immediately to the font. Here she went down on one knee, continuing to whisper, and then dipped a hand into the water, sipping a few drops carefully. She stood then and stared for a long moment at the urn to one side of the font. As she reached out toward it, Hayes realized that Rose had risen from his place.

"What are you doing?" he hissed, but it was an accusation, not a question.

She turned and glared at him as he came to the foot of the stair. And then with a quick motion and some half-whispered words, she spun and descended the far stair, crossed the chamber and disappeared through the arch at the far end.

Rose stood and watched her go, hands on his hips. For a moment Hayes was certain that the priest would follow, but instead he returned to his place and lay down on his side facing the nance.

Hayes was certain that Anna had gone up the stair again, making him wonder if there was not something more to this place than she claimed.

He noticed then that Erasmus, too, was watching the priest. Hayes lay back down, wondering what he had just seen. Wondering what would happen to them. There was not time to fight among themselves, he was sure.

We are trapped with no hope of escape, he told himself, but found he could not believe it.

Erasmus lay for a long time listening to the even breathing of the others. The questions he had asked all his life seemed no closer to being answered. Some part of him had always believed that one day he would find these answers. He had a fantasy that, once the mage had passed on, he would hear from Walky, still miraculously alive, and from the old man he would have all his questions satisfied. But not now. In a matter of days he would certainly be dead. It made all of his years of searching for knowledge seem terribly futile.

What had he to show for it? Had his efforts benefitted mankind? Had they even benefitted him?

The answer, undeniably, seemed to be that his efforts had profited no one at all—except perhaps Eldrich—which was, no doubt, what had been planned.

I lured the Tellerites here, he thought. *Despite what I believed, that has been my only purpose in this life.* He felt such a rage toward Eldrich that his muscles began to ache where they had knotted from anger.

Quietly, Erasmus slipped away from his sleeping companions and crossed to the chamber's far end.

Moments later he was ascending the winding stair, his anger driving him quickly on. He wondered what this rather cold and imperious young woman was doing up this mysterious stair. Thinking the end was farther, he rounded the corner to find Anna collapsed against the stair's end. Her knees were drawn up and her face was buried in her arms.

Hearing him she looked up, her face shining with tears. She let her arms fall limply by her sides and laid her head back against the stone, and still she cried as though she were alone, utterly alone.

Erasmus stopped, so taken aback that he had no idea what to do.

"Bastard," she said through her sobs, "he trapped us here. I was a fool . . ." and then she began to sob so violently that she could not go on.

Unable to bear it any longer, Erasmus came and sat on the step near to her, reaching out and taking her hand tentatively. She leaned forward and buried her head in his shoulder and continued to sob. Erasmus laid a hand awkwardly on her shoulder.

He found himself making soothing sounds, saying the meaningless things that people say to comfort each other, though he did not believe them. They were trapped without hope—that was the truth. Buried alive.

It was a long time before Anna began to recover, and then she finally pulled away from him, rubbing at her eyes with the heels of her hands.

"I haven't even a clean square of linen to offer," Erasmus said.

"And you call yourself a gentleman?" she said, a weak jest. "I have been down here long enough that I would accept a soiled one, I think."

Erasmus produced his handkerchief. She held it up to examine it, and then laughed. "I guess I have not been down here quite as long as I thought." She returned it to him. "I must look a fright."

"You are the most beautiful woman in this entire system of caves," Erasmus said, his tone mockingly solemn.

She laughed. "Ah, when you are the only woman trapped with a roomful of men, you finally hear the things you wish to hear."

"Shall I leave you alone?" Erasmus asked.

"I gather I am not quite as beautiful as you suggested?"

"Not at all, it's just . . ."

"That you have no idea how to deal with crying women?"

Erasmus shrugged. "Something like that."

"I'm all right now. I will pass beyond it if you can."

Erasmus nodded. He was not quite sure what he would say, now that they were alone. Why had he come up here in the first place? To speak with her, certainly, but now he was not sure why.

"I had no part in this," Erasmus said suddenly. "I was manipulated and trapped, like everyone else."

She nodded. "I believe you. Eldrich is a mage, and loyalty is unknown to them." She looked up at him, her eyes still wet with tears. "But what do we do?"

Erasmus shook his head. "I don't know. I feel certain that there must be another way out, for surely the tiny hole we used to find our way in here is not the main entrance. I'm not sure I even understand its purpose." He reached up and flattened his hand on the rock. "This is the mystery to me. Clearly one did not climb all the way up here to admire a single character. Once, it must have gone somewhere, or been intended to go somewhere. Hayes believes the outside world might lie only a few feet away. Clarendon and I have studied the survey, but it is not clear how close to the surface we might be." He looked at her. "Banks said he did not understand the purpose of this stair. Is that so?"

Anna twisted her head around, looking up at the wall. "Do you know this character?" she asked.

"It is the Darian equivalent of our 'L'."

"Exactly . . . or almost so. Spoken, it is not voiced as it is in Farr, or perhaps is only half-voiced, so that it is softer, almost a whisper, and hard for many to master. But it is Landor's initial and was used as his signature. Centuries later, Lucklow would pattern his own distinctive L on this one." She turned her head and looked down the stair, pondering. "I have been thinking much about this. In fact, I came up here to be alone and contemplate it more, not to collapse in tears as you saw." A tear streaked her cheek again, but she had mastered her emotions now and did not give way to them. "This entire chamber is bespelled, and with a sophistication that I can hardly begin to understand, let alone explain. The men—and women, for there were both in the seven who made this place—were skilled in the arts far beyond any who came after. Look at this chamber. It is true that it is hidden beneath the surface, but even so it is untouched by time. When the outer passage collapsed, the dust that at first blew into the hallway was then forced back out again.

Did you not realize? One moment we were choking in dust and debris, and the next the air was clear. This chamber is protected, and Eldrich could only collapse the entrance." Anna paused, and Erasmus was sure tears would appear again as she remembered her colleagues who had died just beyond the safety of the chamber. "But we were allowed in, which indicates that it was meant to be discovered." She looked up at Erasmus again. "And in the vault which contains Landor's crypt, we find your likeness carved in stone."

"But could you read the text around it?" Erasmus asked quickly, "I couldn't make sense of it."

She nodded, still staring at his face. "It is a confusing phrase for a direct translation is not possible. 'The last keeper of the gate,' is how I would render it."

These words chilled Erasmus utterly. He felt himself push back against the wall, as though drawing back from the meaning. "What does it mean?" he asked, afraid that he already knew.

For a moment she didn't answer, but continued to stare. "I am not completely sure. What I find odd is that the likeness is not more exact. Though perhaps there is a simple explanation for that. Halsey might know."

Erasmus didn't want to ask if Halsey was one of the people killed in the collapse—he assumed he was. "But what of the face of the woman? Why was it never finished?"

She looked at him oddly. "But these were not carved by human hand," she said, a bit incredulous. "Did you not know? The face is emerging, slowly. I don't know the role of the woman, but the face will form when it is clear who she will be."

"Clear to whom?"

She shook her head, puzzled by his response. "To no one. It is like augury, though it is a spell that was cast centuries ago. At some point the vision will be complete and the identity of the woman will . . . *emerge*. There is no human agent. The spell is the agent. Do you see?"

Erasmus had only the vaguest sense of what she meant. "Is it you?" he asked.

Her look suddenly changed and her eyes glistened again. "That is what Banks believes. . . ." She could not speak for a moment. "I don't know. If it was meant to be me, I think the face would have formed by now. I can't imagine why it would not." She shook her head. "I don't know enough to understand." She looked up and touched the wall, tracing the bottom of the character with delicate fingers. Erasmus realized then how young she was—barely into her twenties, he thought—and at the moment she looked even younger and quite vulnerable.

"But this gate, I began to say. . . . It has a spell about it, if I can use that term. You understand, Mr. Flattery, you worked through some part of the primer. But I am not skilled enough in the arts to understand it. Unless there is some clue written in the main hall, I fear we shall never unlock this gate. And even if we could, there is no guarantee that it would lead to the surface."

"Are you saying it would lead to this other land? Is that where it goes?"

She shook her head. "No, it is not that sort of gate. It might open into another chamber, one that was not meant to be penetrated by anyone but a mage, and perhaps not just any mage. But I suspect we will never know, Mr. Flattery, for we haven't the skills even if we had time."

Erasmus reached down and worried the edge of the leather that flapped over a hole worn in his boot. "I am not the sort of man who will sit idly by and starve to death. I must try to find a way out. I can't believe there is nothing we can do." He banged his fist against the wall. "If we give up now, then we're certainly walking about in our own crypt, and I'm not ready for that. I'm not. . . ."

She nodded agreement, rather unconvincingly. "Nor am I, Mr. Flattery. But I am not sure what we can do. Even if we could unravel the spells that surround the urns on the *nance,* I'm not certain we would be further ahead."

Erasmus looked at her quizzically. "I think you assume I know more than I do. What is this about urns?"

"I thought you'd read the primer," she said, surprised. "The urns contain the king's blood, or so I surmise. I can't imagine they would be so protected if they were empty. Can you?"

"I do remember references to king's blood. But I never understood what they meant."

She drew her head back, her look quizzical. "I am amazed, Mr. Flattery, but then I suppose the book was not meant to be read without guidance. King's blood is a plant—beyond rare. There are references to it in the chamber below."

"Yes! Of course, I saw one, but could make nothing of it."

"The seed is a powerful herb. It is said to be a physic able to cure the worst illnesses, and it is also believed that the seed was the source of the mages' long lives. But it does something more. It wakens the talent in individuals, if there is any talent there to begin with. But it is said that the seed exacts a price, for all who use it becomes habituated unless they have an iron will, or take certain precautions. But it was a key to the mages' powers, and they guarded it even more closely than their knowledge.

"The legend tells that Landor bore the king's blood with him from beyond, and it grew here only under uncommon circumstances. But if the urns contain seed . . . well, we must study the text on the walls with care and examine the chamber meticulously. Banks believes that it is even possible that there is a hidden door—an entrance from the surface. We must look. It could be anywhere. We must focus all of our energies on this task. All of us. Even this priest, Rose, will have to put his secret knowledge at our disposal."

Erasmus wanted to jump up and begin immediately, but Anna did not look ready to start just yet.

"How did you come to be down here?" Erasmus asked suddenly. "Were you following me?"

She pulled the stray hair that had escaped from its braid away from her face. "We knew that this young man Kehler was searching the archives at Wooton for Skye. His interest in certain events had caught our attention. We watched him as we could, for we are wary of the priests and thought they might be using him to tempt us. For some time we didn't realize that there was a connection between Kehler and yourself—Mr. Hayes. When we did discover this, we realized that . . ." she searched for words, "events were converging. Happenstance is not something I believe in, not where certain individuals are concerned. Through Kehler, Skye was seeking the secrets of Baumgere, which we believed were likely hidden in Wooton, where we dared not go.

"When Skye set off for Castlebough, we felt almost certain that the time to approach you might be near. You see, the similarity of your life to Teller's is undeniable—or so we thought. You both apprenticed to a mage yet left his service. Both you and Teller spent your lives thereafter seeking out the secrets of the mages, or so it seemed to us.

"We practice augury—it is not so reliable that we base all our actions upon it, but we consider it in our decisions. We had a vision that you played a part in, Mr. Flattery. And here you were in Castlebough meeting up with this young man who had been in Wooton."

"What vision?" Erasmus asked, his tone flat, for he felt a little apprehension.

Anna did not answer, but he thought she colored a little. She simply could not answer.

"You are filling me with fear," Erasmus said quickly.

"No need," she said, her voice pitched very low, as though afraid they would be heard. "I have had two visions in which you played a part, or so I believe. In the first Skye opens an ornate bronze gate set into a stone wall. I pass through and inside I find a man who offers me a book and a white blossom—king's blood. . . . I could never see the man's face, though I long believed this might be you." She looked away. "The second . . . the second was not so . . . significant."

"Why do you say that? This first vision seems to have been wrong, entirely. Perhaps the second has more meaning?"

She took a breath, as though steeling herself. "We were on a hillside, you and I, beneath the stars, with trees all around. There was a bed of soft moss, and we. . . ." She had looked down, but now she glanced up at him, not raising her head, and she colored, making her hair suddenly appear more red.

"I see," Erasmus said softly, feeling his own cheeks warm.

"It does not necessarily mean that we will. . . . It is a vision and must be interpreted."

Erasmus nodded quickly. For a moment he sat looking at her, and she did not meet his eye. He thought of the countess, comparing her to this young woman before him, in her boy's clothes, her hair a mess, her face streaked with dirt from her tears. And he realized that he felt immense pity for her, trapped here so young. She looked more vulnerable than he could imagine—unlike the countess who seemed so in control—in control of every situation.

He reached out a hand and touched her shoulder softly, meaning to offer her comfort in some way, but she moved forward immediately and came into his arms, pressing herself close to him. She did not raise her face, but kept it close beside his own so that he could not see her, but only hear her breathing close to his ear. Hear her catch her breath.

"Perhaps there is more truth in your vision than you know." Erasmus whispered. "Perhaps we will escape yet to see the stars."

Chapter Forty-three

THE message found Kent pacing the room, his confusion and chagrin not even slightly reduced. He had not slept that night and his exhaustion made his entire situation seem more dire. After hours of turmoil he'd sent a note off to the countess, hoping that she would see him so that he might try again to persuade her that he had been telling the truth. Even if she did not choose to travel with him, she must flee. It was imperative to her safety.

But his note had gone unanswered for several hours now, and he had begun to despair of it ever receiving a reply.

A knock caused Kent to start, and he rushed to the door, hoping that it was not merely a chambermaid come to change his bed. At the door he found a young local man, who presented him with an envelope.

"From Miss Edden, sir," the man said, waiting expectantly.

Kent handed the young man a coin, hardly aware of its denomination, and closed the door with barely a nod.

He began to tear open the envelope, but paused, knowing full well that a reply from Marianne Edden, not the countess, meant that his overture had been rebuffed.

He lowered himself rather gently into a chair and stared at the envelope, too dejected even to be angry at Marianne. Slowly he opened the letter, pulling the single page free and shaking out the folds.

My Dear Mr. Kent:

Please, come at once! I clearly owe you an apology. Please, please make all haste, I cannot tell you how worried I am.

Fearing the worst, Kent snatched up his frock coat and bolted out the door.

When he arrived at the house of the countess, he was met by a maid who looked near to tears. Kent felt his heart sink utterly. The countess could not be dead . . . ? She could not.

"Oh, Mr. Kent, thank Farrelle you've come," she said. "Miss Edden is beside herself with worry."

Marianne appeared behind the servant, her usual quiet demeanor swept away entirely.

"Lady Chilton has gone," she said.

"Gone? But where?"

Marianne took his arm and drew him hurriedly into the house. "I was out visiting in the village and learned of her departure only when I returned. Gone without explanation." She looked expectantly at the maid, who stood twisting her apron in her hands.

"Yes, Mr. Kent," the maid said. "A small man came to the door asking for my mistress, and within moments Lady Chilton had me throw a few belongings into a trunk, and she went off with him. Went off without saying where, or even when she might return."

Kent closed his eyes for a second. "Did this man come in a large, old-fashioned carriage?"

The maid nodded. "A coach and four. Yes, sir. And a smaller carriage followed behind."

"She did not even leave me a note, Kent," Marianne said. "Not a single word. I've known the countess for years. She would never, never have done such a thing. I—I. . . ." She completely lost what she had meant to say.

The maid interjected. "Has the countess eloped, do you think?"

Marianne looked at Kent; clearly she no longer doubted his story. She dismissed the maid and took Kent into the sitting room.

"I should have listened to you, Kent," she began, keeping her voice low, though it was filled with emotion all the same. "This is entirely my fault. It was just that . . . I have seen men concoct the oddest stories to gain the attention of the countess. . . ."

"It's too late to worry about that, Marianne," But Kent did not finish his sentence, for at that moment the Earl of Skye arrived.

"Ah, Lord Skye," Marianne said. "I cannot thank you enough for coming so quickly." She glanced oddly at Kent, who was sure he looked at her like a betrayer. "I'm sure you've met Mr. Kent? Yes? I hardly know where to begin."

With Kent filling in his parts of the story, they related what had occurred.

"You believe it was Eldrich?" Skye said, when the story was completed. "You're sure?" He shook his head.

"I'm afraid there is no doubt of it. If only Mr. Flattery were here," Marianne lamented. "He might be able to tell us what to do."

This caught Skye's interest. "Perhaps we could speak with Mr. Flattery. I've heard he is traveling in company with a young gentleman of my acquaintance. Someone I would like to speak with in any event. Do you know where Flattery is staying?"

"Yes, but he remains down in the cave searching for those young men."

Skye looked up quickly. "You don't mean Hayes and Kehler?"

"Yes, that sounds right . . . but I don't remember exactly. Elaural mentioned their names only in passing."

"Farrelle's—" He let the curse go unfinished for Marianne's sake. "And is this the cave where Baumgere's confessor self-murdered?"

Marianne shrugged.

Skye rose and paced across the room, pausing before the windows.

"But what shall we do?" Marianne said.

"What?" Skye turned back to the others. "Well, you should have heeded Mr. Kent's warning," he said. "If the countess is in the hands of Eldrich, then the Farr army will not pry her loose." He turned back to the window again, obviously disturbed, but Kent was not sure it was by the plight of the countess.

"There is only one road from Castlebough back into Farrland," Kent said. "We can catch them yet—if we ride at once."

"And do what, exactly?" Skye said, whirling to stare down at Kent. "He is a mage, Kent." He paused, looking at the painter and

Marianne, his features softening a little. "I'm sorry about what has happened to the countess, but there is nothing anyone can do. And to be completely logical about matters—you don't know that she didn't go of her own accord. It's true that the countess did not leave Miss Edden a note, and she rushed off in terrible haste, but—" He raised his hands. "You might catch them up, Kent, and if Eldrich is not inclined to cripple you on the spot, then the countess could just as well lean out the window of her carriage and tell you to turn around and bother her no more. And whether she says this of her own choice or not, we will never prove. I'm sorry. But there is nothing to be done." He looked from one to the other. "How long has Mr. Flattery been in this cave?"

Marianne shook her head, hardly able to follow the change in conversation. "I don't know!" she snapped. "Four days, perhaps."

"Well," Skye answered, "there is someone we can help. If Mr. Flattery hasn't appeared by tomorrow, I suggest we organize a search. At least *he* is not in the clutches of a mage."

Kent was beginning to feel the effects of lack of sleep, but he forced himself up the stairs to Sir John's rooms. The knight had obviously been sleeping, but when he saw Kent, he came completely awake.

"Eldrich has taken the countess away," Kent announced.

"Flames," was all Sir John could manage. "Come in, man, come in."

"Is this man Bryce still in Castlebough?"

"No. No, he's gone. Why do you ask?"

"I don't know. He is a servant of Eldrich. Perhaps . . . perhaps he could assure me that the countess went of her own choosing. That she is in no danger." Kent sat in a chair, hands on his knees, his head hanging down as though he had not the energy to raise it. "I must go after her," he said.

"Take hold of yourself, Kent, you're not making sense. You're not some hero off to rescue a maiden in distress. You're a painter, for Farrelle's sake. Come to your senses, man. There is nothing you can do. And do you even know if Lady Chilton was taken against her will?"

Kent looked up at Sir John, who asked the same question as

Skye. "The countess had no memory of her meeting with Eldrich. The very thought of it caused her the greatest revulsion. How can I assume that anything but an abduction has taken place?" Kent sat back in the chair, letting his arms fall loosely to his sides. "Flames, I wish Erasmus were here."

"Flattery, you mean? Could he help?"

Kent shrugged. "He has a certain . . . affection for the countess, I believe. And who would know more about the mage than Erasmus? Assuming he had nothing to do with the countess' disappearance."

Sir John shook his head. "If Eldrich is out in the world again . . ." he muttered, letting the sentence die. "Can Mr. Flattery be reached?" the knight asked.

Kent shook his head. "I don't know. He has gone exploring one of the local caves for some unknown period of time. I cannot say if he is still there, or if he has, perhaps, emerged and even returned to Avonel."

"Well, let us endeavor to find out before you do anything rash."

Kent felt a bit embarrassed at his state. He knew that he had no claim on the countess and was acting a bit of a fool. "I don't think I can wait, Sir John. I need to know where he has taken her, at the very least. Perhaps you could take on the contacting of Erasmus Flattery? And I will send word back to you as to the whereabouts of the countess. I feel sure Erasmus will help."

Sir John did not look like a man who felt any degree of confidence in Kent's plan. "I think it more likely that he will try to dissuade you from interfering. Though I'm not sure, now, what my own situation is. I received a note from Mr. Bryce this morning saying that he was leaving Castlebough immediately and that I was free to return to Avonel. In other words, I have been dismissed—temporarily." Distress seemed to draw his face taut. "He has gone off after his master, I assume." Sir John lowered himself into a chair, staring at a spot on the floor just before him.

"I don't know, Kent. It is all very odd. Eldrich was in Castlebough for a reason. Bryce insisted I accompany him here, but now I'm not sure why. Whatever purpose he had came to nothing, it would seem. But even so, I have a feeling that something occurred here. And not something insignificant either." He pressed fingers into the corners of his eyes, clearly still tired. Then he looked up at

Kent, his eyes red from exhaustion and worry. "Well, Kent, what will you do? I hold little hope that you'll listen to reason in this."

Kent knew the man was talking sense, but it did not matter. "I will heed your advice, in part. I will keep my distance from Eldrich and try to discover where he will take the countess. I'll then send word to you. If you will attempt to speak with Mr. Flattery. . . ." Kent paused for a moment, finding it difficult to keep his train of thought. "Skye is worried that Erasmus has been gone too long, that he has met with misadventure." Kent shook his head. "I can't believe it. Erasmus Flattery is an enormously competent man. I'm sure no evil has befallen him. If you will tell Erasmus what has happened when he emerges, I will set off immediately so that Eldrich does not outdistance me."

Kent shook his head, trying to make his mind function. Was there anything else he should say to Sir John? Unable to think of anything, he forced himself up. "Good luck to you, Sir John."

"And to you, Kent. Safe journey." He rose from his chair, reaching out to clasp Kent's hand warmly. "But, Kent, do keep your distance from Lord Eldrich. It is likely he has already learned of your interference. Take no chances, Kent, I implore you."

The painter nodded. Sir John pressed his hand firmly and then released it, and Kent went out thinking that Sir John treated him like a man going off to war. Like a man who would not be seen again.

The countess realized that she had been staring for a long time at the scene before her, but it had not registered until now. She shook her head and blinked, her eyes feeling like they had been scoured with sand.

Eldrich roused from his reverie and looked at her. "Ah, there you are," he said as though she had just appeared.

"Indeed. . . ." She felt a peculiar confusion, as though just awakened from a deep sleep. "But where am I?"

"In a carriage traveling through the Caledon Hills. We have come from Castlebough."

She nodded. Yes, Castlebough. "My mind . . . it is not clear."

"It will become so in a few moments. Do not be alarmed," Eldrich said, his tone musical but not terribly soothing. She felt as though he mocked her; she was not sure why.

She pressed her eyelids closed for a moment, relieving the pain in her eyes, and tried to order her thoughts. She had been in Castlebough. With Marianne! Yes, now it was coming to her. They had gone there after Skye, though she could not recall the reason. . . . She took a long breath and searched her memories, which were terribly fragmented. A feeling deep in her center was familiar. Had she taken a lover there? Something told her she had; in fact she seemed to remember—everything but his face and name.

Erasmus! That was it; Erasmus, but she felt an odd sense of disappointment, though she was not sure why. Had it ended unhappily? Was he inadequate? Neither of these seemed to be true.

Putting this line of inquiry aside, she tried to remember the reason she had gone there in the first place. Skye. She was certain it had something to do with Skye. And his paintings! The Peliers. And this priest Baumgere. She took a long breath. It was coming back. But why was she here?

Certainly she knew Eldrich, but how? She was sure that she had not encountered him before her journey to Castlebough, but she could not remember when they had first met. One did not forget meeting a mage. Curious.

She opened her burning eyes and focused on Eldrich, who looked at her with disturbing disinterest.

"Why am I here?"

He did not answer but continued to stare, almost as if he had not heard. She was about to ask again when he spoke.

"The explanation is lengthy, and I have provided some of it already. It will come back to you. Give it time, something we have in abundance, for the next few days, at least."

The countess straightened her skirt. "At least I have clothes," she said, not sure why.

Eldrich smiled in amusement. "Are you disappointed?"

"No, I think not. What have you been doing to me?"

"Not what you suspect at the moment, though I will confess that I have been tempted. But that would be tempting fate, quite literally, wouldn't it?"

"Would it?"

He did not answer.

The countess sat up straight, suddenly feeling very vulnerable.

"Well, you have all the advantage of me. I do not know where we are going or why."

He nodded agreement but did not offer an explanation.

One hand had gone to sleep, and she rubbed feeling back into it. "Nor do I remember agreeing to such a journey."

"Were your relations with Erasmus intimate?" Eldrich asked suddenly.

"Sir! I am shocked that you would ask such a thing."

"In fact, you're not. And I'm glad to find that they were—intimate, that is."

She was about to protest, but he turned and looked out the window, as though no longer interested in this matter. She thought his face changed a little, the mockery replaced by sadness.

"Something has happened to Erasmus," she said suddenly.

He turned back to her, his look a bit surprised, or perhaps more impressed. "Erasmus is perfectly hale, I can assure you."

"But where is he?"

"Do you really care?"

"Yes, of course I do."

He nodded, though she was not sure why. "It is often said that to practice the arts one must give up one's heart." The look of sadness returned. "But I will tell you that it is not so simple."

She did not quite know what to say, but suddenly her conviction that something had happened to Erasmus was not so solid. Did she care for Erasmus? She remembered their night of love. Certainly it had given her great pleasure. But had Erasmus engaged her heart that night? It almost seemed that if the question needed to be asked, the answer must be "no." And this made her a little sad.

"You did not answer my question," the countess said.

Eldrich looked at her sharply. "Have you not heard that it is unwise to anger a mage?"

She did not answer, feeling suddenly frightened, but frustrated and angry at the same time. Eldrich turned again to survey the passing countryside.

She felt a stirring inside and a blush spread across her skin. A memory of desire came back to her, but it did not seem to be connected to Erasmus. Eldrich. . . . She had felt this desire for him—at his command, it seemed. And now the memory of it washed through her again.

Is this his doing, she asked herself, *or are these my feelings?*

Fear—she also felt fear. Fear and desire. The idea that these two emotions could live within her at one time she found loathsome, but her body did not care. And worse, she sensed a hunger in him that she had not felt before—hunger for her. It was hidden behind his mockery, by his stillness, but, even so, she felt it. She was desired by a mage. . . .

"I still do not remember consenting to this journey," she said, hoping that speaking would take her focus away from the confusion she felt.

Eldrich turned and looked at her, drawing himself up in his seat. "Do you know my age?" he asked, as though he had not heard her.

She shook her head.

"One hundred and thirty-three years. All other estimates you have heard are inaccurate. In fact it will be my birth day in just over a fortnight." He paused, watching her reaction to this information. "I am stronger than men a century my junior, my mind is still sound in all its parts. In every way I am a man in his middle years, except that, like all my kind, I cannot father children." He raised his eyebrows, cocking his head a little, as though a bit proud of these facts. "I will not stoop to asking how old I appear, for politeness begs a lie, even in my situation, but I do not look like an elderly man, of that I am aware." He paused again—his conversation was punctuated by pauses, all a little too long, and the effect was to discomfit those he spoke to, or at least it had that effect on the countess. "Do you know Lady Felton-Gray?"

She nodded, wondering if his mind was as sound as he claimed, for there was no apparent thread to this conversation.

"She is eighty-some years old, I believe. When she was your age, I thought her the most beautiful woman I had ever seen. At the risk of being terribly unkind, she is now a crone."

"It is rather more than unkind," the countess said before she thought. "Lady Felton-Gray is a woman of great distinction, I think."

He nodded. "But the men of Farrland, and even farther afield, sing the praises of the Countess of Chilton, not Lady Felton-Gray. You, Lady Chilton, are the great beauty of your generation. In ten years you might still look much as you do now. Oh, your hair will not be so thick and lustrous, and your skin will not have the glow that it does today, and lines will have begun to form at the corners of your eyes. But you will still be thought a great beauty. In twenty years you will be replaced by someone half your age. In thirty years you will be thought handsome and perhaps well-preserved. In forty years people will marvel that men whose names you did not know once fought duels over you. And when you are the age of Lady Felton-Gray. . . ." He shrugged.

"And it gives you some pleasure to remind me that I am merely mortal and will suffer the same indignities that befall us all?"

"It might give me some small pleasure, I suppose, but that is not why I brought it up. I have been confronted recently with a dilemma, but I think I have found a solution. Would you not like to stay much as you are now far into your old age?"

"What are you saying? You can give me such a gift?"

He paused, and then nodded slowly, watching her face.

She looked at the man sitting before her and thought that he did not truly look like an evil man, yet she felt terribly threatened by him all the same. What he felt for her was not tender, she was sure of that. He did not care for her or anyone else. Eldrich was not a man as other men were. "I assume you will require something in return?"

He nodded again, but did not offer further explanation.

"And what might this be, pray tell?"

"Most would say that long life, youth, and vigor could not have too high a price," he said.

"I have read stories of people who made bargains with devils, Lord Eldrich. They never had happy endings."

He actually laughed, as though he found the comparison flattering. "Life never has a happy ending, Lady Chilton—old age, infirmity, death. One can only aspire to a rich life, and a fullness of years. But I am offering more: a chance to prolong your youth in all its parts. Your beauty and vigor and all your mental faculties. All of them. Youth, Lady Chilton—or at worst, middle age—until you have passed your centenary. Passed it by half a lifetime as men measure such things.

Some part of her brain believed she was being mocked or made to look the fool, but another part of her was not so certain. *Youth*—not eternal, but for many years. Oddly, tears welled up, and she struggled to keep them back as a flood of emotion swept through her.

She knew now that there was something more here—something more between them. She remembered their first meeting and the things he had intimated. The idea of becoming part of his world was too frightening, too alien.

"I think I shall have . . ." she pushed her emotions down, "have to decline your generous offer."

Eldrich did not answer but only stared so that she looked away, casting her gaze out the window into the darkness. The carriage had slowed to negotiate one of the road's many tight turns, and suddenly it stopped. She heard voices—the driver apparently speaking to someone on the road.

Eldrich opened the door and stepped out, lowering the stairs and holding out a hand to her in a manner that was less than polite. For a second she demurred, but then remembered that he had said he was not a gentleman, and she reached out and took the offered hand.

She climbed out, unaware of anything but the touch of his skin—infinitely soft, like the skin of a child. And warm, so unlike his manner.

Warm hands, cold heart, she remembered her mother saying.

"Why do we stop?" she asked, a bit short of breath.

"There seems to be someone on the road. Walky? What is it?"

"A woman, sir. She seems to be wandering, lost."

They rounded the team and, there, in the light of the coach lamp, found an elderly woman standing by the small man the countess had met before. Clearly the woman was confused, staring around her as though she could not understand how she had come to this place. Her motions were exaggerated and not perfectly controlled.

"My dear!" the countess said, going immediately to the woman who was clearly not a peasant. "Has there been an accident? What's happened to you?" The countess took the woman's hand, cold as snow. "Tell me, madame, what's happened? From where have you come?" There was no smell of drink on the poor woman's breath but she was not steady on her feet.

She stared at the countess curiously as though she recognized her. "I . . . I don't know. Where are we? What place?"

"The Caledon Hills, my dear. Near Castlebough. Is that where you've come from?"

"I don't know. . . ."

The woman sagged suddenly, clutching the countess' hands, and the countess tried to bear her up.

"Oh, Mr. Walky, can you lay down your coat?"

Walky quickly did so, and they lowered the woman to the ground where she lay, still confused, but conscious.

"Can you tell me your name, dear?" the countess asked.

"Name. . . ? Oh, yes. It's. . . ." The poor woman squinted, trying to force the words up from her memory, but then she shook her head, and tears glistened in her eyes.

"Lord Eldrich," the countess said, "is there nothing you can do for her?"

"I don't think she wants my assistance," he said firmly.

The woman touched the countess' hair. "And who are you, child?" she whispered.

"The Countess of Chilton, my dear. If we help you, can you get into the carriage?"

"But you can't be," the woman said, her look even more confused. "I am the countess. There can't be two?" The old woman began to cry in earnest now. Pitiful tiny sobs. "You can't be me. . . ."

The countess felt herself draw away, staring down at the wrinkled old woman in some horror.

"You will be surprised how quickly youth is spent," Eldrich said. "How everything you take for granted crumbles and fades. And here you meet your future, Lady Chilton. Not eighty years, and not even your memories to bring you comfort. Stay with her for a while. Contemplate the choice you are making."

"I've seen enough," the countess said, starting to rise, but the old woman clutched at her clothing, holding her still. And the countess felt as though a vision of death had its cold hands upon her, dragging her down toward the earth. She pulled sharply away from the whimpering woman, feeling both guilt and revulsion—but revulsion was the stronger.

It is an apparition only, the countess told herself. *An apparition and nothing more.*

She turned to Eldrich, but the mage was gone, leaving her standing there in the coach light, confronted by her future. The common future.

For a long moment she could not tear her eyes away from the poor woman, who still held out her hands to her, begging her help. A wave of nausea passed over her, and she felt the world spinning, endlessly spinning. She turned quickly away, stumbling into the carriage.

Hanging her head, she closed her eyes and tried to control her breathing, her tears. The animal fear of death had come over her, and she knew that she was ready to fight to the last breath to stay alive.

Look what he has done to me, she thought. *He has stripped away my honor, my dignity. Reduced me to a beast, growling at threats in the darkness, prepared to do whatever is necessary to preserve my precious self.*

The vision of the ancient woman appeared in her mind.

Farrelle's blood, she thought, *preserve me from becoming that.*

What a monster he is. What a terrible monster.

The coach lurched into motion again and as it rolled the first few feet the countess stiffened, afraid she would hear the terrible whimpering. Blessedly, she heard nothing.

"Perhaps," Eldrich said softly, "we should begin this conversation anew. I require your cooperation, Lady Chilton, and in exchange I am able to offer something that no other living man might offer. What say you now?"

Chapter Forty-four

ANNA and Banks bent together over their translation of the wall text, hoping to uncover some hint that might indicate some way out of the crypt into which they'd been sealed. Occasionally they consulted with Erasmus who seemed to be remembering more of his boyhood lessons by the hour. Only Deacon Rose continued to claim that he could offer nothing, though clearly the Tellerites did not believe him. If the priest could not help, he certainly kept his eye on all progress, and his actions were creating a palpable tension.

The others examined every inch of the chamber that could be reached, searching for a seam in the stone or any other sign of an exit. Hayes and Kehler worked together, starting in the long hallway. The walls seemed flawless to them, the rock carved and finished to a consistent texture, as though it had been meticulously shaped by hand, though from what Anna had said, there was some doubt that craftsmen had worked here at all.

"I am beginning to think this is futile," Hayes said, lowering himself to the floor to rest for a moment. His stomach growled, for the most recent "meal" had been so absurdly inadequate that Kehler had actually laughed when he first saw it, though the laugh had died rather abruptly and he'd been left with a dark look in his eyes.

Small amounts of food seemed to waken the appetite, and Hayes began to have some pain from his stomach and even a burning in his esophagus. A headache had come to reside in his temples, and he had to be careful to rise slowly or his head would swim.

"Perhaps it is futile," Kehler said, responding to Hayes, "but have we something better to do?" He pushed his back to the wall, bracing his legs out. "I put my hope more in the efforts of Anna and Banks. Perhaps there will be something written here that will help us." Kehler looked around the chamber. "I can't believe that our route in here was the only entrance."

"Nor can I," Hayes said, his tone a little defeated. "I think that our passage was left open so that the chamber could be discovered one day. So that the accomplishments of Landor and the others would be remembered. In some ways I think of this shrine as an act of colossal vanity. Can you imagine building a shrine to yourself?"

"Look at all the great houses and palaces in Farrland, Hayes. What are they but monuments to their owners, many of whom accomplished next to nothing?" Kehler fell to thinking. "And," he pushed himself up, "how many of these homes had passages built in them to allow escape in uncertain times?" He paused. "There must be a way out. I cannot believe otherwise. And we must find it before we're too weak to make use of it."

Two hours later they came to the end of the hallway and were in such despair that they could not look at one another. It was finally sinking in that they might die here, and their failure to find anything that might facilitate their escape only made that worse.

"Shall we go over it again?" Hayes asked, no great hope in his voice.

Kehler shrugged. "Do you think there's any chance we'll find something we've missed?"

Hayes looked out into the chamber where the others had gathered in the middle of the floor. "No. I'm afraid we'll find nothing more. Let's go see what the others have turned up."

The gathering in the chamber's center was a somber one. Hayes and Kehler sat down among their fellow inmates, and listened to the terrible silence for a few moments. No one seemed at all hopeful, and only the priest seemed at peace with their situation.

"Is there nothing useful in the text, then?" Kehler asked quietly.

Banks shook his head. "Nothing, though it is certainly a fascinating document, if one can call it that. Of course there are sections we cannot translate, but it seems a good part of it is a history. A history of the mages' arrival in Farrland from Darr."

"But do you believe this, Banks?" Kehler asked. "Do you believe the mages came from some other land that cannot be reached by mundane means?"

Banks glanced at Anna, a bit guiltily. When she did not react, he nodded. "I do, yes. But there is other evidence. You yourself were interested in the Stranger of Compton Heath, Kehler, and certainly that man was not from our own world—not even some unexplored part of it, I'm sure. And a mage took him away, for the mages have greater interest in these matters than anyone else."

"You know it was a mage?"

"Have no doubt of it," Anna said firmly. "It was a mage. Eldrich, I would say."

"And what became of the stranger?" Hayes asked.

Anna shrugged.

"More importantly," Erasmus took up the argument, "how did he get here, and why did he not simply return?"

Banks motioned with his hand as though about to speak, and then paused, perhaps finding his explanation inadequate. "There is no agreement on this matter, but I believe it is possible that there are times when the worlds touch and natural portals occur. I cannot explain how this happens, but it seems to me that at times individuals have come through these openings: the Stranger of Compton Heath; 'Mad Nell,' as she was known; a boy found nearly frozen to death in Doorn. There are any number of others. They were all confused, more surprised to find themselves here than we were to discover them."

"And do you agree, Miss Fielding?" Erasmus said.

Her mouth turned down. "Recently I have been forced to admit that this explanation is very likely true."

"You have met a stranger," Clarendon said quickly.

She pressed her lips together, barely shrugging, and looked down to her hand which traced a circle on the stone floor.

"Well, if we are not to get out this day," Rose said, his manner composed, as always, showing no trace of despair, "then who will be next to tell their story?" He looked evenly at Anna and Banks.

"No," she said putting her hand on Bank's arm. "We will not reveal our secrets to you until we are sure there is no escape."

The priest nodded, casting his eyes down deferentially. "Who then?" he asked quietly.

"Why don't you tell everyone how you trapped my brothers

and burned them for the crime of causing harm to no one?" Anna said.

"I was not alive when this occurred, Miss Fielding. I can, however, tell you another story—equally sad—but I think somehow you will want to hear it." Rose looked around at each person in turn. "I can tell you how the mages trapped the Followers of Teller and destroyed them."

"You know this story?" Anna said, looking up sharply. "The true story?"

Rose nodded once. He put his hands on the floor behind him and tilted his head to look up at the ceiling for a moment. And then he began. "After the terrible conflict that has come to be known as the Winter War," he said, his voice faltering. He stopped and worked some moisture into his mouth. "In the year 1415, a final great battle took place, though it was not between nations, and few ever heard of it. The field of this battle was somewhere near the ruin of Tremont Abbey—some say the abbey itself was the site." The priest looked around at the others. "The followers of Teller, who had hidden themselves for uncounted years, centuries in fact, made a grave error. They underestimated the patience of the mages."

Anna hung her head so that her face was hidden by her hair, and she became utterly still. Hayes wondered what went through her mind. Beside her Banks looked like a man at a reading of his own funeral rites. Color drained from his face which seemed drawn and rigid.

"No one knows how the mages learned of their rivals' plans, or even of their existence, for the followers of Teller hid themselves not only by normal means, but by means arcane as well. They believed that augury would not detect them." He leaned forward now, sitting cross-legged and putting his fingertips together. "But perhaps the story had its beginning an age earlier, in the tenth century. It is true, as is often speculated, that Teller's master died before Teller had completed his apprenticeship. The war between the Church of Farrelle and the mages was nearing its height then. Teller offended the mages somehow. One contemporary who actually met Teller claimed that he had delved into Lapin's books after he died. He even stole some of the texts to have for his own, hoping to make himself a mage without sanction from the other mages." He closed his eyes and drew a long breath. "For some reason Teller believed the mages would not allow him to complete his transformation to a mage. No one knows exactly why, but he fled them, and eventually came for a time to serve the church in the long struggle." He paused, thinking, the way he held his fingertips together reminding Hayes of making a church of his hands when he was a child. The priest stared into this structure as though it were an aid to meditation.

"Teller was only a reluctant ally, I think. Not caring for the word of Farrelle, but for a while he helped immeasurably. No one knew more of the mages and their ways than Teller. The mages did not expect to be countered by sophisticated arcane means, and though Teller was no mage himself, he was endlessly inventive. A genius, many thought. But when it became apparent that the church would not win, Teller vanished. The mages questioned the seniors of my church at length, but their renegade had slipped away.

"But miraculously the church was allowed to continue, much reduced in its power, but even that was something to be thankful for. In a rite that horrified the fathers of the church, they swore never again to employ the arts of the mages, and never to have commerce with a renegade servant of a mage. The penalty for ignoring this would be complete destruction of the church.

"Afterward, members of the church realized that much of what Teller had been doing during his time with the church was preparing his escape. Preparing his escape and hiding the texts and knowledge he had stolen from Lapin. Somehow Teller eluded the mages, which must indicate both great talent and skill in the arts. The Society of Teller was created. More clandestine than any secret society, for one whisper of their existence would see them destroyed. And there was something more, some other crime that Teller had committed: he had stolen a secret herb from Lapin. King's blood, as we have read here. And this, above all things, was a crime that could not be forgiven.

"There is no document that I know of that tells the story of those years, though perhaps Mr. Banks and Miss Fielding know more. Certainly Teller shared his knowledge with his followers, and increased his own, for he had escaped with a number of books. But it seems likely that those who came immediately after him had less of the talent needed to truly master the arts, for they couldn't recruit just anyone, no matter how talented. The society dwindled in power, if not numbers—each successive generation less skilled than the last. For centuries this dwindling of power went on, while the few who even knew of Teller thought his knowledge had been lost.

"But as will happen in any art, there was a renewal, a golden age, where men of successive generations were born with talent. The arts were greatly restored among the followers of Teller, and they grew in confidence. Finally, during the Winter War, the decision was made to perform a rite—I cannot tell you its exact nature—but it was believed that it would give them power. Perhaps it was the ritual performed to make a true mage—that is what some think. And they went to Tremont Abbey. There is an ancient lay. . . ."

"Mr. Flattery knows it," Clarendon said quickly.

Rose recited the words of the song that Erasmus had sung at Clarendon's home.

A delro, a delro. Ai kombi aré," Banks repeated.

"Meaning what?" Kehler asked.

" 'We are here, we are here. At the world gate,' " Anna answered, "or as we would render it: 'At the gate of the world.' It could also be translated: 'we are here at the beginning of the world,' but in this case I think it means 'gate.' "

"But what happened at the abbey?" Kehler asked, impatient for the story.

"To the few who know the story, it has long been said that only the five mages know for certain, but I will tell you now that this is not so. There was a young priest of Farrelle on a pilgrimage to pray in the holy places. He had stopped at the ruin of the abbey for the night when the followers of Teller came, singing their song of power, if we are to believe the ancient lay. They passed down into the cellars of the abbey, leaving him wondering what they did. But there was something forbidding about these men, so he stayed where he was, hidden in the ruin.

"The five came by moonlight, 'more ghostly than men,' but they did not ignore a pilgrim monk; in fact, they seemed to know he would be there. 'The witness of the Holy See,' they greeted him, and took him with them, down in the cellars. Brother Stephen, was his name, and he is the only man who saw what befell the followers of Teller.

" 'Before they descended into the cellars of the ruined abbey,' he later wrote, 'they drew a pattern upon the stone of the nave with the ashes of my fire, and then, with a candle, spread wax over this same pattern. A vial of starlight, or so they called it, was used to mark a second pattern within the first, and this glowed ghostly light on the floor. At a word, the outer pattern took fire and burned in thin, unbroken lines as fire should not. Many words were spoken in a foul tongue, and spells were woven and enchantments cast. Not till the mages were satisfied with their monstrous work did they descend the stair. Down we went, into the bowels of the old abbey. Down a passage unknown to men, and a secret stair that wound its way into the earth like a serpent hiding from the light. Down . . . until we came at last to an opening in the solid wall.

" 'There the seven who had gone before performed a rite of terrible splendor. So involved were they in their wicked pursuit that they did not see the five who came; the five and the one who watched. Seven columns stood in a half circle around a font, above the base of which sculptures of a man and a woman had been cut from the rock. Lines glowed like starlight and moonlight on the floor, and the men cried out in inhuman voices in strange tongues.' Brother Stephen claims to have stopped up his ears, but it did not matter. He heard every dreadful word. 'From the font emerged a column of fire, and the man chief among them spoke to it in words of power and it obeyed him.

" 'But then the mages began to chant, nearly silently, and around them dazzling patterns appeared in the air. Their voices grew until we could no longer hear the song of the seven. Suddenly the mages burst into the chamber, casting before them the white down of birds, which caught flame where it fell. With silver daggers they slew the seven to a man, slew them singing a horrible dirge. And the flame exploded around them, sweeping out across the floor, and the ceiling opened up to the vast dome of the sky, and we seemed to spin among the stars in the heavens.' Brother Stephen claims that he passed from consciousness then, believing that he was dying, and praying to Farrelle for his doomed soul.

"But he did not die. 'When I awoke, I lay in the sweet grass of a meadow beneath a warm sun. A spring bubbled a few feet away, and as I sat up in this fair setting, I realized I was not alone. One mage remained. "Drink from the spring," he said, "before you follow the path that will lead you back. And then travel to the seat of your Order and tell them what you have seen this night. Take them this warning." And he left then. Left me in this place which I think today is the fairest place I have ever seen. And so I drank from the spring, and by and by I followed the path beneath an arch of stone, out of the wood.' "

Rose looked around at the others. "Brother Stephen did as he was instructed, recounting the story as he understood it, and writing it down in the secret annals of the church. I confess to have read it many times, and apologize, for this has been a truncated, paraphrased version. But the center of the story is true to the original. Ah, there was one brief corollary: Brother Stephen returned to the abbey years later and could find neither secret passage nor stair. Nor could he find the beautiful meadow he described as the 'fairest place on earth.' Could not find it though he claimed it was but a short walk from the abbey. Some do not believe his story at all, but the song came from the others: 'the orphan, the maiden, the man,' and so I believe it, for it is too close to the story of Brother Stephen who was, by all accounts, of sensible disposition, and in all his later years blessed in every way; 'from drinking the water of the spring in that fair bower.' " Rose stretched his legs before him.

"That is the story as it is known to the church. Even the mages believed the followers of Teller destroyed. At least for many years they believed that. It seems they never suspected the hidden meaning of Teller's sign: three vale roses. One for each secret company he left behind, each unknown to the others. Or so I have come to believe." He looked at Anna who still hung her head, and even Banks would not confirm or deny the man's speculation.

Suddenly Anna rose to her feet, and stepping deftly among the seated men, walked off across the chamber, her head up now, her manner stiff but filled with rage and dignity. Banks watched her with great distress, and then he rose and followed, without looking at the others.

"Perhaps, Deacon Rose, you did not choose the most appropriate tale to tell in these circumstances," Clarendon said, fixing the man with a hard look.

"In truth, Mr. Clarendon, I think that Miss Fielding wanted to hear that story. It is a piece of their history that has likely never been clear to them, for the other groups were never known to them until after their destruction."

"Perhaps, but she is like a child whose entire family has been destroyed, even those distant relatives she has never met. And now she, too, is trapped and doomed to die. I think it was cruel, Deacon Rose, cruel and unnecessary, but I'm sure it gave you great pleasure at least." Clarendon pushed himself quickly up, and walked off, disappearing into the crypt.

Erasmus thought that the priest did not look so concerned with the idea that he would die in this place as everyone else. "You are quite happy to die here as long as the followers of Teller die with you, aren't you, Deacon?" Erasmus said.

"You do me injustice, Mr. Flattery. I believe that I shall live beyond this life. That I shall be reborn in a better world. A world without poverty and sickness and strife, where only the virtuous live. Believing this, why would I be unhappy?"

Kehler got up and went to the corner of the large chamber, and began examining the wall with great deliberation. Hayes went to help him, and a moment later Erasmus rose and disappeared down the hallway. The priest was left alone, seemingly unaffected by his rejection by the entire group.

Erasmus set foot on the bottom stair, wondering if he did the right thing. Should he interrupt Banks and Anna? Clearly Banks had gone to comfort her, and Erasmus was sure that the young man held her in affection. Perhaps it was not his place to interfere.

Footsteps came down the stairs, and Erasmus stepped back into the hall, going to one of the stone faces and pretending to examine the text.

"Ah, Mr. Flattery." It was Banks coming from the stairwell. "Anna would like to speak with you, if you . . . would be so kind." He tried to smile as he spoke, keeping all signs of emotion from his voice, but Erasmus heard it all the same. The poor young man felt some pain at her asking for Erasmus. Pain that he tried not to show.

Erasmus nodded, not knowing what to say, and turned to ascend the stair, before realizing Banks had not quite finished.

"I think you have something more to say, Mr. Banks?" Erasmus said.

The young man struggled for a few seconds. "Do you think there is any chance we will get out of here?" he asked, though Erasmus knew this was not what Banks wanted to say at all.

Erasmus shook his head. "I don't know, Mr. Banks, but if we give up, we will certainly never escape. I don't want to die here, that is certain."

"But perhaps you won't, Mr. Flattery."

"What do you mean?"

" 'The last guardian of the gate.' Perhaps you will live on to fulfill your purpose."

Erasmus felt something indescribable inside—as though his heart paused to listen to something utterly horrifying. "You cannot be serious."

"It is not impossible. We are dealing here with an art so deftly managed that we cannot even begin to guess what it could do. No, Mr. Flattery, I'm afraid it is entirely possible." He nodded toward the opening. "She is at the top of the stairs."

Erasmus ascended slowly, wondering if Banks had meant what he said, or if it were merely jealousy driving him to cruelty. He hoped it was the latter.

He found Anna at the stairhead, sitting with her legs drawn up and her chin on her knees. She stared off at nothing.

"You keep returning to this place," Erasmus said.

She shrugged, but offered no explanation. "Erasmus . . . may I call you Erasmus?"

"Certainly."

"I have been thinking and I'm convinced that Rose will not let us escape, even if we do find a way out. At least he will try to prevent Banks and me from getting away. I'm not sure about the rest of you."

Erasmus looked off at the same point in the distance that had so drawn her attention, and wondered if they saw the same things. "I'm not sure about the rest of us either, but it's possible he would prefer to see us all buried with what we've learned. If we discover anything at all that might help us escape, we must keep it from Rose. I'm not sure how we'd do it, but we would have to slip away without him." He pushed a hand into his hair. "Not an easy task, for I fear there are several among us who are not skilled at subterfuge."

"Poor liars, you say? Well, you cannot possibly mean Banks and me, for we have spent our lives hiding the truth. . . . Though look where that got us." She turned her head so that her cheek rested on her knees and she looked sideways at Erasmus. "It maddens me the way the priest seems so unaffected by our situation. I cannot believe that he has no fear of death—I do not care what his beliefs are. Men fear death. It is in their nature."

Erasmus nodded, still staring off at some point in the impossible distance, some point beyond the cave. He thought of the countess.

Was she worried for him? Would she mourn when he was finally given up for dead?

And what of Rose? Why was he so. . . ? It was an odd epiphany, yet in this place it seemed completely natural. There was a very obvious reason for Rose's equanimity.

"Perhaps Rose is more devious than we realized. He didn't choose to tell that particular story just to cause you distress and to gloat about the triumph over the Tellerites. There was something more, I felt it even as he was talking. 'Why this story now?' " He turned and looked at Anna. "He believes he is to be the witness for the Holy See. That is why he shows no fear. Rose believes he plays the role of Brother Stephen."

Anna sat up straight against the rock, and closed her eyes. She was so still that Erasmus thought she forgot to breathe, but then she let out a long sigh and took in a quick breath. "I should have realized," she said, still not moving. "I don't know what's wrong with me. I seem to be missing everything. Eldrich lured us down here like fools. And then this priest follows us. 'Everyone has their part.' I believe that is true. Rose's part must be to witness for the church."

"But I don't understand why," Erasmus said, leaning back, trying to find a position that was comfortable.

Anna shook her head, her eyes still closed, as though she were afraid to open them, afraid of what she might see. "Why didn't the mages destroy the church? It is a question we have long asked. The usual answers are not even close to the truth, I suspect. There was something, some reason to let the church survive. It is almost as if the church had some hold over the mages, though I cannot imagine what that could be."

"Nor can I. But you're right. There is no explanation that I find adequate. It seems most likely to me that the mages found some use for the church. They would never have let it survive otherwise."

A silence settled around them, but it was not terribly awkward. The silence of people pursuing their own thoughts. The silence that existed between people who were not familiar enough with each other to know what the other was thinking.

"I saw you on the *nance*, examining the urns," Erasmus said. "Is there any hope that we could reach the seed? Would that help us?"

"It could, yes. The seed is necessary to the arts of the mages. If we could find some way to get at it, we could take it, you and I, and we might find that some secrets of the chamber would be revealed. The chamber is sensitive to our presence—Hayes and Kehler said there was no light when they first looked in. When I performed the proper rites, light appeared in the crypt." She waved a hand around them. "And now we have light here as well—ever since Banks and I ascended. I believe that someone who is on the path, someone with talent who had taken the seed, might gain control of some of the chamber's functions."

"But we haven't the knowledge, unless you are keeping much from me."

She shook her head. "You are likely right, though how will we ever know unless we try? But every time I go near the urns, the priest comes and stands by, watching me. He must guess what's hidden there, even if he will not set foot on the *nance*." She rubbed her hands over her face and pressed her fingers to her eyes, shaking her head. "I don't know why I am suggesting this, I don't know enough. It is very unlikely that I could break the spell. It is more than unlikely," Anna said, any small hope that she had expressed earlier abandoning her. And Erasmus felt it, too. He stifled an urge to beat on the walls as though he could demand to be set free.

They sat in silence for some time, pursuing their separate thoughts. Erasmus found himself wondering what this woman felt about him. She had pressed herself close to him before. They had kissed—only once—but it had been a kiss full of promise, Erasmus thought. Now he found himself wishing that she would touch him again. He wanted to reach out and put his arms around her, but something stopped him. The countess came to mind, and he felt a twinge of guilt.

But I am likely going to die here, he thought. *Should I deprive myself comfort? Is that not foolish?*

He realized suddenly that Anna was gazing at him, her eyes moving slowly over his face. "You have the eyes of a poet," she said, a small smile appearing, as though she were a bit self-conscious.

"Haunted, a bit mad, suicidal?" Erasmus asked.

"No. A bit sad and very thoughtful. And focused inward, not upon yourself, but not focused on the world around you."

"Distracted, you mean?"

She laughed. "You will not take a compliment, will you?"

"Ah, it was a compliment."

"Well, there is more implied in what I said, you see. I was telling you that you had beautiful eyes." She looked at him, the playfulness disappearing from her face.

Erasmus leaned forward slowly, and they met halfway, kissing tentatively. A smile lit Anna's face—a bit smug, Erasmus thought, and then she moved closer to him.

She whispered something to him in another language.

"What's that?"

" 'My heart lifts like a water lily rising from the depths.' It is far more beautiful in Darian."

"There is love poetry in Darian?"

"Oh, yes. The mages had a book of lore and history and poems. It was called *Owl Songs,* though we have only fragments of it now. So much has been lost over the years of secrecy."

"Lost how?"

"Too much has always been trusted to the minds of my brothers and sisters—for the written word can give one away. But over centuries people die unexpectedly, and knowledge is lost before it is passed on. So our powers dwindle, and what we learn anew does not compensate."

"And the seed? Did Rose not say that Teller had seed? What became of it?"

She shook her head, close beside his own. "We had so little, and the secrets of cultivation were lost, or the seed, which is treacherous, betrayed us. It has been gone now for many years. We have failed in our endeavor. There was some hope that you might be our new Teller, Erasmus—that you might renew us—but you are here, trapped like the rest of us." She pushed herself closer to him, seeking contact.

"I was nothing but a lure set out to tempt you." He closed his eyes, seeing poor Percy staggering toward him, his terrified face enveloped in flame. It occurred to him that this was what the church did to heretics. "I had no other purpose."

I have always felt cut adrift, he thought. *As though my purpose was kept secret from me. All the years I sought to understand why Eldrich had taken me into his house, I never suspected the truth.*

"But you have a purpose now," she said, her fingers cool on his face, touching him as though she were without sight and wanted to know him. "Escape from Eldrich's trap. Escape, ultimately, from Eldrich. We have ways of hiding ourselves. We can slip away, as long as he believes, at least briefly, that we are dead." Her fingers traced his brow. Erasmus closed his eyes and felt her touch, cool and gentle on his skin.

Erasmus felt the unreality of the moment touch him. "I can never escape him," he said. "You don't know. Eldrich lets no one go. He would find me. Even if he had no further use for me, he would never let me escape."

She pulled him very close to her.

"But Eldrich does not plan to live in this world much longer. There is a reason he has sacrificed seven. He hopes to open the way one more time and slip through. That is his plan, I'm sure. If we can escape, we will strand him here. Eldrich will be trapped. Her voice seemed very hard suddenly. "I am not as kind a person as I seem for the idea of revenge seems sweet to me now. To strand Eldrich in this world he would escape, and trap the priest here, alone, in this netherworld. These are the thoughts that bring me comfort, the weapon I use to drive away despair. Only let me live to have revenge. If I could appeal to a higher power, that would be my prayer."

Chapter Forty-five

ERASMUS lay looking up at the dome of the chamber, so like a star-filled sky that he could almost imagine that he had escaped to the world above. He drifted in and out of sleep, rising to clouded consciousness, sinking down into the depths of dream. They were all becoming more and more lethargic—all except Deacon Rose and, oddly, Clarendon.

Erasmus tried to force himself to the surface, back to consciousness, but a current took hold of him, spinning him slowly, pulling him down. Erasmus could feel the great chasm below him, leagues of dark, silent ocean—the place he would drift for eternity, tugged this way and that, half in dream. The cold of the limitless sea seeping into him. A world of cold blue.

He tried to call out, but no sound came.

Swim, he thought. *I must swim.*

Up, if only I could. . . .

Suddenly he was swimming, following a trail of bubbles that escaped his lips. Up, straining toward air and light. Starlight.

When he broke the surface Erasmus found himself sitting up, gasping for air, covered in a cold sweat.

"Flames," he whispered. "Bloody blood and flames."

He looked around. The others lay here and there about the chamber, their posture strange as though they'd collapsed and were too weak to arrange their limbs for comfort. Anna and Banks lay near the crypt, Rose between them and the *nance.* Hayes and Kehler sprawled by the door to the hallway, and Clarendon stood silently, staring at the wall as though reading what had been written there.

Erasmus forced himself up, his head throbbing. Vertigo gripped him, and he braced himself, waiting for it to pass. A moment later he made his way slowly to the stream that emerged from beneath the *nance.* He knelt down and drank from cupped hands.

If only I were a fish, he thought. *I could dive into this stream and find my way out, out to the sunlight.*

He moved across the chamber, staring down into the opening that drained the water from the font. Clarendon appeared beside him.

"Are you well, Mr. Flattery?"

Erasmus continued to watch the water spin down into darkness.

"Mr. Flattery?"

"How wide do you think this opening is, Randall?"

Clarendon stopped, considering. "More than a foot. A foot and a third? Perhaps as much as a half?"

"That's what I would guess." Erasmus glanced across the chamber to where Hayes and Kehler slept. He pitched his voice low so that anyone who might still be awake would not hear. "Can you pass through such an opening?"

"One not filled with water, certainly. I think you could yourself, Mr. Flattery, though it would not be comfortable, but even so, I think you could."

Erasmus nodded. He crouched down, examining the small trench that carried the water across the floor. "How could we not have seen this? Look, Randall—what if we were to take rubble from the collapsed tunnel and dam the flow of water? We could build up a small dam down this side of the channel, across it diagonally to the wall. Do you see what I mean? Force the water out onto the floor and into the hallway. There must be gaps among the fallen blocks of stone—enough for water to find its way—and beyond the chamber the floor of the tunnel slopes down." He looked back at the opening in the floor. "It might be hard to stop all the water, but if we could reduce it substantially we could explore this pathway. We have a rope. We could lower you. . . .

Clarendon stared down into the darkness where the water disappeared. "And if our dam gave way?"

Yes, Erasmus thought, that was not impossible. He thought of the boy in flame. "I will chance it. It could hardly be a death worse than the one we live now."

Clarendon nodded once, then glanced over his shoulder. "Come away from here for a moment." He led Erasmus to the chamber's far end as though he would show him something. "But what of Rose?" he whispered. "He will not allow these Tellerites to escape—not if he can in any way prevent it. I'm not convinced he will even let us escape. Did you not say that he believes he is to be a witness? That somehow Eldrich will free him?"

"It is possible, yes."

"Then all he must do is wait, and somehow this unholy bargain between the church and the mages will be honored. Perhaps our own deaths are even necessary." He put a hand to his brow, suffering the same throbbing ache as everyone. Erasmus almost reached out a hand to steady him, but thought better of it. Clarendon was a proud man.

"I'm not certain your idea will work, Mr. Flattery—we have such poor material to make a dam—but it our best hope and I feel we must try it." He cast his gaze once more across the chamber. "Leave Rose to me."

"But, Randall, certainly we can't . . ." Erasmus had almost said "murder the man," he was so unsure of anyone's judgment. They were becoming desperate.

"I will not harm him if it can be avoided, but I don't know how we can take him with us either. We shall see. I will speak to the others. I think Rose is watching us this moment, afraid that we'll find some way out. Perhaps your plan has already occurred to him, but he has said nothing. Leave it to me, Mr. Flattery."

Clarendon went to Hayes and Kehler and roused them gently, leading them off, still half-dazed, down the *Hallway of the Seven,* as they had learned it was called.

Erasmus wanted to examine the opening in the floor again to be sure his judgment was not wildly mistaken, but he didn't want to arouse the priest's suspicions. The man hardly seemed to sleep, and was always watching.

A spasm of abdominal cramping bent Erasmus double, and he lowered himself to the floor, resting his back against the writing on the wall. A cold sweat broke out across his brow again, and in spite of himself he moaned quietly. If they didn't get out soon, they would certainly be too weak. They might not have the strength to follow Erasmus' scheme as it was.

Some time later Erasmus had gone to the end of the hallway and was examining the rubble that had fallen, blocking their exit. Although massive blocks predominated, there would certainly be a quantity of smaller material, more or less suitable for their purposes. Getting it out without causing further collapse would be the problem. They would likely need several cubic feet of material, which would make a hole in the rubble large enough to be dangerous—or so he thought. He was no quarryman, after all.

As he stood there considering the possible problems, a sudden cursing and shouting came from the main chamber, then the sounds of a scuffle. He ran as best he could and arrived in time to find Kehler, Hayes, Clarendon, and Banks wrestling Rose to the ground, Anna standing near, making quick motions in the air before her.

"You must gag him quickly. . . . Banks!" she said.

A moment later Rose was thoroughly bound, both hand and foot, and a filthy handkerchief had been used to gag him cruelly.

The others were near to collapse from the effort, and Rose was glaring at them with a viciousness that Erasmus would not have thought possible of a priest.

Clarendon saw him coming and raised his hands. "Now, I know you did not agree to this, Mr. Flattery, but we do not trust this priest to let us go. If our plan works, and once we are all safely away, you may release him and make your way out together. We are sure he will do nothing to harm you for fear of Eldrich."

Erasmus had not been warned about this speech, but it made immediate sense. Better Rose did not think he was being left behind.

"Why would he fear Eldrich on my account? The mage trapped me here as well."

"That might be so, Mr. Flattery, and I cannot deny that Eldrich has dealt with you in the worst manner, but we all know mages have their own ideas of justice and do not brook interference. I think this priest knows enough of Eldrich that he will not dare interfere with you."

Erasmus glanced at Deacon Rose, wondering if he believed this act, though Clarendon, at least, was quite convincing.

"I haven't the strength to argue," Erasmus said resignedly, having no difficulty finding the right tone, for he truly was exhausted. "We must be sure to let him drink, and to do him no harm. But let us get on with our task, while we have some strength left."

No one had imagined how arduous an endeavor they had taken on. Removing material from the collapsed passage proved both more difficult and more dangerous than expected, and the rocks and smaller fragments that they could get free made only an indifferent dam. Water poured through it as through a sieve, and though its flow was reduced, it was not reduced enough that anyone would dare the opening.

Exhaustion and hunger wore away at what little strength they had, and reduced them to taking longer and longer rests between trips to their quarry. Erasmus did not like the looks in the eyes of any of them, for he could see the doubt there—doubt that they could accomplish the task at all. And if they did, who would have the strength left to crawl down into this tiny passage that they all knew would steal their strength away in fifty feet?

Their labors drove them all to consume quantities of water, but no amount of water was a substitute for food, and they were all soon so exhausted that a few moments of effort were followed by many more of recovery—and occasionally one of them would fall into a sleep that could not be fended off.

If we had only come in here with our reserves undiminished, Erasmus thought, *but the journey through the cave taxed us all more than we expected.*

Anna emerged from the tunnel carrying a boulder the size of a skull—not such a burden really, but she struggled with it as though it were a hundred-weight.

"Is this any use?" she asked, nearly dropping the rock to the floor, and then sinking down beside it.

"I'm sure it is," Erasmus said, putting a hand on her shoulder. "Rest a moment," he said. "We must pace ourselves if we are to succeed."

She looked down at the stream of water that found its way through their makeshift obstruction, and Erasmus thought she might begin to cry.

"Clay is what we need," he said quietly. "Something to fill all the crevices." The problem of engineering their dam had fallen to him, and he did the best he could with it, while trying to keep up a brave face, which was the harder part.

Kehler and Hayes had proven themselves adept at extracting stone from the pile of rubble, and soon invented any number of dodges to shore up the pile while they pulled loose some stone. Every now and then they would stand back and heave rocks at the pillars they had made as braces and the pile would collapse again. Dangerous, Erasmus was certain, but no one had a better suggestion.

"How are they doing out there?"

Anna nodded. "Well enough. They have a bit of a stockpile waiting now. How much more do we need?"

Erasmus looked at their efforts. They had filled the channel for about three feet, but the dam was so porous that the water had not yet overflowed its banks. They had also built up a small dike along one side of the channel, but this would likely need more material if they ever succeeded in forcing the water to back up.

Anna pressed her hands to her eyes for a moment, and then forced herself up. She crossed the chamber stiffly and a moment later returned with a coat. "Try this," she said. "Perhaps it will stop up some of the holes."

Erasmus spread the coat over the inside of his dam. For a moment they waited, watching.

"It was a foolish idea, I suppose," Anna said.

"No, wait a moment yet. It is having some effect I think. And you've given me an idea. Kehler and Hayes dragged much of their gear in here. Did they not have oiled cotton bags?"

These were found, one split and laid in place, and they were rewarded by a noticeable backing of the waters.

They all stood watching the miracle, the water finally overflowing the banks of the channel. The low dams that were to direct the water away from the opening in the floor were only partly effective, but signs of success energized them all for a while. Two hours later a shallow pool of water covered the floor to one side of the channel and the *nance*, flowing slowly out into the hall and disappearing into the pile of rubble.

They all lay on the hard floor on the dry half of the chamber, unable to move, it seemed.

"We must not wait too long," Clarendon said, "for we cannot know how long the dam will hold."

Although several heads nodded, no one rose to begin their efforts. Hayes and Kehler were snoring.

They had consumed the last morsels of their food some hours earlier and Erasmus was now regularly seized by spasms of abdominal cramping that would last several minutes. He noticed that Banks suffered the same, though the others were less affected. He'd begun to wonder if he would make it out even if the passage proved viable.

Erasmus glanced over at the *nance,* with its macabre figures. What purpose did trapping them serve? Destroying the followers of Teller, clearly, but Eldrich could likely have done this less elaborately once they had revealed themselves. No, Erasmus was certain that Anna was right—they were a sacrifice. But was it that simple? Had they nothing more to do than die? It made so little sense. . . .

Rose squirmed around on the floor near the door to the crypt, and this prompted Clarendon to rise and check the man's bindings. They let him drink by soaking the handkerchief used as a gag, for Anna and Banks were afraid to let the man speak, which seemed to indicate that Rose might have more skill in the arts than Erasmus had believed. Not enough to loosen his ties, apparently.

As much as Erasmus knew Clarendon was right, he felt sleep drawing him down, into the infinite blue, at the mercy of currents and undertows and upwellings.

Something brought him to the surface, though he could not say what. A strange warmth and tingling, almost luxurious, as though he had just had love. As though he had never gone into that hard, lightless place inside the earth, far beneath the roots of the great trees that bathed in sunlight.

His vision would not quite clear. Light, pale and cool. Starlight. He could hear a mumbling, almost singsong chant. And then—there—Anna standing beneath the masked figures. What was she doing? Erasmus tried to move his head for a better view, but he could not.

I'm dreaming, he told himself, for often, in his dreams he was frozen, immobile.

But then he heard Anna speak, her voice cracking and almost overcome with exhaustion. "Teller be praised," she whispered, "I've done it. . . ."

Erasmus tried to speak, but only a hoarse breath escaped him. Anna came down from the *nance,* Banks rushing to support her, comfort her.

Someone else was trying to speak. Erasmus could hear strange, gargling vowels, cursing.

And then the sea took hold of him again, rocking him on its gently lifting breast beneath a star-scattered sky.

"Mr. Flattery?"

Someone shook him from his sleep, from his drifting toward darkness. Clarendon.

"They've gone, sir."

"Wha. . . ? Who's gone?" He propped himself up on an elbow, somehow surprised to find himself still in the chamber.

"Anna and Banks, sir."

Erasmus came fully awake, though his mind could not quite escape the dream-fog. He looked across the chamber. Their dam still held, the mirror-calm pond spreading across the floor. Then he noticed the rope knotted around one of the urns on the *nance* and leading to the opening in the floor.

"When?"

"Just a moment ago, I think," Clarendon said, putting a hand to his head. "I watched but could not move. I—I'm not certain our sleep was quite natural." He shook his head, pressing his eyes closed in apparent pain.

Hayes stirred nearby, moaning. And Rose, Erasmus realized was wide awake, his eyes wide with frustration and rage.

"Why did they go without us?"

Clarendon helped him to his feet. "One of the urns on the nance is opened, Mr. Flattery. It would seem clear that they managed to break the charm and fled with the contents. King's blood? Is that what you called it?"

Erasmus nodded.

Rose began to make a terrible choking noise, writhing on the floor. In an instant Erasmus and Clarendon had his gag off and were pounding him on the back.

For a moment Erasmus thought they would have to bear the

responsibility of the man's death, but then he managed to catch a breath, and then another.

"They took the seed," Rose said, his voice only a hoarse whisper. "Water. . . . Please. . . . Water."

Erasmus untied the man's legs and they bore him up, supporting him for a moment on weak limbs, then led him to the dammed stream and lowered him to where he could drink his fill, slurping up the water like an animal.

"I'm not sure he will harm us now," Erasmus said. "It must be clear to him that Kehler and Hayes are not in league with the Tellerites." The priest's condition was causing him some guilt.

Clarendon hesitated, and then nodded once and addressed himself to the knots that held Rose's hands behind his back. Free, the priest staggered to his feet, and before either Erasmus or Clarendon could move, Rose threw himself at the dam, breaking it down with his weight and the force of his lunge.

Water flooded through the gap, taking parts of the dam with it, filling the channel, and swirling down the opening. Erasmus and Clarendon leapt to save the ruins of their effort, dragging the priest out of the mess, not without a few cuffs, shoving him rudely aside. Erasmus struggled into the rapidly dissolving dam, grabbing for the oiled bags that had held the water back. Without them they had no chance of rebuilding, though Erasmus wondered where they would find the reserves to perform such labor again.

Hayes and Kehler came up, wading into the rapidly receding lake, pulling out the stones they had collected at such cost, glaring at Rose, who knelt in the shallow pool, his eyes cast down, perhaps in prayer.

"I could not let them escape," he said, meeting no one's eye. "You do not realize what you would have set loose on the world. These Tellerites, they appeared to be the most gentle of people, but they are ruthless. Do not doubt it. They will stop at nothing to achieve their goal. And now two of them are free, and they have the cursed seed. You do not realize what that means, but it will give them power, a hundredfold. Our only hope now is that they have drowned, or that the passage does not take them to the surface. Only Eldrich can stop them otherwise. Once that trollop has begun to take the. . . ."

Clarendon hurled a rock at the man, and dodging it ended his tirade. No one wanted to hear the priest's rantings. All they could think of was that their only hope—the only possibility of escape—had been closed, and no one knew if they had the strength to open it again.

"There's nothing we can do until the water has all drained away," Erasmus said, looking at the currents that now flowed toward the opening in the floor. They would defeat any efforts they made. The water might only be three inches deep over the floor of the chamber, but that added up to substantial volume, and now it was all running toward the opening. They struggled to preserve what was left of their efforts.

Rose retreated toward the hallway, wading across the pond, and disappeared through the archway. This left Hayes and Kehler free to curse him, which they did with a passion.

An hour later the floor of the chamber was rapidly drying, only a few small puddles remaining. The group collected on the steps of the *nance,* staring at the destruction Rose had caused.

"It will not be so bad this time," Erasmus offered. "We have no need to collect or carry stone from the tunnel and this time I need make no experiments in dam construction. We know what needs to be done. It shouldn't take us three hours working together. And the result will be stronger, I'm sure.

"But what of Rose?" Kehler asked. "Will we leave the man behind? There is no trusting him, that is certain. I for one won't go easily down into that hole thinking that the priest will send a stream of water down to drown me."

The others nodded agreement. There was no sympathy for the priest at that moment, but nor were they certain they could subdue him again, now that they would have no element of surprise.

"I don't know what to do about Rose," Erasmus said. "Let us rebuild the dam and guard it carefully. That is all we can do. That, or give up and die, and I, for one, will not give up."

They began again, working more slowly this time, but as Erasmus had said, experience informed their efforts and the dam began to take shape, despite their exhaustion. Clarendon and Erasmus made the younger men pace themselves reasonably, and they all took frequent rests, at which they were too drained to speak, but sat with their heads hanging like beaten men.

But they were not defeated yet. Perhaps eight hours passed in this labor, and finally the water rose so that only a trickle found its way into the opening in the floor.

Clarendon argued with Erasmus about who would go down into the shaft first, and Hayes and Kehler lent their support to the small man, forcing Erasmus to concede, though he did not do so easily. Anna and Banks had managed it and though she was slim and likely more flexible than the men, Banks was of normal size—at least as big as Hayes and Kehler, though not so large as Erasmus.

The small man went down into the hole in the floor, holding tightly to the rope, scrabbling with his feet for purchase on the passage walls. Watching him go, Erasmus realized that he had come to view Clarendon differently after their few days together. His small size was no longer the characteristic that stood out—his indomitable will had superseded that. The man had courage out of proportion to his size. And here, where many passages were so small, his size was a great advantage. Clarendon led the way and the rest followed.

"How does it seem, Randall?" Hayes asked, trying not to show his own fear of the tiny passage.

"Big enough, I think," Clarendon said, trying to look down, his voice distorting strangely up the shaft. He worked down a little farther. Erasmus could see that he was struggling, weakened by his labors. A trickle of water still made its way through the dam and this was enough to keep the shaft wet and soak the rope, making both slippery. He only hoped that it was not far to the bottom, for a fall was a real danger, and injury would leave Randall unable to climb up again. Against Erasmus' urging, Clarendon had refused to let them tie a line around his waist and lower him down. The passage was small enough that he went with one arm down and the other stretched over his head, which could make it impossible to release a knot if it became necessary. Either way there was risk, and in their desperate state Clarendon had made the more courageous decision—though not the one with the least risk.

Clarendon's feet slipped suddenly, and his hand skidded on the rope before he checked his fall. Erasmus could hear his harsh breathing. They were all so frightfully weak. . . .

"How do you go, Randall?"

He saw the small man's head nod, though he spared no breath for speech. The size of the passage made it dreadfully difficult because it was all but impossible to look down and there was no way to carry a lantern. Clarendon had gone about ten feet now and already he was losing the light from the chamber. Soon he would be in utter blackness.

"You're all right, Randall?"

A grunt in response.

They should have sounded the shaft first, Erasmus realized. It would have been easy to do, but their wits were so clouded.

Fifteen feet now. The rope had originally been a hundred feet, but a section had been cut off to bind the priest.

Twenty feet.

If Clarendon slipped, how far would he fall? No one knew. It could be ten feet to the bottom, it could be a hundred. The small man was only just visible, but from the sounds Erasmus could tell that he was laboring cruelly.

Don't fall, Erasmus willed him. *Please don't fall.*

"Randall? Are you bearing up?"

"Well enough." The terse reply funneled up the shaft.

Forty feet.

They could hear Clarendon gasping for breath now. His strength was fading fast, and they all knew that in their exhausted state there were no reserves to call upon. One could not force one's strength to hold that moment longer. When it gave out, it did so immediately and without recourse.

Hold tight.

Forty-five feet.

"Flames!" Clarendon swore. "Thank Farrelle."

"Randall!" Are you all right?"

"Yes," came his tired voice though the relief was clear. "I found a little ledge for my feet and just in time. If this shaft tightens down to nothing at the bottom, I don't know how I'll get up again."

Erasmus did not like to think that Clarendon might come down upon the drowned corpses of Anna and Banks. "We'll draw you up, Randall, don't you worry. Is there any sign of the bottom?"

"I'm in the dark, here, Mr. Flattery. It could be ten feet or ten miles, there is no way to be sure. Let me rest a moment, and then I'll press on."

It was a long moment, which worried the others, for not only was Randall tiring quickly, but it did not bode well for them when their own turns came.

"Randall?" Erasmus said when his concern would let him wait no longer. "Can you go on?"

"Yes, Mr. Flattery. Best to rest while I can when the bottom is some unknown distance away."

Hayes glanced at Kehler, the meaning clear. They all worried that they would not be strong enough to make their way out.

Erasmus ran his eye over their dam, which so far appeared to be holding, but it was yet another cause for concern, They had been tending to it regularly, and how would the last man down manage that?

"Mr. Flattery? I'm going to go on," Clarendon called up, though he did not sound confident, as though he realized that no amount of rest would restore him to any greater degree.

"Take care, Randall."

Almost immediately they heard the small man's breathing grow harsh and quick, partly from fear, they were sure. They could not see him now, but marked his progress only by the sounds. The dull scrape of boots and the rasp of his clothing against the too-smooth stone.

"How far is he?" Kehler whispered.

Erasmus shook his head. "Sixty feet? More? I cannot say. Light the lantern, Hayes, and we'll see if we can cast some light down to him. It might bring him comfort at least, even if it does him no real good.

"Randall? How goes it?"

"I cannot hold much longer," he said, his voice surprisingly calm, though very small.

Hayes jumped to light the lantern, fumbling with the flint, as though light would make a difference. They could hear Clarendon's breath coming in short, quick gasps now. And then suddenly, unmistakably, the sounds of him falling, and then, only a second later, silence.

"Randall?!" No response. "Randall?"

"I seem to be down," they heard the small man say.

"Are you injured?"

"No . . . not so much. I have wrenched my knee cruelly, but nothing seems to be broken. The passage turns here. Give me a minute."

They waited. Hayes lifted the lantern over the opening, and cast its dim light down into the darkness. They could make out something, perhaps Clarendon's fringe of white hair. Movement. Erasmus thought it might be a hand waving.

"Mr. Flattery? Can you send down the lantern?"

Quickly, Hayes hauled the rope up, and the lantern was sent down more slowly, care being taken not to shatter it against the stone. Finally Clarendon appeared in the descending illumination, though, still, he could not be clearly seen. He released the lamp from the rope, and then began to wriggle, painfully, disappearing from view.

The next minutes crept so slowly by that the others began to worry that something had gone wrong—Clarendon had passed out, or fallen again.

"Perhaps one of us should go down," Hayes said. "I will do it," he offered, showing his character, for surely none of them wanted to attempt this difficult descent less than he.

"A moment more," Erasmus said. He glanced around at a sound and there, by the door to the hallway, stood the priest, watching. For a moment Erasmus met the man's stare, but then turned slowly back to the opening in the floor.

Hayes and Kehler looked at Erasmus expectantly, clearly wanting him to make a decision. He took a deep breath. "As things stand," he said, "the three of us can likely draw Randall up again if the passage goes nowhere, but if one of us goes down after him, I don't think that the two who remain will have the strength to bring anyone up. We must wait, I fear, although Randall might be in danger, until we are all but sure, he will not return."

They stared down into the darkness of the shaft, wondering if this pit offered any hope at all.

A splash behind him caused Erasmus to whirl, and there stood the priest, only a few feet away.

"Stay away from this dam!" Erasmus ordered, and Hayes put himself quickly between the dam and Rose.

"You need have no fear," the priest said. "The Tellerites alone were my concern. Even Kehler's betrayal of trust is of little matter, now. . . ."

"As though we would take you at your word, priest," Kehler spat out.

"But what I say is true, nonetheless," Rose said, his voice so utterly reasonable, that even after what he'd done, he made Erasmus feel as though they were persecuting him. "And besides, I can help you. As Mr. Flattery knows, I have spent some little time wandering in the hills and mountains. I know how we can all descend safely, and if need be I can help draw a man up. I will tell you honestly, that I no more wish to die in this foul place than do you."

"You want to pursue the Tellerites, if they survived your attempt to drown them," Hayes said.

"I wish to live, Mr. Hayes, just as you do."

Just then a dim light appeared at the shaft's bottom, and then the lantern appeared, followed by Clarendon's too white face.

"Mr. Flattery?" he called up in a thin voice. "It goes. . . ."

Erasmus felt Hayes clap him on the back, such relief on the young man's face that Erasmus thought tears might appear.

"What could you see, Randall?"

"Only a small passage with a stream running in it. Very wet, but hopeful. All the hope we have at least. It might come to nothing in a hundred feet. Perhaps only one more should come down so that we can explore. I'm a bit crooked, I think—this leg. . . ."

"Who will go?" Kehler asked.

"Either you or Hayes," Erasmus said, knowing he must stay to watch Rose. "Whoever feels stronger."

The two candidates looked at each other, and then Hayes spoke up. "I feel quite recovered," he lied. "Let's get on with it. I fear Mr. Clarendon's injury could be more serious than he is saying."

Rose took a step forward, and everyone glared at him, which stopped him in his tracks. "I can make your descent much safer, Mr. Hayes, if you will allow me."

Erasmus looked at Hayes and nodded. He did not trust the priest at all, but he was quite sure the priest badly wanted to know if the Tellerites lived, and would pursue them if so, and that made it unlikely that he would try to destroy the dam again.

"If this is treachery, Deacon," Kehler said, "I swear, I will throttle you myself."

Rose did not respond, nor did he show anger, but only looked down at the floor—the posture of a man unjustly persecuted by his fellows. He stepped forward, his manner humble, his voice as reasonable as ever. "It is a simple thing, Mr. Hayes. Sit here, on the rim. Now take a turn of the rope around your boot and then hold it in your left hand. Yes, like that. There will be enough friction that you can control your speed easily—but you must keep your leg utterly straight and never let the pressure off, or the loop might come off your foot. If you feel it running off toward your toe, point your toe down a little. With your other hand, grasp the rope above your head. That's it. You should have no trouble, but have Mr. Clarendon move to safety, all the same."

"I am clear," came Clarendon's voice up the shaft, for clearly he heard every word.

Hayes let himself over the edge, letting the rope run jerkily through his hands.

"Good, good. That's it," Rose coached. "Try to let it run more smoothly, and then stop every few feet, for you will certainly burn your hand if you go too quickly and then you risk losing control of your descent entirely."

"Are you all right, Hayes?" Kehler asked.

"Yes. . . . This works well enough, though I fear I'm sawing my poor foot in two. Better than falling to the bottom, though."

They watched him make his slow descent, the rope hissing slightly at each drop, until he disappeared into the darkness. Every few moments they called down and he answered, and then, unexpectedly he was at the bottom.

"It is easier than a stair," he called up, a bit of laughter in his voice. They heard him speaking then but could not make out his words. "Erasmus? I will go on and have a look at this passage and see where it might go. If it appears to go some distance or branch, I will come back and you can follow. The dam is holding, I take it?"

"Yes, but go with care, Hayes," Kehler called down.

The men remaining retreated to the steps of the *nance,* for the entire floor had some water on it now, and here they collapsed, Kehler clearly fighting to stay awake, not wanting to leave the priest unwatched, Erasmus thought.

But try as they might, sleep would not be denied, and one by one they slipped into troubled dreams, dreams in which food figured largely.

Erasmus awoke when someone shook him, and found Kehler doubled over on the stair, his eyes dark, his face somehow seeming years older. "I heard a call," he said.

Erasmus started up, his wits still fogged. Rose awakened as well, looking around as though unsure of where he was. Immediately Erasmus went to the well.

"Hayes?" he called down.

"Ah, there you are. I thought you had all expired or escaped some other way. I cannot tell how far it goes, but some distance at least. There is a falls that will have to be negotiated, and once we've done that I doubt we'll get back up again, but I think we should chance it. Is there any way you can bring the rope with you? It would make the falls less treacherous, I'm certain."

"I don't know, Hayes. You've been down the shaft. Can one of us climb it without the rope?"

The hesitation was answer enough. "No. . . . I don't think you should try it. No, we'd be better to take our chances with the falls."

"How is Randall?"

"Injured. More than he is letting on, that is certain. He will need all the help we can provide. Fortunately much of it is crawling, which he seems more able to do. Are you coming now?"

"Yes. As soon as we've looked over our remaining gear to see if there is anything to bring. Stay where you are a moment and we will lower down our last tin of lamp oil and the few candles."

Light, Erasmus knew, would be their greatest problem. Once the lamp oil ran dry they would be forced to use candles—and even if they could keep them lit in the wet passage Hayes described there were only a handful. Kehler had done an estimate and thought they might have eight hours of light—no more. It was fortunate that Anna and Banks had not taken all they had.

Once the few things had been sent down, Kehler took his place on the edge of the shaft, and following Rose's instruction, let himself down. Having the example of Hayes no doubt helped, for he went easily down without mishap, touching the bottom in no time.

Erasmus looked around for Rose and found the man carrying a large stone across the pool.

"I don't know if it will work, Mr. Flattery, but if we can jam a stone tightly in the channel and set it upon small rocks so there is a space beneath it, then we can wrap the rope around it. It will be doubled then, and may not reach the bottom, but, with Farrelle's help, we may be able to bring it down after us by hauling on one end. But first you go down as it is, and I will come after and try to bring the rope."

"But if this stone does not lodge properly, Deacon, you might bring it down on top of you."

Rose looked up sharply at Erasmus. "But will that not be the best of all possible worlds, Mr. Flattery? You'll be rid of me, and have the rope as well. Do not concern yourself with my welfare, but get yourself down unharmed and quickly. We have light for a few hours only, and once that is gone, the chances of us finding our way out are. . . . Well, only Farrelle can help us in that event. On with you, sir. Just as I've shown the others."

Erasmus went down into the black well, lowering himself with the rope around his foot, water trickling down his neck as he went, running coldly down his back and chest. He hoped his ruined boot would stand up to the rope abrading it, for his chances of getting out of the cave barefoot would be slim. A broken foot or toe down here could mean disaster. Which made his concern for Clarendon all the greater.

For the first time in days Erasmus felt his hopes rise, even as he slipped down the shaft into the passage below. If only his strength would hold. Even using Rose's method for descending, he felt completely spent when he finally struck bottom, stopping with a jar that sent hot pain shooting up his back.

"Erasmus?" It was Hayes. There was some light around his feet, he realized. Erasmus stood in the tiny well, for he could do nothing else, leaning his head against the wet stone, the pain in his back so severe that he did not dare move.

"Erasmus?"

"Yes," he said through clenched teeth.

"You must come out feet first. It is a bit of a trick to get oneself into the passage and then turned over, but once done, it is no more than ten or twelve yards out into the larger passage. Light will do you no good, I'm afraid. Can you manage it? You're not too fatigued?"

"I'll manage," Erasmus said, not certain that he would. The thought of getting down into another cramped little passage had little appeal to him, but standing here waiting for the dam to burst and water to flood down was even worse. If the pain would just stop. He waited a moment more, the pain slowly ebbing, though not disappearing entirely.

"Mr. Flattery?" Rose called down, his voice echoing loudly in the well. "Are you clear? May I come down?"

"A moment."

Slowly Erasmus lowered himself, trying to slip his legs into the bending passage. For a moment he thought he was lodged and would have to try to pull himself up. Panic set in, and he cursed loudly. He was taller than Hayes and perhaps could not fit.

So frustrated and frightened was he that he felt tears sting his eyes, but then with a thrust he forced himself through, tearing the skin off his shins and knees. He slipped down into the passage that ran only slightly down, slopping about in the stream of water. He realized that if Rose released the dam now, in his weakened state he would certainly drown.

He will do no such thing, Erasmus told himself, but even the thought of it was almost unbearable. This was not the place he wanted to die.

Forcing himself to move, he began the painful crawl out, more difficult for it being feet first. He seemed to be inching along for hours, stopping to rest after every effort, each attempt carrying him a shorter distance, until he was resting every few inches. For a some moments he actually fell asleep, one side of his face resting in the cold stream. Clarendon's voice called him back and the horror of what he wakened to drove him on again. Finally he felt hands take hold of his ankles and they drew him slowly out.

The passage he emerged into was small—not a yard high and perhaps half again as wide, but it seemed enormous after what he'd been through. He found his friends, sprawled in the water, too exhausted even to try to keep dry. Kehler and Clarendon were shivering, which did not bode well. They looked frightened and despairing, as though they had not really escaped at all, but had come from a place well-lit and dry, to this. A passage that they all knew would likely flood if there was a rain storm above. After the enchanted light of the chamber, the lamplight was pitiful, Erasmus thought, and it seemed to exaggerate the haunted looks on the faces of the others.

The passage sloped at an angle of some twenty-five degrees, water tumbling down it into a series of pools, one of which they all sat in now. Below them the passage extended the few yards the lantern illuminated, looking much the same.

"So this is our salvation," Erasmus said, but no one answered.

Erasmus leaned his head back into the dark tunnel and called up. "Deacon Rose? You must hurry. We are wet and cold and must go on quickly. Deacon Rose, can you hear?"

From far off a distorted, macabre voice echoed to him, the words incomprehensible. Erasmus thought he was hearing a voice from another world.

"How far to this falls, Hayes?" He did not really care but felt he had to bring some focus to this group, who looked more defeated than at any other time.

"Not far," Hayes said softly. "Fifteen minutes."

"Might I see your knee, Randall?"

Clarendon nodded, shifting slightly, which caused him to wince. The small man managed to prop himself up against the wall so that his knee came clear of the water. Hayes moved the lantern to give better light.

Clarendon's breeches had been slit, and the knee was blue and already badly swollen.

"Can you put weight on it at all?" Erasmus asked, his tone solicitous.

"I don't know, Mr. Flattery. Perhaps if I could get started on it and work past the pain. But don't you worry, I will go on one leg and two hands if I must. Or on my belly if need be, but I will not stay here."

"Well, a physician would recommend you bathe it in cold water and elevate it, but I think we can only manage one of those. But as for the rest of us, we should try to get up out of this water or it will sap away what little strength we have. Is there nowhere we might sit up on dry stone?"

"Down the passage," Hayes said, gesturing.

"Then let us go there, and I will come back with the lantern for the priest. Come along. Except for Randall's knee, we must try to get dry. We'll huddle together for warmth. Up with you." He took the lantern from Hayes, trying to hide the pain shooting up his back. Fortunately Hayes and Kehler helped Clarendon, for Erasmus was certain his back would not allow it, and they made their slow, painful way down the passage.

Erasmus had to rest for a moment before starting back, and when he got there Rose was calling, convinced he had been left behind in the dark. The truth was that Erasmus would have been tempted to do so, but with a little luck, the priest was bringing the rope, which they might well need. And the priest seemed to have retained more of his strength than the others, for he had spent none of it building the dam. He also possessed skills from his climbing outings that they might require. It was a sad irony that now they might need the man.

"Deacon Rose? Are you down?"

"Ah, there you are, Mr. Flattery. I thought you'd . . . all been swept away. Have I far to come?"

"Have you negotiated the corner? Then it is not too far. Did you manage to bring the rope?"

"I have it."

"Well done!" Erasmus thought they might have to forgive the man if he managed another miracle like that one, though he suspected the others would not agree.

A few moments later the priest emerged, clutching the end of the rope. He quickly drew it out, coiling it in shaky hands, and dropping the coil over his shoulder. With a nod to Erasmus they set out, half-crawling, half-slithering from one pool to the next.

In a moment they found the others, huddled in the dark. Erasmus could not remember seeing a more sorry company. Filthy and shivering, their eyes sunken and haunted. He thought then that if the surface was not very near they would never make it. They had used the last of their reserves to get to this place—a worse grave than the one they'd escaped.

"Can you go on?" he asked, afraid the answer might be "no," but they all nodded.

And so they went, slowly, taking turns to carry the lantern and bundle of candles, for they were so weak that any weight quickly became more than one could bear. Rose assisted Clarendon, whose condition was far worse than Erasmus had hoped, and Clarendon accepted the help, desperation having replaced pride. Every hundred feet they stopped to rest, Erasmus choosing a place where they could sprawl out of the water, though it hardly mattered, they were all so wet and cold that they shivered uncontrollably, barely able to master their limbs.

Erasmus did not speak his fear that this passage would continue down and down until it ended in a pool, and that would be their final resting place. As they went, he searched the walls for openings, hoping to find a passage that might lead them off in a more likely direction, but only one passage was found and it was filled with flowing water, which swelled the stream they waded through and made the going more difficult.

They came to the falls Kehler had mentioned and rigged the rope as a hand line. It was not really so steep, perhaps forty degrees, but more water seemed to be flowing here and they had so little strength.

They went down one at a time to save the rope, which Erasmus was beginning to distrust—it had been severely strained and wet now for days. Rot would have to set in and weaken it.

Clarendon had to make his way down alone, clinging to the rope, sliding on his seat, buffeted by the current, gasping for breath. Twice his hands slipped on the slick line and he slid, crashing down on the rock, but both times he recovered before another could go to his aid. They all came down with only minor injuries, but were soaked again and had expended too much of their already reduced resources.

They rested, no one speaking, all hanging their heads, mouths agape, as though they had no strength to spare to keep them closed and no concern for appearances.

"On," Rose said over the sounds of the running water. "We must go on."

No one even nodded agreement, but Kehler pushed himself up, and staggered down into the next pool, Hayes following, and then the others. At least the passage had opened up so that they could walk upright, but Erasmus had examined the walls as they went and was sure, from the signs of scouring, that water ran at all heights here at different times of the year. Even a passage this size could be flooded. Spring rain, not an uncommon thing, could be their end.

The slope was less, now, allowing them easier passage, but even so, the stops were more frequent and longer. The lantern had been turned down to save fuel and the darkly orange flame cast the faintest light through the smoke-stained glass. Erasmus shook the lamp gently, and despaired to hear the tiny swish of oil within. It would not last the hour, he was certain.

Hayes looked up at him, and grimaced, as though telling Erasmus that he knew the truth. They would not find their way out—even if there was a passage they could hardly go another hundred yards. Both Kehler and Clarendon had begun to shiver with such violence that the others crowded around them and they held the lantern close to capture its almost inconsequential heat. They stayed like that for over an hour, turning occasionally to warm their exposed sides, no one speaking. The truth was there was little warmth in their frames to share, but eventually there was some small improvement. Food was what they needed, for they were travelling on nothing but willpower and desperation.

The lamp flickered suddenly, and Hayes produced a candle, lighting it from the shrinking flame. A moment they all watched, and then the thin little flame guttered inside the glass, brightened for an instant, wavered, and disappeared in a sigh of smoke.

More than one of them drew a quick breath, as though they had been holding their breath. There was silence, the small flame of the candle flickering, barely lighting the walls a few feet away.

The sounds of their rough breathing were like words—the language of despair and fear. The last flicker of their hope had gone, Erasmus realized. They would sit here until they died of exposure. Shivering out their last reserves in darkness.

"I think we will need to light a second candle," Clarendon said, his voice thin and a bit shaky yet. "If that one goes out, we will never use a flint in these conditions." The others nodded, though all knew this would mean they would have light for only half as long. Better light for a shorter time than none at all.

They still huddled around the lantern, drawing the last embers of heat from it, and then Erasmus took it and removed the glass chimney. With great care he cleaned this with his shirt, and then did the same to the bronze fitting where the wick emerged. Using a knife to bend the thin metal, he wedged a candle into this with difficulty, for his cleaning had not removed the residue of oil and wax did not stick so well. Lighting the candle, he replaced the glass and held this aloft, swinging it from side to side to see the effect. The flame wavered a little but held.

"Ah, Mr. Flattery," Clarendon said. "That will brighten our future, and extend our hours of light." He tried to make his voice steady, and push back the despondency in his tone.

They smothered the other candle and put it away, risking going on with one, knowing that if it went out, they would be consigned to darkness, which would much reduce their chances of escape. How easy it would be to be injured or to pass by openings in the dark.

With their candle lantern held aloft, they set out along the passage. Clarendon, bringing up the rear with Rose, spotted a small opening that the others had missed, which concerned Erasmus. How many others had they passed by? Kehler volunteered to explore it, and crawled in with the light, leaving the others to sit in the darkness, imagining an opening to the soft world above. Barely able to let themselves hope. A few moments later Kehler emerged, saying nothing, only shaking his head when he saw the others staring at him. Perhaps the hope on their faces stole his voice.

They let Kehler rest a moment and then went on, needing to pause within fifty feet. Then on again.

Suddenly Hayes, who was leading the way with the lantern stopped, bent over a pool. He reached out tentatively, and then drew his hand back.

"What. . . ?" but Erasmus saw what it was. "Banks?" he said, and Hayes nodded.

"Yes, though one would hardly know it. Look how battered he is."

They all stood staring, no one even glancing at Rose, for they could not bear to see the satisfaction that was, no doubt, written on the man's face. They body floated heavily in the pool, the skin white and swollen where it was not purple with wounds.

"He has been swept down here from much higher up," Erasmus said, "that is why he is so battered." He did look up at Rose then. "You should be proud, Deacon, no doubt your flood drowned him in the first tunnel. Likely we will find Miss Fielding not much farther on."

Erasmus had barely thought of her since they had begun rebuilding the dam, but now he felt an odd sensation. Was she dead, too, lying facedown in a pool, her faded gold-red hair streaming in the current?

Hayes handed the lantern to Erasmus and bent to rummage the body, hoping to find candles, or anything they might use, but he found nothing.

"There is no seed?" Rose asked.

Hayes shrugged. "Search him yourself, Deacon," he said, and turned away, moving off a few steps.

The priest bent quickly over the man, searching him, and then he made a sign to Farrelle in the air, muttering some words that Erasmus was not sure were last rites.

They stumbled down the passage, a vision of death traveling with them. It was no mystery now. That is what they would become if they could not find a way out. It stunned them into silence, and both drove them forward and filled them with despair.

A second candle was wedged into the lantern as the first burnt down to a stub. Erasmus estimated that they had two hours and a little more from that candle—not very long—and they had only five more. A dozen hours of light, at most. And then they would be left wandering in the darkness—just as some myths of the netherworld described. But not wandering endlessly.

Down they went again, descending a small falls that left them all sprawled on the rock, gasping, their heads spinning from the effort. One more such obstacle and that would be the end of Clarendon, Erasmus was certain. The poor man had to expend so much more energy to move, and he was in constant agony now. It was written on his face. Even Hayes looked as though he would soon give up.

The passage had opened up considerably, until the ceiling was almost twenty feet over their heads and the walls almost as far apart. A torrent of water plunged down this in rapids, swirling into pools. Erasmus was not certain why the volume of water was so great. Either it rained in the world above and this had swollen the underground streams, or hidden passages added their water to the flow—he suspected it was the latter. Either way it made progress more difficult, and certainly more treacherous. But the increase in the passage size seemed a good sign to them and raised their spirits a little. At least they were not crawling through tiny holes more fit for rodents than men.

They struggled on, assisting each other more often—taking turns providing encouragement, convincing the others to go on. A third candle went into the lantern, and they stopped for a long rest, most of them falling into an odd sleep, rousing every few moments, but unable to stay awake. Erasmus did not sleep but watched the irreplaceable candle burn too quickly down—wasting their invaluable light—but it could not be helped. The others had passed beyond the limits of their endurance.

When he had seated the fourth candle into the lantern, Erasmus roused the others, forcing them up, making them all drink. They were cold again, and shivered terribly, but there was no time to warm themselves. They had, at most, five hours of light, and once that was gone, they were all sure that no hope would remain.

Clarendon argued that they should explore on without him, and come back if they found a way to the surface, but the others would not even discuss it, but simply bore him up, and he was too weak to argue. They took turns helping him now, two at a time, and changed this duty frequently.

They came down a steep section of tumbling water, and at the bottom found what Erasmus had most dreaded—a pool. Both

Hayes and Kehler cast themselves down on a rock hiding their faces for they knew there was no way out, now.

"We could have died in the light, at least," Clarendon said, as Rose and Erasmus lowered him to a rock.

"I cannot believe that I have come so far at such cost only to end here," Hayes said. "Flames, I will go with a curse for Eldrich on my lips!" And he put his head in his hands and silent sobs shook his shoulders.

"What will we do now?" Clarendon said, taking up the task of providing hope. Or at least an example of resolution.

Erasmus looked at their candle, which had burned down to its final half inch. Only one remained. "I will take the lantern and go back up the passage. Perhaps there is an opening we missed."

The priest shook his head. "Five pairs of eyes searched as we descended, Mr. Flattery. Looking again will be of little use."

"Have you a better plan, then?"

Rose thought for a moment. "How high are we, do you think?"

Erasmus was taken aback by this. "Why do you ask?"

"There are openings into the lake that are only accessible at the low waters found in summer. Could this pool connect to the lake? Clearly the water must go somewhere."

This caught the attention of everyone and they fell to musing.

"I think we are above the lake by some distance yet," Clarendon said, his voice drawn taut by pain. "The chamber was above the Fairy Galleries and they are quite high up the hillside as it is. We have come down only a little more than halfway, I think."

Silence followed his words, and they all sat apart, shivering, thinking about the end, and the two hours of light that the last candle would bring. Erasmus picked up the lantern and walked along the edge of the pool, holding the light high so that it would penetrate to the farthest reaches of the chamber. His efforts only proved that the dark patches were shadows, and not openings as he hoped. Disheartened, he sat down again. There was no exit from this room except the way they had come. It was the end.

He stared down into the black waters where a few bubbles floated, caused by the water falling into the pool. They bobbed across the pool in a fan, disappearing as they went, so that only a few touched the far shore.

Erasmus stood suddenly, holding the lantern high again. "Have a look here," he said. "Do some of these bubbles seem to disappear, there, in the far wall? Is that another shadow or a small opening?" He pointed. "Do you see where I mean? Just in the center."

The others gathered about and Erasmus handed the lantern to Hayes and put his foot into the water, testing to see if there was a bottom. Taking the lantern back, he waded out into the water, which was almost immediately chest deep.

"It is an opening!" he called back. "Right at the surface. Flames, it is small." The bottom dropped off so that he could no longer walk, and Hayes plunged in after him and took the lantern, holding it up as best he could while Erasmus swam the few strokes to the far side.

The current here was far swifter than he expected and almost swept him into the opening. He grabbed the rock and felt inside with his hand, and then a foot.

"It is deep. No. I can touch the bottom, but just."

The current grabbed him but he hauled himself back by gripping the stone.

"I don't know if it has air in it for any distance. There is less than a foot clear just inside."

"Sailors say that drowning is painless," Rose said, "though I don't understand how they would know."

"It likely doesn't have air for far," Erasmus said, "but give me the end of the rope and I will explore what I can. I would rather die trying than huddling in the dark."

Erasmus swam back to the others and Rose knotted the rope about his waist.

"Your voice will likely be indistinct, Mr. Flattery, so call like this. Call 'out' once for more rope, and 'in, in' for us to draw you back. Your words will likely be distorted, but we will be able to distinguish between one word and two."

"Will you take the lantern?" Hayes asked.

Clarendon nodded. "You must, Mr. Flattery. We will light the last candle and guard it here, while you take the lantern."

Erasmus considered this. The idea of going into darkness was terrifying, but he was sure the candle would be doused in a moment, for he would need both hands to make his way in the current.

"Keep it here, but hold it low to the water and I will have some light for the first few feet. It likely goes no further than that."

Erasmus went back into the cold water, knowing that he would lose his strength within minutes, so there was no time to spare. He forced his muscles to obey, floating quickly into the opening, grabbing the sides as he could, but carried swiftly in. He would never be able to swim out but would have to trust to others and the rope.

The feeble light from the lantern disappeared in a moment and he was in darkness, trying to feel ahead of him in case the ceiling came down and knocked him senseless. His strength faded, and soon he was swept along, struggling to keep his mouth above the surface. And then suddenly the rope went taut, cutting into his middle.

"*In, in!*" he hollered. "In, in!" he shouted again. "Flames, I will die here in a moment."

There was a tug on the rope, and then a harder one that pulled his head under, but he pushed himself up, bracing his feet against the sides.

Bit by bit he was drawn out, scrabbling against the sides of the passage, fighting to keep his head above water. Many mouthfuls of water later he caught a glimpse of fitful light, and a moment later he was out in the pool again, and splashing across to the others.

"Does it go?" Hayes asked, wading out into the water and helping Erasmus to the shore.

"I—I don't know. There was air as far as I went, but beyond that I can't say. Certainly I could not have come back without your help."

They all looked at each other, Hayes and Kehler shaking their heads.

"It is a great risk," Clarendon said.

"But certainly death will find us here," Erasmus said. "In two hours we will be in darkness, huddled together, starving, though we will die of lack of heat before." He looked back at the tiny opening not sure that he was really ready to go in there again, in with no chance of returning.

Hayes rose to his feet. "Look, we can tie the rope around that horn near the opening. That will give us at least twenty feet more rope." He looked at Erasmus. "I will try it this time."

"No, Hayes. . . . It will be difficult if you can't swim."

"Yes, but if it goes anywhere, we all must go into it, and none but you can swim, Erasmus. Is it not narrow? Can I not pull myself up on the walls?"

Erasmus shook his head. "Not easily. You're so weakened. We

are all so weakened. No, I will try it once more. Give the rope to me."

"Then I'll come with you," Hayes said. "In some of the deeper pools I felt myself float up, and by moving my arms and legs, I managed to propel myself forward. I'm willing to try. Better you not go alone."

Erasmus looked at the determination on the young man's face—far preferable to the despair that had been written there. Erasmus nodded and they plunged into the pool. Hayes tied a loop over a horn of rock, for Erasmus' fingers would not work, and then they took the rope in both their hands and went into the passage, their legs streaming out behind them.

Twenty feet in, Erasmus felt his fingers slipping. "Hayes! I can't hold on." Erasmus felt Hayes hand take hold of his shirt, and they hung there for a moment, gasping for breath but unable to go back. Hayes was spitting out water, struggling to keep his head above the surface, and then suddenly Erasmus' fingers slipped, his shirt tore away and he was swept into the darkness.

"Go back!" he yelled and went with the current, no strength left to resist.

Hayes called his name, and then Erasmus was fighting to keep his head above water, the walls tearing at him as he swept by on the current. Once the ceiling dropped down, cracking him hard on the forehead, forcing him under, but he fought his way back up and found air again. Then he plunged down a smooth slide, coughing up water, scrabbling to rise, but the current had him, and he felt himself surrender. He could fight no longer. And the darkness took him.

Just as Erasmus felt he was lost, he found himself suddenly floating in calm water, coughing up great mouthfuls of the stuff. Rock came under his feet and he stood, stumbling back into the water, and then rising again.

"Flames. . . ." he whispered. "I'm alive. Bloody. . . ." He was racked by coughing, and fell again, but now the water was so shallow that he sat with it not even to his chest.

And then he heard splashing. Though he felt barely able to move, he plunged back into the water, thrashing around with his arms, searching the darkness. "Hayes. . . ? *Hayes!*"

He moved toward the sound of splashing and suddenly gripped a handful of hair and pulled the young man up, spluttering and coughing.

"Don't struggle! I have you. Damn it, man, don't struggle. Just here you can stand." He hauled the choking boy into the shallows and pounded him on the back. For a moment he thought Hayes would expire, and Erasmus began to beat him with all his remaining strength, and suddenly Hayes twisted away from him.

"You don't need to . . . murder me," Hayes gasped, and was gripped by another spasm of coughing.

Not knowing what to do, Erasmus kept dragging his companion into shallower water until they were on dry, smooth stone where they lay, shivering and coughing.

"Well, here we are," Hayes said at last, his voice coming out of total darkness, and though they were only a foot apart the sound seemed to have no source. "And the others will never know what has happened."

"And I'm not sure we're better off," Erasmus said, feeling an exhaustion in his limbs such as he had never known. "I haven't the strength to go another step."

"No. . . ." Hayes stopped. "Listen! Did you hear that?"

Erasmus tried to control his gasping for breath. "Are they calling?" He forced himself up, swaying on his knees. "Where is it coming from?"

In the darkness sounds echoed, seeming to expand to fill the chamber, their source mysterious. It was even difficult to tell where Hayes' voice was coming from. Erasmus waded back into the water, feeling the current and pushing against it. Hayes shouted behind him, the sound echoing around the chamber for an impossibly extended moment.

"This room must be enormous," Hayes called to him. "Where are you, Erasmus?"

"Here. Let me try to find the way we came in."

The flow of the water became stronger and pushed him away to one side, but finally he found the source. An opening much like the one they'd first entered, but discharging a strong flow of water. He pulled himself along the rock wall, leaning his head out so that he could call into the opening.

He shouted as loudly as he possibly could—no words, for none would carry—just a sound. Anything to let the others know he was alive. There was a long silence, and then a dull echo, garbled, unintelligible, as though the rock complained of its ancient pain. Erasmus shouted again. He waited and there was a response. Two distinct noises this time.

"Hayes? Is that an echo, do you think?"

"I . . . it is impossible to say. Call again."

Erasmus tried to copy what he'd heard, in both number and duration.

Three distinct calls returned. Erasmus called four, so they would not think it an echo.

"That is them," he said to Hayes. "It must be."

"What will they do, Erasmus?" Hayes asked. "Will they try to come through?"

"I don't know. All we can do is call and hope they realize we're still alive." Silence. Only the sound of water moving, and dripping down from overhead.

Erasmus did not know what to do. He shivered uncontrollably, now, his fingers slipping on the stone. He let the current take him, drifting him back.

"Hayes? Speak so I might find you."

"I'm here." They both floundered around in the water for a moment, and lumbered into each other, causing Hayes to fall, where he sat in the water, laughing.

"I don't know how in this round world you can laugh, Hayes, but I do admire it."

They helped each other onto the stone, sitting back to back for the little warmth of contact, wondering what they would do now.

"If you were the others, what would you do?" Hayes asked quietly.

Erasmus considered a moment. "I would likely try to come through, but then I can swim and haven't such a fear of the water."

"I would do the same. So we should be ready for them," Hayes said. "If one of them is rendered senseless as he comes through, he could float right past us and we would never know."

"Yes," Erasmus said, gently exploring the wound on his own forehead. "But if we go stand in the water, we will be even more cold than we are now, and I am near to freezing."

"I am as well. . . . Then we must listen."

They fell silent, imagining white swollen bodies floating by in the darkness.

"Do you think she got out?" Hayes asked suddenly.

"Anna? I don't know. She could not have been far ahead of

Banks, so it is unlikely. I'm surprised we didn't find her, though. Can you imagine doing this on your own? No, even if she survived Rose's flood, she would likely not have made it through the tunnel that just vomited us out here."

"Yes, but what if she found some other way that we missed? It's not impossible."

"No, it's . . ." But he did not finish for the sound of something floundering in the water stopped him.

Both Erasmus and Hayes leaped into the water, calling, and suddenly Hayes cried out.

"I have him!"

For a moment Erasmus could not find them, though he could clearly hear someone coughing and another pounding him on the back, but try as he might he could not get closer to the sound. Then his hand found Hayes in the darkness.

"Who is it?" Erasmus asked.

"Kehler, I think," Hayes said. "He makes a very distinctive sound when he's trying to drown. Kehler? Are you whole, man?"

Kehler continued to cough and it was some minutes before he could speak. "Rose and Clare. . . ." He began to cough again.

"Clarendon, yes. . . . What of them?"

"They're going to come through together. Bloody martyr's balls, that was the most terrifying experience of my life."

Erasmus found the young man in the dark and put a hand on his shoulder. Certainly it had been no less awful for them.

They fell silent, only their breathing and something that Erasmus identified after a moment as his own teeth chattering.

They listened, and suddenly heard the sounds of the others splashing. Hayes and Erasmus plunged back into the water, and in a moment had Rose and Clarendon out on the rock. For some reason they were not so badly off, and recovered more quickly.

The five of them huddled there in the dark, shaking violently, wondering what they would do now.

"Whose turn is it to t–tell their story?" Hayes whispered, and the others actually managed to laugh.

"Do we have the rope?" Erasmus asked?

"I tried to bring it, but it snagged and was lost," the priest said.

"Well, I thought we should tie ourselves together like blind men, but we will have to stay close. I have some strength left, enough to explore this chamber. There must be a way out. The water has to go somewhere."

"I will not go into another such passage," Kehler said, "Do not even ask me."

"I will stay here and die with Kehler," Hayes said. "But if there is a dry passage, I might manage a few more feet."

Erasmus pushed himself up.

"I will help you, Mr. Flattery," Rose said. "I will search one side of the chamber if you will tackle the other."

Erasmus went back into the water, not caring how frigid it was. He could not possibly be colder than he was. He swam a few strokes until his hand found rock, and then he lumbered awkwardly up onto a ledge. Here he began to search with his cold and battered hands until he found a wall, and this he explored as high as he could reach until the ledge ended in water. Making a mental note that the water's edge beyond this would need to be explored, he went back the other way, deciding to stay dry for now. He searched it all again for he could not tell where he had begun, but nothing felt familiar. His mind was not working as it should, that was certain.

"What are you finding?" Hayes called out.

"Rock," Erasmus answered.

"The same," Rose said quietly.

"I think we are in a giant stomach," Erasmus said. "We have been swallowed up by the world."

Erasmus tripped and fell hard to the stone, laying there for a moment, too exhausted to get up.

"Erasmus? Deacon Rose? Are you all right?"

"Yes. I stumbled," Erasmus said. "But I'm unhurt. Just need to rest a moment."

He lay there wondering if he would bother to struggle up again, his sudden energy gone, but then he imagined a passage just ahead. A flat, easy passage, dry, tall. And down it came the sweet scent of pine.

"I have something!" Rose called out.

"What? What is it?" Hayes called, his voice echoing from everywhere at once.

"An opening. Not large, though not so small." A pause. "I can fit into it easily, though I think I must rest before I attempt it."

Erasmus forced himself up, going carefully back into the water.

"Keep talking, Deacon, though quietly," Erasmus said, "and I will cross to you."

Out of the darkness came a sweet song, a hymn of sad beauty, and Erasmus stopped for a moment, so surprised was he to hear something so lovely in this harsh world. He followed the air, which echoed around the chamber so that it sounded like an entire choir, a choir singing in a great cathedral.

"Here you are," Erasmus said as he found the man, and the singing stopped, much to his disappointment. "Where is this opening?"

Rose led him to it, and Erasmus explored it with his hands, like a blind man would.

"It is not so small," he said. "Let me try it now. If I wait, I think I will grow weaker, not stronger."

Not waiting for Rose to agree, Erasmus pushed himself into the opening on hands and battered knees, ignoring the pain, and the humming in his ears. He stumbled down the passage, feeling before him as he went. It sloped up, not steeply but unquestionably up.

For a moment he stopped to rest, odd lights swimming before his closed eyes. *This is it,* he thought. *This is all the effort I can make. I'm too cold. Too exhausted. Flames, I am tired.*

He lay still, feeling sleep reach out for him. Warm sleep. He imagined a soft breeze caressing his face, the smell of fallen leaves. A smile touched his lips.

"Mr. Flattery," came a voice.

Erasmus shook his head. "Yes."

"What have you found?"

"Nothing yet," he called, forcing himself up on his elbows. He shook his head. "Ten feet," he whispered. "You can go ten feet."

He struggled on, not even rising to his knees, his head swimming now, a terrible ringing in his ears, like the body's own dirge for its passing. Even crawling, he lurched to one side, losing his balance in the dark. He collapsed again. And lay shivering, gasping for breath from his effort. His empty stomach heaved, and there was a hot burning in his throat. He heaved again and spat out bile, letting it dribble down his chin, uncaring.

"Flames," he muttered. "Flames. . . ." Then, "Ten feet, man. Any weakling can crawl ten feet. Percy would have managed it."

A murmuring seemed to fill the passage, and he stopped to listen, not sure what it was, then picking out the sound of voices. The others had gathered about the opening. Perhaps they came after him.

He forced himself to move his limbs, crawling through his own bile. He shook his head, trying to clear it, for he was dizzy and nauseated. Strange lights moved before his eyes now, even when they were open.

But he crawled a few feet. Rested a moment, his back spasming, and when that let up a little, he made himself go on. Five feet this time. Just five feet.

He saw a strange pinpoint of light that wavered and blurred, but at least it had the decency to disappear when he pressed his eyes shut. Five feet more.

There was some rubble of rocks on the floor of the passage now, and he crawled across this, the scream of pain from his poor battered knees and elbows seeming so distant.

"Mr. Flattery?"

Go away, he thought. *Can't you see I haven't the energy to spare to answer.*

He forced himself on, ignoring the calls of the others, though they seemed closer, now.

I'm delirious, he thought. *I'm half out of my wits. Is this what you feel before you die?*

He went another few feet, before being overcome by nausea again. When he opened his eyes, the point of light returned.

What if it is the proverbial light at the end of the tunnel? he thought. *But it is so small. . . . It would have to be a mile away.* He couldn't possible crawl a mile.

He squinted. Could it be sunlight infinitely far off? Or worse, could it be a tiny hole allowing light in but not large enough for any man to pass? Would he die with a view of the outside world?

He crawled a little farther, banging his head hard. He lay stunned for a moment, and then reached out with his hand, but it was not such hard stone. He put his cheek against it.

"Flames," he whispered. *Is this delirium?* He ran his hand over the surface, then rolled onto his back looking up.

The world seemed to spin and he shut his eyes. *But it was a tree!* And those were stars overhead, and that *was* the scent of pines. He had crawled out into the world. The world of light and air and trees and grass.

Erasmus tried to call out, but only a faint whisper emerged. A mumbling came to him, like someone chanting. A voice spoke his name a few feet away. Hayes. The others were near, crawling out into the delirious warmth of a spring night.

He felt himself convulse oddly, and sob. And then he lay, curled up like a child, hot tears running down his cheek, collecting on a fallen leaf. A breeze moved the branches overhead, whispering in a soft, green voice, welcoming him back to the world, to the brief life of men.